BLACKTHORNE ACADEMY

Year One

Zoe Dunn

For every woman who has ever been told to dim her light or stay small, this book is a reminder that you were never meant to be ordinary. You were built for fire, for magic, for more. May these pages remind you that your strength, your scars, and your magic are what make you unstoppable.
And to Pam and Janny, thank you for being the kind of friends who prove every day what extraordinary truly looks like. Your strength, humor, and unwavering belief remind me that extraordinary women aren't confined to stories but walk beside me every day.

CONTENTS

CHAPTER ONE

Bechora

The glitter caked to my skin was making me itch as I crept through my sleepy apartment toward my bedroom. I wanted nothing more than to scrub my body clean and then collapse into bed after working a long shift at Sinful Seduction. My feet ached from the pink platform stilettos currently dangling from my fingertips, and my shoulders screamed from a night full of pole work. The fresh-linen scent of my bedroom was a welcome relief from the cigar-smoke-filled strip club, and I was nearly tempted to forgo cleanliness for a few extra moments of comfort in my bed.

Dropping the small duffle bag that held my stage clothes from my shoulder and the stilettos from my hand, I moved toward my small, rickety dresser instead. Not bothering to turn on my lamp, I pulled open the top drawer, riffling through it in the dark to find a pair of sleep shorts and a tank top. My movements caused something to slide roughly across the top of the dresser, and my free hand hurried to jerk the chain of the standing lamp beside it.

"What on Earth?" I murmured, catching sight of the thick envelope with my name scrawled across the front in calligraphy.

My brows furrowed, and I freed my other hand from the open drawer, sliding my index finger beneath the sealed flap. Inside was what appeared to be an invitation printed on thick, black cardstock, the fanciful lettering penned in a bold red. A crest containing the letters B and T wrapped in thorns adorned the top, and I couldn't help wondering where it could have come from.

Bechora Knight
We are delighted to extend our warmest congratulations and
welcome to Blackthorne Academy for Supernaturals. Only those
identified as holding immense potential are admitted to our
prestigious halls. As you have been identified as a late admission,
your elective courses have been preselected for you. Should
you find issue with these selections, you will be able to discuss
scheduling changes with your Head of House after orientation.
Additionally, transportation has been arranged on
your behalf to ensure you arrive on time. You will
receive further details during orientation.

Frowning, I set the strange invitation back on my dresser and grabbed my intended pajamas from the top drawer, before padding barefoot down the hallway to shower. My mind worked over the card as I scrubbed myself clean, and by the time I was wrapped in a towel, I'd come to the only logical conclusion. My roommate, Geordie, was the only one who could have left something like that for me, and he'd thrown theme parties in our small apartment before.

Geordie had always been enamored with the fantastical and magical. It was something that made him a target growing up on the streets, and in some strange way, what drew me to him. I'd already been on my own for nearly a year when I found him being cornered by some of the other teens from the runaway shelter. Geordie had been small for our age. At sixteen, he looked no older than twelve, and his obsession with some magic card game made him stick out as one of the weak. Something about seeing five kids, ranging from fourteen to seventeen, surrounding the terrified boy enraged me. The result was three of the five in the shelter's infirmary, and my being banned for assault. Geordie and I had been together ever since, eventually managing to afford our rundown apartment.

Climbing into bed, I set my phone alarm so that I could be awake when he got home from his first job, before drifting off to sleep with memories of our years together on the street.

The shrill sound of my phone alarm caused me to bolt upright in my bed. The blackout curtains on my window meant the only light was coming from my cell like a beacon, which I promptly reached over to shut off. The muffled sounds of Geordie's footsteps reminded me why I'd set the alarm to begin with, and I tossed my blanket away with a groan.

Rubbing the grit and sleep from my eyes, I followed the sounds to our small kitchen. Geordie was humming an oddly familiar song to himself as he flitted between the fridge and the stove. I took a moment to look him over. He seemed slimmer than the last time I'd had a good look at him, and I couldn't help but wonder if I should worry.

"Hey, B!" Geordie called over his shoulder. "I didn't think you'd be up before I left."

He moved to our small coffee pot and clicked it on before moving back to the stove.

"I wanted to talk to you," I shrugged. "Between my hours at the club and all the doubles you've been pulling lately, I haven't seen you in weeks. I only know you're alive because I wake up every evening to food, and the coffee pot ready for me to turn on."

"Someone has to make sure you're fed and caffeinated, B." He chuckled, as the scent of bacon started filling the small space. "You're always taking care of me; this is the least I can do for you."

"You don't have to take care of me, Geordie," I said, momentarily forgetting why I'd gotten up early to speak with him.

Geordie took a deep breath and turned from the stove to face me. "That's what family does, Bechora. You taught me that."

"Geordie...."

"Bechora," he replied flatly, narrowing his eyes at me. Puffing out a breath, I held my hands up in defeat, causing him to smile. "So, what did you get up early to discuss? I know it's not just because you missed me."

"Oh," I replied, moving around him to grab my favorite cup from the cabinet and pour myself coffee. "I saw your party invitation."

"Party invitation?"

"Yeah, I know you love throwing those theme parties, but I'm not really sure I'm up to hanging out with your friends. I don't really fit in with that crowd, so I was thinking maybe I'd pick up an extra shift at Sin and let you do your thing."

"B," Geordie drawled, pulling the pan of bacon from the burner. "What party invitation?"

I shot him a confused look over the rim of my cup as I took a sip of my coffee. "The Blackthorne Academy thing. You left it on my dresser."

"I'm not having a party, B," Geordie replied, cocking his head slightly to the side.

"Are you serious right now? Why would you leave an invitation on my dresser and then lie to me about the party when I say I don't want to come?" I demanded. Whatever Geordie was up to, I hadn't had enough sleep for it.

Geordie raised his hands in front of him. "I swear, B, I don't know what you're talking about. I'm not planning any parties. I'm pulling doubles for at least the next month so I can get tickets to a con."

Slamming my half-drunk coffee cup on the worn counter, I stomped through the apartment to my bedroom to grab the invitation. After a beat, I heard Geordie's footsteps following after me. Tearing into my bedroom, I made a beeline for the dresser to grab the invitation and wave it in his face. Except... it wasn't there.

"Where did it go?" I shouted, pulling open the top drawer and shuffling clothes around before dipping down to check the floor around and behind the dresser.

"Where did what go?" Geordie asked.

"The damned invitation! It was sitting right there," I pointed angrily at the dresser top, "when I got home this morning."

"B," Geordie started slowly. "Are you sure you didn't imagine it? It wouldn't be the first time you thought you saw something after a long night. Remember about a year before we found this place and were sleeping in the park? You swore you saw a man having a conversation with a wolf."

"It was here, Geordie!" I huffed, plopping onto my unmade bed. "I wasn't that tired when I got in last night, and I'm not crazy."

Geordie moved to sit beside me on the bed and gave my hand a gentle squeeze. "I didn't say you were crazy. Obviously, there's no invitation here, so maybe it was just a really vivid dream, B. I know I've had some pretty out there ones that took me days to realize were just dreams."

Taking a deep breath, I blew it out slowly. "Yeah, okay. It could have been a dream." I conceded.

"Look, why don't you go back to sleep. You don't have to be up for the club for a couple more hours, and I doubt you're resting if your dreams are that vivid. I'll have the coffee pot set up for you and a BLT in the fridge when you get up."

"Yeah," I replied, yawning suddenly. "That's probably a good idea. I'm sorry I snapped at you, Geordie."

"It's okay, B." Geordie chuckled, standing up from my bed before tucking my blanket against my chin once I'd gotten comfortable. "Get some rest. I need to hurry up before I end up late to work."

I mumbled a response, sleep already sinking its claws into me and working to drag me under. Geordie's footsteps retreated to the door, and I could have sworn I heard him mutter an apology before my door clicked shut behind him.

The strange invitation and murmured apology were both long forgotten by the time I pulled into the gravel employee parking lot at Sinful Seduction for my shift that night. The club was packed, the front parking lot overflowing into the street. Waving at the security guard posted on the back door, I slipped inside and hurried to the dressing rooms to change. The thumping bass vibrated through the souls of my worn-out sneakers and sent a trill of anticipation through my body.

"Hey, B!" One of the other girls called out, as she adjusted the barely-there strip of material that acted as a skirt.

"Hey, Nat." I answered, "Good crowd tonight?"

"Oh, yeah. Owen said they're turning people away at the door tonight." She grinned. "Loads of big spenders tonight, too. It's like there's something in the air."

"Fan-fucking-tastic!" I cheered back, moving to my cubby and working to change quickly.

I'd been working at the club since I was eighteen. Without an education or G.E.D., there weren't many options for a barely legal, homeless kid. Four years in and several clubs later, I'd long since learned that there weren't any places I could pull in the type of money I did at Sinful Seduction. It didn't hurt that Sin had strict rules about touching the girls. Any would-be creep trying to cop a feel would be bounced before he knew what happened. Owen, the bouncer who usually manned the main club, seemed to have a second sense when it came to keeping us safe.

When I was finally changed, I made my way to the main club and couldn't help the smile that split my face. Nat was right. The club was packed. I let myself get lost in the music, working the crowd and picking up tips in between my turns on stage. As the night wound down, I had made nearly enough money to surprise Geordie with the con tickets he was working so hard for. The thought was enough to convince me to take one last private dance just before closing.

The club was all but deserted when I led my patron back to the main club to cash out his tab. Owen hovered nearby as I made my way behind the bar to close the man out, following a few steps behind once he was done to see him out.

"I'll be back in a sec, if you need someone to walk you out!" Owen called over his shoulder.

"I'm good, thanks!" I replied with a wave.

There were still a few members of the bar staff cleaning and preparing the club for the next night's opening when I was finally changed into a baggy T-shirt and a pair of gray sweatpants. Securing the large wad of cash into the inside pocket of my duffle bag, I called my goodbyes into the main club and made my way to the back exit.

The streetlights flickered with the first hints of daylight, and my eyes scanned over the nearly empty lot. A shiver ran up my spine, and I stiffened when my eyes landed on the large man leaning against my rusted-out Corolla. His muscular arms were crossed in front of his chest, causing his biceps to bulge and his light gray t-shirt to strain against his chest. My mind screamed for me to turn around and head back inside, where it was safe. For me to grab Owen and have him scare the stranger off, but my body had another idea.

Gravel crunched under my shoes, causing the man to straighten to his full height. My hand instinctively reached for the pepper spray in my duffle bag as his arms dropped loosely to his sides and his eyes raked over me from head to toe. The man was at least six-and-a-half-feet tall, my head tilting farther back to keep his face in view the closer I got to him. I couldn't make out his features, obscured as they were by a puff of steam he'd blown through his nose, so thick it could be mistaken for smoke.

My mind finally seemed to catch up with my body, and I stopped just out of arm's reach. Craning my neck back, I could just make out the amber color of his eyes and the way his nostrils flared as he leaned toward me.

"Bechora Knight," He spoke, his gravelly voice sending a pulse of need straight to my core. "I've come to escort you to Blackthorne Academy."

I blinked at him slowly, his words taking a moment to register. "I—"

"We must be going, Ms. Knight." He spoke, cutting off my confused protests and reaching for my arm.

The moment his rough palm touched my bare skin, a jolt of lightning shot through me. A needy whimper tore from my throat, and the man frowned, his hold relaxing for just a second before tightening painfully. My mouth gaped open in shock, my eyes flitting between where he held me and the molten amber of his eyes as my tired mind tried to figure out what just happened. A low growl seemed to vibrate from his chest as he waved his free hand, and a large, black hole opened behind him just before he pulled me through.

CHAPTER TWO

Bechora

My vision went black, and my stomach felt turned inside out. The strange man held onto my biceps as I stumbled forward and hunched over, dry heaving. My brain barely registered that we were standing on strangely colored grass instead of the gravel parking lot of Sinful Seduction.

"Just breathe," the man grunted. "You'll be fine. Portals take a little getting used to, but as long as you breathe, the strangeness you're reacting to now will pass."

"What the fuck," I managed to get out between heaves.

The man didn't answer, and I was tempted to aim for his expensive-looking shoes if I finally did vomit. Taking shallow breaths, I swallowed down the saliva pooling in my mouth as my stomach slowly began to settle. The stranger didn't release his hold on my arm until I finally righted myself.

"What the hell did you do to me?" I demanded, whirling on him and jabbing his brick wall of a chest with my finger. I winced as my finger bent backward, instantly regretting the decision to poke the man.

"As I told you, I am your transport to Blackthorne Academy. Did you not read your welcome letter?" The man replied, frowning.

"That was a stupid theme party invitation!" I shrieked. "This is... You've kidnapped me!"

The strange man scrubbed a hand over his face in irritation. "I assure you, Ms. Knight, the welcome letters from the Academy most certainly were *not* party invitations. We take educating the next generation of supernaturals quite seriously here. Now, if you don't mind ceasing the dramatics, you have an orientation to attend."

He moved forward, crushing the odd orange grass underfoot and leaving me standing in stunned silence as he strode away. Nothing about my surroundings was familiar, and I couldn't understand how I'd been at work only moments before. The longer I stood there, letting distance grow between me and the stranger, the more insistent the strange tug in my belly from the parking lot became. It wasn't long before I was chasing after him.

"You can't just kidnap someone and then call them dramatic." I huffed out between heavy breaths once I finally caught up to him. "Where the hell are we going, anyway?"

"As I said, Ms. Knight, you're due for orientation. The Academy is just beyond those trees up ahead."

I reached out and grabbed his arm, that strange jolt shooting through my hand again as I did. Jerking it back, I shook it out and scowled. "Hey, can you just... slow down. You're fucking giant, and I'm practically running here to keep up with you, *and* I have questions."

I could have sworn a muscle in his jaw ticked as he clenched his teeth, but he shortened his long strides so that I could finally walk at a normal pace.

"You'll get all the answers you need at orientation, Ms. Knight," he bit out as he scowled at me.

Deciding it was useless to press for more from Mr. Scowly, I followed him in silence as he led me down a dirt path through a copse of deciduous trees. I allowed myself to marvel briefly at the strange coloring of their leaves. Pinks and purples blended into more sedated reds and browns, with the occasional blue peeking out. I was about to ask my grumpy escort how they managed to get the leaves such strange colors when a massive brick wall appeared, seemingly, out of nowhere.

We passed under a stone archway centered in the wall that looked straight out of the Middle Ages, and into a large courtyard brimming with activity. Everywhere I looked, people were milling about. Some of them were dressed in black slacks or skirts, with pressed white button-down shirts and a black tie. Others were dressed more casually in outfits meant for weather ranging from the tropics to the Arctic. Mr. Scowly drew to a stop just near a group of nervous-looking teens as I gawked at the surrounding people.

"You will follow the First Years to orientation. The instructors will get you settled from there." He said, pointing at the nearby group.

"You can't just kidnap me and then leave me here!" I whisper-shouted as he started to move through the crowd toward a nearby stone building.

"I've done my duty by escorting you here, Ms. Knight," Mr. Scowly replied, grabbing my shoulders and turning me toward the group he'd singled out before and giving me a push. "I have other duties to attend to."

I stumbled forward, colliding with a short, white-haired girl dressed in all black. Mumbling an apology, I looked back for the man who'd brought me here only to find he'd vanished.

"How do you know Professor Thrackborne?" a melodic voice spoke, calling my attention back to the goth girl with pale white hair.

"Professor who?" I asked.

"The dragon shifter you were just talking to."

"Uh, he kind of kidnapped me from work and brought me here." I deadpanned, not sure what to make of the girl.

She let out a tinkling laugh. "Human realm, right?" She asked, not bothering to wait for me to answer. "That's okay; you can stick with me for orientation. My sister just graduated from here last year, so I'm pretty familiar with the campus."

"Thanks, I think." I frowned. "But would it be possible for you to tell me how to get back home?"

"First Years aren't allowed off campus. I'm Shadrie, by the way," she beamed, grabbing my arm and looping it through hers. "I'm an ice mage. Do you know what you are yet? If not, don't worry. They'll sort you out during orientation. Not everyone manifests before the school's magic enrolls you in the academy. I only manifested a month ago. I was so sure I was going to be a dud because everyone else in my family manifested on their sixteenth birthday."

"A what? I'm sorry, but I'm not following anything you just said."

"Oh, I suppose this would be pretty confusing if you just came from the human realm." Shadrie frowned before dropping her voice to a whisper as she began to lead me across the courtyard. "A dud is a supernatural that never manifests. When I didn't manifest any abilities by my eighteenth birthday, I was pretty sure I was one. Before I could pretend I was just a late bloomer, even though the rest of my family manifested at sixteen like clockwork. But look at me now, just turned twenty-one, and I have ice magic!"

I rubbed my eyes with my free hand before mumbling to myself. "Maybe Geordie was right, and I need more sleep. This has to be a fucking dream."

Shadrie shot me a confused glance before tugging me into a building that looked like a massive cathedral with stained glass windows. Hundreds of people were seated in long rows of pews, the sound of their conversations a dull roar to my ears. The raised dais, where an altar should have been, sat three long tables with neatly stacked envelopes on them. Three women and two men dressed in long robes stood before the tables, watching as the rest of the students filed in. More people moved into the cathedral behind us and jostled me closer to the front just as a woman's voice boomed out through the crowded room.

"Welcome, students," she spoke as I looked around for the speakers that had to be there, making her voice echo over the crowd. "Welcome to Blackthorne Academy. Today, we will sort you into your houses based on your magic. Those of you who have already manifested, please move to the tables in the left transept. Professors Griselda and Malgarn will provide you with your house and room assignments."

"That's my cue," Shadrie smiled. "It was nice meeting you…"

"B," I replied.

"B." Her smile widened, and I wondered if I'd just made a mistake giving her my name. "Good luck!"

Shadrie gave me a small wave and disappeared into the crowd, moving to the left of the cathedral. The roar of conversation kicked up again briefly, and I was pushed closer to the dais as people moved around me.

"Now," the woman's voice called out again. "The rest of you will be tested and then given your house and room based on the magic revealed in our testing." The din of excited voices kicked up again. "If you would please form orderly lines, we will begin."

The crowd surged again, and I felt myself pushed forward, stumbling into the back of a thin boy. He turned toward me and reached out his hands to grab my shoulders and steady me. His light brown hair and round face reminded me of Geordie.

"You alright?" He asked, pushing up the black frames of his glasses before his hazel eyes scanned the crowd behind us. "Bit rowdy today."

"I'm good. I should be asking if you're okay since I fell into you and all." I replied.

"Not your fault. My name is Miles, by the way." He smiled.

"I'm B. Nice to meet you." I paused for a moment, committing his name to memory. "Miles, huh. That's the most normal-sounding name I've heard since I arrived."

"I grew up in the human realm." He shrugged. "My coven was thrilled when I got accepted to Blackthorne Academy."

"The human realm? That's the second time someone has said that to me. Do you know how to get out of here?" I asked, my voice harder than I intended, causing Miles to frown at me and shift from side to side in discomfort.

"First Years aren't allowed to leave campus," Miles said, moving forward with the crowd. "You need a special pass that they don't give us until Second Year."

"That can't be legal."

Miles shrugged. "It's been a rule for centuries, from what I understand. Something to do with a Fae manifesting and accidentally hurting a lot of people when it happened." My face blanched, causing Miles to flutter his hands in front of me. "Oh no, don't freak out. It's rare that someone manifests out of control, and that can't happen on school grounds, anyway. The campus is spelled to prevent anyone's magic from hurting someone like that, and the Academy's magic is pretty good at detecting those who might manifest in a dangerous way before they do. It helps prevent accidents."

"That is not at all comforting." I drawled, moving along with the crowd and realizing we were only a couple of students away from the dais. "How do you know all this if you're from the human realm?"

"Oh, I'm not the first from my coven to attend the Academy, just the first in a long time. I grew up hearing all about the place and how only the strongest of our coven was always selected by the school's magic to attend." Miles' cheeks tinted pink as he spoke. "It was a big deal for me to be selected. My parents and coven leader think I'm going to be the one to restore our magic to its former glory."

I cringed. I couldn't imagine the amount of pressure that had to put on Miles. "How old are you?"

"I just turned eighteen." He replied before a woman in a long black robe motioned him toward the empty place in front of her on the dais. "Well, looks like it's my turn. Good luck, B! I'm sure we'll see each other around."

He gave me a small wave before moving in front of the woman. She cupped her hands in front of her and muttered something I couldn't hear. Craning my neck to see around Miles' body, I saw her puff her cheeks and blow, just before small bolts of electricity sparked from Miles' fingertips. The woman beamed at him and waved her hand, a manila envelope flying through the air toward her. She caught it between her fingers and murmured something else to the boy that I couldn't hear before handing it to him. Miles turned back to me with a wide grin and another cheery wave before bounding off the dais toward the back of the cathedral.

The woman turned her attention to me, motioning for me to take his place. Taking a deep breath to steady my nerves, I stepped onto the dais and paused in front of her. Her eyes scanned me from head to toe, in a quick once-over.

"Sparkling, perhaps a bit of pixie in you." She murmured, noticing the glitter that still graced my skin. "Your build would lend credence to the idea, but we shall know for certain momentarily."

"Listen, I don't know what's going on here, but I am positive I don't belong… wherever this is. If you could just tell me how to get home."

The woman wasn't listening to me, muttering something in a language I didn't understand over her cupped hands.

"Really, I don't want to waste anyone's time. I'm pretty sure there's been a major mix-up somewhere. I promise I'll keep my mouth shut about everything I've seen here. I just need to-" The woman blew on her hands, sending some sort of dust into my face, and I sneezed. Flames burst from my lips, and my mouth fell open in shock.

"Not the typical manifestation for a fire mage, but I don't sense any shifter in you." She smiled as if she'd just given me a gift.

"What the absolute fuck did you just do to me?" I demanded.

"Now, dear, I've done nothing but uncover your magic." She smiled, patting my shoulder as a manila envelope flew into her other hand. "I know it can be startling sometimes, especially for our students from the human realm, but you should be pleased. Fire mages are quite powerful once they learn to harness their magic."

"Absolutely not. I'm not a mage. I'm not magical at all. I'm telling you, there's been a mistake."

The woman frowned at me. "No, dear. I assure you there has not. The school's magic doesn't make mistakes, and the test has shown you're clearly a fire mage. There is a map inside the envelope that now holds your house and room information. It is spelled to show you the way. Hurry along now; there are more students who need to be tested." She said, shoving the envelope at me.

I sputtered in shock as she leaned around me to motion the next person forward in a clear dismissal. With no other recourse, I looked around the packed cathedral and spotted the exit in the back, heading toward it as I opened the envelope she'd thrust into my hands. Inside were a handful of papers. As I slid them out, I noticed a detailed map on top. There was a red dot labeled with my name and dotted lines leading to a building labeled 'Magus House'. As my eyes scanned over the map, I realized there were no exits from the campus anywhere. The archway I'd entered the grounds through with Mr. Scowly wasn't even on the map.

"Fucking hell!" I muttered to myself before slipping through the back door of the cathedral. My eyes widened in shock as the red dot that represented me moved along the marked path on the map. "Guess we're not in Kansas anymore, Toto."

CHAPTER THREE

Caulder

Bechora Knight was going to be a problem. My dragon perked up the moment she stepped out of the seedy strip club, and I caught her scent, pressing for control hard enough that smoke blew from my nostrils. Two hundred and thirty-five years of control were the only thing that kept him in line when I touched her to pull her through the portal. The electric current that shot through my body confirmed the tiny woman was my mate.

I stalked through the crowd of students toward the white brick building that held my office. As if sensing the storm brewing under my skin, students moved out of my way, none of them daring to make eye contact. My office door was open slightly when I arrived, further adding to my irritation. Stepping inside, I scanned the room and found Vallynn sitting in my chair, his pristine boots propped on my desk.

"Get your feet off my desk and your ass out of my chair before I fry it," I growled at the dark-haired fae.

"What's got your tail in a twist?" He smirked, moving his feet to the floor.

"None of your fucking business, Vallynn. Why are you here?"

"That's no way to speak to the crown prince, you overgrown lizard." Dante, the Fae's gargoyle bodyguard, spoke from beside the window.

I eyed the other raven-haired male, wondering if he was worth the trouble it would cause me to let my dragon eat him. Before I could decide, Vallynn cleared his throat, drawing my attention back to him as he moved around my desk. I moved to my chair and began sorting the papers he'd kicked around, ignoring the presence of both males. The high and mighty Prince Vallynn would tell me why he was in my office when he was ready. I'd learned early on that not even my dragon could scare him into speaking before he wanted to.

"Professor Waylon is missing." He spoke after several minutes of silence.

"Yes, well, he always was a bit flighty," I replied dryly. "Why is this news?"

"I have reason to believe my father had him taken."

My eyes snapped up from my desk and scanned over Vallynn, really taking him in for the first time since I'd entered my office. While he was dressed in the Academy's standard black uniform, his tie was slightly askew, and there was a slight, nearly unnoticeable wrinkling to his white button-down shirt. The fae prince was nothing if not always perfectly put together, with never a single hair out of place.

"What do you know about Waylon's abilities?" Vallynn asked.

I leaned back in my chair, my brows drawing down as I worked to recall everything I knew about the missing professor. "He was an air mage. A powerful one at that." I started, rubbing my hand over my

chin. "He also had the ability to manipulate other supernatural's shields if I recall correctly."

Dante hissed and moved to one of the empty seats opposite my desk, collapsing into it. The high-backed chair groaned under his weight in protest.

"Break my chair and I will eat you, Gargoyle." I snapped.

"Try me, lizard," he smirked in response. "I've heard stone is rather hard to digest."

"How did I end up stuck working with such an impudent child?" I huffed, a puff of smoke blowing from my nose.

"Because you tried to storm the castle like an idiot after my father slaughtered your clan," Vallynn replied. "You're only lucky that it was Dante that caught you and not one of the other gargoyles that guard the castle. You'd be one very dead dragon otherwise."

A low warning growl rumbled in my chest, but I forced my dragon to calm his temper. Vallynn, the arrogant prick, was right. When I'd returned from the human realm nearly three years ago and found my entire clan slaughtered, their magic drained entirely, I'd followed the scent of their attackers back to the palace. I didn't have a plan, only sheer rage and grief driving me forward.

It had been reckless of me. If Dante hadn't dropped on me from above and managed to bring me to the ground during my single-minded focus, I'd have been at the executioner's block for treason the next day. Vallynn appeared shortly after the Gargoyle subdued me and gave me a new purpose to channel all of my anger.

I'd been in disbelief when the fae prince told me his father was behind the missing supernaturals. That the King was draining them of their magic and slaughtering entire families to cover his tracks. If Vallynn had not used his magic to show me proof, he never would have convinced me. The disappearances were being blamed on the thinning veil and our people choosing the human realm over our own. With the decline in births from all species and the lack of true mate bonds in the last century, it made sense that people would defect to another realm in hopes of finding their mate or building a family. No one would believe their King was the true source of the disappearances.

I'd been working at the Academy ever since. The position allowed me to meet with Vallynn without raising any suspicions, though the information he was able to pass along was becoming harder for him to obtain. We were saving fewer and fewer of the King's intended victims, and Waylon was a stark reminder of that fact.

"If the King has already taken Waylon, there isn't much we can do about it," I said, forcing my mind back to the present.

"I am aware of that." Vallynn clipped. "But for someone to go missing *from* the Academy raises some concerns."

I rose from my seat so fast my chair flew into the wall behind me and slammed my hands on my desk. "Why didn't you tell me he went missing from the Academy before you started asking about his abilities? *That* is the sort of thing I need to know!"

An image of Bechora's heart-shaped face surrounded by her wild, red hair flashed in my mind, and my dragon strained against my skin. If people were being taken from the grounds, my mate was in danger. That was something my dragon couldn't abide; my need to maintain my position at the school to continue my work with Vallynn be damned.

Vallynn waved his hand, his magic wrapping around me and forcing me back to my seat. "Calm the fuck down, Thrackborne. I did not mean he was taken from the campus itself; the wards only allow staff and students through. Not even my father can access the grounds without permission. He was, however, taken from his lodgings just beyond the Academy's barriers."

"In case your lizard brain is failing to understand, those are the professor's accommodations provided by the academy," Dante interjected with a smug grin. I was definitely going to eat that fucking gargoyle once my work with him and the prince was done.

"Is the Dean aware of this?" I demanded.

"Yes, and no." Vallynn shrugged. "There was a note claiming Waylon was defecting to the human realm. Same as some of the others we've been too late to save. I was able to convince her to extend the warding, however. It wouldn't do for the crown prince to disenroll from the academy over safety concerns."

I rolled my eyes. Blackthorn Academy was the most prestigious school in the realm. Their elitism was rivaled only by the royal court itself. Dean Femirea would do anything the prince wanted just to keep him enrolled and protect the Academy's reputation. As much as Vallynn grated my nerves with his pompous entitlement, he wasn't wrong.

"Fine," I gritted out, barely managing to soothe my beast. "If the wards have been extended, what exactly is it that you want me to do?"

Dante's smirk grew wider, and he leaned forward in his chair, placing his elbows on his thighs.

"Waylon was the head of Magus House. I've arranged for you to take that position so that we can, hopefully, prevent more missing people. If you're my head of house, I have more reason to be seen meeting with you. With how difficult it's becoming to even get the information before my father has abducted his targets, I thought this would allow us to act faster."

"How the fuck am I supposed to head a house of mages and fae?" I snorted. "You do understand, Princeling, I am a shifter, and the heads of house are supposed to mentor the students in their house."

"Dragons really do have tiny brains." Dante snorted. "You have more innate magic beyond your shifting ability, you idiot. We all do."

I snarled at the gargoyle, letting my dragon break free just enough for my nails to shift into claws and dig into my desk as smoke poured from my mouth and nose.

"Enough!" Vallynn bellowed. "Dante, stop taunting the dragon. Thrackborne, I do not care *how* you mentor the students of Magus House; you can send them to their damned professors for help for all I care. But this *is* happening. There were over seventy disappearances over the summer. We cannot keep playing catch-up with my father if we want to stand a chance at saving any that are to come."

The gargoyle paled and went still. If not for the rise and fall of his chest, I'd almost have thought he'd transformed into his stone form. Easing my claws free of my oak desk, I forced my breathing to slow and pulled my chair back toward me to sit.

"Have you gotten any closer to uncovering his end goal?" I asked.

"No," Vallynn replied, his face tightening with anger. "But

I did look into the missing we are aware of. They each had particularly powerful magic, and based on their locations, it appears my father is homing in on the Academy."

"His inability to snatch anyone from the grounds aside, what would he want with a bunch of untrained children?" I mused.

"Really, Thrackborne? You can't think of a single reason he might be moving to target the Academy? Students leave with their magic bound all the time, not to mention those who go missing or die during the trials at the end of the year," Vallynn answered. "Second Year class alone has nearly thirty fewer students than we did our first year, and the trials only become more deadly as we progress through our studies. Then there's the magic of the Academy itself. You know as well as I that this place has a magic all its own that goes well beyond selecting names for admission. If my father found a way to steal the Academy's magic, who knows what he could do with it."

Gold and red scales erupted along my arms, and I struggled to maintain my hold on my dragon. If the princeling's theory was right, my mate was no safer here than she had been in the human realm. My instincts were screaming at me to find her and steal her away somewhere we'd never be found, but that wasn't possible. She hadn't seemed to feel the bond, and even if she had, I needed to be here to continue the work I'd started with Vallynn and his annoying gargoyle sidekick.

I couldn't do anything that would cause the dean to suspect Bechora Knight was my mate, or I would lose my position. The academy had strict rules around fraternization between staff and students. While the Dean would never fault me for finding my mate, she wouldn't allow me to remain on staff to prevent any interference in my mate's studies. I'd be banished from the grounds, and Bechora would be given the choice to continue her training or have her magic bound in order to leave the academy with me. It would be better for both of us if she and the Dean remained ignorant of our connection. At least until I'd help Vallynn expose his father's misdeeds and placed the princeling on the throne in his stead.

"I am working on getting close to my father's inner circle," Vallynn spoke, pulling me from my thoughts. "He's growing more paranoid by the day, and it's making it difficult, but I believe I may be able to turn one of his newer cohorts against him with the right leverage. In the meantime, we have no choice but to stay alert and do our best to get to his victims before he does."

The Fae prince's eyes flicked over my head, and he suddenly stiffened before shooting a glance at Dante.

"What?" I demanded, turning my head to look at the clock on my wall.

"We should go; the Dean will be on her way to inform you that you're now head of Magus House any time now. It would be best if she didn't know that Dante and I were here already."

I gave Vallynn a tight nod and watched as he and Dante made their way from my office before turning my attention back to the papers on my desk. This year was going to be a nightmare.

CHAPTER FOUR

Bechora

If I had any doubts left after everything I'd already witnessed, the map changing to show the interior and guide me to my room eliminated them. I stood just inside Magus House, eyeing the stairs that were off to the side of a large open common room, wondering if I had the energy to follow the dotted line leading to them.

"They just let anyone in this place these days." A nasally voice spoke behind me.

I turned my head to find a fit blonde raking her eyes over me with her lip curled in disgust. She looked like she'd just walked off a runway. Somehow, her pointy ears made her seem more ethereal. I studied her for a moment before turning my gaze to the curvy brunette beside her. Both of them looked to be around my age, but they clearly came from money.

"Come on, Maera, let's wait in Vallynn's suite," the blonde spoke, still sneering at me. "Don't want to risk the smell of trash rubbing off on us."

Maera, the brunette, laughed, exposing slightly pointed teeth before nodding at the blonde and moving toward the stairs.

"Great, not only do I not know how to get home, I have to deal with mean girls," I muttered to myself, shifting the strap of my black duffle bag to a more comfortable position on my shoulder.

I waited until they were out of sight and made my way up the stairs, following the dots on the map until I reached the fourth floor. When I stepped onto the floor's landing, I could have sworn the hallway shimmered. Rubbing my exhausted eyes, I shook my head and looked back at the map, noticing a gold star was marked on a room numbered four-hundred-fifty-eight. The black dots told me it wasn't far, and I sighed in relief. Mr. Scowly snatched me from the parking lot at work when all I wanted was to go home, shower, and collapse into my bed. This place wasn't home, but until I could find a way back, it would have to do.

What I found when I opened the door to my room caused my jaw to drop open. Shadrie, the goth girl who led me to orientation, was flitting around what appeared to be a smaller version of the common room, shooting icicles from her hands, causing them to wrap around twinkling lights.

"Holy shit, Elsa!" I managed in my shock.

Shadrie squeaked and whirled around to face me. "You startled me!" she shouted before the corners of her lips tugged down into a frown. "Who's Elsa? I'm Shadrie, remember. We met earlier."

"I know," I replied, stepping into the room and shutting the door behind me with my foot. "Elsa is from a movie."

Shadrie burst into laughter. "I know. I'm just fucking with you. We get movies and stuff from the human realm. Ours are better though, if I'm honest. Most of the human films about us get things crazy wrong. It's super annoying." She moved toward me as she talked, reaching out and tugging my duffle bag from my shoulder. "I'm super glad we're roomies! I know a few people, but most of them are stuck-up bitches. You seem like you'd be fun."

I reached out to take my bag back, but Shadrie was too fast. She turned and was headed toward a door across the shared space. I raced after her, barely noting the tiny kitchenette tucked in one corner, before she disappeared inside another room. She was already standing in front of a closet with my stage outfit from the night before in her hands, her nose scrunched in disgust.

"Are you a stripper or something? Girl, we have to get you

more clothes." She snorted.

"Uh, yeah. I am actually."

Shadrie's eyes opened wide, going round as saucers, and her face flushed red as she slowly turned her head to look at me. "I- Oh, no. I'm so sorry. I didn't mean it that way. You just don't have much in this bag, and I was..."

I raised my hand and waved her off. "It's fine. I'm used to getting that kind of reaction over my job. But the money is... well, I guess was... good, and it's not like Mr. Scowly gave me time to pack anything else before he snatched me from outside the club."

"It's a good thing classes don't start for a few more days in that case. The academy usually gives students enough of a heads up that they're packed and can pick out any electives, but not always." She smiled. "There's some bedding and toiletries already in your closet, so you're set there. In the meantime, we can order you a new wardrobe and some uniforms. There's a cute shop on campus that my sister showed me when she went here that we can check out for anything else you need."

"Actually, I'm exhausted. I'd really love to just shower and get some sleep. The clothes I've got on are clean enough, I can make them work for tomorrow." I quickly lifted the collar of my gray t-shirt and gave it a sniff to confirm.

"Umm, okay. I might have some pajamas you can borrow." Shadrie said, making her way out of what was apparently my room and across the common space to her own door.

Too tired to argue with her, I moved to the closet where she'd mentioned I'd find bedding and toiletries. Tucked away on a metal shelf that ran the length of the space were towels and travel-sized soaps, shampoos, toothpaste, and a single unopened toothbrush. Just beside those sat a black bedding set complete with pillows. Grabbing the bedding, I made the bed first, knowing once I was clean, I'd probably pass out as soon as the bed was back in sight. Then I grabbed the towels and toiletries and headed into the common area of our dorm. Shadrie was emerging from her room just as I made it to the middle of the room.

"These should fit you," Shadrie smiled, handing me an oversized black sleep shirt and a pair of shorts. "The bathrooms are coed here, but you should be fine. Most people will still be exploring campus."

"Thanks," I replied, taking the clothes and snagging my map from my bedroom to follow to the bathrooms.

The long hallway was deserted as I made my way to the showers showing at the end of the hall on my map. Cracking open the door, I listened for anyone inside for a moment before walking in and looking around. It looked like what one would expect of a college bathroom. There were rows of stalls opposite sinks and mirrors, and beyond those were rows of shower stalls with opaque white doors. Stepping into the first shower, I quickly hung my towel and clothes on the hook and turned the water on. Steam filled the space as I let the hot water wash over me and soothe some of the ache that came from dancing all night before I washed up as best I could with the travel-size soaps and shampoos. My hair was going to be a nightmare without conditioner, but that was a problem for after I'd slept.

Just as I was drying off and dressing in my borrowed pajamas, I heard the door to the bathroom swing closed. A distinctly male voice rumbled through the room, muttering something I couldn't quite catch. His heavy footsteps echoed past the shower stall I was in, followed shortly by the sound of the water turning on in another stall. Not wanting to deal with another person when I was dead on my feet, I quickly threw my hair into my towel, ignoring the few wet tendrils plastered to the side of my face, and slipped from the shower. I cringed when the stall door slammed behind me.

"Fuck's sake, are you so desperate you have to follow me to the shower-" the male spoke behind me, causing me to turn toward him. "Oh, sorry. I thought you were someone else."

Gorgeous was an understatement for the man before me. My eyes tracked down his body, from his short black hair, his stormy gray eyes, to his face that looked like it had been chiseled from stone. My breath caught in my throat, and I had the strangest urge to lean forward and follow the droplets of water that trailed from his broad shoulders down his muscular chest and stomach with my tongue.

"Hey, you good?" He asked, his brows knitting together.

My eyes snapped back to his face, and I flushed in embarrassment. "Yeah, I'm good. Sorry, I'm just exhausted. I haven't slept in God knows how long. Speaking of, I should uh, get back to my room. Sorry about, whatever this is." I was babbling.

The gorgeous male chuckled, flashing unnaturally sharp canines, as the sound caused a warm vibration in my chest. "Nothing to apologize for, Red." He winked. "I don't mind a little gawking."

"I was not gawking." I retorted.

He took a few steps toward me, closing the distance between us and gently tugging a wet tendril of hair that escaped the towel on my head. "It's alright. It's normal betwee —"

"Did you fall in there, B?" Shadrie's voice called through the bathroom door, interrupting the man. I jerked away from him and turned to find the tiny goth girl looking at us with a frown. "What are you doing in the fourth-floor showers, Dante? Don't you and the prince have special quarters upstairs?"

"Shadrie," Dante drawled. "I see you're still as annoying as ever."

Shadrie flipped him off and moved to grab my elbow, tugging me toward the door. "It's not my fault you're such an asshole, you bring it out of me, Dante," she retorted. "Come on, B. Let's get back to our room, some stuff showed up for you."

I shot Dante a puzzled glance over my shoulder as Shadrie dragged me through the door. The smirk on his face told me whatever transpired between us before she interrupted was far from over.

"Stay away from him, B," Shadrie warned once we were

out of earshot. "Dante Vazgurr is incapable of being decent to anyone except Prince Vallynn, and between the pair of them, I'm not really sure who's worse."

"Wait, what? How do you know him?"

"My uncle was part of the King's council when I was growing up. We'd summer with him, and I spent a lot of time with Dante and Vallynn as kids. They were nice at first, but then they hit puberty, and if you weren't one of their little groupies, they made it a point to terrorize you."

"I take it you weren't a groupie?" I snickered.

"Nope. I had no problem telling Vallynn and Dante just where they could take their egos and shove them. Unfortunately for me, that meant I was the target of some pretty cruel pranks, and one of their little followers even tried to drown me one summer."

"That's horrible, Shadrie."

"Yeah, I know. Just stay as far away from Dante and the Prince as you can. You really don't want to end up on their radar if you can help it," she said as she opened the door to our dorm. "Anyway, enough about those assholes. There's like four boxes that showed up while you were in the shower. I had them put in your room."

"Weird. Did they say who they're from?" I asked. Shadrie just shrugged and shook her head. "Okay, I guess I'm going to deal with the boxes, and then I need to crash."

"Cool, cool. I can wake you in time for dinner or something. I think we've already missed lunch." Shadrie replied.

I agreed and made my way into my room to find four large boxes surrounding my bed. Shutting the door behind me, I moved to the first one, looking for anything to tell me who they were from. All I found was my name listed on the label. Opening the boxes proved just as fruitless. There wasn't a note with any of the items in the boxes. Instead, I found a bunch of clothing and sleepwear in my size, uniforms, brand new bedding that looked extremely soft and expensive, and a myriad of school supplies, including a laptop. Shaking off the creepiness of someone I didn't know sending clothes in my size, I put the last of the items away, telling myself it *had* to be something from the academy and climbed into bed.

CHAPTER FIVE

Dante

I didn't need a shower, but it was the only thing I could think of to escape Vallynn's vapid fiancé, Daena and her crony, Maera. It was a small miracle they hadn't brought the third musketeer along before I managed to escape Maera's obsessive clutches. I'd *actually* thought she was desperate enough to follow me to the fourth-floor coed bathrooms, but instead I found myself staring at a lean redhead.

The brief moment when our eyes met, electricity shot through me, and I knew I was looking at my mate. She'd seemed embarrassed to be caught staring at me, but before I could reassure her that it was more than okay, Shadrie Nightshade stole her away. The petite white-haired mage held a grudge. Vallynn and I became real assholes to her when we became interested in impressing girls. We'd both apologized, but Shadrie was having none of it. I'd have to get creative if I wanted to get to know my mate as long as the little ice mage was around.

I took my time showering after my mate vanished through the door with Shadrie, working to direct my thoughts back to the most recent disappearances. We'd missed them for so long, it was a wonder we'd caught on at all. The memory of Vallynn's ashen face and trembling hands as he told me what his father was doing fought its way to the surface of my mind. He still hadn't told me how he'd learned his mother was one of his father's victims, but even I'd been suspicious of her sudden retirement to the countryside. The Royals didn't just retire. I'd grown up being groomed to protect Vallynn with my life;

most of my kind served the royal family in the same manner. I knew how things at court worked, and I knew the Queen. She wouldn't have left her son or her ladies behind. I still woke up to Vallynn's haunted cries from the night he discovered what the King did to her. It was one of the few things I hadn't been able to protect him from.

Vallynn was pacing the living area of our suite when I returned from the fourth-floor showers.

"The blonde banshee and her familiar gone?" I asked, causing him to stop pacing and look at me.

"There you are. Where in the seven hells did you disappear to?" Vallynn replied, ignoring my question.

"I went to shower. I had to do something to get away from Maera. Selir knows that harpy would have followed me if I tried to escape to my room or worse, the en suite."

"Fine, whatever. You're here now," Vallynn said, resuming his agitated pacing.

"Vallynn, what's wrong? Something has you out of sorts, and I know it's not just Professor Walyon's disappearance."

He sighed heavily, raking a hand through his short hair before collapsing onto the sofa. "You're right. Daena informed me that the rituals to prepare for our marriage have been moved up." Vallynn grabbed a rolled-up piece of parchment from the coffee table and handed it to me. "My father has sent word confirming what that soulless bitch said. My father has decided they will begin at the end of the academic year. I can't bind my life force with hers. I just can't. But until we find a way to deal with my father, I don't have a choice."

My brows raised in alarm. Vallynn was set to wed Daena after his schooling was complete on the king's orders, with the extra demand that they complete the Fae soul bonding. The rituals to prepare them both for binding their souls took time and focus when the couple weren't fated mates. The practice was something that fell out of favor because of the danger that came with exerting the amount of power, during each ritual, required to complete it. Even with a Fae's fated mate, it took a lot of power to seal the bond. With a chosen, it took so much more. Vallynn would be nearly depleted and weak after each ritual required to forge the sacred connection. That knowledge was enough for me not to envy the Fae's way of solidifying their mating bonds. I was grateful that, as a gargoyle, all it took was a claiming bite.

"We should bring my father in, if your father is moving up the timeline, he has to know he's risking your safety. He wouldn't do that unless he suspected you were already working against him." I said as I moved to sit in the recliner opposite him.

"No! Absolutely not. It was clear from the way Daena was preening about it that my father is doing this to keep her father loyal. He doesn't suspect me, not yet. Even if he did, I am still his only heir. He won't risk my life, but any leniency I can have extended to you on that account won't go further. He will execute your father for treason—if he doesn't drain his magic first."

"Vallynn... You may not even be able to sway the king to spare me. That's a risk I willingly took, but with more help, we're more likely to succeed. My father could help us. It's not like we haven't recruited others already. How is putting me or them at risk any different than my father?"

"Because you were already at risk by virtue of your position, and *they* were all planning to act against my father already, Dante. Even if you had chosen not to help me—if I released you from your position—my father would have hunted you down to discover what you knew of my plans. The others who've joined would have failed and died for nothing. They've thrown in with us so that their deaths can count for *something*."

"Vallynn... My father has experience with stuff like this. He would gladly risk his life if he knew what your father was doing."

"I said no, Dante. Besides, I've heard from Linoran. He's keeping an eye on the dungeon for any new arrivals and may have found us a way around my father's warding to track him with the mirror."

"That's a huge break. If we can spy on him with the mirror, we have a much better chance of identifying his targets and getting them underground before he takes them." I replied, leaving further arguments for later. Vallynn had dug his heels in; there would be no swaying him to enlist my father's help for the time being.

"I know." Vallynn grinned. "He's also compiling a list of all the missing. It should arrive next week. We'll need to go through it and see if we can find anyone we missed. The ones we *know* are victims of my father have already started to show a pattern, but I feel like the whole picture is just out of reach. Like, if we could discover some of his earlier targets that have gone unnoticed, we can figure out what connects them and why he's abducting people to steal their magic."

"Do you realize how many supernaturals go missing at any given time? It's going to take us months to sort through a list of all of them, Vallynn. We're going to need help."

"Selir sake, Dante. Why do you think I had Thrackborne placed as our new head of house?" Vallynn drawled, pinching the bridge of his nose. "It wasn't just for us to pass information faster. Now we have a reason to visit his office whenever we need, and it won't seem strange for us to take papers along when we do."

"Right." I smiled, clapping my hands together as I stood from my seat. "And in between all the clandestine adventuring, we show out like we own the place. At least maintaining our cover comes with a side of fun. Starting with the annual start of term bash."

Vallynn chuckled, the tension in his body easing slightly. "There *is* that."

CHAPTER SIX

Bechora

Gentle hands cupped my face, and the soft sounds of murmured conversation filled my ears.

"This is the only way," a woman sobbed. "Selir willing, I will see you again, my little star."

Suddenly, I was falling through darkness, my arms flailing as I fought to find balance.

I jolted awake, my arms windmilling as if I were still falling. My room was freezing, and my teeth chattered against the cold just as I noticed a thin layer of ice coating every inch of the small space.

"What the fuck." I grumbled, wrapping my blanket around my body and climbing from the bed.

I carefully made my way to the door, planning to rip Shadrie a new one for her little prank. I'd asked her to wake me, but *this* wasn't what I'd meant. Jerking the door open, I startled back. Shadrie was just on the other side, her hand poised to knock.

"You're awake," she smiled, before her eyes moved to my room. "Holy shit, girl! You didn't tell me you're an ice mage, too!"

"This isn't funny, Shadrie. You could have given me hypothermia!" I bit out. "Get the fucking ice out of my room."

Shadrie's brows dipped down, and she frowned. "You think I did this? I swear to you, B. I didn't. I've been in my room organizing my things since you lay down."

"I don't have ice magic, Shadrie!" I shouted. "When they did whatever the hell they did to me at that weird ass orientation,

I sneezed fire!"

"Wait... Then how..." Shadrie's eyes widened. "I promise, B. I didn't ice your room; I barely have enough control over my magic to encase the lights in the living area. Even if I could do this, I wouldn't."

The sincerity on her face caused my anger to deflate, and I scrubbed my hands over my face. "I don't understand what is even happening." I groaned.

"You should probably schedule a meeting with the head of Magus House. There's a chance that not all of your abilities manifested during orientation, and you're a true elemental mage." Shadrie said, patting my shoulder in a comforting manner. "Come on, grab some clothes, and you can get dressed in my room. Once you leave your room, the academy's magic will deal with the ice. It'll be like nothing ever happened by the time we get back from the dining hall."

I carefully turned and slid my feet across the ice to make my way to my closet. "I don't plan on staying here long. As soon as I find a way home to Geordie, I'm leaving." I called over my shoulder as I grabbed a pair of jeans, a light blue long-sleeved shirt, and my sneakers.

"Oooh, who's Geordie? Is that your boyfriend back in the human realm?" Shadrie asked as I made my way back to my bedroom door.

"Eww, no. Geordie is family. My only family, really, and I'm sure he's worried sick about me by now."

Shadrie frowned and motioned for me to head to her room, shutting my bedroom door for me. She waited as I slipped into her room and closed the door to change.

"Is Geordie supernatural?" her voice called through the door.

"No," I called back as I pulled the jeans on. "I'm not even sure I believe I am."

"B, you are most definitely a supe. But if Geordie isn't, the Academy would have made sure to leave a cover story for your absence, so the human authorities don't get involved."

I pulled the sweater on and slipped my feet into my shoes before opening the door. "Geordie knows I wouldn't up and leave him behind, no matter what cover story the Academy spins. I *have* to get back to him, Shadrie. We're all each other has."

Shadrie opened her mouth to reply, and my stomach growled loudly, causing her to laugh instead. "Listen, let's get some dinner and then I might have a way for you to check up on Geordie."

"Really?! Don't play with me, Shadrie."

"Really, really." She beamed, linking her arm through mine and dragging me from our dorm.

I let Shadrie lead me across campus to a large dining hall. Long tables with bench seating sprawled across the cavernous space. My eyes nearly bugged out of my head as I took in the high arched ceilings and stained-glass windows depicting various supernaturals I'd only heard about in myths. The dining hall wasn't as crowded as the cathedral for orientation had been, and I couldn't help wondering if most of the new students were still there as Shadrie tugged me toward the far wall lined with buffet tables.

"Look at this spread! My sister always raved about the food here." Shadrie squealed.

I followed her to the line, and we grabbed our trays. Each buffet spread offered something different. There were foods I recognized, like pizza and fries, and things I didn't—like the strange purple mushroom that was the size of a plate. I settled on what looked like a club sandwich and a small salad. Shadrie, on the other hand, had something that looked like purple rice and orange flowers. I couldn't help scrunching my nose at her meal.

"What?" she asked, arching a brow at me. "Your human realm food looks just as weird to me."

Shaking my head, I followed her to an empty table and sat down to eat. Shadrie filled the meal with talk about her family and the various types of supernaturals she spotted in the dining hall. I tried my best to listen, but my mind was trying to process everything that happened while I worried about Geordie. It was a relief when we finally returned to our dorm, and I could ask her what she'd meant about having a way to check on Geordie.

"My sister taught me this when we were kids. We were always pretty close, but as she got older, she decided she preferred spending summers with her friends instead of our uncle." Shadrie babbled as she slipped into her room and grabbed a hand mirror from her vanity. "Anyway, it only goes one way, but you'll be able to see and hear Geordie."

"A mirror?" I asked skeptically. "How is a mirror supposed to do all that?"

"Well, I mean, not yet. I have to spell it first."

"Right, so a magic mirror, like some Beauty and the Beast shit. You have got to be screwing with me."

Shadrie smirked. "You'd be surprised how many of the fairytales in the human realm hold some truth. If I remember right, that one was actually based on a wolf shifter and his mate. It doesn't have a very happy ending, though. Our version was basically a warning against the dangers of exposing our true nature to the human realm."

She shuddered before moving to the couch in the middle of our living area and placing the hand mirror on the table in front of her. I moved closer to watch over her shoulder as she produced a fine-tipped pen and began to draw symbols I didn't recognize on the top, bottom, and each side of the mirror, mumbling something I didn't quite catch as she worked. After a moment, she leaned back with a grin on her face.

"Done, now all you have to do is ask it to show you Geordie!"

Shooting her another skeptical look, I moved around the couch and sat down beside her.

"This feels ridiculous," I muttered, picking up the mirror with the handle and holding it at face level. "Show me Geordie." Geordie's face filled the mirror, and I gasped, dropping it. "Holy fucking shit."

"Magic, B." Shadrie giggled, nodding for me to pick the mirror up again.

I grabbed it from where it landed on the floor and took a calming breath before looking into it again. Geordie was there, but he wasn't anywhere I recognized. He leaned against the trunk of a strange colored tree; his hands folded in his lap as if he were waiting for something. Narrowing my eyes, I took a closer look and noticed the sharp point to his ears.

"What the fuck?" I breathed.

Geordie's eyes popped open as if he'd heard me. "Bechora, I know you're watching. I saw it in a vision."

"How?"

"There's a lot I can't explain right now, but whatever you do, do not leave Blackthorne Academy."

"What the fuck, Geordie? What is going on?" I demanded.

Shadrie nudged me with her elbow. "He can't actually hear you, B."

"I don't know how much time I have before I need to move again now that I'm back in this realm, but I need you to stay where you are, Bechora. I promise, as soon as it's safe, I will come to you and explain everything. But until I can, you need to use the Academy to learn what you are and master your abilities. And whatever you do, Bechora, don't ever, under any circumstances, leave the grounds. Trust the ice mage, she can help you figure this out."

I glanced over at Shadrie to find her wearing a confused expression.

"Don't use the mirror to find me again, Bechora. They can't know that you've returned, and they will find you if you do." Geordie said. "Everything I've done has been to keep you safe and to lead you to the Academy. I promise, you will be safe there."

He waved his hand in the air, and suddenly, I was looking at my own reflection, more confused than I'd been when Mr. Scowly pulled me into this realm.

"Holy shit, B, you didn't tell me your friend was a seer,"

Shadrie whispered, pulling my attention to her. Her face was pale and her eyes wide as saucers.

"I-I didn't know." I stammered. "We met as kids in the human realm. I swear, he was human the whole time I've known him."

"Glamour. All fae have the ability to glamour their appearance." Shadrie shrugged. "A fucking seer, though. That's intense, B. And a little creepy, if I'm being honest."

I placed the mirror on the table and dropped my head into my hands. Nothing made sense anymore. Even with his warnings, I wanted to find Geordie and make him tell me what was going on. I didn't understand how the kid I met on the streets could be some supernatural being, and I'd never seen the signs.

"I need to find him. Did you recognize anything about where he was?"

Shadrie placed a hand on my arm and frowned. "I don't think that's a good idea. He said for you to stay on Academy grounds. He's a freaking *seer*, B. If he's saying you need to stay here, you need to stay here. I'll help you figure all this out," she insisted before muttering to herself. "A freaking seer, I've never been part of a seer's vision before. Selir, that's intense."

"Selir?"

Shadrie blinked at me before bursting into laughter. "Right, human gods are different. Most supernaturals aren't religious, so Selir has become more of a swear for us, but at one time, there were really insane rituals involved in worshiping her. She's like, our goddess or whatever."

I leaned back against the couch and sighed. "This is all insane."

"We'll figure it out, B." Shadrie smiled, patting my thigh. "You're clearly not just a fire mage, and something tells me that if we figure out what you are, we'll find the answers you need."

CHAPTER SEVEN

Bechora

Classes didn't officially start for a week. I spent most of that time in my room, reading every book I could get my hands on about the strange new world I found myself in. Shadrie helped by giving me a crash course in all things supernatural. She even brought me meals from the dining hall, and I found myself enjoying the often-strange selections she made for me.

"Okay, B, you've been holed up in here long enough," Shadrie spoke, causing me to look up from the latest book I'd found to see her standing in my doorway. "It's been five days of cramming, and we both need a break. The annual start-of-term party is tonight, and we're going."

"I'm not stopping you, but I'd rather finish up—" I paused, flipping the book to find the title. "Creation of the Realm."

"It's been five days, Bechora. You need to get out and meet people, get the full Academy experience. Besides, Geordie said you'd find answers here, not that you had to avoid all fun to do it. So, get your ass dressed. We. Are. Going."

The petite ice mage crossed her arms in front of her chest and scowled at me. Part of me wanted to laugh at how hard she was trying to appear stern, but I knew she'd just continue to argue with me until I gave in.

"Fine," I sighed. "An hour. I'll go for one
" I held up my index finger, "hour, and then I'm coming back here to finish this book."

Shadrie clapped her hands and squealed. "You won't regret it, I promise. Now put on something sexy and let's go!"

She bounced away from my room, and I uncurled my body

from my seat on my bed. Stretching to work out the stiffness that had set in from being bent over a book for hours, I shut the door and headed to my closet. Grabbing a clean pair of jeans and a black spaghetti-strap shirt, I quickly changed out of my pajamas. I'd agreed to go to the party, but no way in hell was I dressing "sexy" like Shadrie insisted. Giving myself a once-over in my vanity mirror, I applied a small bit of makeup to cover the dark circles under my eyes and ran my hands through my red hair to tame it into beachy waves.

"That is not at all sexy," Shadrie pouted when I stepped out of my room. "You're dressed like my grandma."

"I am not," I huffed. "Besides, I said I'd go to this stupid party, but I never agreed to dress sexy. This is comfortable and cute. Best I can do."

"Ugh, fine. Next time I'll pick your clothes, though," Shadrie replied, motioning for me to follow her. "The party is in the woods behind Versipellis House. It's the only place on campus where we can throw a rager without being noticed."

"Versipellis House—that's the shifter house, right?" I asked, working to recall what she'd told me about the Academy's four houses. If memory served, there were originally only three; Noctus House was for the vampires on campus. The fourth was added some time later.

"Yep. They have a massive forest within the Academy's magical protection barrier, so they can shift and run as needed. Keeps their aggressive tendencies in line. And it's way less creepy than the demon house, Daemonium." She gave a slight shudder. "My sister was friends with a demon here, and the pictures of their house she showed me over the summer were just creepy. It's like a freaking mortuary."

"And they're into that sort of thing?"

Shadrie shrugged. "Some, but for the most part, they're like anyone else."

"Aside from the creepy house, you mean?" I laughed.

Shadrie stopped walking and turned to look at me. "I mean, there used to be a lot of prejudice against them. It makes sense that when the school was founded, they'd have made their house somewhere other supernaturals didn't want to go."

"So…not evil, then." I laughed, causing Shadrie to blanch.

"You can't say things like that, Bechora!" Her eyes darted around, checking to see if anyone overheard. "It's like a slur to call a demon evil. They're just a different kind of fae that got a bad rap because of the deals their kind likes to make."

My brows knitted together, and I pinched my mouth shut as I considered her words. Seeming satisfied with my response, Shadrie started walking again, leaving me to follow her through the dormitory and outside. We walked in silence as we made our way across campus toward Versipellis House and into the forest behind it. It was clear that even with all the reading I'd done over the last several days, I still had a lot to learn about the supernatural world.

I was pulled from my thoughts by the glow of a large bonfire and the sound of music. Shadrie led me into a wide clearing where people were dancing and chatting around the massive fire in the center. Music blared from the tree branches in familiar beats that made me almost feel like I was at a party back home.

"I'm gonna grab a drink—do you want anything?" Shadrie asked, nodding toward the far side of the clearing where a table with cups and a keg sat.

"Water, please," I replied. "I'm gonna hang here and get my bearings."

"You better be here when I get back, Bechora! You promised me an hour," she shouted to be heard over the music as she moved away.

I shook my head in response before scanning the crowd. There were so many people in the clearing, I was a little surprised that anyone had room to move, let alone dance. My eyes stopped on Dante Vazgurr and the dark-haired male beside him; their heads tilted in hushed conversation. I hadn't seen the man since our encounter in the co-ed bathroom, so I was surprised to find him standing across the clearing in a tight gray T-shirt and fitted jeans. My gaze shifted to the man beside him, noting the way he held himself as if he were above everyone here. As if sensing me studying him, his head turned toward me and his eyes widened. I could have sworn shock and longing flashed across his face before his expression shuttered and he scowled, turning his attention back to Dante. Weird.

A body slammed into mine from the left, and I nearly toppled over before warm hands grabbed my bare shoulders, sending an electric shock through me, and righted me. Whirling around to give whoever knocked into me a piece of my mind, I found myself staring at a hard chest wrapped in a black T-shirt that left every muscle on display. Craning my neck, I looked up —way up—into the smiling face of a gigantic blond man.

"Dilectus," he purred, his hands sliding from my shoulders down my arms. "I never thought I'd find you, and yet here you are."

"Uh...okay, buddy." I patted his chest and freed myself from his hold. "I think you have me confused with someone else. My name is Bechora, not Dilectus."

He grinned wider. "Bechora..." The way he spoke my name sent a shiver down my spine. "That is a lovely name, Dilectus."

"Yeah, so...this is weird, and I'm gonna go." I backed away slowly.

His brows dipped before his face split into another grin. "Ah, I see. I will prove myself worthy then, Dilectus."

"You...do that." I eased my way into the crowd, not taking my eyes off him.

I waited until there was a small group of people between us before turning my back on him and looking for Shadrie. I found her only a few feet away, holding a bottled water and a silver cup, her mouth hanging open in shock.

"Thanks," I said, closing the distance and snagging the water. It seemed enough to shake her out of her stupor.

"Oh, my Selir! Bechora, what did Zypher Morningstar say to you?"

"What? The weird guy?" I tossed a glance back at him. "I

think he had me confused with someone else."

"Zypher Morningstar doesn't get confused, B." She rolled her eyes. "Spit it out—what did he say?"

"Uh, I'm pretty sure he does, because he was clearly looking for someone named Dilectus."

Shadrie's cup paused mid-sip, and she choked on her drink, face blanching. I grabbed it from her hand, balancing it with my water bottle, and slapped her back.

"He called you Dilectus? Bechora, do you know what that means?" she sputtered, wiping liquid from her chin.

"Clearly not. Why don't you explain it to me like I'm from the human realm?" I deadpanned.

Shadrie burst into laughter, then sobered. "Zypher Morningstar is basically demon royalty, B. His father is Lucifer Morningstar. You're about to be one of the most hated females on campus for taking him off the market. Honestly, the only way you could paint a bigger target on your back is to attract Vallynn and Dante's attention."

"I'm one thousand percent sure I'm not taking anyone off the market, Shadrie."

"B, Dilectus is what demons call their mates." It was my turn to blanch. "They find their mate through skin-to-skin contact, and they never use the term Dilectus with anyone that isn't their mate."

"Absolutely not. No way in hell am I anybody's mate," I argued. "Especially not if that means what I think it does!"

"It absolutely means what you think it does, and you don't really get a choice in the matter, B." Shadrie sighed. "I mean, I guess you could reject the bond, but why would you want to? Fated mates are rare—super rare—these days. Supernaturals spend their entire lives looking for theirs because they're supposed to be your perfect match in every way. Fully dedicated to your happiness."

"Why would anyone want to be with someone who doesn't have any choice but to be with them?" I retorted.

"It's not like that, B." Shadrie winced. "Okay, maybe a little.

But you do have a choice. People can reject the mating bond if they want to. I know you grew up in the human realm, so you're not used to how things work, but I don't understand why you wouldn't want to be with the person literally made for you."

I scanned her face, taking in the wistful expression she wore. "I'm not saying I'm rejecting him, Shadrie. It's just weird to me, y'know? Like, maybe I'd like to get to know someone before I'm supposed to be theirs forever."

Her face split into a grin. "That makes sense. Just don't let all these jealous bitches get to you before you get to know him. The second they realize he's off the market, they're gonna have it out for you, girl."

"Real comforting, Shadrie." I drawled.

"Don't worry, I'll ice their asses for you." She laughed. "Now, come on, you promised me an hour, and I want to dance!"

I let Shadrie drag me into the dancing crowd, and before long, I was lost in the music. We danced until my legs burned, and I was shocked at how quickly time slipped by. Wiping sweat from my brow, I leaned toward Shadrie to be heard over the music.

"I need another drink!"

"I'll come with you!" she yelled back. "I'm dying of thirst!"

"B!" A familiar voice cut through the noise. I scanned the crowd and grinned when I spotted Miles from orientation. "I was wondering if we'd see each other again."

"Hi, Miles." I threw my arms around him for a quick hug. "It's good to see you!" A throat cleared beside me, and I grinned. "This is my roommate, Shadrie."

"Nice to meet you, Shadrie." Miles gave a small wave.

"You didn't tell me you knew anyone else at the Academy, B. I'm mad you kept this cutie away from me." Shadrie smirked, elbowing me.

Miles flushed red, the color traveling to his ears.

"You're embarrassing him, Shadrie," I scolded, before turning to him. "Sorry about her. She's had too much to drink and lost her brain-to-mouth filter."

"It's alright. Thank you for the compliment, Shadrie." Miles smiled uncomfortably.

"Apologize, Shadrie—you've made the poor boy uncomfortable as hell."

"Sheesh, alright. I'm sorry. Can't blame a girl for shooting her shot when he looks like that."

"Oh, um…that's very kind, but I'm…not into girls." Miles rushed out.

"Figures." Shadrie pouted, making him shift again.

"Shadrie!"

"Oh no, I didn't mean anything bad by it!" she nearly shouted, moving toward him. "It's just—B found herself a mate and you've got this whole sexy-nerd thing going on, but we could totally wingman for each other."

The corners of Miles's lips ticked into a smile. "I can get on board with that." He chuckled, eyes flitting to me. "You have a mate? Congratulations. They're incredibly rare. My coven has hosted a few wolf shifters who came to the human realm hoping to find theirs there."

"See? I told you." Shadrie smirked, poking her tongue out at me. "Bechora isn't happy about the whole mate thing. I practically had to *beg* her not to reject him and at least get to know him first."

"You did not." I scoffed. "There was no begging. I just think the whole thing is weird."

"Oh, you've got your hands full with this one, Shadrie." Miles laughed. "I'm honestly surprised she didn't run to her head of house the first chance she got and ask to have her magic bound so she could go back to the human realm. B was really freaked out by the supernatural stuff when we met at orientation."

"I know, right? She probably would've, too, if Magus House knew who our replacement head was already."

"No way! I'm Magus House, too. Electricity mage." Miles grinned.

"Ice mage." Shadrie beamed, raising her hand and calling ice to her fingertips. "They said Bechora is a fire mage."

"How have I not seen you in the common room?" Miles gaped.

"She's been locked up in her room for the last five days. If I hadn't brought her food, she'd probably have starved to death by now," Shadrie answered for me.

"What the hell? What is this—gang up on Bechora hour?" I snapped. "I was literally just trying to learn what I could about the place. It's not like I even knew it existed before I was dragged here against my will."

Miles reached out like he might pat my shoulder, then dropped his hand. "I get it. I grew up hearing about the supernatural realm and the Academy, but it can still be overwhelming. If you want, I'd be happy to help and tell you everything I know."

"That would actually be really nice, Miles." I smiled.

"I have a feeling we're all gonna be the best of friends. I'm so excited!" Shadrie squealed.

CHAPTER EIGHT

Vallynn

"We have a meeting with Thrackborne tomorrow after he's named head of house," I murmured to Dante as he sipped his ale. "Linoran has passed coordinates for a new target."

"I'll be ready," Dante assured me.

Whatever I was going to say next fled from my mind as I felt a strong tugging sensation low in my gut. Glancing up, I locked eyes with a stunning, petite redhead across the clearing. The air around me felt charged with electricity, and I could feel my shadows aching to slip free and close the distance between us. Whoever the woman was, she was my mate.

"Fuck," I hissed, just before a slim hand ran up my back and over my shoulder. I tried to tear my eyes away from my mate before Daena could follow my gaze, but I was too late.

"Really, Vallynn?" she hissed in my ear, her nails digging into my chest through my shirt. "I know we both have our dalliances, but she's below you. I ran into her on orientation day—she's just human realm trash."

"Daena," I gritted out, forcing myself to look the shrew I was betrothed to in the eye. "I had no intentions of seeking out anyone else's company this evening."

"Good," Daena replied, plastering on a saccharine smile. "I'd hate to think you'd lower yourself to slumming with the likes of her."

I gave her a tight smile and caught Dante's eye over her shoulder. Much to my relief, my friend wasn't too drunk to catch my unspoken request. Clearing his throat, he slapped Daena hard on the shoulder.

"Daena, a pleasure as always, but we've been summoned. Vallynn, if you'll follow me," he said in a tone that shouldn't have allowed for argument.

"Really, Vallynn?" Daena hissed. "You're going to let your stone-brained guard talk to me like that? I'm going to be your fucking queen. I deserve the respect that entitles me."

"Don't make a scene, Daena. You know how my father feels about women who make a scene," I warned. "If you want to remain at my side, you'd do well to remember that."

Daena paled and pressed her lips in a thin line. Dante barely stifled a snicker as he led me through the crowd and into the forest. He didn't press for answers as we made our way across campus back to our dorm room. Dante knew I'd explain myself once we'd reached our suite.

"What was that all about?" he asked once our door shut behind us and I'd cast a silencing spell around the room. "I know Daena is a piece of work, but you're supposed to be keeping up appearances."

"My mate was there," I replied before running my hands through my hair and tugging at it hard. "I didn't think it was possible. There hasn't been a fae that's found their mate since before I was born, but she was there."

"Fuck. This is bad," Dante breathed. "If your father catches wind of this..."

"I know." I groaned as I started pacing the floor in front of our sofa. "At best, he'll imprison her to use against me. At worst..." I couldn't bring myself to say what my father would do. The thought alone was enough to make me feel like I was being torn apart.

"Vallynn!" Dante barked, causing my head to jerk up.

"Shit!" I'd lost control—my shadows flooded the living room of our suite, and Dante shifted to his stone form to prevent them from injuring him.

Gritting my teeth, I fought to regain control. When my shadows finally succumbed to my will and slid back into me, I let out a breath of relief.

"Did she sense the connection?" Dante asked gently.

"No, I don't think so." I shook my head.

"Good, that's good. We just keep her away from you, then," he said, nodding his head to himself. "What did she look like? It'll make it easier to run interference."

I closed my eyes and pulled the image of her standing across the clearing to mind before describing her in great detail to Dante. When I opened my eyes, my friend went so still I almost thought he was still in stone form.

"What?" I demanded.

"Nothing. It's just...I had a run-in with her a few days ago. She's Shadrie Nightshade's roommate."

Tilting my head, I frowned at him. I knew Dante well enough to know he wasn't telling me everything. "Shadrie would castrate us both and eat our still-beating hearts if she could."

"She would," Dante grinned. "It'll make it easier to stay away from her. That's good. This is good."

"And if she starts to feel the pull of the bond? We were both taught about these things as children," I cautioned. "She may not feel it now, but my soul will continue to call to her until she answers."

"We take a page from Daena's book." Dante winced. "Make her hate you so much she stays as far away as she can."

I collapsed onto the sofa and threw my head back with a heavy sigh. My magic was restless under my skin, almost angry at the idea of doing anything to harm my mate in any way. But I knew my father, and he'd become increasingly unhinged over the last decade. Since the night he stole my mother's magic and murdered her, he'd been on a paranoid downward spiral. He was even starting to suspect that I was working against him—his paranoia getting something right for once. If there was even a whisper of me having more than superficial feelings for a female who wasn't his chosen bride for me, her life would be in immense danger.

"If this isn't what you want, say the word, Vallynn," Dante said, interrupting my thoughts. "We'll talk to Thrackborne and figure out how to keep her safe from your father another way, even if it means hiding her somewhere." He sounded almost hopeful, something I wasn't ready to look deeper into.

"The safest place in both realms is the Academy. Besides, it would be cruel to have her cut off from her magic, not to mention dangerous. The Academy's magic wouldn't allow her to leave unbound, not until she's learned control."

"Then we have no other choice." Dante sounded pained, and his face was rife with remorse. "Avoid her as long as possible, and turn to cruelty when that no longer works."

"Selir forgive me, because I'm not sure, at the end of this, my mate ever will."

CHAPTER NINE

Bechora

The morning after the party, I woke up trapped in my room. We were meant to be in the common room by ten for the new head of house announcement. Instead, I found myself held hostage by an invisible barrier preventing me from leaving. Shadrie attempted every spell she knew to break a shield to get me out before leaving with the promise of finding help. Much to my dismay, help arrived in the form of the grumpy Professor Thrackborne. He glowered at me while he worked, snapping the barrier with ease before demanding I meet with him in his office after my last class the following day.

After the handful of strange occurrences that seemed to happen while I slept, the normalcy of the first day of term was almost a relief. I was showered and dressed in my uniform before Shadrie even rolled out of bed.

"Damn, B, you look hot." Shadrie whistled as she stumbled out of her room. "Zypher won't know what hit him."

"It's not my fault. Whoever is in charge of uniforms has a schoolgirl fetish." I rolled my eyes.

"What's your first class today?"

"Um, Spellcasting 101," I replied, pulling my course schedule out of my bag.

"You'll like that one. It's a required course for all the students from the human realm, but from what my sister told me, it's really good for getting them up to the same level of spellcasting as those of us who've been doing the basic spells our whole lives," she said, strolling over and snagging the paper from my hand. "Ooh, Intro to Supes, that's a good one too. All the reading you've been doing should make that one an easy pass for you. I'm sad we don't have any classes together today, but at least we can meet for dinner after your combat training class."

"I wish. I have to report to Thrackborne's office immediately after my last class, remember."

Shadrie scrunched her nose. "I forgot about that. I don't know what you did to get on the dragon's bad side, but girl, I would not want to be in your shoes. The man is smoking—no pun intended—but scary as hell."

"I totally needed you to make me even more nervous than I already was about having to meet with him," I drawled. "Can we please not talk about my meeting with the scary-ass dragon and get something to eat before classes start? I'd like to pretend I'm actually going to survive my first day."

"Yeah, yeah. Give me like thirty and I'll be ready." Shadrie waved a hand over her head as she headed for the door, carrying her shower caddy.

While I waited, I unpacked and repacked the messenger bag I'd found included in my school supplies, making sure I had everything I needed for the day. As resistant as I'd been when I arrived a week ago, I had to admit, I was excited to learn actual magic. I'd just repacked my bag for the tenth time when Shadrie returned, ready to head to the dining hall.

The early morning light bathed the campus in a soft glow as we exited Magus House. I was so captivated by the sight that I didn't notice Zypher Morningstar standing a few yards away from the entrance until Shadrie elbowed me in the side. As if sensing my presence, Zypher's eyes landed on me, and his face split into a brilliant smile.

"Dilectus," he purred, his long legs closing the distance in only a few strides. "I've come to escort you to breakfast."

"Oh, um, thanks. I think." I managed.

"It is my honor." He grinned, bowing slightly and motioning for Shadrie and me to continue walking.

I wasn't really sure what to think about the massive demon as he fell into step beside me. Shadrie encouraged me to give him a chance, but I had no idea where to start.

"So, Zypher, you're a Third Year, right?" Shadrie asked, breaking the awkward silence. "That means you've manifested all your abilities?"

"That is correct. Although demons don't manifest in the same manner as mages. We attend the Academy to master our more unusual gifts."

"What are yours?" I asked, my curiosity getting the better of me.

"I am pleased you wish to know, Dilectus," he said, smiling down at me. "Beyond my demonic abilities I've had from birth, I am able to create shields and illusions."

"Illusions? Is that why you don't have horns?" I asked, causing Shadrie to cackle.

Zypher let loose a deep, rumbling belly laugh. "No. I only have horns in my demon form," he answered, his unnaturally blue eyes sparkling as he dipped down to whisper in my ear. "I'd be pleased to show you sometime, Dilectus."

My face flushed red as Zypher straightened back to his full height and shot me a wink. Unsure how to respond, we fell into silence again as we continued on to the dining hall. Once we arrived, Zypher found us a table and moved toward the buffets. When I tried to follow, he insisted I sit and wait. Shadrie and I settled in at his request, and she gave me a knowing stare as I wondered what the giant was up to. My eyes nearly bugged out of my head when he returned with several plates overflowing with food and set them in front of me.

"Eat, Dilectus. You will need your strength for classes." Zypher murmured before wandering off to grab his own breakfast.

"You should see your face right now." Shadrie laughed. "Your eyes look like they might pop out of your head at any second. This is the most entertainment I've had in ages."

"Not cool, Shadrie. What the hell am I supposed to do about all this food? No way I can eat it all."

Shadrie shrugged and snagged one of the overfilled plates from in front of me. Zypher returned moments later with his food and sat in the empty seat beside me. I couldn't help stealing glances at the gigantic demon out of the corner of my eye. He wasn't anything like I'd imagined a demon being, aside from his massive frame. Instead, he was breathtakingly gorgeous. His luscious lips tipped up in the corners as if he were perpetually happy, and his blue eyes seemed to glow every time they turned to me. I wasn't sure if it was relief or torment that whipped through me when we finally parted ways for classes.

I was still trying to puzzle out the strange feeling when I strolled into the amphitheater-style classroom. Biting the inside of my cheek, I looked around for a place to sit and smiled when I caught sight of Miles across the room, waving to get my attention. Hurrying over to him, I slid into the chair next to his and pulled the textbook for Spellcasting 101 out of my messenger bag.

"I was hoping we'd have this class together." Miles grinned. "It's always a little weird not knowing anybody."

"Me too." I smiled, trying not to chuckle at his disheveled appearance. "You might want to fix your tie."

Miles blinked at me and then looked down to where his tie sat crookedly around his neck, his brown hair flopping into his eyes. "Oh, right. Thanks."

"Good morning, class." A tinkling voice called through the room, drawing my attention to a woman no taller than three feet with sparkling wings and purple hair. "I'm Professor Snowthistle." I tracked her movements as she fluttered toward the front of the room, taking her place in front of the long blackboard. "For those of you who aren't familiar with my kind, I am a Pixie. You will learn more about Pixies and other supernaturals in your other courses. This course is Spellcasting 101. It's my duty to teach you the groundwork and basic spells that all supernaturals raised in this realm are taught from childhood. Are there any questions before we get started?"

"Yeah, what's the point of this? I could just shift and eat you. I don't need spells to do that," a male voice called out.

"Is that so?" Professor Snowthistle asked, arching a purple brow at the muscular boy seated near the back of the room. "Would you care to assist me in a demonstration then, Mr. Vohs?"

"I'd hate to hurt you, Prof." The boy smirked.

"Please, by all means, Mr. Vohs. It would be a great service to us all if you would assist me by shifting and going on the attack."

"Your funeral." He muttered, standing from his seat and stripping his uniform as he strolled to the front of the classroom.

My eyes widened in horror as he stripped bare, and his nude form shimmered and changed. In the blink of an eye, a wolf appeared in his place, taking up most of the empty space between the front row and where the professor stood. Professor Snowthistle's small hand twitched, signaling him to attack. I gasped as the massive beast lunged forward, jaws snapping at the woman. I barely noticed the motion of her hand or the words she muttered under her breath, clutching my chest in horror over the certainty she was about to be eaten by the wolf.

The classroom erupted into laughter as the wolf slammed into an invisible barrier with a yelp. Professor Snowthistle's hands moved in rapid succession, her voice too low for anyone to hear, and suddenly the beast was bound and suspended near the peak of the vaulted ceiling.

"Now, class, as you can see, I have successfully shielded myself from attack and subdued my attacker. While the second spell I used is something you will learn in more advanced courses, shielding is one of the foundations you will learn here." She smirked, waving her hand and causing the wolf to fall to the floor with a thud. "If someone would be so kind as to take Mr. Vohs to the infirmary, I'm sure that landing was quite painful."

"Holy shit," I breathed.

"I know, badass, right?" Miles replied in awe.

Professor Snowthistle clapped her hands together, calling the class back to order as a girl who was seated next to the wolf boy moved to drag his unconscious form from the classroom.

"Our first lesson will be creating a light orb. If you would turn to page fifteen in your textbooks, you will see the sigil you need to draw out with your hand as well as the coinciding spell."

I turned my attention to the text, opening to the correct page as the professor waited for everyone. Once she was satisfied we'd all followed her instructions, she carefully went over the steps laid out in the book, producing a brilliant yellow orb of light in her palm. After a few more demonstrations, we were instructed to try the spell on our own as she flitted around the room to help.

The sigil seemed simple enough as I moved my hand in the jagged lines displayed in the text. After a few failed attempts, I began to grow frustrated.

"Lux or," I huffed, dragging my fingers through the air to the left, then upward to the right before flipping my hand palm up.

"May I?" Miles asked from beside me, his hand reaching as if to grab mine before pulling away.

"You can touch me, you know." I chuckled. "I don't bite."

Miles flushed a bright red all the way to his ears. "It's not that. I just don't want to end up pounded into oblivion by your mate."

"What?" I demanded, my jaw falling open in shock.

"Most male supes can scent other people, and they get pretty territorial about their mates. I don't want to leave my scent on you and end up getting my ass kicked because of it. I don't know if you've noticed, B, but I'm kind of wimpy compared to most of the guys here."

A shocked laugh burst from my lips before I clapped a hand over my mouth. "I promise I won't let Zypher hurt you," I said when I finally dropped my hand. "Next time I see him, I'll make sure to lay down some ground rules. I didn't know about the whole scent thing, or I'd have told him to keep that alphahole shit to himself this morning."

Miles chuckled and shook his head. "I'd love to witness that. Anyway, I can help you with this spell if you want. The problem is your fingers."

"Show me," I said, holding my hand out for him to manipulate.

Miles carefully folded my hand into a fist before straightening my index finger and forcing my thumb flush with the side of my hand. My eyes narrowed in concentration as I tried to memorize the way my hand felt as he sliced it through the air in the correct pattern, before forcing my remaining fingers open mid-turn.

"See, you're just opening your hand a little too late. Now you try."

I closed my eyes and took a breath before moving my hand the way Miles had. "Lux or," I whispered.

"Look, B, you did it!" Miles cheered, causing my eyes to pop open to find a small glowing yellow orb floating just above my palm.

"Fuck yeah, I did!" I whooped, throwing my arm around his shoulders. "Thanks, Miles, you're the best!"

The rest of the class went by in a blur of practicing the light orb spell. Miles helped make little adjustments to my hand motions until I had it down, having learned the spell in his coven already. By the time we were dismissed, I was able to consistently cast the orb without any issue.

My second class of the day, Introduction to Supernaturals, wasn't nearly as interesting as I'd hoped. Professor Sabelus introduced himself as a vampire before instructing us to read the first chapter of our textbooks in silence while he napped at his desk. When he finally dismissed class, I was all but certain Shadrie had been right about the course being an easy pass for me. I hadn't learned anything new from the first chapter after the books from the library I'd spent my first several days at the

Academy reading, and the professor hadn't bothered to do any actual teaching. I was so desperate for coffee to perk me up after such a boring lesson that I didn't notice Zypher outside of the classroom until I ran face-first into his rock-hard chest.

"I am pleased to see you too, Dilectus," he chuckled, using one hand to steady me while handing me a steaming go-cup of coffee with the other.

"How did you know?" I asked, nodding toward the cup as I took it from him.

"Sabelus teaches a few upper-level courses. Even when he's not sleeping at his desk, his method of instruction will bore anyone to tears." Zypher smirked. "I noticed you heading into the classroom and knew you'd need a pick-me-up."

"Thanks," I replied, taking a sip of coffee and nearly moaning in delight. "This is amazing."

"It pleases me greatly to hear that." He grinned, tucking a stray hair behind my ear. "I wish for nothing more than your happiness, Dilectus."

"Woah there, big guy," I said, patting his chest. "Let's get to know each other first, yeah?"

"I would love nothing more. Perhaps we can dine together again this evening?"

"I would, but I have a meeting with my head of house this evening." I cringed. "Maybe tomorrow?"

"Certainly. I will see you then." He smiled. "Unfortunately, I need to get to my next course, but I look forward to spending more time with you, Dilectus."

I smiled and shook my head at the strange demon as he took my hand and kissed it before turning and leaving. Not really sure what to do with myself, I headed to the dining hall and grabbed a sandwich for my lunch before heading to the library. If Professor Sabelus wasn't going to teach us anything, I was going to have to take it upon myself to learn about the world I found myself immersed in—starting with figuring out the whole demon mate thing.

CHAPTER TEN

Bechora

My lungs burned as I raced across campus to the training pitch. I'd lost track of time in the library, reading through the handful of books the librarian helped me find about *mates*. I'd managed to read through two of them fully, not finding much about demon mates, before the clock above the librarian's desk chimed out, causing me to realize I was going to be late to combat class if I didn't hurry. I skidded to a stop at the end of the line of students just as the professor strolled onto the field.

"Greetings. I am Professor Rumlock, and this is combat training." The tall, muscular fae spoke, his voice booming across the pitch. "Our first lesson will be spent working to gauge your current combat abilities. Once you've all changed into your training gear, we will go through a series of warm-up exercises, and then I will pair you off to assess your skills."

Nerves fluttered in my stomach as his eyes moved along the line of students, the white scar cutting across his left eye down the side of his face, giving him a severe look. Something about the male screamed violence, and I worried I would be found lacking. Sure, I'd lived on the streets, fighting for literal scraps to survive, but I'd never had any formal training.

"The male's locker room is to the left, and the female's to the right. You will find lockers with your name on them containing your gear. You have fifteen minutes to change and be back on the pitch ready to go," Rumlock barked out.

We scattered like mice, hurrying to our designated locker rooms. It was almost shocking how normal the girls looked. There were rows of lockers with benches in front of them and shower stalls tucked away in the far corner. The familiarity of it was comforting as I scanned the labeled lockers, finding mine. Tucked inside were a pair of black, form-fitting pants littered with various weapon sheaths, a long-sleeved black shirt, and a vest. I changed as quickly as I could, trying not to marvel at how sturdy the material felt under my fingers, before putting on the black tennis shoes provided for me and making my way back to the training ground.

In the short span of time since we'd left the field to change, it had been transformed. In place of the green field were various training mats and weapons racks. Professor Rumlock stood in front of the nearest mat; his arms crossed over his chest as he watched students file out of the locker rooms. His hard expression was the only thing that kept me from gawking at the new setup.

After several more minutes, Professor Rumlock dropped his arms to his side and began calling out orders, organizing us into neat rows. Once he was satisfied with our formation, he began a series of exercises meant to get our heart rate up and muscles warm. The warm-up alone worked muscles I didn't realize I even had, which was saying something considering all the ways I'd worked my body on stage at the club.

I was starting to think the combat professor just enjoyed torturing us with the insanity he called a warm-up when he finally started splitting us into pairs. There didn't seem to be any rhyme or reason to the way the professor paired students off as I watched girls be paired with boys and take their place on the mats. I felt a brief moment of relief when I was partnered with another female—at least until she gave me a predatory grin once we faced each other across our assigned mat.

"You will be allowed to use your abilities when you spar. This will help you hone them as tools in your arsenal. The pitch is spelled against lethal actions, so this is the one place on the grounds you will be able to use your magic to its full extent. As I'm sure many of you have noticed by now, the rest of the campus prevents some of the more harmful magic from being used outside of specific spaces. That is not the case in this class. Many of you will be carried off the mats today and taken to the infirmary."

My heart dropped into my stomach as Professor Rumlock continued his speech. I had no idea how to access my magic. Everything I'd managed so far was an accident while I was sleeping. Looking across the mat to find my sparring partner still wearing a feral grin, I knew I was going to have to fight dirty—and even then, I would probably still be one of the students carted off to the infirmary.

"You may begin!" Rumlock's voice boomed across the pitch.

My partner immediately shifted into a bear without a care for her training uniform.

"Oh shit," I squeaked as she swiped a large paw at me.

I barely managed to dodge the swipe, her claws snagging on one of the weapon slots on my right thigh and tearing it open. She lumbered backward before letting out a roar and charging me. I dove to the mat, avoiding the impact and finding myself under her furry belly.

"Come on, come on, come on," I gritted out, shaking my hands in the hopes that something would happen.

The bear chuffed almost like she was laughing at my inability to defend myself against her and swiped a paw under her body where I lay on my back. I screamed as her claws tore through my vest and shirt, digging deep into my shoulder.

"How the fuck am I supposed to fight a bear?" I whimpered, grabbing my wounded arm and kicking my feet at her belly as hard as I could.

Somehow, I managed to get out from under her and scramble to my feet at the far side of the mat. She paced on her side, her lips pulled back in what I could only describe as a twisted, taunting grin. My eyes roamed over her massive form, looking for any weak points, but I didn't know anything about bears to know what I should be looking for. The girl stopped pacing, and I could tell she was about to charge when a bolt of lightning struck her in the back, crashing from the sky with a loud crack. My mouth fell open in awe as the scent of burnt hair and flesh overtook my senses.

"Sorry!" a curvy blonde called from a few mats away. "Sorry, I wasn't aiming there!"

"Ms. Forrester!" Professor Rumlock's voice called out. "Aim for your own sparring partner!"

"Yes, sir! Sorry!" the girl squeaked out.

My stomach roiled in relief as I eyed the now unconscious bear splayed out on the opposite side of my mat. I kept my hand pressed against my injured shoulder, blood pouring through my fingers as I waited for the professor to make his way to me.

"Mr. Dreadgrave," he barked out, catching the attention of a lean-built male with brunette hair twisted into a bun at the back of his head. "If you would please take Ms. Tarrene and Ms. Knight to the infirmary."

"Yes, sir," the guy called out, moving from his mat to mine so fast that he was a blur.

"And Gabriel, I feel compelled to remind you that, though Ms. Knight may be bleeding, she is not your thrall. Fangs to yourself," Professor Rumlock said sternly.

Gabriel chuckled under his breath as he lifted the unconscious bear over his shoulder with ease. He jerked his head for me to follow and headed off the pitch. I kept some distance between us, the professor's words still ringing in my ears.

"You should pick up the pace," Gabriel called back to me, not bothering to take his eyes off the direction he was walking. "I don't need eyes to know you've lost a lot of blood. I can smell it."

"You... you can *smell* it?" I squeaked out, picking up my pace.

"Well, yeah. I'm a vampire. Of course I can smell it." He scoffed.

"And it doesn't, like, send you into a frenzy?"

Gabriel stopped walking and turned to face me with a scowl,

shifting the bear's weight on his shoulder as he did. "Do you always ask such invasive and ridiculous questions? No, I do not go into a frenzy. My kind is taught from birth to control our urges so that we're prepared when we ascend." He narrowed his eyes and stepped closer. "You should learn to watch what you say before you end up in more trouble than you can handle."

"Hey, I can handle myself just fine, asshole." I huffed.

Gabriel tilted his head back and laughed. "Right, and that pathetic display on the training pitch was just to get Esmara to let her guard down. You'd have totally had her if Kiri didn't have shit aim."

My face flushed with embarrassment at his sarcastic words. "It's not my fault the professor paired me up with a freaking bear. Who stands a chance against that?"

"Everyone except you, clearly." Gabriel chuckled. "It didn't slip my notice that you didn't use your ability to protect yourself. That tells me two things, Ms. Knight"—his tone grew menacing, and he crowded into my space—"you're a dud, and you're the weakest supernatural currently at the Academy. How the Academy's magic made the mistake of enrolling someone like you is beyond me, because it's only a matter of time before you get yourself killed. You'd do well to remember that the next time you think of challenging me."

Gabriel stepped back and turned around, stalking off in the direction we were headed. I sucked in a relieved breath, my hands shaking. Gabriel Dreadgrave's behavior may have screamed *bully*, but he was right. I needed to be more careful, at least until I could defend myself. Keeping a few yards between us, I followed him quietly the rest of the way to the infirmary. I didn't relax again until he'd finished telling the healers what happened with the bear and left.

"Selir's sake, what is Rumlock thinking pairing a First Year mage with a Second Year shifter, and on the first day of class, too?" tutted the gray-haired, matronly woman inspecting my shoulder.

Her fingers prodded the gaping wounds, and I winced just before soft green light glowed in her palms.

"Will she be alright?" I asked, curious about the condition of my sparring partner.

"She'll be fine. Nothing a few days here won't cure. The spell around the training pitch prevented serious internal damage. Just some bad burns to salve and heal, don't you worry," the healer replied as she continued to work.

The skin at the edges of my shoulder wound began to itch furiously, and the matron slapped my other hand away as I tried to scratch. I could almost swear I felt my flesh knitting itself back together, but aside from the itching, there wasn't any pain. After a few more minutes of her green glowing palms and feeling like a colony of ants lived under my skin, the sensations stopped.

"There you are, dear. Good as new." She smiled, patting my now unblemished shoulder. "Don't fret about combat training either, dear. I'll be having a word with Dean Femirea about Rumlock's extreme pairings. Won't be having my infirmary full up from his sessions again this year."

Though it was clear the woman meant to comfort me, her words caused me to pale. I couldn't help wondering how many students Professor Rumlock's teaching methods sent to the infirmary, for her to find it problematic. Before I could ask, she shooed me off the exam table and motioned for me to be on my way, handing me my uniform and messenger bag. I had no idea how either arrived at the infirmary, since I hadn't brought them with me or seen anyone else enter after I had, but I was relieved I didn't have to trek back across campus to retrieve them.

My stomach growled loudly as I made my way from the building. A quick glance at the sky was enough to tell me it was close to dinner time. It didn't take mastering telling time by the stars to know that the sun being close to the horizon meant it was well into the evening. Digging my campus map out of my bag, I studied it for a second to get my bearings and then headed toward the dining hall. I was halfway there, according to the magical dotted path that appeared, when a surly voice boomed across the open quad.

"Ms. Knight, you wouldn't be trying to skip our meeting now, would you?" Professor Thrackborne scowled, his arms crossed as he stared me down.

CHAPTER ELEVEN

Caulder

Bechora turned toward me slowly, her lips pressed together in displeasure. Dropping my arms to my side, I stalked toward her. She stood her ground, glaring at me as I closed the distance. My mate's lack of fear in the face of an angry dragon pleased me. The pride I felt in my little mate was quickly replaced by boiling rage. She reeked of blood. It blended into the black of her training uniform, but the jagged tears in the top were enough to tell me it was hers.

"You're injured," I growled, smoke billowing out of my mouth with the words. "Who?"

"What? No, I'm fine. It was just a training accident," she said, scrunching her face.

"Who?" I demanded again, clenching my hands into fists to combat the urge to grab her and steal her away somewhere safe.

"Dude, what is your damage? I told you I'm fine."

"You are not fine. Your shirt is shredded, and you're soaked in your own blood." I snarled, reaching out and tugging at the rip near her shoulder.

She jerked out of my grasp and scowled at me. "Hands off. Whatever *this*"—she waved a finger in some semblance of a circle in my direction—"is, I'm not with it. I wasn't trying to skip the meeting, I just forgot. I imagine being mauled by a god damned bear would cause anyone to forget. You don't get to manhandle me over it."

She was yelling by the time she finished speaking, and all I could do was blink at her in stunned silence. Crossing her arms in front of her chest in a mirror of my own stance moments before, she tapped her foot on the pavement.

"Look, if we're done here... I'm starving. I'd like to get something to eat from the dining hall and then shower off this awful day before I crash."

"We're not done here." I scoffed. "We had a meeting scheduled. We will have it. Follow me to my office, Ms. Knight." I turned back toward the admin building, listening for the sound of her footsteps behind me. When I didn't hear them, I paused. "Ms. Knight, unless you would like a detention, you will follow me to my office for our meeting."

She let out a huff, but I could hear her moving toward me. I continued my way toward the lone black tower that held the administration offices before heading inside and climbing the winding staircase to the fifth floor. Bechora wisely followed behind me in silence. While I was pleased that she didn't cow before me as my mate, her desire to verbally spar with me made it difficult to maintain the boundaries between us.

When we finally entered my office, I moved behind my desk and motioned for her to take one of the empty high-backed chairs on the other side. Her eyes flitted around the small space, taking in the dark decor and massive bookshelves behind her. Smiling to myself, I stooped down and pulled a Tupperware container with homemade stir fry from the bottom drawer of my desk. Wrapping my hands around the container, I muttered the words to release the cooling spell and called forth the heat of my dragon. Once I was sure it was adequately warmed, I strolled back around my desk and handed it to Bechora.

"Eat," I commanded.

She shot me a suspicious look and opened the container. "I didn't know Tupperware existed here. Is this actually safe to eat?"

"It's not poisoned, if that's what you mean." I snorted. "It's stir-fry. I picked up the recipe during a trip to the human realm, along with a handful of those plastic containers.

They're almost as handy as magic."

"This is real stir fry?" she asked, sniffing at the food as she removed the fork I'd attached to the lid. "It's not some weird fairy shit that you cooked up to look like stir fry?"

"For the love of Selir, would you just eat?" I groaned. "You said you were hungry, and I would like for that to *not* be a distraction during our meeting."

Bechora scoffed but did as I asked. I moved back to my chair and settled in, trying to busy myself with anything I could to avoid staring at my mate. She let out a soft moan of pleasure, and I stiffened, my eyes shooting to her face.

"This is actually really good," she said before shoveling another bite into her mouth.

"Yes, well, I take great pleasure in perfecting recipes. I'd be truly surprised if you didn't like it."

"That's surprisingly human, albeit arrogant as fuck." She laughed.

"It's not arrogant when it's true." I smirked, forgetting for a moment that I needed to maintain my distance. "Dragons are known to have a great many skills."

"Alright, Gordon Ramsey. Whatever you say," she said, rolling her eyes.

"I know not of this Gordon of which you speak."

"Of course not." She snorted before turning her attention back to her meal.

This time I couldn't take my eyes off of her. She was almost beastly in the way she shoveled the stir-fry into her mouth. I'd never once found myself aroused by the way a female ate, but there was something so wild and carefree about Bechora inhaling food I'd made that it didn't take long before I was adjusting myself in my slacks. I wasn't sure if it was the mate bond or her, but it was making me question my resolve. The only thing that kept me in check was the knowledge of what would happen if anyone found out she was mine.

"Thank you for the food," she said softly, leaning forward to set the now-empty dish on my desk. "Would you mind telling me what this meeting is about?"

"Yes," I said, pausing to clear my throat. "I scheduled this meeting as I thought it would be useful for you to work on your shielding ability outside of classes."

"I don't understand. It's a pretty common ability, from what I read before the term started."

"Shielding is a common ability. Even those who cannot produce them on their own can create one with a spell. What isn't common is the ability to create nearly impenetrable shields, which you did. Your roommate told me everything she'd tried to break it, and any one of the spells she used would have broken a normal shield summoned by a novice." I didn't bother telling her that I suspected the only reason I'd been able to break the shield was because I was her mate. "Only two others on campus can create a shield that strong. One of them is Dean Femirea, the other is a third-year student."

"Oh," she replied, her eyes wide. "But at orientation, they said I was a fire mage."

"It's not uncommon for supernaturals to have a second ability. Typically, their primary ability will manifest during the orientation rituals, and their secondary will appear shortly thereafter."

Bechora frowned, her lips pursing for a second before she spoke. "What if there are more than two?"

"It's rare, but true elemental mages do exist. They can control all of the elements: fire, water, air, and earth. Depending on parentage, they could have innate shielding abilities." I studied her reaction closely, noting what appeared to be disappointment. "As I said, true elemental mages are incredibly rare. It's far more common to have one or two abilities."

She wiggled her finger in a circle as if to physically bring us back to the point—"how do I access it? Because I gotta be honest, it would have been insanely useful in combat class today. I wouldn't have ended up mauled by a damned bear."

My dragon bristled at the mention of her sparring accident,

and I made a mental note to have a word with Rumlock.

"We're going to attempt a visualization exercise to locate your power."

Bechora let out an amused snort. "Just close my eyes and go to my happy place, then?"

"Not exactly," I replied. "But yes, it's easier if you close your eyes." I waited a moment for her to do so, watching as she relaxed back into the chair. "Most supernaturals describe their magic as feeling like a ball of energy within their core. I want you to mentally work your way through your body, starting with your toes, and just feel."

She cracked one emerald-green eye open and pulled her lips into a frown. "This—"

"Seems silly," I interrupted. "I am aware, but if you can recognize how the rest of your body feels, you will be able to recognize when something is different. In this case, the difference we're looking for is your magic."

"Fine," she huffed, closing her eye.

I took the opportunity to study her. This was probably the closest I would be able to get to my mate until either my work with Vallynn was complete or she graduated from the academy. Even knowing secrecy and distance were necessary, I couldn't help the pang of longing that settled into my chest.

My eyes roamed over her, taking in the way her red hair framed her heart-shaped face. I'd learned through her file that she'd produced fire magic at orientation, and for some reason, the color of her hair made it feel obvious that my mate would control such a wild and reckless element. My fingers itched to tuck the fiery strands behind her ear, just so that I could have even the briefest moment of connection with her.

"This isn't working," she groaned, her long lashes fluttering open.

"What did you feel?" I asked, forcing my eyes away from her plump lips.

"I felt nothing." She shrugged.

"Nothing at all?" I arched a brow at her. "That's not

necessarily unusual. It may take a few attempts for the visualization to help."

"No," she replied, shaking her head. "It wasn't just nothing, it was... like a void. Just a massive, empty void. Look, can we pick this up another time? I'm honestly just exhausted, and if this is going to take some time to actually help, it would probably be better trying it when I'm not ready to collapse into my bed and sleep for a month."

My lips pressed into a firm line, and I nodded. As she slipped from my office, I mulled over what she'd said about feeling an empty void. I'd never heard any supernatural describe such a sensation, not even their first time with the technique. While I was relatively new at using it with Academy students, I'd spent enough time in the human realm with another dragon clan, helping their young unlock their dragons, to know it was abnormal. It didn't make any sense. She'd manifested at orientation and then later with the shield. Shaking my head, I stood from my desk. There was something unusual about my little mate, and I needed to get to the bottom of it.

CHAPTER TWELVE

Bechora

I trudged my way across campus to my dorm room and gathered my things for a quick shower to get the blood off of me. I wasn't sure what to do about my ruined training uniform, but that was a problem for tomorrow. By the time I scrubbed the dried, flaky blood from my skin and dressed in my night clothes, I was so exhausted that I was seeing things. For a brief moment, I thought I saw fur spread across my face when I caught my reflection in the mirror. Blinking my tired eyes, I dragged my feet back to my room and collapsed into bed. There wasn't anything unusual when I checked my reflection in my vanity mirror the next morning.

"This place definitely has me hallucinating," I mumbled to myself as I smoothed my hair down.

I groaned as I stretched my stiff, sore muscles and slowly made my way to my door. Even though I'd slept, I felt like I'd done ten rounds with Mike Tyson. Everything ached.

"Oh, good! You're up." Shadrie beamed when I strolled into the living area of our dorm. She lifted a small brown package and waved it at me. "This came for you."

"What is it?" I frowned, taking it from her hands.

Shadrie just shrugged and motioned for me to open it. Carefully, I peeled away the tape, sealing the package and retrieved a small vial of liquid from inside. There was a brown tag tied to the neck of the bottle that read *Drink Me.* My brows knit together as I studied it, tilting the bottle side to side as I watched the shimmering blue liquid slosh around.

"Damn, B, someone's sending you the good stuff. I bet it was

Zypher."

"Uh, what the hell is it?" I asked.

"It's a restoration potion. Those things are expensive as fuck, too."

"What is a restoration potion?"

Shadrie blinked at me for a moment in silence. "It's only the best recovery potion ever made. I'd kill for one right now. My entire body aches from combat training yesterday morning. You take that and you'll feel brand new. No sore muscles, no brain fog, nothing," she said with a dreamy sigh.

"I'm trusting you, Shadrie," I said, eyeing her. "If this does something weird to me instead of making me feel better, I'm going to find a way to dye all your clothes pink."

She let out an offended gasp and clutched her chest, her voice a hushed whisper. "You wouldn't dare."

"I would. Especially if you're pulling some *Alice in Wonderland* shrinking potion trick on me."

"Cold, Bechora. Very cold." She playfully scowled before waving her hand toward the vial. "I promise it won't do anything weird to you."

I squinted at her before uncorking the vial and downing the contents. My eyes grew wide at the taste of cotton candy and the sudden warmth that traveled down my throat. The warmth seemed to spread to my limbs in a matter of seconds, and I couldn't help the squeak of delight that left me as I realized I wasn't feeling stiff or sore any longer.

"See?" Shadrie grinned, waggling her eyebrows at me.

"I'm going to have to make sure to thank Zypher. That potion is a fucking miracle," I replied.

"Speaking of, he practically interrogated Miles about the human realm when he sat with me at dinner. Where were you, anyway?"

"I had my meeting with Professor Thrackborne," I replied, letting my face show my irritation with the dragon professor. "He threatened me with detention if I didn't follow him to his office for our meeting, as I was on my way to the dining hall. It didn't occur to me at the time, but it's ridiculous that detention is a thing. We're adults, for fuck's sake."

"What do you think detention entails?" Shadrie asked. The tone of her voice told me that my answer had no chance of being correct.

"I mean… I'd assume you're stuck in a classroom with anyone else who has detention, and you just have to sit there until they release you. That's how it is back home, but they don't have detention past high school."

"Oh, you sweet, ignorant thing. No." Shadrie laughed, causing me to scowl at her. "A guy in my potions class has detention all week. You know what they've been having him do? He said they alternate between planting for the potions master and cutting crystals for advanced spellcasting, which is not nearly as easy as it sounds. My sister even told me about a student who had to use his abilities to repair one of the old stables. I can only imagine what sort of twisted punishment Thrackborne would concoct."

"That sounds intense. How do they get away with that?" I demanded. "There have to be laws against using students as laborers."

"It's not like the human realm," Shadrie shrugged. "The Academy can do whatever they like so long as it hones a skill."

"That's really messed up."

"Welcome to the supernatural realm, B." She grinned. "We should probably head to breakfast before that mate of yours comes looking for you, though. After the way he acted at dinner, I'd bet my life Zypher is impatiently waiting for us outside."

Shaking my head at how absurd it was that the Academy could abuse its power the way Shadrie described, I snagged my messenger bag and followed her from our dorm. I caught sight of Zypher waiting just outside of Magus House for us, two paper cups in his hands. Some part of me was soothed by his presence, but I wasn't sure I wanted to examine that feeling any closer yet.

"Good morning, Dilectus." He smiled, handing me one of the cups.

"Good morning," I replied, taking a sip from the cup he'd handed me and nearly groaning in satisfaction as delicious coffee filled my mouth. "God, this is good. Thank you. And thank you for the potion, too."

"You are very welcome for the coffee, Dilectus. I noticed it was your preferred morning beverage yesterday. However, I didn't send you any potion."

"Well, somebody did. B had a restoration potion sent to her this morning," Shadrie chimed in, linking her arm through mine and turning me so that I was between her and Zypher.

"Maybe it was from the infirmary. I did have to go there yesterday after Rumlock paired me with a fucking bear for class," I said.

"He did what?!" Zypher demanded, pulling me free of Shadrie and positioning me in front of him so his eyes could scan over my entire body.

"I'm fine, big guy." I smiled, patting his chest. "I got swiped on the shoulder, but the infirmary fixed me right up. And I'm not even sore thanks to the potion I got this morning."

Zypher's chest rumbled under my palm as he let out a low growl. "Unacceptable. You should have *never* been injured. I will speak to Rumlock."

"You really don't need to," I replied.

Zypher looked down at me, his gaze softening. "I do, Dilectus. I told you that I would prove myself worthy the night we met. I cannot do so if I knowingly allow you to be injured again."

"Just go with it, B," Shadrie spoke, grinning at me.

"Fine," I said with a sigh. "But nothing crazy, okay?"

"On my honor," Zypher grinned. "Now, let's get you fed, shall we?"

We chatted about our class schedules for the day as we made our way to the dining hall. Zypher was a third-year student at the Academy, and his commentary about some of the professors was enlightening. By the time we entered the dining hall, I'd learned that Professor Vatorgan, who taught astrology, was an elemental mage who'd once served at court. With the strange abilities I'd been manifesting in my sleep, I was looking forward to my first class of the day despite my personal thoughts on astrology being a sham.

"Sit, Dilectus. I will retrieve your breakfast." Zypher smiled as we stopped at what was becoming our usual table.

I opened my mouth to argue with him just as a body slammed into mine, knocking me off balance. Faster than I could blink, Zypher steadied me and grabbed the person who'd run into me, slamming them into the table. My mouth fell open in shock as I recognized Gabriel being pressed into the wood by the back of his neck so hard it bowed slightly. His honey-brown eyes locked on my face, and his lips twisted into an angry scowl.

"You dare touch my Dilectus?" Zypher snarled, squeezing Gabriel's neck slightly.

"I see the dud has found a powerful ally," Gabriel hissed. "What did you promise the demon to keep you safe?"

Zypher growled, lifting Gabriel by the neck and slamming him into the wooden table again. I shifted uncomfortably on my feet as the attention of everyone in the dining hall turned our way.

"Zypher," I said softly. "I'm sure it was an accident. Just let him go, and let's get our breakfast."

Gabriel let out a derisive snort and rolled his eyes. I reached out my hand and ran it down Zypher's arm, drawing his gaze away from the rude vampire. Unsure how to proceed, I glanced over my shoulder at Shadrie, who just shrugged.

"His accident"—Zypher started, saying the word like it left a foul taste in his mouth—"could have caused you to become hurt."

"I'm okay. I promise. I don't think he meant me any harm," I said, flicking my gaze to Gabriel. "You didn't mean anything by it, right?"

A muscle ticked in Gabriel's jaw as he clenched his teeth. His face was painted with so much fury and loathing it nearly stole my breath, and I couldn't understand why it was directed at me. Sure, I'd clearly made a faux pas when he'd led me to the infirmary after combat class, but I didn't think I'd given the vampire a reason to dislike me.

"Right," Gabriel spoke up finally, not bothering to hide the malice in his gaze.

Zypher squeezed the back of Gabriel's neck one more time before jerking him upright. "If you are smart, vampire, you will stay far away from my Dilectus. I am not as forgiving as she is, and I will have no problems tearing your heart from your chest should you touch her again."

Gabriel gave Zypher a tight nod, and Zypher released his hold on him. The vampire shot me an angry scowl before moving toward the exit faster than my eyes could track.

"Selir, that was hot," Shadrie spoke, fanning herself. "What I wouldn't give to have a guy go all beast mode for me."

I thrust my elbow back, catching her in the side just as Zypher turned his attention to me.

"Are you alright?" he asked, his gaze softening.

"I'm good," I smiled.

"Good. Though I would caution you to keep your distance from that vampire." Zypher replied as he tucked my hair behind my ear.

"Get a room, you two." Shadrie laughed as she moved around me toward the food buffets.

Zypher's eyes heated with desire, and his nostrils flared. "Say the word, Dilectus."

Heat crept up my chest and into my cheeks as I flushed under his intense stare. Shadrie cackled loudly, and I cleared my throat before patting Zypher's chest.

"Why don't we focus on getting something to eat?" I said.

"Of course," Zypher winked. "Sit, both of you. I shall bring your breakfast."

CHAPTER THIRTEEN

Bechora

After breakfast, I made my way across campus to the tall tower where my astrology class was held. It was in a secluded area, but it wasn't hard to find since the building was the tallest on campus. The circular building lay empty aside from a lone winding staircase that left me winded by the time I reached the top. Slipping into the classroom, I noted the seats were spread out around the wall and the large telescope in the center of the room, just near a large wooden desk where the Professor stood.

"You're the last to arrive, Ms. Knight." The portly, balding man spoke with a smile. "That will make you today's volunteer."

I bit back my retort as Professor Vatorgan motioned for me to stand beside his desk. My eyes scanned the smug faces of my classmates, catching sight of the rude blonde girl and her friend from my first day at the academy. My pulse quickened when my eyes landed on Dante, the guy I met in the communal bathroom, seated beside her. As if sensing my reaction to him, he smirked and shot me a wink.

"Prince Vallynn, if you would be so kind as to be my other volunteer for today." The professor spoke, causing my gaze to fall to the handsome male rising from his seat beside Dante. "As those of you raised in the realm are aware, Vallynn's chart was completed upon his birth, as are those of any royal. It will provide an excellent example of what you may find in your own, while we use Ms. Knight to show you how to get started."

Vallynn prowled through the circular room and stopped just

beside me without a word. Before I could politely introduce myself, Professor Vatorgan leaned toward me and asked my birthday.

"November fifteenth," I replied quietly.

"And do you know the time of your birth?" he asked.

I shook my head in response. It was a miracle I knew my first name and birthday to begin with. I was found wandering the streets alone when I was three, with only the name Bechora and *born November 15* scrawled on a piece of paper clutched in my tiny fist. The social workers weren't able to locate my birth parents, and by the time I fled my latest foster home at sixteen, I'd given up hope of ever knowing where I came from.

"Very well, your chart may not be as accurate, but it will be close enough." The professor smiled before waving his hand in the air. "Now, if you will all turn your attention to the ceiling."

Tilting my head back, I let out an awed gasp. Sparkling along the ceiling was a system of planets and stars unlike anything I'd ever seen. The lack of similarity to my own solar system only made it clearer that I wasn't in the human realm anymore. The Professor's hand waved again, and a series of golden lines formed, connecting various stars and planets.

"This is Prince Vallynn's star chart, plotted along the galaxy." Professor Vatorgan started. "Would any of you like to make an attempt at interpreting part of it?"

"I will, Professor." A nasally, feminine voice called out.

"Very good, Daena. What do you see for the prince based on his chart?"

"His chart starts in planet Nomia, like all royals," she began, "but then it reaches out to the star Etraalis, which means a happy soul bonding."

Vallynn stiffened beside me, and I could have sworn I heard him mutter a curse as Daena shot him a saccharine smile.

"Excellent." Professor Vatorgan praised. "And what of the placement of Mebiphus in his chart?" I couldn't help the satisfaction that rolled through me when the blonde fae frowned, unable to answer. "Anyone?"

"It means I will be tested," Vallynn spoke, his voice rolling through me and causing me to shiver. "That the outcome of whatever trials lie ahead for me could alter the course of the rest of my chart."

"Exactly!" The professor clapped. "Which brings me to a very important point. While our charts can often provide a clear picture of what is to come, there are times they can be altered. Given the proximity of Mebiphus to Nomia in Vallynn's chart, it is likely the tests he will face are the academy's own trials. Which, as you are all aware, can alter the course of any student's life." He waved his hand again, and new silver lines appeared. "This is Ms. Knight's star chart, based on the date of her birth."

"Professor," Daena interrupted. "Are you sure that's right? Her chart starts in Nomia, too."

Professor Vatorgan frowned and moved his fingers in the air as if recalculating something. "Are you quite sure that you were born on November fifteenth?" he asked me.

"As sure as I can be," I frowned.

The professor studied me closely for a moment, his brows knitted together. "Most interesting," he mumbled before addressing the class again. "While not common, we have seen historical accounts of star charts starting in Nomia for non-royals. It seems Ms. Knight is one of those rare instances. Now, would anyone like to take an attempt at interpreting part of her chart?"

Tilting my head back to study the illusion above us, I tried to make sense of it. While I didn't know any of the planets or stars floating near the ceiling, I didn't miss how many of the silver lines of my chart followed a similar path to the golden lines of Vallynn's.

"Etraalis connects to Zoax," Dante snickered. "Looks like Ms. Knight is gonna have a hard time keeping her mate."

The rest of the class laughed along with him, and I felt myself flush with embarrassment. I was seconds away from racing from the room just to escape the laughter and taunts when

Professor Vatorgan got the class back under control.

"Mr. Vazgurr's interpretation brings me to my next point." The professor spoke. "If one stops too soon with their interpretation, they miss the true meaning of the chart." He traced the line from a dark, angry-looking planet to a bright star slightly to the planet's left. "Okraxih would indicate the struggles that Ms. Knight and her mate will face are ones they will work together to overcome." With another wave of his hand, the illusion above us vanished to reveal the dome ceiling. "Thank you for your assistance. You two may take your seats now."

Vallynn moved first as my eyes worked to find an empty seat. When I found one three rows behind his friends, I moved toward it, walking behind the prince. I'd just started to pass Daena when she slid her foot into the aisle, causing me to trip and stumble forward. Vallynn moved as quickly as Zypher that morning, turning to face me and catching my bare forearms in his hands faster than I could blink. Heat shot through me as I steadied myself against his hold and looked up into his face. Our eyes locked, and my mind struggled to comprehend the unrestrained awe shining in his gaze.

"Vallynn," Daena called, her tone harsh. "What in the realm are you doing?"

The reverence in his face dissipated, and his expression smoothed into a mask of disgust. Shoving me back slightly, his upper lip curled. "Ensuring the trash doesn't molest me further."

"Fuck you," I hissed, shoving past him and stalking to the empty seat I'd spotted.

"I doubt he'd touch you with Professor Vatorgan's cock," Dante snorted, causing Daena and her friend to snicker.

I flipped them off over my shoulder and took my seat, slumping down in a poor attempt to disappear. The rest of the class went by in a haze of growing anger, and I barely heard anything the professor said as he talked us through the first few chapters of our textbooks and walked us through the steps of utilizing our birthdate, time of birth, and name to create our star charts. The moment he dismissed us, I fled the tower for the safety of my dorm room.

"What's wrong?" Shadrie asked, jumping up from our sofa as I slammed the door behind me.

"Fucking mean girls." I snapped.

"Tell me who and I'll ice their asses."

I began to pace angrily, staring at the floor as I told Shadrie what happened in astrology class. Replaying the scene only served to make me angrier, and I was boiling with rage by the time I finished talking.

"Oh, shit. Bechora." Shadrie squeaked, causing my head to snap up. "What in the seven hells? How do you have shadow magic?"

The common area of our dorm was rapidly filling with inky, black shadows that seemed to suck all the life and heat out of the space. The edge of them brushed against Shadrie's calf, causing her to cry out in pain before she jerked backward toward the door.

"Call them back, Bechora!" she called out.

Panic laced through me as I looked at my friend. "I don't know how!"

"Fuck, fuck, fuck." Shadrie chanted. "Selir damn it! Stay here, I'm going to get help."

"Please, hurry," I wailed, the shadows growing thicker in my panic.

Shadrie nodded and ran for the door, letting it slam shut behind her. I begged, pleaded, and sobbed aloud for the shadows to stop, but they seemed to be fueled by my distress. I was in near hysterics when Dante burst into the room, his body made of stone.

"You have to calm down," he shouted, grabbing me by the shoulders. I blinked at him in surprise. "That's it. Take a deep breath in and let it go slowly."

I did as he instructed, letting him talk me down through a simple breathing exercise. Each breath calmed me a little more than the last, and the shadows slowly began to recede until they'd disappeared entirely. The moment they were gone, it dawned on me that Dante was gently stroking my hair with a hand made of granite.

"What the fuck?" I demanded, jerking out of his reach.

His head snapped back like I'd slapped him, and he frowned as his body shifted from stone to skin. "I should be asking you that. Shadows are Fae magic, and unless you're hiding under a glamour, you aren't fae."

"Get out, Dante," Shadrie ordered, stepping into the room from the hallway.

"You're the one that dragged me out of the common room up here to help," he retorted.

Shadrie placed her hands on her hips and stared the male down. "Because I knew you'd know what to do after being with Vallynn for so long. You served your purpose, now get out before I call the head of house and report you for trespassing in our room."

Dante shook his head. "Whatever, Sha. Next time your roomie implodes, you can sort it out on your own."

"Oh, go take Vallynn's cock up the ass, gravel for brains." Shadrie snarled. "It's all you're good for outside of skulking on buildings."

"Skulking on buildings?" I asked, trying not to laugh at her ridiculous insult.

"He's a gargoyle. They love hanging out on ledges and shit. When they're not being massive jerks."

Dante scowled at Shadrie and opened his mouth as if to speak before snapping it shut again. With a low growl, he stalked from our dorm and slammed the door behind him. My roommate smirked before turning to face me.

"So... that was interesting." She started, her expression growing serious.

"I don't know what happened." I sighed, moving to sit on the sofa. "This has to be that elemental mage stuff you were talking about."

Shadrie shook her head and sat beside me. "I don't know how you manifested shadows, B, but Dante was right. Only fae have that ability."

"I'm not fae, though." I frowned. "I think I'd know if my ears were pointed."

"I know." She replied, grabbing one of my hands and giving it a gentle squeeze. "Even if someone glamoured you to hide it, the magic would be broken to reveal you as fae at orientation."

"What is happening to me?" I whispered.

"I don't know, B." Shadrie shook her head, squeezing my hand again. "But I promise I'll help you find out."

CHAPTER FOURTEEN

Bechora

Shadrie and I sat in silence on the couch for hours, both of us lost in thought. I'd missed the rest of my classes, including combat, but that was tomorrow's problem. I was currently too busy freaking out about whatever was happening to me. It wasn't until there was a knock on our door that either of us snapped out of it. Shadrie jumped to her feet, giving me a soft smile as she moved to open it.

"Professor Thrackborne!" Shadrie squeaked.

The surly dragon strode into the room, glowering at me. "You're late for our meeting, Ms. Knight."

"Shit," I hissed, standing from my seat. "I'm sorry, I lost track of time."

"And what exactly has you so distracted you forgot you have a meeting with your head of house, Ms. Knight?" he drawled, his nostrils flaring. "Is the paint on your walls that interesting?"

"It's my fault, Professor," Shadrie interjected, her eyes pleading with me to roll with it. "I was having some trouble with an assignment, and I asked Bechora for help."

"Is that so?" Thrackborne arched his brow. Shadrie paled under his intense stare but nodded. "Very well, come along, Ms. Knight. We can salvage what's left of our time."

I hurried to grab my bag and followed the grumpy male from my dorm, gently grabbing Shadrie's hand and squeezing it in thanks as I passed her. Professor Thrackborne strolled through Magus House at a clipped pace. I was practically jogging to keep up with him, afraid to ask him to slow down. We didn't stop until we were inside his office, and he motioned for me to take a seat as he leaned on the front of his desk.

"This is the second time you've attempted to skip our meeting, Ms. Knight," he drawled, crossing his arms in front of his chest. "If you aren't going to take this seriously, you won't make it at the academy."

His intense gaze caused me to squirm in my seat, and I picked at imaginary lint on my uniform skirt just to give my hands something to do. "I'm sorry. It wasn't intentional. This whole... everything... has just been a little overwhelming."

I glanced up in time to see the dragon's eyes soften. "That is understandable," he sighed, running a hand through his short brown hair, causing the muscles in his arm to flex. The urge to run my fingers along his bared skin gripped me suddenly, causing me to nearly miss his next words. "Am I correct in my assumption that you've missed lunch?"

My mouth opened and closed in shock. I didn't know what I'd expected him to ask, but it definitely wasn't about whether or not I ate lunch. Thrackborne watched me expectantly, and I finally managed to nod. His jaw clenched, and he moved around his desk, dipping down to pull a Tupperware container from a drawer. He murmured under his breath as he held the container between his hands and then moved to hand it to me.

"Eat."

"Thank you," I managed to get out as I opened the container.

Delicious, savory scents filled my nostrils as I took a moment to study the meal Professor Thrackborne handed me. The bright colors, so unlike anything I'd come across at home, instantly told me that it wasn't anything from the human realm. Cautiously, I speared the fork attached to the container through an orange, meaty substance and took a bite. Flavors exploded on my tongue, and I let out a low groan as I reveled in them. My life in the human realm left me ill-equipped to describe the taste, but I was eager for more, hurriedly stuffing my mouth with more of the strange food.

Thrackborne cleared his throat as I devoured the last bite,

my taste buds tempting me to lick the container clean. My eyes shot to where he stood stiffly behind his desk, his eyes a molten amber as they burned into me. I could have sworn the temperature in his office ratcheted up as flush crept into my cheeks and I carefully placed the empty Tupperware on his desk.

"So..." I started, repositioning in my chair and twisting my hands in my lap.

"We will try the visualization again," the professor said with a slight nod of his head. "Close your eyes."

I let my eyelids fall closed and waited for his next instruction. My body relaxed into my chair as Thrackborne began to speak. His voice wrapped around me like a gentle caress, and something in me wanted to reach out to pull him closer. The room seemed to warm around me, and a smoky scent filled my nose. It was almost like I was hypnotized, my mind following his whispered instructions without a thought as the sensations around me lulled me into a peaceful calm.

My senses felt heightened with each mental prod of my body, and while I still hadn't uncovered the well of magic these sessions were meant to uncover, there was a strange, insistent pull toward the cranky dragon. My fingers curled in my lap, nails biting into my palm as I resisted the urge to do something reckless, like stand from my seat and launch myself at the professor.

"Bechora," Thrackborne drawled. His voice held a hint of warning, as if he'd detected the direction of my thoughts. "Focus."

Opening my eyes just enough to glance at him through my lashes, I blew out a puff of air. "I am focused, Professor. Have you considered that maybe this just isn't working?"

"This is only our second attempt. It will work... in time."

Shaking my head, I closed my eyes again and began to feel my way through the rest of my body with Thrackborne's guidance. I was ready to make a sassy remark and demand we call it a day when I found myself on the edge of the vast void I'd sensed the last time. The yawning chasm felt like it stretched for miles, though it was impossible for it to be so large inside of me. I hesitated in my mental explorations, wondering at the depths of the void and the aching emptiness it seemed to fill me with. Except, that wasn't quite right this time. Just on the edges of my consciousness, I could feel something writhing within the void. A spark of power that seemed familiar.

"Bechora!" Thrackborne barked, causing my eyes to fly open.

Without realizing it, I'd reached a hand out, palm up, and it was slowly filling with shadows. They weren't nearly as intense as the shadows that erupted from me in my room. Instead, they were slightly translucent, as if whatever fueled them was waning with each second that I held them in my palm. The small spark of power jerked free of the void within me, and the shadows sputtered out.

"That is not the power of a fire mage," Thrackborne said slowly.

"But mages with more than one ability are a thing, right? You said they exist."

Thrackborne narrowed his eyes at me, one hand rubbing the light stubble on his chin. "Elemental mages do exist, yes, but shadows are a fae magic, and even then, they are exceptionally rare."

"You sound like Dante." I snorted before I could stop myself.

"You've summoned the shadows before? In front of the gargoyle." Thrackborne stalked toward me, his nostrils flared, as smoke puffed out on each exhale, and his eyes screamed murder.

"It's not like I did it on purpose." I scoffed. "It just happened. I was just venting to Shadrie about that absolute dickbag of a prince and his cronies, and the next thing I knew... shadows. I couldn't stop them, so she went for help."

If you asked me in that moment why I was spilling my guts to an extremely intimidating and pissed-off dragon, I wouldn't have been able to tell you. Part of me seemed to understand that he was one of the few I could tell, even though everything about his reaction screamed that I was one wrong word away from being dragon-flamed-Bechora.

Thrackborne gripped my wrist, sending an electric shock through my arm, and pulled me to my feet. His nose was nearly touching mine as he stooped to my height and growled. "You can't tell anyone about this. Not until I figure out what you are."

Jerking my arm free, I tried to take a step back, only to have the chair behind me hit my thighs. Unable to get away from the dragon crowding into my space, I put my hands on his chest and shoved. "I didn't plan on telling anyone other than Shadrie a damned thing. She actually wants to help me, unlike whatever this weird alphahole shit you're pulling is. You're my professor, not my father."

His lips peeled back as he bared his teeth and backed away from me. "You're correct, Bechora. As your professor, I must insist you keep this and any new abilities you manifest quiet until we know more. This isn't the human realm. Revealing abilities you shouldn't possess to the wrong person can get you killed, and by my count, you're up to three abilities that do not make sense when added together. You've manifested fire, a nearly impenetrable shield, and now fae shadows."

"And ice," I interjected thoughtlessly.

Thrackborne stiffened, his eyes widening in shock. "Ice? What else have you been keeping from me, Bechora? I can't help you if you insist on keeping me in the dark."

The smartass response on the tip of my tongue was cut off by a knock on the office door. Thrackborne shot me another angry scowl before stomping over to jerk the door open to reveal Dante standing on the other side with a lopsided smirk on his face. His expression fell into a mirror image of the surly dragon's when his eyes landed on me.

"We'll continue this in our next session, Ms. Knight," Thrackborne clipped, motioning for me to leave. "It seems my next appointment has arrived."

CHAPTER FIFTEEN

Dante

I didn't miss the way Thrackborne's hands clenched into fists as Bechora Knight brushed by me on her way out of his office. The overgrown lizard stared after my mate in a way that made me want to snatch her up and lock her away in a tower, high enough only I could ever reach her, which would be impossible considering the male I wanted to snatch her away from was a dragon. My sudden possessive streak was going to be an issue if I didn't get it under control.

"Slumming with mages now?" I managed to say as I painted on a smirk and stepped into his office, closing the door behind me.

"I am their head of house thanks to Vallynn's meddling," he drawled, arching a brow at me.

Sometimes it seemed like Caulder Thrackborne could read the thoughts I kept hidden away. His posture was a challenge, but whether it was one meant to make me spill my secrets or one meant to lay claim to the woman who'd just vacated the room, I couldn't be sure. Neither option sat well with me. I wasn't about to tell the dragon the fiery redhead was my mate, not after I'd kept it from Vallynn.

Vallynn, feeling the pull of a fated bond to the female, put her firmly off limits, no matter my own connection to her. Anything less would have been cruel. After everything we'd been through, I wouldn't parade my connection to the female in front of Vallynn, knowing that he couldn't ever acknowledge their connection without painting a target on her back. None of that meant I was going to roll over and let the feather-brained dragon take her, though.

"Where is the princeling?" Caulder asked, moving to sit behind his desk.

"Just me today, flames," I grinned. "Vallynn felt it would be better if he were seen on campus courting his fiancée and appearing to bend to his father's wishes."

Caulder opened a drawer in his desk and retrieved a pass for leaving campus before hastily scrawling his signature along the bottom. "Very well. You know where to meet, you can give me the details there. The sooner we get this done, the better."

"Got big plans there, Smokey?" I snorted, snatching the slip from his outstretched hand. Caulder merely scowled as a plume of smoke flowed from his nostrils and obscured his face. "Fine, don't tell me." I shrugged.

The dragon growled, and I flipped him off as I strode toward the office door. I couldn't help the nagging sensation that his irritation was more than his usual annoyance at my presence. If I were a paranoid male, I'd almost make the leap that he was angered over my interrupting his meeting with Bechora. By the time I reached the campus gates, I'd resolved to figure out what the damned dragon was doing in his meetings with my mate.

Caulder was waiting for me, pacing impatiently, when I made it to the small, secluded lake off campus. I could have shifted into my gargoyle form and flown, but I couldn't resist needling the dragon by taking my time walking instead. Scales rippled over his bare arms, and each puff of his breath contained sparks of flame. I couldn't stop the satisfied grin that split my face over how much I got under his thick hide.

"You walked," he snarled as I drew to a stop a few yards away from him. "Did you forget that time is of the essence in these little missions of ours?"

"Chill, we have time," I replied. "Our information says the King is still planning his attack. We have at least a few more days before he sends someone after the female. A few extra minutes for me to stretch my legs isn't going to change that."

"A female?" Caulder asked, tilting his head for me to continue.

"A sphinx, from what Vallynn has been able to gather."

Caulder stroked his chin thoughtfully. "Sphinxes are rare, and their ability to see the future makes them nearly impossible to be found if they don't want to be. The princeling's informant is sure this is the King's next target?"

"Positive. The King's scribes found something in the historical archives that would help him avoid the female from foreseeing his movements, but they're missing Selir knows what to make it work. He's sent someone to the human realm to retrieve whatever it is they need."

"How can we even be sure the location we're headed to is where we'll find her?"

"Simple," I shrugged. "She contacted Vallynn and told him where to find her before his father can make his move, and our informant gave us the rough timeline for the excursion to the human realm."

"Fine. Lead the way," Caulder replied, motioning for me to step back so he could shift. "Just know, if this turns out to be a trap of some sort, you'll be digesting in my stomach faster than you could make any of your smartass remarks."

I rolled my eyes with a snort and let my stone form take over as I moved out of range of the shifting dragon. Not waiting for him to transform, I launched myself skyward and turned north. The loud flapping of dragon wings echoed behind me as the other male took flight. I didn't bother goading him as I focused on navigating to our destination as night bloomed over the land. Gargoyles had nearly unmatched night vision, but I needed to focus on the landmarks speeding past below us to ensure we reached our destination.

We flew for hours, cities and towns falling away until there was little more than trees beneath us. As much as our realm's advancements seemed to mirror those of the human realm, the northernmost parts of our lands remained wild and untainted. It was almost like the magic of our homeland protected the region from even the thought of altering it in favor of technological and industrial change.

"There," I called over my shoulder to Caulder as I spotted a small cabin built into a large, old tree.

Caulder blew out a puff of smoke and dove toward the ground. Tucking my wings tightly to my side, I let myself fall like granite toward the earth, smiling at the idea of aiming for the lizard's back as my landing spot. At almost the last second, I opened my wings, letting the air buffer my fall and slow my descent until I landed gently on the purple grass a few feet from the cabin door. Caulder landed at the same moment, allowing the shift back to his human form to take over just before his feet touched down.

"Show off," I grumbled.

Caulder shot me a smirk before whipping his head in the direction of the cabin. The sound of movement inside drew my attention just as the door swung open wide. A short, round woman with gray hair thrown into a loose bun bustled outside to greet us. My eyes widened at the two plaid-colored suitcases, almost the size of the woman, tucked one under each arm. I had to bite the inside of my cheek so as not to chuckle at her overall appearance.

For a powerful sphinx, she was much less put together than I expected. Her bright pink sweater was clearly made from homespun yarn and had a smattering of small holes from missed stitches. The pants she wore were patched more times than I could begin to guess, only the tiniest hint of their original orange color peeking through. To top it all off, she had human realm combat boots on her feet, laced halfway up to show the green and beige striped socks beneath.

The strange female stopped abruptly and dropped her luggage, the whites of her eyes clouding them over as she took us in.

"A creature strong with noble grace. In tales of old and whispers new. A pairing that the ancients knew. A union forged, yet hearts must choose. To seal the fate or risk to lose. A balance swayed by mutual will, if just one walks, chaos reigns, and peace stands still." Her melodic voice called out before she blinked rapidly and smiled.

"What?" I asked dumbly.

"It's a riddle, pebbles for brains," Caulder grunted.

"A riddle, a prophecy. To-may-to, to-mah-to," the sphinx shrugged. "They are much the same to keepers of powerful secrets such as my kind."

"How the hell does telling the future help anyone when you make it a puzzle nobody can figure out?" I huffed, moving to grab the female's suitcases.

"A future clear to anyone is a future lost," the sphinx replied. "Now, away with us, if you please."

I shot Caulder a helpless look, causing the dragon to bark out a laugh at my expense. Scowling, I shifted, grabbed the other suitcase, and launched myself into the air. It was stupid to think the dragon would take any pity on me and explain the sphinx's words. Scoping out the landscape was the perfect excuse to gain a moment's reprieve from his taunting laughter. My eyes scanned over the dark horizon, ensuring we were still alone, and I whistled to let the dragon and sphinx know they could join me in the air.

When they joined me in the sky, we turned to the west, heading for a portal to the human realm. I wasn't sure if it was luck or the sphinx's gifts that caused her to settle so close to a long-abandoned portal. There were so many throughout the kingdom that many fell into disrepair and were forgotten. Vallynn found scrolls tucked away in the palace archives when we were children that held the location of many of the older portals, and the information came in handy a number of times on our covert missions. The fact that none of them were uncovered by the King was almost enough to make me believe Selir existed and was on our side.

It was nearly dawn by the time we saw the sphinx safely through the portal and returned to the academy. I spent most of the journey trying to work out the riddle she'd spoken the moment she laid eyes on us. I was no closer to solving the thing when I finally collapsed into my bed than I was when the sphinx first spoke it, but I couldn't shake the feeling that the answer to her riddle could hold the solution to dealing with the King.

CHAPTER SIXTEEN

Zypher

I hadn't seen Bechora since breakfast. I was tempted to seek her out at Magus House, certain that she would be there, but I learned a bit about human realm customs from her mage friend, Miles, over dinner the evening before. The small male's terror permeated the air until I made it clear I meant him no harm and merely wanted to understand more about the human realm.

A plan forming in my mind around the male's advice, I made my way to the training arena in search of Rumlock. The electricity mage seemed sure that interfering with the professor would only anger my *Dilectus*, but it was the one thing my instincts refused to compromise on. Besides, the combat professor was half-demon—that made him my father's subject, and I was within my rights as heir to question the male.

The hybrid demon-fae was overseeing his last class of the day when I strolled onto the training pitch. Placing his fingers between his lips, he let loose a sharp whistle and dismissed his students.

"Prince Zypher," he nodded respectfully.

"Rumlock," I grunted, waiting until the last student was out of earshot. "What is this I hear about you pairing my *Dilectus* with a bear shifter for her first combat class?"

"I needed to speak with you," Rumlock shrugged.

"Haven't you heard of sending a message? You didn't need to send my fated to the infirmary with a training injury. I could have your head for that."

Rumlock turned to face me, his lips pressed into a thin line that caused the scar across his left eye and cheek to pucker. "What do you think the bear was, Prince Zypher? Would you have me seek you out directly and out myself as half demon against your father's orders?"

"My father's machinations are none of my concern. The well-being of my *Dilectus*, however, is," I replied dryly.

It wasn't a secret among my kind that my father placed a spy within the Academy to ensure the safety of our people on campus. Lesser demons started vanishing decades before my birth from these hallowed halls with no explanation. They were written off as fleeing the Academy for any number of reasons, because anything else meant someone was working against the inherent magic that kept students and staff safe. The disappearances stopped in recent years with the suspicious rise of other supernaturals eloping to the human realm, which only furthered my father's belief that something was amiss.

"You know my gift, my prince?" Rumlock asked.

"Of course. *Filum Viden* is the rarest gift of our kind, one of the few remnants of our origin. Your ability to see the threads that connect us was invaluable on and off the battlefield."

"Yes, well, it helps to know who you can turn against your enemy and who to cut down to weaken their resolve."

"I'm not certain why your ability led you to pair my *Dilectus* with a bear shifter, causing her to become injured. Nor why you felt that was the appropriate message to send." I drawled, crossing my arms over my chest.

"It's quite simple, my prince. I saw her threads, and the darkness attempting to choke them out."

My eyebrows rose sharply at his words. "Explain. Now, Rumlock, before I lose patience with you."

"It's common for the females of our kind to have many *Dilecti*. Rare for those not of our kind, but as she is your fated, it would make sense that she shares some traits with our own females."

"Yes, I am aware of this," I interrupted with a wave of my hand. "My own mother, Lilith, was mated to Adam as well as my father. It is well known that Adam's rejection of their fated bond weakened her power. My *Dilectus* having multiple mates doesn't concern me. So long as they accept their bond, they will strengthen her. I am not a spawn that requires reeducation in that regard, and I suspect the darkness you have seen is the true reason for seeking me out in such a dangerous manner."

"As you say," Rumlock nodded. "The darkness that covets her threads is the true concern. There are forces at work intent on keeping your *Dilectus* from completing her bonded *Vinculum*. For a female to have so many fated at risk can only mean something is coming that will either restore or completely shatter the balance."

"How many fated threads does she hold?"

Rumlock clucked his tongue. "You know that is information I cannot share with you, my prince. To speak such things is to invite dark forces to meddle further."

"You're a superstitious old man," I groaned, wiping a hand roughly down my face. "Why tell me any of this if you're just going to speak in vague riddles?"

"It's not superstition when I've seen the results of speaking such information aloud. Not when my own whispers have snapped fated threads before they could bond." Rumlock scowled. "I may not be able to tell you more, but you know the signs of a fated pairing. What little I've been able to share should be enough for you to suss out the rest of your *Vinculum*."

I took a second to consider his words. Even if he refused to tell me how many mates would be part of our bonded group with my *Dilectus*, he still gave me enough to watch for the signs and find them on my own. If Bechora's bonds were truly at risk, I needed to move up my timeline to woo her and begin introducing her to more demons until we found the others.

"One last thing, my prince," Rumlock spoke, interrupting my

thoughts. "You may want to extend your vernacular for your *Vinculum* to include brood, lest you waste time searching in the wrong direction."

"Vampires?" I asked. Rumlock pressed his lips together in a firm line and narrowed his eyes at me. I let out a heavy sigh and shook my head at his refusal to answer. "Very well. I will brush up on the terminology for other supernaturals. You have done well bringing this to my attention, though I must caution you to find other means of getting my attention in the future. I will not tolerate putting my *Dilectus* in danger a second time."

The professor let out a derisive snort. "She was never in danger. The magic in the arena wouldn't have allowed her to come to mortal harm. But I will account for your most protective instincts should I need to speak to you outside of classes in the future. I wish you luck, my prince, and will pray to the Morrigan on your behalf."

"I doubt the Fae goddess cares for our kind, but I thank you anyway," I replied with a curt nod before turning to leave.

"Who better to care for a species born of war than the Goddess of death and war herself?" I heard him call out as I strode from the training pitch.

I couldn't help but chuckle at how Fae the half-demon seemed in his belief before letting my mind mull over the information he'd given me. The professor provided enough clues to figure out that Bechora had more mates than was usual even for my kind, and unlike other females who mated into demon *Vinculum*, not all of her *Dilecti* would be demon-kind. I was going to need allies, to not only win her over and complete our bond, but to help find her other males. A wide grin split my face as I decided I knew exactly who to ask.

I arrived at Magus House moments later. Several mages milled around their common room, giving me wary glances when they noticed my presence. Not wanting to waste time assuaging their unwarranted fear of my kind, I grabbed the collar of the nearest male mage.

"I'm looking for Miles Dalton. Where is his room?"

"Room two-oh-one," the male squeaked out.

"Thank you." I smiled, releasing his collar and patting him on the shoulder before making my way to the stairs on the other side of the room.

It took me a few minutes to find the correct room, but I was pleased when Miles opened the door after the first knock. The sudden loss of color in his face that greeted me was another story.

"Are you well, Miles?" I asked, studying the lean male for any signs of injury.

"Uh, um, Zypher. Hi, uhm, hello. What can I help you with?" His words came out jumbled with a slight tremor.

Grabbing his shoulder gently, I turned him and walked him into his dorm. "If you are unwell, I can return another time. I simply wished to ask for your assistance. The knowledge of human realm customs that you shared with me over dinner allowed me to realize I will need to... date... my *Dilectus* if I wish to win her over." Miles shuddered under my grip. "You are unwell, I will come another time."

"N-n-no," the mage stuttered. "I'm not sick. I'm just..." He paused, looking over his shoulder at me as if to gauge my reaction. "Honestly, a demon showing up at my door is terrifying enough, but you're... well, you and I know B said she'd make sure you didn't rip me apart for touching her hand in spellcasting, and I washed my hands at least a hundred times just in case—"

"I see. You're babbling, but you're afraid of me," I interrupted, causing Miles to pale further as his eyes widened. "I have no wish to harm you. Even if you weren't friends with my *Dilectus*, your consideration for the impulses males have toward their fated is enough to know you're no threat to me."

"Uh, good, that's... that's really good," Miles mumbled, pushing his glasses up his nose with one finger.

I released his shoulders and let him lead me to the couch in the communal space of his dorm room. Miles motioned for me to take a seat while he nervously gathered up textbooks and loose papers spread along the coffee table.

"You said you needed my help with something?" he asked without lifting his gaze from the items he gathered up.

"Yes. I'd like to plan one of these dates you spoke of at dinner. Something that will impress my *Dilectus*."

"I'm not really sure I'm the right person for the job," he replied with a wry smile. "I mean, I barely know Bechora. Shadrie would probably be able to provide you with better information on what she likes and dislikes."

"I'm sure the ice mage would tell me what I wanted to know, but you are less likely to spoil the surprise. After all, us males need to stick together, yes? I think that's called bro code."

Miles' head snapped up, and he let out a laugh of disbelief. "Who taught you bro code?"

Letting my amusement show clearly on my face, I grinned at him. "I may not have had reason to learn your realm's customs before Bechora, but I met others from there. This is my third year at the Academy; it's not like I could avoid them completely."

"Why would you go out of your way to avoid supes from the human realm?"

"They tend to hold the most unflattering beliefs about my kind." I shrugged. "Listen, Miles, I will make you a deal."

The mage paled again, his body going still. "No, no deals."

I couldn't help the frustrated sigh that left me. It was obvious the male had learned some of the more unsavory beliefs about demons and our penchant for deals. Contrary to what many believed, we didn't steal the souls of those we made deals with, nor did we eat babies, as I was once accused of doing. We simply provided our end of the bargain for them to act as a conduit that enabled us to access the innate magic of their world—magic we wouldn't be able to access and wield otherwise.

"No deals. Not like that," I assured him. "I simply wish for us to be friends and for you to help me plan a date with my *Dilectus*, if you're willing."

Miles' posture relaxed, and a small smile spread along his lips. "Okay. I still think Shadrie would be the better option because she knows B better, but I'll do what I can to help."

"Perfect. Now, tell me how these dates work in your realm."

CHAPTER SEVENTEEN

Bechora

I woke up the next morning to another package waiting on the counter. Someone had noticed I'd missed most of my classes the day before and gathered notes from them for me. Shadrie insisted it wasn't her, that the package was left in front of the door to our dorm, and whoever delivered it seemed to have vanished into thin air the moment they knocked.

"Thank Selir, it's Friday!" Shadrie groaned as we gathered our bags to head to class. "We should totally veg out and watch trash TV this weekend to celebrate surviving our first week."

"That sounds great." I smiled. "It didn't look like I missed much yesterday, just a couple of reading assignments for Elemental Magic and an ass-kicking in combat training. I just have one class this morning and combat training this evening, so if I hit the library after my first class, I can free up my weekend."

"Perfect. Oh, we should invite Miles. After the way your hunka-hunka demon mate interrogated him the other day about the human realm, I bet he could use a veg out too."

"Shit, that reminds me. I need to try to find more information on demon mating stuff while I'm at the library. Zypher's been pretty chill, but it would be nice to know what he's expecting to happen, and the one time I managed to look into it, I didn't find anything helpful."

"You mean other than laying that Demon Daddy Dick on you?" Shadrie cackled.

"Shadrie!"

My roommate shot me a bemused grin and shrugged. "I'm

just saying, the guy is over seven feet tall, no way he's not proportional. Don't try to tell me you haven't thought about it yet, either. That demon is hot as hell, no pun intended."

"Would you shut up before he hears you?" I squeaked, motioning toward the doors leading outside from Magus House.

Shadrie mimed zipping her lips and then grinned. "I'll shut it for now, but I definitely want details when you finally take him for a ride... Oh, look, there he is now."

My eyes followed her gaze to find Zypher waiting a few yards down the sidewalk, balancing four coffee cups between both hands. We made our way to him, and he greeted me with a warm smile, handing Shadrie and me each one of the cups.

"Who's the spare for?" Shadrie asked, tilting her head toward the fourth coffee.

"Miles. We are... bros now." Zypher chuckled when Shadrie's mouth fell open at the word *bros.* "Ah, here he comes now. If you would be so kind as to deliver this to him and give me a moment alone with my Dilectus, I will be in your debt, ice mage."

"Sure thing, Triple D." Shadrie winked with a mock salute before taking the extra coffee from Zypher and turning back to meet Miles on his way out of Magus House.

Zypher snagged my free hand in his and pulled me so we were facing one another. "I have been researching the mating customs of your realm, and I would like to take you on a date this weekend."

The gentle tone of his voice made my heart flutter, and I almost said yes before I remembered I'd already made plans with Shadrie. "I already promised my roommate we'd veg out." I sighed. "But maybe you could join us if you'd like? We were going to invite Miles, so I doubt Shadrie would be mad if I invited you, too."

"Ah, like a group date. I was told those are sometimes a first-date custom in your realm, to make things less awkward between the courting pair. Had I realized the mages were also courting, I would have suggested something similar."

I nearly choked on the coffee I'd just taken a sip of. "Miles and Shadrie? They're not courting, big guy."

Zypher gave me a puzzled look before tilting his head toward where the pair stood with their heads together like they were plotting something. "Their behavior would indicate otherwise, Dilectus."

"Trust me, whatever that little secret sesh is about, they're not courting. Shadrie doesn't have the right parts for Miles."

The demon's brows furrowed, and his eyes flitted between our friends and me. Understanding slowly bloomed on his face after a few moments. "Oh… Oh! I see. Should we find partners for our mage friends to attend the group date with?"

I couldn't help the small laugh that left me as I patted Zypher on the chest. "No, it's not a group date. It's just friends hanging out."

"But I am more than your friend, Dilectus. We are fated."

"Boyfriends attend group hangouts," I said before I considered my words.

Zypher's face split into a stunning grin. "I see. Then I shall endeavor to learn the customs of 'boyfriend attending group hangout' by the weekend."

"I didn't mean… You know what, nevermind. It's fine. There's not really anything special you need to do, just be yourself, and it will be fine."

Before either of us could say anything else, Shadrie and Miles stopped next to me.

"Time's up, Triple D., I am starving, and we have class soon," Shadrie said before turning her attention to me. "Miles is in for a group veg. We decided we're going to watch that sister wives show from the human realm—apparently it's our friend here's guilty pleasure, and he made sure to find out when it would be available in our realm the second he got settled into his dorm on orientation day."

Miles blushed furiously, and his eyes dropped to the ground. "I can't help that I like the drama."

"I, too, find drama can be quite enjoyable." Zypher grinned, slapping Miles on the shoulder.

Shadrie cackled, and I shook my head before gesturing for us to get moving. We made our way to the dining hall in comfortable silence before Shadrie and I settled in at what was becoming our normal table. Miles shot us a horrified look as Zypher pulled him along to the buffet to gather our breakfast. My demon mate didn't seem to notice as he chattered away at the poor mage.

"So, you only have the one class this morning and then combat training?" Shadrie asked as the guys placed overflowing plates on the table and settled in with us.

"Yeah. Somehow, I ended up with Human Studies as an elective." I frowned. "Which is weird considering I'm, y'know, from the human realm."

"I mean, considering orientation day, maybe not." Shadrie shrugged. "If the academy's magic enrolled you late, you probably got stuck in whatever elective was available to meet your credit requirements."

"We have a class together, Dilectus," Zypher spoke, causing me to turn my head to look at him.

"You're taking Human Studies? Isn't that a low-level elective?" Miles asked.

"Yes. Most demons take the course, though I put it off until I couldn't." Zypher shrugged. "My procrastination seems to have worked in my favor, as I will have an expert on the subject matter in class with me."

"Not sure I'd call myself an expert." I laughed. "The human realm is complicated, even for those of us who grew up there, but I'll do my best to help you keep up."

"It's not that in-depth a course anyway," Miles added, pushing his glasses up his nose. "I read up on it when I was selecting my courses. Mostly, it covers a handful of common human customs and then the major ones of each region. It's meant to keep supes from insulting any humans they might encounter if they visit the human realm."

"My sister took that class when she went here. She said they do a section covering region-specific myths caused by supernaturals of certain species gravitating to those areas," Shadrie added.

"Maybe this won't be a waste of time for me after all." I smiled, finishing my food. "I was never big into myths and shit, that was more Geordie's thing."

A twinge of sadness raced through me at the thought of Geordie, and I didn't miss the sympathy on Shadrie's face. We hadn't spoken about my friend-turned-fae seer since the night with her mirror. Before I could spiral into self-pity, Zypher gently stroked my arm to get my attention.

"We should head to class, Dilectus. Professor Kragmane enjoys finding any excuse he can to exert the power of his position over his students."

We said our goodbyes, leaving Shadrie and Miles to finish their breakfast, and headed to one of the old stone buildings in the southern portion of campus. I noticed the professor first when we entered the auditorium-style classroom. For what the squat, white-haired professor lacked in height, he made up for in the ferocious glare he wore. I turned to whisper a comment about little-man syndrome to Zypher and stopped short. Seated in the classroom were the three males who seemed to loathe my existence for reasons unknown to me.

"Ignore them, Dilectus," Zypher murmured, placing his hand on the small of my back to guide me to a seat when he noticed Dante, Vallynn, and Gabriel. "They will not bother you if they know what's good for them."

As if he could hear Zypher's words, Gabriel's eyes sought me out, and he scowled, flashing his fangs at me so quickly I almost didn't catch the unspoken threat.

"Don't worry, Zypher," Dante called out. "You're the only one here interested in stooping so low."

Zypher growled, his hand on my back tightening into a grip on my blouse. "Mind yourself, gargoyle. Even your prince knows the only reason we demons bow is because we choose to."

"Take your seats," Professor Kragmane called out before the males could continue posturing.

I slumped into the nearest empty seat in relief, Zypher sliding into the one next to me. He reached over and took my hand in his, stroking the back of it with his thumb while the remaining students filtered in and took a seat.

"Excellent, you've all arrived on time." Kragmane clapped once the last student was seated. "If you would please open your syllabus, we will cover what is expected of you this term, and then I will be assigning groups for the first project."

The lesson went by relatively smoothly as Kragmane covered the items in the syllabus. Human Studies seemed to be exactly as Miles and Shadrie described, though I had to stifle a snicker when I realized there was a section on *human sexual customs and behaviors.*

"Now, the first major project for the term will see you split into groups of five," Kragmane said once he'd finished covering the rest of the syllabus. "Each group will be assigned a region of the human realm and must present a thorough report covering unique customs of the region and how these customs were influenced by supernaturals. It is important to note that I expect each group to provide as detailed a timeline covering the evolution of these customs. You will have exactly one month to prepare your presentation, as some of the research can be quite time-consuming. Once you've been assigned a group and given your region, you are dismissed. Any questions?"

"Do we get to pick our groups?" Dante called out. I couldn't help rolling my eyes because, of course, he would ask that.

"No, I have already assigned them, and there will be no changes under any circumstances. If you dislike a member of your group, I strongly suggest you get over it," Kragmane answered.

His reply felt like a bad omen, and that sensation only settled in deeper as he began to call students to the front in groups of five before handing them an envelope with their assigned region. There were only fifteen students left when Zypher's name was called off first for the next group. As if sensing my distress, he squeezed my hand gently before moving to the front of the room.

"Vallynn Evarian, Gabriel Dreadgrave," Kragmane called out, and I couldn't help the flash of hope that I'd end up in the next group. "Dante Vazgurr, Bechora Knight."

My stomach plummeted, and I forced myself out of my seat. Keeping my eyes on Zypher for reassurance, I moved to stand with the rest of my group. I couldn't help but wonder if we could convince the other three to work on portions solo; even Zypher in the group wasn't enough to override the dread I felt at being stuck with the others for the next month. I barely managed to grab the envelope with my copy of the assignment and move out of the way for the next group to be called before Vallynn spoke.

"I will take the evening to review our assignment before I email you all plans for how to proceed with the project."

"Excuse you," I snapped. "I'm the only one here actually from the human realm, so what makes you think you should be in charge of the project?"

Vallynn tilted his head and smirked before waving a hand at himself. "Prince."

"Yeah, and?" I asked, jabbing a thumb in Zypher's direction. "Pretty sure he's a prince too."

"Let the fae have this one, Dilectus." Zypher snickered. "He is not used to not getting his way, and we wouldn't want the resulting tantrum to interfere with our project."

I could have sworn shadows swirled around Vallynn's hands as he crossed his arms over his chest, his lips set in a haughty scowl.

"Yeah, okay, big guy, you've got a point there," I replied before narrowing my eyes at the fae and jabbing a finger in his direction. "Don't expect me to be at your beck and call when you can't figure something out about the human realm, though. The library here seems pretty well stocked. I don't want to have to deal with your entitled ass more than necessary."

Vallynn's mouth fell open in shock as Zypher slid an arm around my shoulders and led me from the classroom.

"If I didn't have another class, Dilectus, I would show you exactly how much I appreciated you putting the fae in his place," Zypher whispered in my ear, causing me to shiver at the insinuation.

"How about we get through this weekend, you fill in any blanks I have about demon mating rituals, and then we see what happens from there?" I countered.

"You're interested in learning my culture?" Zypher raised to his full height in shock. "Specifically, the mating rituals?"

"We've only known each other for like a week, but yeah." I shrugged. "I'd like to know what I've gotten myself into, even if you are already starting to win me over."

"I can skip my next class and tell you anything you want to know." Zypher grinned.

"No." I laughed. "I'm heading to the library to get some work done for my other classes. If you want to help now, you can tell me what books to check out while I'm there to get a head start."

I couldn't help the grin that plastered itself on my face as Zypher excitedly rattled off a few titles before dropping me off at the library. It was almost enough to make me forget I was stuck dealing with three douchebags for the next month.

CHAPTER EIGHTEEN

Gabriel

Bechora Knight was the bane of my existence. Everything about the woman seemed crafted to tempt me, from the curves of her petite frame to the sassy mouth she let loose without care for the consequences. She was temptation incarnate, packaged neatly in the wrappings of a disrespectful dud. Power and station mattered in our world, and she turned her nose up at both every chance she got. I'd been sent to the academy for two purposes: to enhance my abilities and find a match that would raise my family's station. My father would accept nothing less, and yet I found my every thought captivated by the fiery redhead.

My growing obsession with Bechora was so at odds with the teachings my father spent my childhood beating into me that I found myself following her and Zypher Morningstar from our Human Studies class. I was convinced that if I could force her to accept her place, then she would fade into the background of my world. By the time the demon parted ways with her at the library, I'd devised a plan to put Bechora in her place.

There were too many people in the library to act immediately, and I found myself watching her as she worked on various assignments. Each minute that ticked by left me more enraged that a magicless nobody had somehow been selected for the most elite academy in the realm. She didn't belong at Blackthorne, and she sure as hell didn't belong in my every waking thought. If I thought for even a second that I could find a way to end her with the protection magic in place on campus, I'd put us both out of our misery. Instead, I'd settle for making her my thrall. She'd learn quickly enough where she belonged once she had no choice but to follow my every whim. Bechora Knight would be begging to leave the academy by the time I was through with her.

I watched her work for hours, completing assignments while totally unaware of the danger that lurked nearby. My gums itched with the need to drop my fangs and sink them into her neck when she finally stood from the small table she'd been working at and put her belongings in her bag. I only required a moment without witnesses to sink my teeth into her and release the venom that would tie her to me as a thrall. While the Academy had rules around the thrall's consent, we weren't barred from taking one. Once the deed was done, she wouldn't be able to turn me in to the administration for enthralling her against her will.

Following her from the library, I nearly laughed at how perfectly my plans were coming to fruition. Rather than heading deeper into campus, Bechora turned down an abandoned pathway between the library and the building beside it, heading toward the nearest tree line. Glancing over my shoulder to ensure we were truly alone, I closed the distance between us with a burst of my innate speed, grabbed her by her shoulders, and slammed her into the outer brick wall of the library.

"What the fuck! Get off me!" she shouted, her hands clawing at mine.

"No," I replied, letting my fangs free. "I warned you on the first day to be careful, Bechora. You decided not to heed my warning, so now you're going to face the consequences."

"Get the fuck off me, Gabriel, or I swear to God I'll have Zypher tear your ass to pieces," she snarled.

Scoffing, I used my hold on her to pin her higher on the wall so that we were eye level. I nearly laughed when I realized that left her feet dangling just barely off the ground. Unamused, Bechora swung her leg in an attempt to kick me.

"You missed," I smirked, pressing her against the wall harder.

"Now, as I was saying. I warned you about not knowing your place. You're a dud, completely magicless, and from what I've witnessed in combat class, wholly unable to defend yourself. You are the weakest student at the academy, yet you still deem yourself worthy of speaking down to your betters. I'm going to do you one last kindness. I'm going to make you my thrall so that I can ensure you learn your lesson."

Bechora's nostrils flared, my words only seeming to enrage her. She squirmed in a pathetic attempt to break free of my hold, and I smirked at her just as one of her palms cracked across the side of my face.

"Put me down, you fucking piece of shit, or I'll scream," she hissed.

Chuckling darkly, I used one hand to keep her pinned against the brick wall and wrapped the other in her hair. With one harsh jerk, I used her hair to pull her head to the side, exposing her neck, and I struck. The moment my fangs broke her skin, I knew something was wrong. Something inside me took notice and rose up, pulling taut before snapping so hard I slumped against her. I was flooded with a rush of anger and fear that didn't belong to me, and I knew instantly they belonged to her. My head jerked back in shock, and I searched her face for anything that would explain the sensations away as anything other than what I knew had just happened.

"No, no, no, no, no, no. This isn't possible. This can't be possible. I... I didn't." The words spilled from me as my mind raced to figure out how the fuck I'd just formed a mate bond with Bechora Knight.

"Get the fuck off of me, asshole!" she shrieked, shoving her hands against my chest.

This time, the action sent me flying into the wall of the opposite building. My bones rattled and dust flew around me as I slammed into the bricks with a sickening crack. Dropping to my knees, I snarled, baring my fangs at Bechora in warning, before I bolted down the path toward the heart of campus.

"That's right! You better run, bitch!" I heard her call out

behind me.

Under any other circumstances, I'd have turned back, but my mind was reeling from what I'd just done. It wasn't supposed to be possible for Vampires to create a mate bond with a simple bite. Bonding took conscious effort because of the very specific pheromones we needed to release in addition to blood being exchanged by both mates. I'd most definitely not released the pheromones, and Bechora hadn't taken my blood, yet the flow of her emotions and the growing need to be near her were there. As impossible as it was, I had no doubt that I'd managed to bond us as mates with a simple bite.

I raced across campus to my room in Noctus House, barely shutting my bedroom door behind me before I was tearing through my things in search of the phone my older brother had gifted me. The supernatural realm had co-opted quite a bit of human technology, including cell phones, even though we still turned to magic more often than not. When my older brother defected from the brood, he knew he'd need to hide himself from magic to prevent our father hunting him down and ending his life. Though I'd never used it, the phone was his way of ensuring I could find him if I ever needed to, without magic as an option.

Finding the small black device tucked into the back of one of my drawers, I pulled it out and hit the call button on the only number it held. My hands trembled as I put the phone to my ear, panic threatening to overtake me with each ring as the reality of what I'd done settled in.

"Gabriel?" My brother's voice came through the phone in the middle of the third ring.

"Rafe," I choked out, letting my body sink to the floor. "I fucked up."

"I'll meet you in the town outside campus. We can get you somewhere safe before Father—"

"Father doesn't know. He will kill me if he finds out, but I was hoping you might know a way to fix this before he does," I interjected.

Rafe let out a heavy sigh. "Tell me what's happened, and I'll see what I can do to help you."

I paused to gather my thoughts. My brother had defected from the brood because of our father's views on those he deemed lesser and the iron hand he used to foist those views on us. Rafe wouldn't understand my need to put Bechora in her place to please our father. He'd been happy to defect and live a life on the run, leaving me behind to shield our younger sister Dina from Father's cruelty.

"Gabe, are you still there?" Rafe asked gently, tearing me from my thoughts. "I can't help you if you don't tell me what's happened."

Puffing a breath through my nose, I dove straight in. "I mated a dud."

"I see..."

"It wasn't intentional. I just wanted to scare her a little, and before you lecture me about that, I have my reasons."

"I know you think I couldn't possibly understand, but I do, Gabriel. I remember what it was like under his thumb—the threats, the beatings, him always seeming to know what I got up to at the academy, causing me to walk on eggshells. I didn't forget any of that just because I left. There's a lot you don't know about what led up to that, but now's not the time to get into it. Just... just explain to me what happened with this mate bond."

"I don't know," I replied, shaking my head. "I didn't initiate anything; it just snapped into place when I bit her."

"I'm assuming she didn't bite you back."

"No, she didn't. She shoved me off her like she'd suddenly gained supernatural strength."

"If you terrified her enough, she might have, due to adrenaline, but that doesn't solve your problem. You're certain you didn't initiate the bond?"

"It's not something we can do by accident, Rafe," I retorted. "You know this as well as I do. I'm pretty sure I'd remember if I'd said the words 'I bond thee' before I bit the girl."

Rafe chuckled. "I just had to be sure."

"Well, now you're sure. What the hells am I going to do to fix it?"

"I don't know. I've never heard of a vampire mating bond falling into place from just a bite. I'll have to do some digging and see if I can find anything to help you. You need to prepare yourself for the fact that there may not be anything you can do. Mating bonds aren't normally something you can just undo."

Scowling at the floor, I forced my voice to remain even. "I know that, Rafe, but there shouldn't be a bond at all to begin with."

"Listen, I need to get going, but I will look into this. I'll text you if I find anything. In the meantime, just do your best to suppress any instincts from the bond." Rafe paused long enough that I checked to see if the call was still connected. "Maybe... maybe consider getting to know your mate as well. If I can't find a solution, or the answers aren't what you want to hear, she may be the only one you get."

No matter what he'd said, I was going to find a way to break the bond. I couldn't be mated to Bechora Knight. For my sake and for Dina's.

CHAPTER NINETEEN

Bechora

I didn't need to know anything about real vampires to know taunting one was stupid. Taunting one who'd just attacked me? I'd lost my damned mind. It was sheer luck that Gabriel hadn't turned around and finished what he started when I yelled after him. Instead, he fled the scene, leaving me feeling as if my heart would burst free of my chest at any moment, and my body wracked with shivers from the lingering adrenaline. I allowed myself to collapse against the wall behind me, the rough, cold stone grounding me. My fingers prodded at my neck where he'd bitten me, and I jerked them back in shock when I felt two raised marks where puncture wounds should have been. My jaw dropped at the absence of blood on my hands.

Panic threatened to choke me as everything I'd read in the library about the Dreadgraves whirled through my mind. Gabriel's family was powerful. His father had been part of the King's inner circle for centuries, long enough to be noted in the textbooks stored in Blackthorne Academy's library. Even if the Academy believed me about the attack, they wouldn't do anything because of who Gabriel was. My back slid down the rough stone wall of the library, the contrast no longer working to pull me from my mounting panic.

Geordie said I'd be safe here, and like a fool, I believed him. My closest friend had lied to me about who he really was for six years, and yet I'd stupidly accepted his word on this. Gabriel's attack made it crystal clear that I wasn't safe at the Academy. Whatever magic I supposedly held was broken. Without it, I couldn't defend myself. More than that, I was a nobody from the human realm. Gabriel could crush me like a bug without lifting a finger. The rules were different here, but one thing remained the same. People in positions of power shaped the world to suit themselves while the rest of us fought for scraps to survive.

Blood roared in my ears, and my heart threatened to burst free of my chest as the realization settled. My eyes darted around the narrow pathway, and I realized how exposed I was. Anyone could stumble upon me and decide to hurt me in a bid to increase their standing. My sweaty palms pressed me off the ground as I scanned my surroundings for signs of danger. The moment I was upright, I ran for the only sanctuary I had. My feet pounded against the cobblestone, sending jolts of panic ripping through me as I raced toward my dorm. By the time I reached my door, I was in a near frenzy. Blowing into the space I shared with Shadrie, I stopped long enough to slam the door behind me and lock it before gulping down air.

"Bechora?" Shadrie's voice was muffled by the sound of my heartbeat.

My eyes flitted to where she stood in the open doorway to her room as my hands clutched at my chest in an attempt to catch my breath.

"Bechora, what's wrong?"

"I-I can't be here," I rushed out, my feet moving once again, this time toward my bedroom. "It's not safe. I have to leave. I need to get away from here."

I stormed to my closet and grabbed my duffle bag from the bottom before leaving it open on the bed. I barely registered the confusion and alarm on Shadrie's face as I tore clothing from hangers and tossed them into the bag.

"I can't protect myself. Geordie lied. I'm not safe if I stay here. I have to go back to the human realm. It's the only way I can be safe."

"Bechora, what happened? Talk to me," Shadrie said, moving to stand between me and my bed.

The words spilled from my lips, my voice reaching decibels I didn't know I was capable of with each one. I began to pace the floor as I told Shadrie what Gabriel had done and what it meant for me. I barely registered her calls for me to calm down and think rationally. It wasn't until her palm cracked across my cheek that my panic released me, anger burning it away.

"Did you just fucking slap me?" I roared, halting my pacing and taking a threatening step in her direction.

"Come at me and I'll freeze your ass in place, B," she replied coldly.

My eyes flitted to her hands, catching the puffs of cold air coming from her fingertips. "You better have a damned good reason for putting your hands on me, Shadrie."

Shadrie heaved out a breath, her shoulders drooping slightly. "You were panicking, and nothing I said was pulling you out of it. I did the only thing I could think of to get you back to reality. Clearly, it worked. You're not raving like a lunatic and trying to pack your bag anymore."

My head jerked back as if she'd slapped me again as my mouth opened and closed. I took a moment to glance around my room and realized that I'd turned it completely upside down. It looked like someone had ransacked the place. I sucked in a deep breath and blew it out slowly before moving to collapse onto my bed next to my duffle bag.

"Tell me what happened, B," Shadrie said quietly, moving to grab my desk chair and sit in front of me. "You were rambling so fast, I only caught bits and pieces."

Shame washed over me, and I stared down at my fidgeting hands in my lap. "I didn't mean to scare you. I'm just not safe here. I feel like a complete idiot for ever believing I was."

"What happened with Gabriel? I did catch his name, but couldn't make sense of how he's involved."

"He attacked me outside the library," I replied, raising my head to look her in the eyes.

"That bastard!" Shadrie hissed, standing from her chair. "He's not going to get away with that, B. I'll go with you, but you need to report him."

"With what evidence?" I said with a sardonic laugh. "I felt my neck where he bit me and there's no marks, no blood. Even if someone would believe me without any of that, it's my word against his."

"Shit," Shadrie muttered, plopping back down into her chair. "You're right. He's a Dreadgrave, he's almost as immune to discipline here as Vallynn and Zypher." She paused for a moment, her eyes lighting up.

"Why do I feel like that look on your face means you're about to tell me something I won't like?" I asked.

"Zypher is the solution, B," she replied with a smug smile. "You're mated to the Demon Prince. The administration might not do anything if you report it, but there's a reason they play nice with the demons on campus. Nobody outside of their own really knows how powerful they are with the deals they make, and rumor has it Lucifer Morningstar could burn the entire realm to the ground if he felt like it."

"I'm not going to use him like that. I haven't even decided if I'm going to accept this mate bond between us."

Shadrie groaned in frustration and rolled her eyes. "It's not using him; he'd happily deal with Gabriel for you. It's kind of a whole thing for demon males to prove themselves to their mates before completing the bond."

"No, Shadrie," I said more firmly.

"Well, you can't leave the academy." Her eyes flitted to my duffle bag in a pointed look. "No matter how much you may want to, it's not allowed unless you have your magic bound. Do you really think Professor Thrackborne is going to do that for you after forcing you to meet with him almost daily to work on tapping into and controlling your power?"

My mind shifted to the grumpy professor. Shadrie had a point; that man was too much of an asshole to bind my magic after he'd invested so much time into helping me with it. It didn't take a genius to figure that out.

"If you're not going to tell Zypher, you need to make Gabriel think what he did had no effect on you. People here view fear as a sign of weakness, so don't let him know that you're afraid."

I considered her words for a moment. They weren't too far off the lessons I learned on the streets back home. Even in the human realm, there was always going to be someone stronger, someone better connected, someone who would take satisfaction in crushing you simply because you were afraid. Not showing that fear was a type of power in and of itself, and exactly why my instincts drove me to taunt Gabriel before I spiraled.

"You're right," I replied finally, squaring my shoulders and lifting my chin defiantly.

Shadrie's face split into a grin. "There's the bad bitch I'm getting to know and love. Now, unpack your bag, boss up, and show that fucking vamp he's not even close to scaring you away from the academy."

Less than an hour later, my room was set to rights, and I was on my way to face Gabriel in combat class. The closer I got to the training grounds, the harder my heart pounded against my ribcage, but I kept my resting-bitch-face firmly in place. My composure nearly cracked when I found Gabriel absent from class. Even as a wave of relief washed over me, I wondered if his absence meant he was plotting something worse for me.

Shaking off the unwanted thoughts, I turned my attention to the lesson at hand. Rumlock was teaching us basic combat maneuvers. After walking us through them a handful of times, he paired us off and sent us to the mats to practice with a partner. I found myself paired up with the girl who'd accidentally struck the bear shifter I'd been against on our first day with lightning.

"Kiri," she smiled as we took position on the mats. "Nice to meet you."

"Bechora," I replied with a smile of my own. "I think I owe you a thanks for our first day of class. Even if it was an accident, you saved my ass."

Kiri leaned forward conspiratorially. "It wasn't an accident.

Esmara bullied me all last term, so when I saw my chance to get a little revenge without consequences, I took it."

I barked out a laugh. "Fuck, that's cold. I like you."

Kiri let out a tinkling laugh and winked just before Rumlock's whistle blew, signaling for us to take our positions. The rest of class flew by. Kiri was a great partner on the training mats. Between her taking the time to make corrections to my stance and movements and the tidbits she gave me about the other students, I left class feeling like I'd gained another ally in this strange realm. She managed to erase the lingering doubts I had about remaining at the academy by the time we parted ways after class.

I found Shadrie perched on the couch in our common space, as if she'd been waiting for me. "How'd it go?"

"He wasn't in class," I shrugged.

"Oh?" she asked, arching a single brow. "Well, that's interesting. Maybe he saw you headed to class and went back to his dorm to nurse his ego over not scaring you away."

"Whatever it takes for him to leave me alone, I guess," I chuckled. "Class was actually really great without him there."

Shadrie waggled her fingers in a "gimmie" motion, and I filled her in on the time spent on the mats with Kiri.

"Kiri Forrester?" Shadrie asked, though her tone said she already knew the answer. "Her mother writes the most popular gossip column in the realm. Rumor has it that after the way Esmara treated Kiri last term, her mother went nuclear and used her connections from the column to completely destroy the Tarrene family's reputation and business."

"Should I be worried?"

"Nah. Kiri is a sweetheart and a good source of information on people. The kind of ally you want in your situation," Shadrie replied.

"So, stay on her good side," I said, blowing out a breath. "If class was any indication, that will be easy enough."

Shadrie stood from her perch and clapped her hands together. "Alright, enough of that kind of talk. I wasn't just waiting for you to see what happened in class. I forgot when we made plans to binge trash TV with Miles and Zypher that I already had plans for tonight. I already talked to the guys, and they're fine with hanging out tomorrow instead. But..." she paused to look me over, "if you'd feel safer with me staying in tonight, I can cancel, and we can have a girl's night."

"I'm fine," I replied. "Seriously, between you and class with Kiri, I am over my freakout. I'm just exhausted after everything, so I want a shower and then my bed."

"Sounds like a solid plan. I'll put a warding spell my sister taught me on our door as extra security, but Gabriel would have to be really desperate to bother you here. Consider it an upside to being in the same house as the asshole prince."

"You will have to explain how those things are connected to me at some point, but not today," I said, shaking my head as I turned toward my room. "Go, have fun. Like I said, shower and bed, that's it for me tonight."

"You're the best, B! I'd tell ya not to wait up for me, but I already know you're going to bed, so... I'll see you in the morning," Shadrie said with a soft laugh before returning to her own room to get ready for whatever her plans were.

CHAPTER TWENTY

Bechora

The trail of blazing kisses left along my inner thigh heightened my desire. When his breath ghosted over my aching core, a whimper of need ripped from my throat, only to be met by a dark chuckle as he continued his path down my other thigh. My hands pulled at him in the darkness, trying to move him where I needed him, but he was always just out of my reach.

The mattress shifted as he pulled away, and I let out a sob of need. Before my pleas could leave my lips, his tongue licked a stripe through my soaked center. With one arm across my hips to hold me down, he lapped at me at a leisurely pace. It was enough to keep me on the edge of oblivion without ever letting me fall. Anguished whimper spilled from my lips as I writhed against his hold. The near-total darkness of my bedroom heightened every sensation he pulled from my body. Just when I was certain I would break under the weight of my need, he pulled away.

"Please," I begged, unable to stop myself.

Without a word, he positioned himself at my entrance, and I let out a sigh of relief. His lips found mine in the dark as he pressed forward. My legs wrapped around his waist, heels digging into his backside, desperate to be consumed by him. His groan of pleasure against my lips as he slid fully inside me sent a shiver of arousal down my spine.

My hands slid along the lean muscles of his back and into his hair, my fingers tangling in the soft strands as I pulled him impossibly closer. It was enough to snap his control. His lips pressed against mine in a bruising kiss as his hips began to piston into me. I moaned against his mouth, and his tongue sought out mine in a brutal dance. The taste of myself on his tongue, combined with the strength of his own need, sent me hurtling toward oblivion.

Wanton sounds ripped from my lips, mixing with his masculine moans to fill my room. My hands moved from his hair to claw at his back as he thrust into me. He slammed into me like a man possessed until there was nothing except the feel of him. The pressure coiling deep in my belly felt bigger than anything I'd ever experienced. As if he could read my body, his hand slipped between us, and his thumb circled my clit.

"Come for me, Noctis Amare, my love, my mate. Come for me, now," he whispered against my ear, his voice tight with his own nearing release.

His lips pressed against the juncture of my neck as he thrummed my clit in time with his thrusts. The sharp sting of his teeth breaking my skin followed, and I shattered completely, calling out his name.

"Gabriel!"

I woke up with a start, sitting up abruptly. I was alone, in my bedroom, the blankets tangled around my legs. It had been a dream, only a dream. I carefully untangled myself from my bedding, cringing at the lingering wetness between my thighs. It wasn't until I swung my legs over the side of the bed that I felt the ache there, as if I'd actually spent the night in the arms of a man.

"There is something seriously fucked up in my head," I muttered, forcing myself to ignore the sensations and climb out of the bed.

I made quick work of changing my bedding and putting on fresh pajamas before making my way to the small kitchenette in the space I shared with Shadrie. I needed coffee and a shower, in that order, to deal with whatever messed-up thought process had caused me to have such a realistic sex dream about a man who clearly hated me. The single-cup machine had just finished when Shadrie burst into the room, looking like she'd been attacked and holding a small package.

"Someone left you another gift," she grinned, stumbling to the counter and setting it down.

"Oh, my God, Shadrie! What happened to you?" I demanded, moving to her side.

Her hair was a wild mess of tangles, her clothing was ripped, and there were bite marks and scratches covering every inch of her exposed skin. Combined with her mildly dazed expression, she looked like she'd been attacked by a pack of wild animals.

"Wolves." She shrugged before waving her hand in dismissal and pushing the package toward me. "Open the package, I wanna see what's inside."

"Shadrie..." I started, reaching up slowly to touch a tear in her shirt. "Whatever is in that box isn't as important as reporting whoever did this to you."

Her brows dipped in confusion for a moment before she burst into laughter. "B, all of this"—she gestured toward herself—"was fully consensual."

"What?!" I sputtered. "Shadrie, sweetie, you're clearly injured. How in the hell could that be consensual?"

"I told you I had plans last night. Well, those plans just happened to include being the mage filling in a wolfie sandwich. Let me tell ya, those wolves sure know how to work their equipment, if you know what I mean."

"Shadrie..." I started.

"Bechora," she deadpanned back. "Listen, I know you're new to all of this, but I promise, I enjoyed getting every single mark on my body. A girl has needs, and the pack took good care of me. Honestly, you'll understand when you have the rest of your mates filling all your holes at once. I could even give you a few pointers to get you prepared."

"The rest of my... what?" I asked, dumbly.

"Your mates, B. You have at least two more besides Zypher. Demons always mate in groups; it's one of the few bits of information that's common knowledge about them." Shadrie paused, taking in my shocked expression. "Didn't Zypher tell you any of this?"

"He did not," I gritted out. "And the books he recommended I check out aren't in the library. The librarian said they don't stock them."

"Oh... Oh, shit." Shadrie grabbed my hand gently and moved us toward the couch, motioning for me to sit down. "Surprise, I guess."

My mouth opened and closed, no words coming out. I had no idea how to process the bomb she'd just dropped on me.

Shadrie sighed and settled onto the couch beside me. "I'm sure Zypher was working up to telling you. It's not like he's been parading you around the other demons to find out who else is part of your mate group. It's pretty obvious from the sidelines that he's taking things at your pace."

"Not telling me something this big is not the same as taking it at my pace, Shadrie. I'm barely starting to know the guy, and now I have to worry about two more? Fuck my life." I groaned, dropping my head into my hands.

"You'll be fucked, alright," Shadrie chuckled, causing me to look up at her with a glare. "Oh, come on, that was funny. Look, Zypher will be here later. Before you freak out too much, just talk to him and find out why he didn't tell you himself."

"Fine, but I want you to tell me what else I don't know about being a demon's mate," I demanded.

Shadrie leaned back against the cushions, her face scrunching in concentration. "Honestly, not much. Demons tend to keep to themselves even on campus. What we do know about them was information they were required to share as part of the treaty between Lucifer and Vallynn's father a few centuries ago. The academy is one of the few places most of us ever encounter a demon."

"But you seemed to know so much about them when Zypher decided I was his mate," I interjected.

"I mean, I knew enough to know what Dilectus meant, and to

know that they aren't evil like most people want to believe. I did spend enough time at court as a kid to learn that much, and Zypher only proved me right," she said with a shrug. "You can't tell me you haven't noticed that male is basically a huge teddy bear."

I didn't reply. There wasn't anything I could actually say in response. Zypher had been nothing but kind and doting since we met. Sensing that I needed time to process, Shadrie stood from the couch and stretched.

"I need a shower and a nap before the guys arrive. Take my advice and talk to Zypher when he gets here, okay?"

I nodded, and Shadrie slipped into her room. Scrubbing my hands over my face, I stood and moved back toward the kitchenette for my forgotten coffee. The small package Shadrie left on the counter caught my attention as I sipped from my cup. Opening the package with one hand, I found another vial of the same potion I'd been sent after my first combat class. Zypher said the first one wasn't from him, but there was no way this one wasn't, which only served to prove Shadrie's point.

After I downed the potion and finished my coffee, I showered, dressed for the day, and threw myself into my homework. Even though I'd spent the day before in the library catching up on the classes I'd missed, I hadn't had enough time to work on new assignments. The academy's workload was no joke, and I still had my textbooks and papers spread across the coffee table in the common room when Miles knocked on the door, Zypher in tow. Shadrie emerged from her room looking well rested, just as the boys stepped inside our dorm, their arms loaded down with familiar snacks.

"You can set that stuff on the counter while I put my books away," I said, hurriedly grabbing my work to stash in my bedroom.

"I'm pretty sure Zypher had someone go to the human realm and wipe out the snack aisle of a grocery store," Miles laughed as they moved to sit everything down.

"Oh! Twizzlers, I love these!" Shadrie cheered. "I've only had them once when I came to visit my sister last year on campus."

Shaking my head, I popped into my bedroom and dropped my things on my bed before heading back to the common room. Miles hadn't been kidding. Our small counter was covered with everything I could possibly want for snacks.

"Wow, you really did go all out, huh?" I mused, causing Zypher to shoot me a sheepish grin.

"I wasn't sure what you liked, Dilectus."

Shadrie gave me a loaded glance, snagging a pack of Twizzlers from the counter and looping her arm through Miles'. "Help me get the show set up, Miles," she said, leading him toward the television.

"Real subtle," I muttered.

"Is everything alright, Dilectus?" Zypher asked, moving to close the distance between us.

Taking a deep breath to steady my nerves, I looked up into his unnaturally blue eyes. "Actually, Shadrie mentioned something earlier that took me by surprise. She suggested I talk to you about it." Zypher opened his mouth to respond, but I cut him off before I could lose my nerve. "Are you expecting me to mate with other demons?"

His eyes widened in surprise. "That is typically the way of my kind. Did you not find the books I recommended?"

"No, I didn't. They don't have them here, according to the librarian. But that's beside the point. That's not something I should have heard from someone else or even read in a book."

"You're right, Dilectus. I apologize. It is true that my kind typically mate in groups of multiple males with one female in what we call a Vinculum. But it's not what I expect of you. The females in my culture choose whether to accept their mates or not, should a male wish to join her Vinculum. It is up to us males to prove ourselves worthy of her acceptance. That was what I wanted you to learn from those books, along with the ways we typically work to prove ourselves."

"Wait, so you believe I have a say in this, even though you

believe we're fated to be together?" I asked, afraid to let myself feel the relief of the knowledge without confirmation.

"You always have a choice, Dilectus," Zypher murmured, gently running his hand down my arm. "Fate only decides who would make a good match should a male prove himself worthy."

The relief I'd held at bay crashed over me in full force, and I puffed out a heavy breath. "You have no idea how much I needed to hear that."

Zypher grabbed my chin and tilted my head toward his as he leaned down toward me. "I will never take your choice from you, Bechora. But do not mistake me, I will do whatever it takes to prove myself a worthy male and earn your acceptance of my place at your side."

CHAPTER TWENTY-ONE

Bechora

"We're all set up, if you two are done," Shadrie spoke, poking her head around Zypher's broad back to look at me. "Just need some help moving the snacks over."

"Are you content with my answers, Dilectus?" Zypher asked, not bothering to acknowledge Shadrie.

I studied him a second longer before patting his chest. "Yeah, we're good. Let's help grab the snacks and get settled so we can binge trash TV"

When I stepped around him, my eyes widened in surprise. Where there had only been a couch, coffee table, and television in our living room space before, Shadrie and Miles had transformed it into a dual love seat sitting area with a raised table, positioned perfectly for snacking without having to do too much moving to reach. Miles noticed my stunned expression as he moved toward the counter, and his face flushed.

"I've been reading a bunch of stuff from the library since I come from a coven and already have a foundation in spell casting. Found a really cool transfiguration spell in one of the books, and Shadrie helped me cast it."

"This is amazing, Miles," I replied, half in awe.

He gave me a sheepish smile and shrugged before gathering an armful of snacks and moving to settle into one of the love seats. I barely caught Shadrie's smirk as she flitted past me to claim the spot beside Miles. Rolling my eyes at her antics, I grabbed what little was left on the counter and jerked my head toward the living room area. Zypher beamed at me, and I nearly laughed as I took him in with his grin and massive arms loaded down with various snack foods.

The love seat that Miles and Shadrie had transfigured from our couch didn't leave much room once Zypher's large frame settled into the empty space next to me. Shadrie muttered something under her breath, and the lights flicked off just as the television turned on with the first episode queued up and ready to start. I tucked my feet under me and leaned against the armrest, away from Zypher, as Sister Wives started to play.

As the episodes played, I unconsciously started shifting closer to the massive demon until I found myself tucked under his arm. Each time his chest rumbled with laughter at the ridiculous commentary my friends were making about the show, I caught myself gazing up at him through my lashes. Without the pressure of losing my choice in our pairing, I allowed myself to really observe him for the first time since we'd met. I was so caught up in just looking at him that I almost missed that Shadrie was talking.

"You know, I don't think I could get down with the whole sister wives thing. It's nice in theory, but I want a mate that absolutely spoils and dotes on me. Not some dude who needs four wives to take care of him. Brother husbands, though... that I could get on board with," she mused before turning her head to look at Zypher. "You think you could take me to Daemonium House to shake hands with some demons and see if I have my own harem of men?"

"Shadrie!" I gasped, jerking forward to look at her around Zypher's massive frame, causing my hair to waterfall across my field of vision.

"What? It's a valid question." She shrugged.

Huffing, I tossed my hair over my shoulder and scowled at my friend. I felt my hair lift from my back before the warmth of Zypher's palm caressed my neck. His hand was so large that it wrapped entirely around my throat, and I could feel the thrum of his thumb as he stroked the nearly invisible bite mark

Gabriel had left.

"Who bit you?" he asked softly.

I jerked upright, his hand remaining in place as I turned my head to look at him. "Nobody. It's nothing."

"It's not nothing, Dilectus. Who. Bit. You?" There was a hard edge to his tone I hadn't heard before as his thumb continued to stroke Gabriel's bite mark.

"Maybe you should—" Shadrie started.

"It's nothing. I took care of it," I interrupted before she could finish her sentence.

Zypher sighed heavily, his thumb stilling on my neck. "This is not nothing, Dilectus. This is a mating mark from a vampire. Given your concern about choice and lack of other suitors, I do not believe this was given to you with your consent."

"What?" I asked dumbly, my mind trying to process what he'd just said.

"It can't be a vampire mating mark," Shadrie interjected. "She'd have had to complete the ritual for it to be that." Her eyes flicked to Miles as if seeking out confirmation, but he only shrugged.

"Their ritual is only required for chosen matings," Zypher responded. "This mark is most definitely a mating mark."

"Absolutely not!" I shouted, throwing my hands in the air.

Magic erupted from the normally empty void within me, enclosing me and Zypher in a bubble that glowed with a slight blue hue. My mouth dropped open in shock, both from his assertions and from the magic I'd just cast. I could feel it surrounding us, and it seemed he could as well. Zypher smiled, raising one hand to caress the magical wall around us, and the sensation sent a shiver up my spine.

"Your shield feels startlingly similar to my own, Dilectus," Zypher murmured in awe, before the shield snapped like a rubber band pulled too tight. His gaze held mine, and a soft smile graced his lips. "I'm happy to provide you with private lessons on how to hold it, if you'd like."

There was an undercurrent of innuendo to his tone that

left me at a loss for words, the conversation moments before momentarily forgotten. I found myself considering what exactly the private lessons would entail. Lurid images flashed through my mind in a tempting display. The sound of Miles clearing his throat snapped me back to reality and caused a flush to bloom across my face. Zypher gave me a knowing smirk before giving his attention to the mage.

"Are you saying Bechora accepted a mate bond?" Miles asked, pushing his glasses up his nose as he gave me a puzzled look.

"I haven't accepted any mate bond," I insisted.

Zypher sighed and removed his hand from my neck. "Do any of you know the history of Vampire kind?"

"They don't really teach anything from before the Dreadgrave line came into power," Shadrie replied.

Zypher leaned back, keeping one hand on my neck, his thumb stroking my skin and causing involuntary shivers to roll up my spine. My body swayed toward him with each pass, unconsciously attempting to get closer to him. He didn't miss the small movement, shooting me a wink before turning his attention back to Shadrie and Miles.

"Before the Dreadgraves took control over leadership of their clans, vampires were classed as demons. Vladimir Banecroft was the last of his line to hold power. He served on the demon council and was well-liked among the clans. Callidora Dreadgrave was his downfall. Her father, Gaspare, wanted more. Power, control—you name it, he wanted it.

It's written in demon history books that he sent his youngest daughter, Callidora, to Vladimir. Her father ordered her to behead her mate so the Dreadgraves could take control of the clans, and she chose to go against their bond and fulfill her father's wishes.

After that, Gaspare set his sights on the larger kingdom. Rather than take a place on the council, he betrayed several powerful demons, handing them over to the Fae king in exchange for a position in his court. That position was passed from him to his son, his son to his grandson, and one day it will fall to Gabriel as the Dreadgrave heir."

"What does that have to do with B's mark?" Shadrie asked.

Zypher inhaled deeply through his nose, letting it out again slowly. "Vampires had soulmates before Callidora's betrayal. We know not if it was actually the betrayal, or what followed, that caused their kind to lose the ability to sense their mates. Without the pull to their Noctis Amare, they took up rituals to claim mates, but it is known throughout demon kind that a true mated pair only requires a bite."

I stiffened at the phrase Noctis Amare. That was what Gabriel called me in my dream. Zypher's head snapped toward me, his eyes locking onto my tensed body.

"Do not worry, Dilectus. That may be a mating mark, but the bond isn't completed unless you have taken his blood." Miles, who had just lifted a cup to his lips, choked at Zypher's words. "You still have a choice," Zypher continued, ignoring my friends as Shadrie moved to slap Miles on the back. "Tell me who bit you and, if you wish it, I will end them and sever the bond completely."

"No," I managed to grit out. "I don't want you to kill anybody on my account. I will deal with this myself."

Zypher tilted his head, studying me for a moment before giving me one sharp nod. "As you wish, Dilectus. It is your choice who you accept into your bonded Vinculum. I will always honor that choice." Seemingly satisfied, his hand slipped from my neck before he clapped once. "Shall we return to our show?"

Miles and Shadrie voiced agreement, and we settled back into our seats. I let Zypher wrap his arm around my shoulders and tuck me in close to his side as he watched the show play out on the TV. I let my body relax into him, but I couldn't focus on anything beyond my own thoughts. If Zypher was correct, Gabriel Dreadgrave was also my mate. The moment he bit me, he marked me as his. I was going to make the asshole pay for it.

CHAPTER TWENTY-TWO

Caulder

My fingers thrummed on my desk as I let my thoughts wander to my mate. I should have been grading papers or dealing with the endless requests from the two houses I was assigned. Instead, my mind was focused on the problem of Bechora's magic. She was a conundrum, with the way her magic seemed nonexistent at times while granting abilities she shouldn't have. I'd gone so far as to seek out the mage who'd determined that Bechora was a fire mage, but she was adamant that only fire had revealed itself on orientation day.

A light rap against the frame of my open door drew me from my thoughts. Mrs. Fiodh, the Academy's librarian, stood in the doorway with her cart. Though she looked no older than forty, the small fairy had been with the school for centuries—possibly even since it came into existence; nobody was actually sure.

"Professor Thrackborne, I have the files you requested," she smiled, pulling three folders and an ancient-looking tome from her cart. "This was provided when I made the request." She tapped the tome. "I'm not sure it's quite what you're after, but the Academy deemed it important to your search, so I've brought it along."

"Thank you, Mrs. Fiodh. These should prove helpful," I smiled, taking the stack from her tiny hands.

There were times the school seemed sentient—the way it decided, without input, which students to invite, and now with the strange tome. They seemed like such minor things that it was easy to forget they ever happened, that the magic fueling the Academy was older than anyone living could recall. Part of me wondered if there wasn't more the school could do that it simply chose not to.

"If you need anything else, Professor, you know where to find me,"

Mrs. Fiodh smiled, fluttering her small wings as she strolled back to her cart.

I called out my thanks again as she pushed her cart out of sight before turning my attention to the three files in my hand. In my search for answers about Bechora's magic, I'd decided to look into past cases of students who came from the human realm and seemed to be magicless. I had a sneaking suspicion that being from the human realm was the key to solving her inability to call upon her magic on demand, but I needed something solid to be sure.

Setting the tome aside, I dropped the files on my desk and opened the one on top. There wasn't much information beyond the students' grades and trial scores—just a single mention of having come from a non-magical family in the human realm and presenting as a mage. Based on the grades alone, something had changed from the beginning of their first term that allowed them to improve significantly, though that could have been something as simple as taking the time to study and practice outside classes. There wasn't anything documented to say otherwise.

The second and third files were almost as empty. Had I not been paying such close attention to detail, I'd have missed the notes scribbled in the margins of their personal information. Neither student had grown up around magic. Whoever had scribbled the note had taken the time to explore the depth and fullness of the students' magical wells, finding them completely devoid of magic. "It's as if the lack of magical exposure in their home realm has left them with a deficit in their well," was scrawled in barely legible writing. Further down, a smeared note in the third student's chart read, "intense magic exposure successful," with no clarification on what that meant.

With the new information in mind, I thought back to the handful of times Bechora had been able to summon her abilities. Our meetings were after her final class of the day, which happened to be combat. Rumlock was known for throwing students off the deep end, starting them on training that utilized their magical abilities right away. The pieces started to click together in my mind as the realization dawned on me that Bechora most likely needed to be exposed to more than just the ambient magic in the realm to fill her well properly, at least for now. It was also something easy enough to test.

Smiling to myself, I reached across my desk, intending to make space to bottle a bit of my magic. My hand brushed against the tome Mrs. Fiodh had given me when she brought the files, and I hesitated. While I was certain I'd already found the answers I needed to help my mate access her abilities, regularly, and keep herself safe, I couldn't snuff out my growing curiosity. My plan temporarily forgotten, I grabbed the tome and studied it closely.

The binding was clearly ancient, but the tome seemed well intact. Carefully opening the cover, I was surprised to see a language I recognized. Ornate Elvish scrawled across the front page, denoting the tome as a historical account from someone named Thaliondil. A faded portrait sat center of the page, displaying a male with long, pointed ears dressed in ancient Elven garments. Shock rolled through me at what I held in my hands. I'd been taught as a hatchling that Elves had long abandoned the realm, taking with them their histories and magic and leaving the Fae to fill the power vacuum left in their place. My people became the history keepers after that. Each dragon was taught to read Elvish, should we ever be lucky enough to stumble across anything the ancient race had forgotten during their exodus. In my two centuries of life, I'd never heard even a whisper of anything left behind, and now, if my eyes were to be believed, I was holding one of their forgotten ancient texts.

Gently turning the page, I worked to recall everything I'd been taught about the ancient language. It was slow work translating the text with how little practice I'd had since childhood. My office was nearly submerged in darkness, my eyes straining against the lack of light, when I'd finally worked out enough of the translation to read a few pages. Pausing long enough to turn on the lights in my office, I returned to the first page. It was titled "I eri o i tinu nall," which translated to "The rise of the Starcaller." I frowned, trying to work out where I'd heard that name before.

The few pages I'd managed to translate so far spoke of an imbalance in the realm and the rise of a champion meant to right the scales. The *tinu nall*, or Starcaller, was said to call the power of others into themselves, granting them whatever abilities they needed to combat the darkness threatening to unbalance the realms. They had no true power of their own, relying primarily on the power of their bonded.

I worked well into the night and the wee hours of Sunday morning, translating the short tome. While I didn't see why the Academy had deemed it important to my search for answers on Bechora's behalf, I found myself fascinated with the history it told. Thaliondil was a skilled storyteller, weaving the tale of the mad Elven king. He'd set about ripping power away from every being in the realm, only to find himself up against the Starcaller. Using the power of her bond through their connection, she was able to subdue the mad king. The Elven queen begged for his life, her love for him more powerful than her hatred of what he'd become in his quest. An agreement was struck: the Elves would leave the realm, never to return, and take with them the knowledge and power the king had used to steal gifts from his subjects. If the tome were to be taken as fact, Thaliondil remained behind, relinquishing his gifts to the realm so that he could write down the history should it ever repeat itself.

My eyes ached from the strain of an entire night translating, and my body was stiff. Closing the tome, I tucked it into the top drawer of my desk as I let my mind work through what I'd learned. I couldn't help but note the similarities between the story of the mad Elven king and King Evarian. Vallynn hadn't been able to determine what his father was doing with the power he drained from the people he slaughtered, but we knew beyond a doubt he was draining it. I couldn't help but wonder, after what I'd read, if the king hadn't happened upon another forgotten tome that might have provided him a way to absorb the stolen magic for himself. The thought caused me to shudder. It was terrifying enough to know he was murdering people and stripping their power. If he had managed to discover a way to take it for himself, he'd be unstoppable.

Rubbing my tired eyes before stretching in my seat, I forced the thought aside. I refused to accept the possibility that we wouldn't be able to end the king's quiet reign of terror. After what he'd done to my clan, I needed to believe he could be brought to justice. I shook my head to further push thoughts of failure away and caught sight of the files I'd left forgotten as I dove into the Elven tome. Their presence was an instant reminder of why I'd ended up with the tome in the first place. I was supposed to be finding a way to help my mate access her magic, not getting lost in what may or may not have been a fictional account of history.

Growling softly at myself, I reached into another drawer and retrieved a small vial meant to contain magic. It had been created to hold even a dragon's flame without shattering under the heat, while being small enough to wear on a chain around the neck. I'd only managed to recover three of them from my clan lands after I'd found them slaughtered and our home decimated. They'd been tucked away in my desk drawer, serving as a reminder of what I'd lost, but now I had a new use for them.

Calling my dragon forth just enough to breathe our fire, I uncorked the small vial and pressed my lips to the opening. Smoke curled from my nostrils, and I let out a gentle puff of flame, filling it with violet flames. I quickly replaced the cork before attaching the glass vial to a delicate golden chain as it transformed itself into a discreet pendant.

Dragon fire was potent magic that couldn't be put out by anyone other than a dragon. Contained within the vial, Bechora would be able to absorb the magical properties of it without fear of getting burned or using it up before her well was filled. Snagging a blank sheet of paper and a pen from my desk, I quickly scrawled a note instructing her to wear the necklace and keep it concealed. I placed the vial and note in an envelope before grabbing a bottle of the restoration potion I'd been sending her every morning, and then stood from my chair. Glancing toward the window of my office, it was still just dark enough that I could make it to her dorm and drop the envelope without being noticed. A pleased smirk tugged at my lips with the knowledge that I was caring for my mate, even if nobody else knew it.

CHAPTER TWENTY-THREE

Bechora

Monday morning came far too soon. I stretched with a groan and forced my tired body from the comfort of my bed. Gabriel still haunted my dreams, leaving me feeling both thoroughly fucked and aching with a bone-deep need I didn't want. If Zypher was correct about the mark Gabriel had left on my neck, I could only imagine whatever magic tied mates together was responsible for the intensely erotic dreams plaguing me.

"You awake in there, B?" Shadrie called through my bedroom door. "There's a package for you."

"Yeah, be out in a sec," I called back, forcing my feet toward my closet so I could dress for the day.

I heard her move away as I pulled a clean uniform from the closet and dressed. A quick glance in the mirror caused me to frown at the state of my hair. It was wild and unkempt, as if I really had spent the night in the throes of passion. With an irritated huff, I dragged a brush through the tangled mass and secured it in a ponytail before exiting my bedroom.

"Package is on the counter," Shadrie called from her room.

Moving to the small island counter that separated the communal area from our dorm's tiny kitchen, I snagged the small package waiting for me. Other than my name, the brown paper was blank, but I could feel magic radiating from within. I'd been at the academy a couple of weeks and never felt anything like it. Even the empty void deep in my gut seemed to take notice, and I frowned as I felt the physical sensation of magic slithering through my system into that hollow space.

I cautiously tore open the packaging and tipped the contents out on the counter. My eyes went straight to the strange glowing pendant on a gold chain before moving to the now-familiar restoration potion. Those potions had been arriving for me every day since the start of classes, and I knew I'd need it at the end of the day. Combat was my only daily class, and Professor Rumlock was brutal in how he trained us.

Setting the potion aside, I picked up the glowing necklace. Power pulsed through my palm and wound through my body, slowly filling the empty void. The sensation was strong enough to nearly steal my breath, and I closed my eyes for a moment before opening them to look at the note attached to the delicate chain. "This will help build your magic stores; wear it at all times, but keep it concealed," was written in an elegant scrawl.

"Ohh, that's gorgeous," Shadrie grinned, sliding up to the counter beside me as I set the note aside and secured the necklace around my neck before tucking the pendant beneath my shirt. "Zypher is really upping his game, but he should probably take credit for all his gifts before someone else does."

"Right. Like anyone else on campus has a reason to send me gifts. His credit is safe, no matter how much he denies it," I laughed. "He sent a note this time, unsigned, but still. Said to keep it concealed."

"I wouldn't be surprised if it was some rare gem or something. Demons have a way of getting their hands on them, so it makes sense he would tell you to hide it. Wouldn't want to risk causing you any trouble over it. Speaking of trouble..." the shift in her tone signaling she was about to bring up the whole Gabriel Dreadgrave mate thing. "Are you doing okay? After our veg sesh, you pretty much holed up in your room, and we haven't had a chance to talk about the massive plot twist Zypher dropped in your lap."

"I wasn't holed up, I was studying and doing my homework. Not all of us grew up in this realm, in case you forgot," I snarked.

"No way, B, you're not getting out of this that easily. Zypher might have dropped it when you wouldn't tell him Gabriel is the one who bit you, but I know, and now we both know he marked you as his fated mate. That's a huge deal, B."

"It's not, really. I'll deal with Gabriel, somehow, but I also don't plan to keep the bond with him. There has to be something in the library—or even something Zypher can get a hold of—for me to tell me how to break it. As long as I don't drink his blood, the bond won't be completed if Zypher was right, so it's a non-issue."

"If you say so," Shadrie snorted. "Whenever you get around to plotting your revenge, know I'm here for you, and I'm happy to ice his underwear."

"You're ridiculous," I chuckled, rolling my eyes at her. "I've got to get to class. I'll see you at lunch."

Shadrie called out several more things she'd freeze on my behalf as I strolled from our dorm. Zypher was waiting outside of Magus House with coffee like he'd done every day since we met.

"You are a god among men," I groaned, taking a sip of the caffeinated goodness he'd brought for me.

"I am pleased you think so, Dilectus," he chuckled. "Perhaps such high praise will lead you to accept my proposal."

I choked on my coffee. "Proposal?" I sputtered.

"I have been studying human mating rituals, and the electricity mage has been tutoring me in your human ways. I have learned that your kind's matings require a special, smaller ritual called a date."

I couldn't help the soft smile that pulled at the corner of my lips at his serious tone. "Are you asking me on a date, big guy?"

"If you would be amenable to such a proposal, then I would like to initiate this portion of your human mating rituals," he replied.

"I am very amenable," I grinned.

A wide smile split his face, and for a moment, I was overwhelmed by how heartbreakingly gorgeous he was. "I am grateful for the chance to court you and prove that I am worthy of being accepted into your Vinculum," he said softly, placing a hand on the back of my neck. His thumb stroked over the mark Gabriel had left as we made our way across campus.

If you'd asked me at that moment why I was dragging my feet with Zypher, I wouldn't have been able to answer. It wasn't like I'd been a saint in the human realm. I'd had a few relationships and my share of lovers before I was snatched away to the Academy. Zypher was possibly the worthiest male I'd ever met, and there was an undeniable draw to be near him that only grew the longer we knew each other. It was the idea of fate that seemed to keep tripping me up. Some part of me needed to know that I chose him for myself and not because some unknown force had decided we were meant to be.

"What troubles you, Dilectus? I can see your mind working." Zypher's voice broke through my thoughts.

"It's nothing, really," I replied with a soft smile. "You're just not what I would have expected had I known supernaturals even existed."

Zypher stopped walking, turning me to face him so that he could look me in the eyes. "We are not all monsters. I cannot speak for the male that left his mark on you already, but for most males in this realm, our females hold the power when it comes to accepting or rejecting a bond. That is especially true among my kind. Our women are our fiercest warriors; we males only wish to offer our Dilectus what she needs to choose her own path in life. Whether that means fighting by her side or allowing her a safe space to be soft, it is always and forever her choice and our honor to provide."

"That's exactly what I'm talking about." I couldn't help but chuckle at the confused look on his face. "Sure, there are some great guys in the human realm, but you have to weed through a bunch of entitled douchebags to get to them—if you find the good guy at all."

"Is this why you choose not to tell me who marked you?" he asked.

"No," I sighed, patting him on the chest and turning to start across campus again. "I'm choosing to handle that asshole my way first. I promise if I can't deal with this on my own, you will be the first to know."

We continued the rest of the walk to my first class in silence, saying our goodbyes before I slipped into Spellcasting 101. So far, it had been my easiest class at the academy. It became apparent within the first few days that you didn't need internal magic stores to cast spells, and with Miles making minor adjustments to my hands, I'd caught on fairly quickly.

Intro to supernaturals followed spellcasting. What should have been an interesting class, now that I'd accepted my new reality, nearly bored me to tears. Professor Sabelus was awake long enough to direct the class to read the chapter on harpies, answer the chapter questions, and put them in the bin on his desk by the end of class. The vampire professor then collapsed into his chair, lay his head on his desk, and promptly started snoring. I'd already read the textbook in its entirety before the start of term, and it took me next to no time to answer the questions at the end of the chapter. I couldn't help wishing for a professor who engaged us and answered questions we couldn't find buried in the text. Zypher was waiting for me after class with a fresh coffee.

"You are a saint," I groaned as I sipped from my cup.

"Far from it, Dilectus," he chuckled. "Though it pleases me to see you happy."

I couldn't help the smile that split my face at his words. Before I could stop myself, I'd stretched onto my tiptoes and pulled him down with my free hand to kiss his cheek.

"I'm headed to the library to start studying up on Serpopards for our human studies assignment. I'll see you at dinner?" I asked as I released him.

"You will," he smiled.

Chuckling to myself, I told Zypher goodbye and headed to the library. I spent the rest of my time before combat class reading through as many books as I was able, only stopping long enough to grab some lunch. Vallynn hadn't emailed about the group project yet, and I was determined to learn as much as I could before he did. The way he'd acted like I was beneath him made me want to prove him wrong in whatever way I could. My head was swimming with information and random facts when I arrived at the training grounds for combat class.

I changed into the new fighting leathers I found in my locker as quickly as I could, ensuring my new necklace was secured beneath my top, before making my way to the training pitch. My eyes roamed over my classmates, and I spotted Kiri waving at me with a grin. Smiling back, I picked up my pace until I stopped to stand beside her.

"Hey, girl!" she grinned. "I was thinking we could be training partners again."

"That would be great, actually," I replied.

"You won't be picking your own partners," Professor Rumlock barked, causing us both to jump. "It is important that you not get comfortable with a single partner, lest you find yourself unable to defend against a different sort of supernatural."

Neither of us replied as we waited for our remaining classmates to arrive on the field. As soon as the last student appeared, Rumlock led us through a series of warm-up exercises, followed by laps around the pitch, before assigning us to our partners. To my dismay, I found myself paired with Gabriel. The vampire scowled at me as if I'd offended him as I made my way to our mat.

"You can stop scowling at me," I hissed as soon as my feet hit the edge of our training mat. "I'm the one who should be pissed. You fucking mated me."

Gabriel's eyes widened for a fraction of a second before narrowing. He moved too fast for my eyes to follow, closing the distance between us until his hand was wrapped around my throat and his nose was nearly touching mine.

"Like I would mate someone as pathetic as you. You don't even have enough power to defend yourself." He scoffed. "You had to stoop to finding a mage to cast a spell for you so that you could pull me into your fucked-up fantasies."

"In your dreams, asshole," I snorted as I tried to push him away.

"So, you know exactly what I'm talking about then, dud." He smirked, shoving me back and releasing my throat.

I felt power swell in the hollow pit of my stomach, winding through my body toward my fingertips. "Fuck you, you elitist prick," I snapped as a flame the size of a baseball formed in my palm.

Moving on instinct, I thrust my hand toward him, sending the flames spiraling through the space between us. Gabriel's mouth gaped open in shock, his body frozen in place as if he couldn't believe I actually had any power. The flaming sphere hit his shoulder, disintegrating with a hiss against his training leathers and leaving a charred circle behind.

His head tilted to the side, a vicious smile splitting his lips. "Oh, little mage, you're going to pay for that."

CHAPTER TWENTY-FOUR

Caulder

Rumlock stood with his hands on his hips, glaring off in the distance as I approached him on the training grounds. He'd summoned me to collect Bechora, though he hadn't said why he'd sent for me rather than a healer.

"Good, you're here," he drawled without looking in my direction.

"You summoned me, Rumlock. Of course, I'm here," I replied.

He tilted his head to where Bechora lay sprawled on her back in a starfish pose on a scorched training mat. "She won't move. Been there since class ended. Figured she's your problem anyway."

I tilted my head, studying the half-demon. While it wasn't obvious that he wasn't fully fae to anyone else on campus, I'd known immediately, my inner dragon alerting me to his presence on my first day as an instructor. What he was, left me curious about his choice of words. His true kind held a grudge against the Fae king, so he wasn't inherently my enemy here, but demons loved to meddle.

"And why is it that she's my problem and not the healers?" I pressed.

Rumlock shrugged. "Ain't injured."

"You can't handle a simple disciplinary issue, so you chose to bring in the current head of her house?"

Rumlock shrugged in response before moving toward the far end of the field, where his small office was tucked away. "Just get her off my field, Thrackborne," he called out over his shoulder.

I watched him for a moment longer, trying to puzzle out why it felt like he knew something more than he was letting on, before finally turning my attention to my tiny mate. She hadn't moved from where she was sprawled out on her mat, the slight rise and fall of her chest the only indication she was simply pretending to be dead.

Closing the distance between us, my eyes scanned her entire body in search of injuries Rumlock had missed. The scent of charred foam and leather was thick in the air around her, but it lacked the metallic tang of blood that would have indicated she was wounded beneath her training gear.

"Are you injured, Ms. Knight?" I asked, unable to identify any reason for her current position.

"Only my pride," she groaned, tossing an arm across her eyes.

"So, this is just a ploy to miss our session? You thought you'd simply lie here and all would be forgotten?"

Bechora slowly removed her arm from her face and propped herself up on her elbows, glaring at me. "No, Mr. Scowly. I thought I might lie here and wallow for a bit before I had to come to your office and discover just how much more inadequate I am as a mage."

"You're not inadequate, Ms. Knight. You simply haven't—"

"Right, not the least bit inadequate. That's why that fucking vampire was able to mark me, and then when I finally got a scrap of power to fight back, even that didn't matter. He slung me around the mat like a ragdoll, dodging every flame I tried to throw at him," she ranted, collapsing back to the ground as her hands waved angrily in the air. "He even had the fucking nerve to smirk about it. The smug asshole."

"Marked you?" I asked, latching onto that part of her story. My dragon pressed forward, causing scales to ripple along my skin, incited at the thought of someone else laying claim to my mate.

Bechora continued to rant, not acknowledging my inquiry. Before I was even aware I'd done it, I'd lifted her into my arms, bridal-style, and clutched her as close to my chest as I dared with her still-flailing arms. The action didn't seem to faze her as she let out a string of colorful curses toward the unknown vampire. The urge to tip my head toward her and sniff in hopes I'd catch the scent of whichever male she ranted about was only stymied by the need to jerk my head out of the path of her constantly moving hands, lest I be hit.

"I should have never been brought here, let alone forced into a combat class," Bechora continued as I strode toward the training pit exit with her still in my arms. "Why the hell is combat class even a thing? It's not like we're being trained for a war or anything... Wait, are we being trained for war?" She bolted upright in my arms, her hands clinging to my shoulders, her face so close to mine I could kiss her. "You didn't snatch me from work just to make me into a soldier, did you, Mr. Scowly?"

I couldn't help it—the look on her face that was clearly meant to intimidate was the most adorable thing I'd ever seen. My head tilted back, and a loud laugh boomed from my throat. I could feel my tiny mate jostling in my arms with the way the laughter shook my chest.

"No, there is no war," I said finally, causing her to relax her hold on me and sink back into my arms. I wanted to ask her if she felt how natural it was for us to be so close, but I feared drawing her attention to the way she settled into my hold. "The class is a holdover from the early days of the academy, when this realm was wilder. Long before the Fae king took the throne, there was a time when species fought for dominance, and then they had to fight to hold their ground against the realm itself."

I paused, continuing to carry her into the forest on Academy grounds meant to give the shifters a place to roam. "I suppose for a while, though, the course was made for generating soldiers. There was a long and bloody war to claim and tame the realm. After that, I can't say for certain why the course was kept in the curriculum, only that it was."

She drew her bottom lip between her teeth and crossed her arms over her chest, settling into silence. I let myself revel in the fact she still hadn't seemed to notice that I held her as we moved toward a clearing in the woods that I often sought out when the need to shift and be alone overtook me. I hadn't intended to bring her here, not at first. After reviewing the few student records that seemed relevant to her case, I'd planned to use my dragon fire in my office as a way to boost the ambient magic and hopefully hasten the filling of her empty well. The second my dragon had her in our arms, the plan changed.

"Where are we?" she asked, noticing that we'd stopped moving.

"The forest on campus," I replied. "I have been looking into your little void problem, and I think I have a solution."

A smile split her face. "Really? That would be awesome, maybe we can fix me, and I can go kick Dreadgrave's ass." She shifted her weight and froze. "Did... did you carry me here?"

"Yes. Well, you were quite preoccupied with your whining, so I felt this most efficient," I replied, forcing myself to sound disinterested as I placed her on her feet. All I truly wanted to do was gather her back up and demand to know if Dreadgrave was the vampire that had marked her before ripping his head from his shoulders.

"I was not whining," she snapped, her cheeks flushing a pretty red as she put her fists on her hips.

"It is of no consequence," I said, waving my hand in the air. "Now, as I was saying. The human realm has less ambient magic than this realm. Simple spells like those you're being taught in spellcasting don't require any magic from the caster, and they temporarily raise the amount of ambient magic in the air. This is why mages in that realm form covens and why others who visit in search of a mate often spend time with the covens. If they let their wells dip too low, they're unable to use their magic, shift, or even recognize the mate bond, defeating the purpose of their visit entirely. Events like a full moon can increase it as well. I suspect this is where your realm's myth about shifters originated."

"What does any of this have to do with me?" Bechora frowned.

"I pulled the records of every student with an issue similar to your own, and each of them had one thing in common. They'd grown up in the human realm, away from anywhere the ambient magic would be thicker. Their wells were completely empty when they arrived at the academy—so much so they'd been likened to dried-out riverbeds—and needed an extra boost above and beyond the ambient magic here to allow them to fill their wells and access their magic properly."

Her brows dipped and her hands dropped from her hips as she considered my words. One hand raised toward her throat before she caught herself and dropped it. The corner of my mouth twitched, threatening to break into a grin when I realized she must be wearing the flame I'd sent her and was keeping it secret as I'd told her to do.

"I wouldn't say it feels like a dried-up riverbed, more like an unending void, but what you're telling me makes sense. That doesn't explain why we're in the middle of the woods, though."

"Simple. I'm going to raise the ambient magic," I answered. "If you don't mind stepping back, Ms. Knight."

She did as I asked, her lips pursed in confusion as she walked backward until I motioned for her to stop. As soon as she was far enough away for me to safely shift, I began unbuttoning my dress shirt. Bechora's eyes widened, and her nostrils flared as I slipped it off, my hands moving to undo my belt as I toed off my shoes. My dragon preened at the hungry way her eyes roamed my chest, dipping down to my hands before her face went scarlet and she yelped, covering her eyes.

"What are you doing?" she demanded, whirling so her back was toward me.

"Shifting. These clothes aren't spelled to shift with me, so unless you'd rather we return from the woods with me in the nude, I have to remove them before I shift."

"You couldn't, I don't know, warn me?"

"Are all from the human realm this prudish?" I retorted. "Nudity is not uncommon in this realm. Even those who aren't able to shift find freedom in being bare."

"Just... just tell me when you're shifted."

"I cannot speak in my other form, Ms. Knight." I sighed, shaking my head as I stripped my pants and underwear off.

Bechora didn't respond, and I let the shift take over. My dragon burst forth, shaking our massive head and fluttering our wings. The beast was eager to meet our mate, gently nudging her with his snout. She stumbled forward a few steps before facing us. I'd expected fear. It was a common response when faced with such a large creature for the first time. Instead, her face was filled with awe and wonder.

Bechora reached out her tiny hand and rubbed our snout. A loud purr rumbled in our chest, causing her to laugh in delight. I allowed myself and my dragon to enjoy her touch for a moment longer before taking control of our form and gently nudging her further back. When I was satisfied with her position, I carefully drew fire into my throat, encircling her in the magical flames while keeping them far enough away not to burn her.

"Uh... What am I supposed to do inside the ring of fire, Professor?" she called out nervously.

I took a moment to consider how I would respond, regretting that I hadn't claimed her as my mate. If I had, I'd be able to speak into her mind while in my dragon form. The ability to speak with their mate in their shifted forms was a trait all shifters shared, regardless of their mate's species. There was even a slight possibility that my inner dragon would be able to communicate with her by sending his emotions and impressions to her mind directly. But none of that was possible since she didn't wear my mark.

"Right, you said you couldn't talk like this," she muttered to herself, most likely unaware that my shifter hearing allowed me to hear her as if she'd meant the remark for me.

She nodded her head as if she'd decided something before sitting cross-legged on the ground. Her eyes fell closed, and her breathing fell into a rhythm I recognized. Bechora was using the technique we'd been working on to seek out her well and determine if it felt different. Eventually, she cracked open an eye and focused on me.

"I don't feel any different than I did when we got here. I don't think this is working." I blew out a puff of air, causing her hair to blow behind her. "Christ, even like this, you're cranky. Fine, I'll wait."

Over the course of the next hour, things continued in much the same way. Every once in a while, I would add more flames to the ring around her, hoping that I'd reach the threshold she needed to finally feel the difference in her well. Each time she opened her emerald-green eyes and pinned them on me, they were filled with growing frustration and disappointment.

When our time came to an end, I recalled my flames, and Bechora collapsed onto her back. Shaking my head at her dramatics, I retrieved my clothes and dressed quickly, not wanting to offend her prudish sensibilities. Once dressed, I moved to stand beside her, my eyes taking in the sweat and dirt streaks across her face.

"You did not tell me it was too hot, Ms. Knight. I would have moved the flames further away."

"Not like it matters. It didn't work anyway," she grumbled, scrambling to get her feet under her. "My 'well' feels exactly the same."

"It may take more time, as you were in the human realm longer than the others," I said, offering a hand to help her up.

Bechora frowned and rolled her eyes, sliding her tiny palm into mine. An electric jolt ran through me from where our skin touched. I recognized it for what it was, a sign of our unsealed mating bond, but there was something else hidden beneath it. My tiny mate gasped, yanking her hand free of mine, and I thought she'd felt the same jolt I had.

"That made it feel different," she said. "Whatever the hell you just did when you touched me, I felt it. The magic filling my void, I mean. I fucking felt it."

CHAPTER TWENTY-FIVE

Vallynn

The moment Bechora swept into the classroom, I couldn't focus on anything but her. Her cheeks were flushed and her chest heaved from exertion, as if she'd run up the stairs to our astrology classroom. I had two classes with her, and both were torturous tests of my self-control. I'd even put off setting up the study session for our Human Studies assignment in an attempt to put some distance between myself and my unsuspecting mate.

"Really?" Daena's high-pitched voice grated across my eardrums. "What is your obsession with the trash? It's not like she even has any power, Val. Rumor has it she's a total dud, and Dreadgrave has already claimed her as his thrall as a reminder of her place."

I forced my mouth into a sneer, directing it at my mate. "I've heard the gossip, Daena. I'm curious how she gained admittance to the academy."

"Vallynn's right. There's no way a dud got in," Dante added. "If she's truly powerless, it's his duty as the crown prince to uncover whatever plot is at play that brought her here."

I didn't add my voice to the discussion, merely nodding along with whatever nonsense tale Dante was about to spin. Instead, my mind drifted back to my mate. Her visage haunted me, clouding my every thought to the point that I was failing in my duty to the realm. The mating bond was an insistent thrum, pounding away in my chest, refusing to grant me solace even in my dreams. On the rare occasion I could wrench control free of it, my thoughts would turn to the horrific ways my father would use my mate if I succumbed to the bond's demands.

"Would you kindly shut up, Daena," I demanded as the female's grating voice broke through the fog clouding my mind while she hissed her disapproval of Dante's every word.

I felt her stiffen in the seat next to mine, her hand curling into a fist in my peripheral. "You cannot speak to me that way. I am your betrothed, the future queen."

"Assuming you make it to the soul bonding, let alone survive the process," I drawled. "The crown still has many enemies, and you, my dear betrothed, have even more willing to slit your throat to take your place."

"Is that a threat?" she hissed.

"Merely an observation," I replied with a shrug, turning my head to look at the scroll spread open on her desk. "A simple look at your birth chart would show you are in a tenuous position. It is my duty to warn you of the dangers that come with tempting fate."

Daena's lips pressed together in a thin line as her face paled. Like most of the better-connected students in the academy, she hadn't created her chart herself. The version displayed on her desk had been created recently by her family astrologer, leaving no room for doubt about the future awaiting her on her current path. My sneer morphed into a vicious smirk as my eyes darted from one alignment to the next, noting that failure lurked at every turn in her future.

"Seems you already have enough troubles on the way," I snickered, just as Professor Vatorgan called the class to order.

Try as I might to focus on his lecture, my attention was constantly pulled to the female who vexed my every thought. Even though I knew burying any hint of what she was to me was the only way to keep her safe, I couldn't help the outrage and fury that coiled tightly in my gut, knowing that two males had laid claim to her. She was mine—my mate—and yet the so-called "prince" of demons, Zypher, had laid claim to her as his fated. Worse, rumors were flying around campus that Gabriel Dreadgrave had made her his thrall, in stark contrast to the rumors about their match in combat class. Her flaming red hair covered her neck, preventing me from seeing any marks the vampire would have left on her delicate throat, but the thought was enough to drive me to madness.

The moment class was dismissed, I stormed from the tower, fighting every instinct to follow my mate. Dante's hurried footfalls echoed behind me as I tore my way across campus to our dorm room. I'd barely made it inside when my friend and bound guardian grabbed my arm and forced me to give him my attention.

"Whatever is going through your mind right now, you need to put an end to it, Vallynn. You've been distracted, and we can't afford to be distracted if we're going to end whatever the hell it is your father is up to."

"I'm well aware," I snapped.

"Are you? Because it seems to me you've forgotten what's important. Instead of helping me go through the information sent by Linoran, you're doing Selir knows what. We haven't prevented an abduction since the sphinx, and there have been reports of more going missing since you sent me with that damnable dragon to save her."

My hands raked through the longer strands of my hair, and I collapsed onto the couch in our common area with a groan. "I know that. It's the bond. The damned thing is insistent, to put it mildly, and leaves room for little else."

Dante grimaced, and I could have sworn I saw a flash of longing cross his face. "I'm sorry," he murmured.

"It's fine. I knew it was possible when I decided to keep my distance from her. The bond doesn't care that I can't claim her if I want to keep her safe; it only cares that it hasn't been completed yet," I replied before taking a deep breath. "We should go over the information Linoran sent. It might be helpful to force myself to focus on our task."

Dante nodded before settling into the recliner opposite me. "I hate to admit Thrackborne is actually useful, but the angry lizard may have uncovered a pattern in the abductions. It seems the majority of the missing have gifts related to shielding, conjuring, ability enhancement, and entire clans of shifters. There's been a few outliers—a handful of seers, an illusionist, and... well, she's not on Linoran's list, but your mother was a dream carver."

I winced at the mention of my mother. She'd vanished when I was barely fifteen. My father told the court she'd simply retired to the country, but I knew better. My mother wouldn't have abandoned me like that. That knowledge was enough to make me dig into her disappearance, doing my best to spy on my father without him noticing. My efforts finally came to fruition shortly after my eighteenth birthday during the royal tour of the kingdom required of all royals upon the age of maturity.

My procession had stopped in Solstway, a small village near the veil that kept the realm hidden. Unlike the other villages, there was an air of disquiet and suspicion that saturated everything. Slipping a few coins into the hands of villagers bought me information about an estate on the outskirts of the village. It was said the estate appeared overnight, wrapped in dark magic that hungered for souls. The villagers who'd traded secrets for my coin swore they had seen skeletal mercenaries patrolling the property and that a strange male appeared every fortnight in the village to steal children away to the estate, never to be seen again.

By some miracle, I managed to sneak out of the inn unseen after my retinue retired for the night and make my way to the estate. Selir must have guided me that night because I made it into the estate without issue and eventually found myself in a secret dungeon standing in front of a cell where my mother was being held. Her movements were unbearably slow, trembling as if each step cost her, as she moved to the bars to get a better look at me. It was clear she'd been suffering, her once vibrant skin seeming to stretch too thin as if it clung desperately to brittle bones. Purple bruises kissed the skin beneath her eyes as she raked them over me.

I couldn't say how long I stood there, my feet rooted to the ground by shock and horror, before she begged me to run, her voice raspy and cracking. Her pleas seemed to hang in the damp air long after her voice failed, rattling through me like a dark omen. I moved closer, despite her warnings, desperate to reach my mother. Guilt twisted like a knife in my stomach. She'd been here for years, suffering, while I did nothing to save her. Her trembling hand reached through the bars, skeletal fingers caressing my cheek just as the tingle of magic crackled through the air.

Once again, her broken voice urged me to run, and this time I obeyed, swearing to myself that I'd find a way to save her. I tore away from the dungeon on silent feet, praying to Selir that I wouldn't be found; that I'd manage to return and rescue my mother. Cold, damp air, thick with power, cut at my lungs, each breath shallow and ragged, but still I ran. I didn't stop until the lights from the inn were in sight. I made my way inside, just barely stepping into my room before Dante pulled my mind away from the horror I'd witnessed. He'd been angry that I'd left without him. He wasn't only my best friend; he was my bonded guardian, and I'd stolen away into the night without him. His face paled, anger slipping away only to be replaced with horror, as I told him what I'd uncovered.

Dante's voice caused the memory to crack like splintering glass, yanking me back to the present. "Vallynn? Did you hear me?"

"I—" I hesitated, not quite sure what to say. The walls of our dorm room seemed to be shrinking in on me, my chest tight with grief over that night in Solstway. I forced myself to my feet, shaking my head to clear it. "I need some air."

His eyes narrowed as he studied my face briefly before giving me a tight nod of assent. It took all my self-control to make my way out of Magus House at an unhurried pace. Grief clawed at my throat. My mother had died before I could return to that cell in Solstway. The broken promise I'd made taunted me now, weaving itself among my latest failures—my people, my mate—all at risk because of my inadequacies.

As if summoned by my thoughts, the mate bond tugged my attention toward a cobblestone path. Bechora moved along it, between ancient buildings, toward the forest, completely unaware of my presence. My heart squeezed at how I'd been treating her. Not cruelly, per se—more like she was invisible, even though she was the planet around which my soul orbited. She didn't know the danger she was in because of the bond that stretched between us —a bond she didn't even seem to be aware of. Nor did she seem to acknowledge the dangers that lurked in the academy for someone like her. The rumors Daena had brought up in astrology flashed through my mind at lightning speed. My body moved without conscious thought, feet carrying me after her as my shadows slipped free to hide me. I couldn't claim her; it was vital that nobody suspected she was mine—but that didn't mean I couldn't keep her safe without her knowing.

CHAPTER TWENTY-SIX

Bechora

Professor Thrackborne didn't have any explanation for why I felt a surge of power when our hands touched. He'd made some comment about needing to look into it and promptly left me to find my way back to my dorm alone. I hadn't seen him since. The scowly dragon hadn't even bothered to show up for our sessions the past few days.

"You're sure it wasn't his dragon fire that gave you the boost?" Shadrie asked, for the hundredth time.

"Positive," I replied.

"Dragon shifters are said to be pure magic; it could be that you needed direct contact with the magic for it to work," Miles interjected, pushing his glasses up his nose.

The three of us were in the living area of my and Shadrie's dorm room. I'd filled Shadrie in on everything as soon as I'd returned from my trip to the woods with Thrackborne, and we'd been trying to figure out what happened since. Miles had a stack of books from the library in front of him on the coffee table and was flipping through one while Shadrie paced and asked the same question a dozen different ways.

What I hadn't shared yet was that the boost seemed to have dissipated, and in its place was a strange, growing draw to five males on campus. I found my eyes searching for Zypher, Gabriel, Dante, Vallynn, and even the crabby Professor any time I left the dorm. Zypher made sense. The growing attraction to him could be the mate bond he claimed existed between us. Especially if what Thrackborne had said was true about the lack of magic in the human realm interfering with the ability to sense bonds. The draw to the others left me feeling somewhat guilty, as if I were betraying Zypher with the unwanted attraction.

"B... You still with us?" Shadrie asked, snapping her fingers in front of my face. "Where did you go? You zoned out on us, and Miles was talking."

"Yeah, sorry. What were you saying?"

"I was saying I remembered a wolf shifter who came to my coven for help. She'd been in our realm for a decade, but for whatever reason, she hadn't been able to stay near a coven to keep her magic stores up. Her well was so empty that our coven had to physically touch her while casting to help replenish her well. It's rare, but it happens."

"What about the pendant?" I asked, my hand moving on instinct to grab it where it was hidden beneath my shirt. "I've been able to summon fire since I put it on."

"Easy," Miles shrugged. "It's obviously enchanted, and it is touching you. Same principle, though it has to be a decently strong enchantment if it's still replenishing your well."

"This would be so much simpler if Thrackborne hadn't vanished, so I could demand some answers." I groaned.

"Answers or..." Shadrie laughed, waggling her brows suggestively.

Miles shut the book he was skimming with a decisive snap. "I think that's my queue to leave. Why don't we table this for the night and pick back up in the library tomorrow? There's a few more books I'd like to check out that could tell us something useful. It might be helpful to narrow things down if you make a list of anything strange you've experienced since arriving here."

"You mean like being snatched through a portal, having strange dust blown in my face, and told I'm a fire mage?" I asked, raising a brow.

"Well, no," Miles frowned.

"She's being sarcastic," Shadrie interjected. "You know he means after that, you know, like icing your bedroom, trapping yourself in there with a shield, that sort of stuff."

Shadrie gave me a pointed look as Miles nodded.

"Fine. I'll make a list," I groaned.

"Perfect. Meet in the Library, let's say, after lunch?" Miles asked as he gathered his books and moved toward the door.

"Sure, I'll make sure B has your list at breakfast," Shadrie smiled, seeing him out. Once the door shut behind him, she turned to face me. "I know you're being bitchy because we don't have answers, but you really gotta give Miles a break. Your seer friend said you have to figure out what you are, right? Well, Miles is the biggest bookworm I've ever seen. If anyone can help us figure it out, it's him."

I let out a heavy sigh. "I know, you're right. I'll apologize to him in the morning. He's been nothing but kind since I got here, and I was being a grade-A bitch just now. He didn't deserve that."

"Good." Shadrie grinned. "Now that we've settled that, I've got a hot date tonight, and you need to get some rest. Those dark circles under your eyes are so not in style."

I rolled my eyes and flipped her off. Shadrie laughed as she strolled into her bedroom. It wasn't my fault that my sleep was being disturbed nightly by dreams about Gabriel. Still, she was right about me needing rest, a fact I decided to act on as I made my way to my own bedroom for the night.

Gabriel prowled toward where I was sprawled out on a bed of black satin. My eyes raked over him, drinking in the lean muscle of his naked chest. Clapping broke through the otherwise quiet space, and I frowned.

"Wow, I knew he was a looker, but damned, B," Geordie's voice called out from somewhere to my right.

The scene before me slipped away like smoke, and I found myself sitting at the counter in the apartment I shared with Geordie. He stood on the other side of the counter, a grin splitting his face as he slid a cup of coffee toward me.

"Wha–"

"I don't have a lot of time," Geordie interrupted. "It took a lot of doing to find someone trustworthy to get me into your dream, but I can't risk being here for very long. I have to keep moving so I'm not found. This realm isn't safe for me."

"What's going on, Geordie? Why did you lie to me about... well, everything?" I demanded.

"I promise, I will eventually give you those answers, but for now, I need you to focus, Bechora. I can't tell you certain things or else the future will change. You need to discover what you are and how to use your magic. Things are progressing faster than I originally foresaw. All I can tell you without risking making it worse is to hurry. Your friends can help, give them the list, and for the love of Selir, accept your bonds. You're going to need them." Geordie's words came out in a rush, and he started to flicker out of existence near the end. "I'm out of time. Do what I said, B. I'll come to you again when I can."

Before I could say a word, he was gone. Our apartment flickered, and a loud crash sounded from behind me. I jolted upright, my eyes flying open as my hands flew to my pounding heart. My entire body was soaked with sweat. I was in my bedroom at the academy, early morning light streaming in through the lone window. Geordie's words echoed in my mind as I forced myself from the bed just as my alarm went off.

I gathered my uniform and shower caddy and made my way to the showers while I mulled over what he'd said. Part of me was angry at him, but another part recognized the underlying fear that had laced his words. I tried to figure out what could have him so scared, as I washed the sweat from my body and hair, but still hadn't managed to come up with an answer by the time I finished.

I reached out of the shower stall to grab my towel from the hook and came up empty. "What the fuck?" I hissed, poking my head out of the stall.

My towel was gone, along with my uniform. I hadn't heard anyone else in the shower, and yet my things were missing, even the pajamas I'd worn. Sticking my head out farther, I looked around and didn't see anyone.

"Shit," I huffed. "Guess someone decided to fuck with me today."

Taking a deep breath, I steeled my spine and stepped out of the shower stall. My head was on a swivel as I looked for the culprit with each step. It wasn't until I made it out of the showers that I found them.

"Someone must be desperate for cash," Daena sneered. "Although I thought strippers were paid to take their clothes off, not start in the nude."

Her posse of mean girls snickered, one of them holding up a cell phone aimed in my direction.

"I thought you might want to see what a tight body looks like," I shot back, refusing to let her get to me. It was obvious the bitch was behind my missing towel and clothes. "It's not my fault your man can't keep his eyes off me."

"You stupid slut," she screeched.

I forced myself to laugh, turning on my heel and striding toward my dorm with a little extra sway to my hips. Daena called out insults, but I ignored them, keeping my head held high. There was no way the photos or video, whichever her lackey had taken, weren't going to be all over campus before the day was out, but I refused to let them shame me with their idiotic mean girl prank.

"Where are your clothes, and why are you dripping water everywhere?" Shadrie asked as soon as I slipped inside our dorm and shut the door.

"Apparently, Daena and her crew decided they needed my towel and clothes more than I did," I shrugged, heading to my bedroom so I could dry off and get dressed.

"So, you just walked back like that?" Shadrie chuckled.

"Yup."

"Oh, Selir, I would have paid out the nose to see her face when you just strutted back like it was nothing."

"If you hurry, you probably still can," I called over my shoulder as I stepped into my bedroom. Shadrie cackled and shook her head, causing me to smile. "By the way, how do people have cell phones here?"

"We copied human tech for some stuff, like computers and phones," she called back from my bedroom door as I disappeared into my closet to dry and dress.

Shadrie was leaning on my door frame, dressed for the day, when I finally reemerged. "I'd ask how, but I'm not sure I'd understand it, so I'm going to ask where to get a phone instead."

"I'll contact my parents and see if they can send one. There's not anywhere on campus to get one," she replied. "I'm surprised you didn't realize we had them before now."

"It's not like the human realm where everyone is always on them," I shrugged. "I didn't even know you had one."

"Magic tends to come more naturally to us," Shadrie shrugged. "Anyway, we need to get moving if we want breakfast before class. Grab your list for Miles!"

Shaking my head, I snagged the list I'd made the night before and followed Shadrie from our dorm.

CHAPTER TWENTY-SEVEN

Zypher

"Good morning, Dilectus," I purred as I handed Bechora a cup of coffee.

The scowl she'd worn as she exited Magus House gave way to a smile that nearly took me off my feet.

"Hey, Triple D, you bring one for me?" her roommate, Shadrie, quipped. I chuckled and handed the ice mage the other cup I'd brought.

Bechora moved to my side, listing closer as we made our way to the dining hall as if she couldn't stand to be apart from me. I reached out and tucked her beneath my arm, practically purring when she didn't pull away. Part of me hoped it meant she was finally overcoming her hangups about our mating, but I wasn't going to press the issue.

"Are you prepared for our human studies group meeting this evening?" I asked.

She jerked, her steps hesitating. "What meeting?"

"It would seem the Fae male has decided it is time for our group to meet and proceed with our assignment. Did you not get the message?"

"No, I didn't." She scowled. "I planned on spending time in the library today."

"Ah, well, there should still be time for that. He is demanding we gather in his dormitory an hour after dinner."

"Fucking Vallynn," she grumbled as we stepped into the dining hall.

I led her to our usual table and helped her into her seat before making my way through the buffet lines to bring her breakfast. By the time I'd returned to the table, her friend Miles had joined our little group, and he was discussing some list with Bechora and Shadrie. To my pleasure, my mate didn't argue when I set her plate before her, choosing to graze from it as she continued her conversation.

After breakfast, I walked Bechora to her first class and then went in search of Gabriel Dreadgrave. My mate had refused to tell me who'd left a mating mark on her neck, but the academy was rife with rumors claiming Dreadgrave enthralled her. I'd made it my mission to seek him out and demand the truth; only then would I decide how to respond. I found him tucked away in the library, scowling over a worn-out text.

"I've been looking for you, Dreadgrave," I spoke, causing him to startle.

Gabriel snapped the book shut, stuffing it onto the shelf behind him. "What do you want, Morningstar?"

"I'm curious why I found your mark on my mate," I replied.

The vampire froze, his back going stiff for just a second before he turned to face me. "Where did you hear that?"

"You don't deny it?" I asked, causing Gabriel to hiss. "I see. In that case, it seems we have much to discuss, starting with taking our mate's choice away from her."

"We have nothing to talk about, Morningstar. As soon as I figure out how, I'm breaking this fucking bond. I don't want your mate."

If he'd hoped to hide the pain that flashed across his face with his denial, he'd done a poor job. Gabriel's words may have denied our mate, but he clearly wanted her. "What's done cannot be undone."

"Bullshit. My brother is looking into it; he'll find a way to undo this because it was a fucking mistake. The vows weren't said; this bond is an abomination that shouldn't exist."

"You know nothing of your own history, do you?" I asked, shaking my head. "Before your clan betrayed demon kind, fated bonds were plentiful. All it took was a bite, and you were bound to your fated for eternity."

"Lies," he hissed.

I sighed and pinched the bridge of my nose in frustration. While I wasn't sure what to expect when I found Gabriel and initiated our discussion, his current reaction was the furthest from my mind.

"I know you're protecting that fucking dud. She probably even put you up to this, but you can tell her I refuse to be bonded to someone like her," he seethed, his chest heaving as anger poured off him in waves.

His words pushed me to act; my hand gripped his throat as I slammed him against a shelf. "You will not speak of our mate that way, do you understand?"

"Fuck you, Morningstar," he snarled. "She will never be my mate."

"If this is how you plan to treat her, then I agree. She will never be yours," I sighed, releasing my hold and letting him drop to his feet. "I suggest you keep your distance, lest I decide I've shown you enough mercy."

The vampire bared his fangs with a hiss and then sped away. Placing my hands on my hips, I rolled my neck to release the tension of our encounter and noticed the spine of the book he'd been reading sticking out from the rest. Snagging it from the shelf, I nearly laughed as I realized he'd been reading up on vampire mating bonds. The tome was old, the pages yellowing as I thumbed through them. Two pages were crinkled near the bottom as if someone had gripped the book so tightly it left a mark.

I nearly laughed when I realized Dreadgrave had been reading about the dreams initiated by the vampire mating bite. The vampire mating bond would drive a fated pair to complete it by drawing them together in dreams, and it only happened for fated pairs. Armed with the knowledge of what the vampire had been reading, I was suddenly looking forward to our study group. It was going to be highly entertaining to watch him and our mate navigate it while denying the truth. I couldn't help but wonder how they'd react with a little nudge.

It was difficult to come up with a plan to tease out Gabriel's attraction to our mate—a fact I was still ruminating on when I met Bechora at the library to escort her to our study group session.

"You're awfully quiet there, big guy." She shifted the pile of books in her arms that she'd refused to let me carry.

"I'm preparing myself." I smiled.

Bechora turned slightly toward me as we continued walking. Just as she opened her mouth to respond, she collided with another student. Her books flew from her hands, scattering on the cobblestone along with books the other female had been carrying.

"Oh god, I'm so sorry," she breathed, rushing to help the other woman up before I could intercede.

"It's fine, I should have been watching where I was going," the female replied just before she looked up and noticed Bechora. Her lips twisted into a sneer. "Oh, it's you."

"Watch your tone," I snapped.

"Me?" Bechora asked at the same time.

The female's eyes flitted to me before moving back to my mate and then down to where Bechora's hand rested on her arm. It took me a moment, but I recognized her for what she was: a succubus.

"Don't touch me," she hissed, jerking her arm away. "It's not enough that you've ensnared our prince; now you're putting hands on me?"

"I—" Bechora jerked her hand away, raising both in surrender as confusion painted her face.

"I've not been ensnared, and you'd be wise to guard your tongue. You will not insult my Dilectus again."

The succubus blanched, her eyes darting to the ground. "Apologies, your majesty. I meant no disrespect."

"Of course you meant it," I scoffed. "I should punish you for it."

"Zypher…" Bechora's voice held a hint of concern. "I'm sure she's just surprised you're not mated to another demon." She turned her attention to the succubus. "Right?"

The succubus bared her sharp teeth and hissed. "I don't need a mage to save me from my prince. Especially not one weaving spells to trap powerful males. We've all heard the rumors."

"Enough," I thundered. "Gather your things and go before I make a public example of you!"

The succubus flinched as if I'd struck her before bowing her head. She rushed to gather her books, where they lay scattered on the cobblestone, and then raced for the safety of the library. I turned to track her movements, tempted to follow through on my threat anyway.

"Let it go," Bechora sighed, moving to gather her own books from the ground. "We don't have time for petty rumors and mean girls."

I ground my teeth, tearing my gaze away from the direction the succubus fled, and bent to help my mate. "She will learn what it costs to speak ill of you."

"She's not worth it, Zypher," Bechora said firmly, rising from her squatted position as she adjusted her books once more. "Let her be bitter and jealous. The kind of misery that creates is punishment enough."

Her words cooled some of the anger burning through my veins, and I reluctantly inclined my head.

"Fine, Dilectus. I will allow her to go unpunished this once."

Bechora snorted and let out a small laugh. "Good. Now let's get to this study group before the fae prince has a coronary."

I barked out a laugh, and we made our way to the Fae's dorm in Magus House. The fae in question glared at us as we entered. His gargoyle guard, Dante, and Gabriel were already seated around the coffee table in the living room area.

"You're cutting it close," Vallynn snapped.

"You're lucky we even showed up, considering you didn't schedule this group session with any real notice," Bechora snapped.

Vallynn clenched his jaw before blowing out a breath. "Just sit down so we can get started."

"A 'please' wouldn't kill you," Bechora muttered, causing me to chuckle as she made her way to the empty love seat at the closest end of the coffee table. "Or maybe it would, and that's why you don't have any manners."

The gargoyle chuckled, and the fae prince growled softly. Neither of us paid any attention to them as we settled into our seats. Bechora placed her stack of books on the coffee table, opening the one on the top to a page displaying a list of Greek customs. I leaned around her to get a better look, intentionally brushing my shoulder against hers as I flicked my eyes toward Gabriel. The vampire's nostrils flared, and he pressed his lips into a thin, angry line.

"With that look on your face, you remind me of Hades denying his want for Persephone," I said with a grin. "So, like a vampire, that one, sulking in the shadows, denying his fate while his heart betrayed him with every glance."

"Speak for yourself, Morningstar," Gabriel snarled.

Bechora narrowed her eyes at me, her hand instinctively moving to Gabriel's mark on her neck. "How?" she hissed under her breath.

I leaned toward her, sweeping her hair over her shoulder to whisper in her ear while keeping my gaze on the vampire. "Rumors can be useful."

"Can we get to work?" Vallynn snapped, pausing briefly. "Please." The word sounded like it pained him.

"Starting with the gods is a good call," Dante spoke. "Their function and worship tend to influence culture, and it evolves from there. If I recall correctly, most of them were based on supernaturals as well."

Bechora's eyes widened in shock. She clearly hadn't expected the gargoyle to have anything nice to say. "Thank you," she said, disbelief laced in her tone.

"Right, we'll start there," Vallynn agreed, taking a seat near Dante.

We turned our focus to discussing various myths and comparing them to information in the books Bechora had brought about modern Greek culture. I'd practically forgotten my desire to taunt Gabriel as we dove deeper into the work. It wasn't until Bechora started shifting uncomfortably, crossing and uncrossing her legs, that I noticed something was amiss.

Bechora shifted again, her thighs pressing together as if even she didn't understand the strange pull rolling off her in waves. The air in the dorm seemed to thicken, heat rising until it felt like we were breathing through honey.

Vallynn's pen slipped from his fingers, clattering uselessly to the table. His jaw tightened, a faint shimmer of shadows sparking in his irises before he dragged his gaze away from her. Dante shifted in his chair like he couldn't quite get comfortable, stone-hard composure cracking with a rare flicker of need etched across his face. Even Gabriel's stillness betrayed him, his eyes narrowing to slits as his knuckles whitened around the edge of the book he held.

It hit me next, the power writhing uselessly against my skin. Realization snapped into place like a lock clicking shut. Bechora was emitting succubus allure, drowning herself and the other three in pure desire. I cursed under my breath and frantically looked around the room for somewhere secure. I couldn't leave the dorm with Bechora, lest the allure snare anyone else. The others seemed to rise to their feet in unison.

Vallynn was the first to move, his usually careful grace abandoned as he circled the table, eyes locked on Bechora like a starving man offered a feast. Dante shoved to his feet, moving with slow, deliberate steps toward her. Gabriel was the most direct, fangs bared, pupils blown wide. He lunged toward where we sat with one hand shot out toward Bechora—possessive, desperate.

I snatched my Dilectus into my arms, noting the dazed expression on her face. Her lips parted on a needy whimper; her face flushed with desire. Bechora's hands moved to my chest, tugging at my shirt as the other males snarled. Snapping my shield into place, I moved, racing toward the nearest bedroom, grateful that I had the rare gift of impenetrable shielding.

"Please, Zypher... I need you." Her voice was breathy and pleading.

"I can't. Not like this," I murmured softly, working to free myself of her roaming hands and sit her on the bed.

"Give her to us," Dante demanded, pressing against my shield as he attempted to force his way into the bedroom.

"No."

"Please, Zypher. I ache," Bechora sobbed.

I clasped her hands together between mine, pressing a soft kiss to her knuckles. "If you still want this after the allure has worn off, then I will give you all of me. But I cannot take advantage of you in this state."

The moan that left her lips at the small amount of contact told me the allure was in full effect. Carefully, I pushed her away from me and walked backward to the door. Dante was standing in my way, his chest heaving as his fingers gripped the doorframe. Gargoyles, on a good day, were difficult to move. They could be as heavy as stone when they wanted to be, without ever shifting to their stone form. Behind him, Vallynn and Gabriel snarled and hissed, pressing against Dante's back and adding to his unmovable weight. I needed help if I wanted to last the night protecting my Dilectus.

There were only two types of supernaturals immune to a succubus' allure: demons and dragons, and I wasn't keen on calling another demon for assistance after our encounter outside the library. Instead, I cast an illusion, seeking out Thrackborne and praying to the gods he came to my aid.

The three males before me slammed themselves against my shield, causing me to wince. They were mindless, seeking out the female who snared them with allure. I widened my shield to ensure the entirety of the doorway was blocked and worked to shove them back. I can't say how long I worked to keep them away from Bechora while she begged for relief at my back. It was long enough that my body physically sagged with relief when the angry dragon professor stormed into the dorm.

"What is the meaning of this!" he bellowed.

"She's leaking allure," I called back, just as Thrackborne's nostrils flared.

The dragon's pupils dilated, and scales erupted along his arms. His chest rose as he scented the air, and then he moved, shoving the other three males across the room with enough force to slam them into the opposite wall.

"Mine," he snarled. Bechora whimpered behind me, but I refused to take my eyes off the dragon. "Let me in," he demanded, his voice rough and unsteady.

His reaction didn't make sense. It was as if he'd fallen under the allure as well, except that shouldn't have been possible. Thrackborne roared, slamming his fists against my shield to punctuate his demands. I shook my head in disbelief. This shouldn't be possible, couldn't be possible. Not unless he was hers.

"Gods," I breathed. "This is going to be a long night."

CHAPTER TWENTY-EIGHT

Bechora

I woke up in an unfamiliar bed. My memory was hazy as I sat up in the puddle of silk sheets draped over my body. Zypher was sitting on the floor, slumped against the open door. I carefully climbed from the bed and moved toward him, peeking into the room beyond, recognizing Vallynn's dorm room. Except it wasn't nearly as put together as it had been when Zypher and I arrived the evening before.

Broken furniture was strewn everywhere, and my books appeared to have been unceremoniously dumped so someone could use the coffee table as a weapon. Professor Thrackborne sprawled on his back across the uneven couch, his feet on the floor with the way that section had been demolished. Gabriel was on his stomach on the floor nearest Zypher, one hand reaching toward the door. Dante slumped against the counter dividing their kitchen from their living room, and Vallynn was curled on his side near him. I nearly laughed at the way the normally put-together prince's hair stuck up in every direction.

Zypher stirred near my feet, and the brush of his arm against my pants leg sent a memory rocketing through me. My face burned with embarrassment as I recalled how I'd begged for these males, desperate for any one of them to fuck me. Flashes of them fighting against Zypher's shield as he tired, and of them fighting one another to be the one to reach me, caused my stomach to roil.

"You're awake." Zypher's sleepy voice drew me from the haunting memories.

"I'm sorry, I don't know what happened." The words spilled out of me without a thought.

Zypher pushed himself up from where he sat in a movement too graceful to be human and smiled. "It's not your fault. It was the allure. Though I am quite curious how you came to possess such a talent."

"Allure?" I asked dumbly.

"Succubus magic." Zypher shrugged.

I frowned. "I… well, I don't know. Just another weird thing for the list, I guess."

"Allow me to escort you back to your dorm, Dilectus. You can tell me about this list along the way."

"Let me just—"

"Never mind that. I'll ensure your books are returned. I want to get you to your room before the others wake, as I do not know what state they will find themselves in when they do," Zypher insisted.

I nodded, not sure whether he meant they would still be under the spell of the allure he mentioned or if he meant something else entirely. Zypher offered me his arm, and I took it, grateful for the support as more embarrassing memories flitted through my mind. The memories were laced with something else, a longing and a draw to the four men passed out around the room, that I wasn't quite ready to face. As soon as we stepped into the hallway, it felt like I could breathe again. A part of me yearned to turn back, but it seemed smaller somehow now that the others were out of sight.

"What is this list, Dilectus?" Zypher asked, guiding me through Magus House toward my dorm.

"A list of all the strange things that have happened to me since arriving here," I replied. "My magic doesn't seem to be normal, and I'm hoping the list will help me figure it out."

"Hmm. Why don't you talk me through it all from the start, and I will see if I can help," Zypher replied.

The sincerity in his words shifted a weight I hadn't known I was carrying. Something about the way the demon prince had been a quiet, steady force since we met, always respecting my boundaries, made me want to open up to him. I realized at that moment he'd chipped away at my reservations little by little until all it took was his offer to help to smash the rest to bits. I told him everything. From the moment Thrackborne yanked me through a portal, to the dream that Geordie appeared in, to all the strange manifestations of magic I'd experienced. Zypher listened quietly, guiding me into my door and settling us on the couch while he waited for me to finish.

"So, that's everything. This allure, as you called it, is just another thing I don't understand."

"And you're working with your friends to figure this out?" he asked, though he wasn't truly seeking an answer. I nodded anyway. "If it is alright with you, Dilectus, I'd like to speak with my mother about this. She may have some guidance that can help us get to the bottom of things."

"Your mother?" I asked, my brows dipping down in confusion. "Why not your father? He's like the oldest demon in existence, right?"

Zypher laughed. "No. My mother, Lilith, is the oldest demon in existence. Followed by Mazun, my other father. Lucifer is my father by blood, but he was the last to join her Vinculum. Mazun prefers the shadows, and my mother prefers her enemies think her weak, so Lucifer wears the crown as far as anyone outside of our family bond is aware."

"Back up. Your mom is Lilith. Like, removed from the bible, Lilith?" I squeaked out the words, just barely.

"Yes and no." Zypher frowned. "My mother's story is hers to tell, as yours belongs to you. She may be able to help us if you allow me to share what you've told me with her."

"If you think she can help, you can tell her everything," I replied. "Thank you. For everything."

I didn't hesitate, pulling him down by the neck and leaning forward to kiss him softly on the lips. Zypher stilled for just a second before his arms wrapped around my waist and pulled me flush against him as he lifted me off my feet to get a better angle. I tore my lips away from his, a little shocked at my own impulsiveness, and his hold loosened slightly.

"I'm sorry, I shouldn't have done that," I murmured, sliding down his body and casting my gaze toward the floor.

Zypher gently tilted my head with one finger beneath my chin, so I was forced to look him in the eyes. "You have nothing to be sorry for. I told you, Dilectus, should you want me with the allure gone, I am yours. Completely and irrevocably, yours."

I didn't resist this time. Instead, I leaned into him again as he bent toward me, capturing his mouth with mine. The kiss deepened quickly, our hunger snapping like a live wire between us. His lips moved with a fierce possessiveness, one hand tangling in my hair while the other pressed firmly at the small of my back, holding me against the solid warmth of his chest.

A soft gasp escaped me as his tongue brushed against mine, coaxing me closer, daring me to lose myself in him entirely. The world outside that moment ceased to exist. There was only Zypher, his heat, his taste, the way his power simmered against my skin like a dangerous promise.

"Well, well, well…" Shadrie's voice rang out, dripping with amusement. "Look at you finally giving in. Took you long enough."

I wrenched myself back, breathless and mortified, but Zypher didn't so much as flinch. His lips curved into a lazy, satisfied smirk as his hand lingered at my waist.

"Oh God, I'm so sorry, Shadrie!" I practically shouted at her, hiding my burning face behind my hands.

"Don't stop on my account," Shadrie teased, leaning casually against the doorframe with her books hugged to her chest and turning her attention to Zypher. "Honestly, this dorm has been entirely too boring lately. You're doing the realm a public service, B has been way too wound up if you catch my drift."

"Shadrie!" I squeaked, jerking my hands away from my scarlet face to glare at her.

My roommate only grinned wider. "Oh, don't look at me like

that. If I had a demon prince offering himself up body and soul, I'd have jumped him ages ago. Now go on, don't let me interrupt, just pretend I'm not even here."

Zypher chuckled low in his throat, clearly delighted, while I wished the floor would swallow me whole.

"Don't encourage her!" I hissed, causing him to shake his head in amusement.

"Don't worry, B, I'm headed to grab breakfast before class. I'll let Miles know you're busy getting that triple D and to come by after dinner so we can chat about anything he found to do with your list." Shadrie cackled, making her way to the door.

"Triple D?" Zypher frowned. "Isn't that what you've taken to calling me, ice mage?"

"Yeah. Demon Daddy Dick. That's you." She grinned, waggling her brows. Zypher burst into a full belly laugh. "Take good care of our girl. I'm out." Shadrie threw up a peace sign and sauntered from our dorm.

"I'm going to murder her," I groaned. "Better yet, I'm going to replace all her belongings with pink, sparkly things, and then I'm going to murder her."

"I find this new vengeful side of you quite appealing, Dilectus," Zypher purred. "Though I suspect you wish to attend class this morning. I shall leave you to ready yourself and return with coffee to escort you to the dining hall."

He gave me one last chaste kiss on the lips before releasing me and exiting my dorm. It took me several minutes to regain my composure and change into a clean uniform. Tossing my hair into a ponytail, I gave myself a final once-over in the mirror before grabbing my messenger bag and heading to meet the others. Zypher was waiting with coffee just outside Magus House as promised, and I couldn't help wondering how he'd managed to get back in fresh clothes with my chosen morning beverage so quickly. Before I could ask, he kissed me gently on the lips and looped my arm through his, turning us toward the path that would take us to the dining hall.

"I still plan to follow through with your human custom,

Dilectus," Zypher said, as if he'd sensed my thoughts shifting to the more passionate kiss we'd shared. "I have planned out our date, and though it seems you're starting to accept our bond, I intend to follow through with my plans."

My breath stuttered. Not because he was putting effort into dating me, but because he'd noticed something I hadn't. My feelings about the bond had shifted; I just couldn't pinpoint when. There was still a small part of me, growing quieter by the day, scared of losing my agency. But the rest, I was noticing, was filled with excitement at the thought of being bonded to the male beside me. I should have been terrified at how quickly my feelings had changed, and yet, I wasn't. Being with Zypher felt right, and after the way he'd protected me from the allure, I couldn't imagine rejecting our bond.

Zypher shot me a knowing smile as if he could read my mind. "Wait until the conclusion of our date to decide, Dilectus. If you wish to complete our bond at that time, I will gladly give you all of me."

CHAPTER TWENTY-NINE

Bechora

After breakfast, Zypher dropped me off at my first class, saying he was leaving campus to speak to his mother and promising to take me on our date when he returned. I had Elemental Magic to start my day, and now that I had some power at my disposal, I was performing well enough to forget the embarrassment of being under the allure. The day went relatively well until I returned to the dining hall for lunch.

I'd noticed the strange looks from students leaving the hall as I entered, but I wasn't sure what to make of them—at least not until I stepped fully inside and saw the video of me strutting naked through Magus House playing along the back wall. Someone had projected the video larger than life, giving everyone in the dining hall an up-close and personal look at every inch of my body. Gasps and laughter rippled through the hall, the sound hitting me harder than the image itself. My stomach dropped, my breath coming in shallow bursts as whispers flitted from table to table.

"Slut couldn't even keep her clothes on in the dorms," someone jeered.

My gaze darted around until it landed on Daena, standing near the center of the chaos, arms folded smugly as if she'd orchestrated the whole spectacle. Her lips curved into a cruel smile when our eyes met.

"Enjoying the attention?" she called, her voice carrying across the room. "You looked so eager for it in the video. Thought you'd like an encore."

Heat flared across my cheeks, part fury, part humiliation, but before I could form a retort, another voice cut across the noise.

"Enough!" Dante stepped forward from where he'd been leaning casually against a column, his stone-grey eyes narrowing on Daena. He didn't shout, but the weight in his tone silenced half the room instantly.

Daena bristled. "What? Just pointing out what everyone's already thinking. She's—"

"She's nothing but a distraction," Dante interrupted smoothly, tilting his head as if bored. His gaze swept the crowd, daring anyone to disagree. "If she wants to parade herself around like some cheap entertainment, fine. But you're wasting my time with this little show."

Daena faltered, her smirk slipping under his scrutiny. "I was just—"

"Trying too hard," Dante said flatly, a mocking edge curling his lips. "If you want to be noticed, Daena, do something worth the effort. This?" He gestured lazily at the projection. "Pathetic."

A ripple of laughter broke out, but this time it was aimed at her. The video abruptly vanished from the wall as whoever had cast it dropped the spell. Daena's face darkened, but she tossed her hair and stalked away, muttering under her breath.

"Show's over, go back to your meal!" Dante ordered the still-gaping crowd. He lingered only a moment longer before striding off as if nothing had happened.

Shocked by his actions, I found myself chasing after him. My footsteps echoed on the cobblestone as I followed him into the dark recess of one of the nearby buildings. I thought I'd lost him in the shadows when I was suddenly grabbed from behind and spun so my back was flush against a stone pillar. Dante stared down at me, his face mere inches from mine.

"Following me, Red?" He smirked, reaching up to tug a strand of my hair.

"Why did you do that? Why did you step in and stop her?" I

demanded.

Dante shrugged, his expression unreadable. "Why not?"

"I don't know, maybe because you usually egg her on if you and your little fae friend aren't treating me like I'm nothing," I snapped.

His smirk widened, though his eyes darkened in a way that made my pulse quicken. "Maybe I got bored of watching her tear you down. Maybe I'd rather have all that fire aimed at me instead."

"Don't play games with me," I warned, but my voice wavered when he leaned just a fraction closer.

"Who said I'm playing?" he murmured, his breath brushing my cheek. "You think I don't notice you, Red? That I don't see the way you burn brighter than everyone else in this place? I could make you forget the sting of every rumor with just one kiss."

For a second, the intensity in his gaze threatened to unravel me. My heart betrayed me with its frantic rhythm, but I clenched my fists against the stone pillar to hold steady. For some ungodly reason, I was drawn to the male before me.

"No." The word came out sharper than I intended, thanks to the guilt from my attraction to him sitting like a boulder in my stomach. His brows lifted in surprise.

"No?" he echoed, tilting his head, clearly not used to rejection.

"I won't be someone's dirty little secret," I said, forcing steel into my tone. "You can sneer at me in public and whisper in the shadows all you want, but I'm not playing that game. If you want me, you don't get to hide it."

For the first time, Dante faltered. The smirk slipped, his mouth opening as though he might argue, but nothing came out. Instead, he studied me in silence, something heavy and conflicted flickering in his eyes.

Finally, he huffed out a laugh that didn't quite reach his expression and stepped back, releasing me. "Careful, Red. You keep talking like that, and you'll make me want things I shouldn't."

I pushed off the pillar, brushing past him with my head high, even though my chest was tight. "Then maybe you should think about what you really want before you corner me in the dark."

Behind me, his voice followed, low and rough, stripped of its usual mocking lilt. "I already know what I want. I just can't have it."

Something inside me urged me to turn back, but I pushed it down, trying to convince myself the pull I felt toward him was a lingering effect of the allure. I was starting to think I might actually be losing my mind with how many males I seemed drawn to. My responses to his declarations only made that conclusion more likely. I had a mate. I shouldn't be lusting after males who weren't him.

Forcing my feet to keep moving, I wandered aimlessly across campus until the sound of two sets of footsteps racing toward me caught my attention.

"B! Wait up!" Shadrie called out, causing me to turn.

Miles ran beside her across the quad, where I'd ended up without thinking, his cheeks puffing with labored breaths. The pair of them looked like they'd just come from combat class, sweaty and red-faced, though I knew better. When they finally reached me, Miles leaned over, hands on his knees, struggling to catch his breath.

"Are you alright?" I asked.

"Asthma." He wheezed between shallow gulps of air.

"We should be asking you that," Shadrie said at the same time. "I walked into the dining hall, and everyone was talking about the show Daena put on and Dante shutting it down. I had to threaten to ice a bitch to get the full story. That's why you asked me about cell phones, isn't it? Because that evil bitch filmed you?"

"It's fine, Shadrie. Really, I'm fine. She tried to embarrass me by plastering that video up for everyone to see, but I used to take my clothes off for a living. That shit doesn't bother me," I said, not sure if I was trying to convince my friends or myself.

"It shouldn't have happened," Shadrie insisted. "At least let me help you get revenge on her. My sister gave me this little book of hexes and pranks when I got my acceptance letter, which I've been dying to try out. Nothing permanent, they're meant to be fun, but some of the stuff in there would absolutely humiliate her."

Miles finally straightened, still pink-faced and wheezing, but listening. "I'm not normally one for revenge, but public humiliation works both ways," he said, pushing his glasses up. "If she wants to play dirty, I can do some digging and find out if there's anything she wouldn't want to get out in her student record. Maybe find out if she's had disciplinary strikes we could use."

"No." My voice came out sharper than I intended. Both blinked in surprise. Softening my tone, I shook my head. "No, I don't need to retaliate or for either of you to do it on my behalf. The last thing I want is more people talking and staring like I'm some sort of spectacle. Besides, mean girls like Daena just want the attention. If I ignore her, she'll eventually get bored and leave me alone."

Shadrie wrinkled her nose. "You really don't understand how things work here. Daena isn't some human realm mean girl. She's not just going to let this go."

"Please, Shadrie. Just do it my way for now," I pleaded. "If I'm wrong and she doesn't get bored, I promise I'll let you get back at her."

"Fine, but one wrong move and I'm hexing the bitch bald," she replied. "And Miles will dig up any dirt he can find in her file for us to use against her."

Miles nodded solemnly. I couldn't help but smile at them. Their reaction reminded me of Geordie enough to make me homesick for our small, rundown apartment. I shook my head to clear away the feeling just as Miles cleared his throat.

"Since that's settled, I wanted to give you an update on your list," he said, the wheeze finally gone. "Which is, there isn't one. I haven't found anything yet that makes it make sense."

"I should probably update that list." I grimaced. "Something happened last night."

"Does it have anything to do with you and Zypher getting hot and heavy this morning?" Shadrie asked before making kissing noises.

I leveled my sternest glare at her, causing her to laugh. "Not exactly."

Miles reached into the messenger bag across his chest, pulling out a pen and notebook. Flipping it to a blank page, he motioned for me to proceed. I rushed through an explanation of the night before, leaving out the embarrassing bits I could remember. When I finished, Miles hummed softly and tapped his pen to his lips.

"So, now we have allure added to the list. This really makes no sense. It's like you're a mixed-up hodgepodge of abilities that aren't found together naturally. It's possible someone is using magic on you, making it seem like these things are coming from you when they're not. Maybe if we start at the beginning and go through the entire day, we can pick up on something you missed?"

My stomach growled loudly, reminding me I had fled the dining hall after Dante before eating lunch.

"Why don't I grab us all something from the dining hall, and we can eat in our dorm. If someone is using magic to mess with Bechora like that, we don't want to risk them overhearing and finding out we're onto them," Shadrie offered.

"Smart thinking. Should I come with you to get the food?" Miles asked Shadrie before turning to me. "I'm assuming you'd prefer to head straight to your dorm after what happened?"

"Sounds like a plan," I replied, grateful for the out. "You two grab food, I'll head back to the dorm. I don't have another class until combat class this evening."

"Perfect. See you there, B!" Shadrie smiled, snagging Miles' arm and dragging him back the way they'd come.

I gave them both a slight wave and headed toward the dorm,

mentally preparing myself to go over every small thing that happened the day before.

CHAPTER THIRTY

Bechora

"Repeat that last part, please," Miles spoke, his pen scribbling across a page in his notebook, rapidly filling with notes about my day.

"We ran into each other, and she got kind of bitchy when she realized who I was." I sighed, pacing in front of the coffee table. "She was pissed about me being with Zypher and acted like me touching her to help her up was the worst thing in the world as soon as she found out. I'm not really sure what else there is to say about it."

"Hmm." Miles hummed, pausing to study his notes. Shadrie sat next to him, skimming what he'd written over his shoulder. A smile broke across Miles' face, and he bolted from his seat. "I have a theory, but I need to check something in the library." His words tumbled out in a rush, his chair screeching back as he grabbed his bag. "Meet me there before dinner!"

He darted from the room, leaving Shadrie and me staring after him.

"What the hell was that about?" she asked, brows furrowed.

I shook my head, still processing how fast he'd moved. "No idea. I was hoping you might have one since you were paying attention to what he was writing."

Shadrie gave a small laugh, though it didn't quite reach her eyes. "I've been helping him dig through books to figure this out for weeks now, and have never seen him act like this. Half the time it ends with stacks of books taller than me and him muttering about some obscure magical theory until he drives himself in circles." She tilted her head toward the door he'd bolted through. "If he's running off like that, he must think he's finally onto something big."

A knot formed in my chest. Miles had thrown himself into my mystery like it was personal, and though I appreciated the effort—more than I could ever say—I didn't dare let myself believe this sudden breakthrough would actually be one. Hope had teeth, and it bit hard when it snapped shut on nothing.

"Maybe," I murmured. "I just don't want to get my hopes up. Thrackborne's had plenty of theories that haven't panned out. What could any of us possibly figure out that he can't?"

Shadrie shrugged. "He's told me a little about his coven back in the human realm. They have stories and myths I'd never heard before. Just because Professor Thrackborne couldn't find the answers doesn't mean Miles isn't onto something." I opened my mouth to retort, but the look she shot me had me snapping it shut with an audible click. "If he's wrong, he's wrong. I'm just saying you can't discount us because we're not some two-hundred-something-year-old dragon."

I shifted on my feet, guilt pricking at me. I was grateful to her and Miles for the lengths they'd been going to, looking for anything that could help uncover the answers I needed. I'd only ever had one person in my life that had my back like that, and Geordie had turned out to have secrets so deep they'd landed me here. The thought of him drew my dream to the front of my mind. Geordie was insistent that I uncover the truth of what I am and claim my bonds. There was something in the way he'd told me to hurry that had desperation and fear coiling in my gut and tightening the knot in my chest. If whatever theory had sent Miles flying from the room didn't pan out, where would that leave us? Would it even be possible to figure this out?

"I can see the wheels turning, B. Your head is practically smoking with how hard you're overthinking this." Shadrie spoke, pulling me from my spiral. "Your seer said to trust me, do you remember?" She paused long enough for me to nod. "So, trust me now. Miles hasn't gotten that worked up the entire time we've been combing through the library. My gut is telling me he's onto something, so let's let this play out and see before we freak too much, okay?"

I blew out a puff of air, forcing the panic trying to claw up my throat back where it belonged. "Okay. I can try to do that."

"Good, and B," Shadrie hesitated. "You should probably run across campus."

My brows furrowed, and I shook my head in confusion. "What?"

"Yeeaaahhh, if you don't run, you're going to be late to class." She grimaced. "You kind of spent too long spiraling out before you snapped out of it."

"Shit," I hissed, my eyes seeking out the clock in our kitchen area and snatching my messenger bag from the recliner where I'd left it while I'd gone over the day before in detail with my friends. "You couldn't have warned me before I spiraled."

"Sorry, B," Shadrie laughed. "I wasn't exactly watching the time, so I only just noticed."

I groaned, slinging the strap of my bag over my shoulder and bolting for the door. The hallway outside was empty, students already in their last class of the day or tucked away in their dorm rooms. My footsteps pounded against the carpets as I sprinted toward the front doors. The academy felt different without bodies crowding the corridors—too quiet, as if the whole place were holding its breath. I shoved through the heavy doors and into the courtyard, the chill of the fading afternoon air biting at my cheeks. The quad stretched out before me, eerily still, the usual clusters of students replaced by empty benches and silent walkways.

I ran harder, bag thumping against my hip, the rhythm of my breathing ragged in my ears. By the time the training pitch loomed ahead, my chest burned, and sweat dampened the back of my neck, pooling between my breasts. Faint shouts and the crack of magic against magic crackled through the air, as if the pitch itself were alive. I slowed only long enough to drag in a steadying breath before stepping through the arched opening in the walls surrounding the pitch.

"Late," Rumlock growled, his gaze cutting to me as he crossed his arms over his chest.

"Won't happen again!" I called back, raising a hand in surrender.

"See that it doesn't." His eyes narrowed before he jerked his chin in the direction of the locker rooms. "Get changed."

Heat flushed my face as a few students nearest the gate smirked, their attention flicking between Rumlock and me like they were waiting for him to make an example out of me. I ducked my head, muttering under my breath, and sprinted for the locker rooms tucked beneath the stands.

By the time I reemerged onto the pitch, the matches in progress were heating up. Pairs of students slammed into each other with fists, kicks, and bursts of power that sent sparks snapping through the air. The warded ground drank up the energy greedily, glowing faintly as it absorbed impact after impact. Rumlock's eyes tracked me the moment I stepped back onto the pitch, his expression unreadable save for the faint twitch at the corner of his mouth that said he was still displeased.

"Dreadgrave," the professor barked, causing me to flinch. "Pair up with Ms. Knight."

My eyes shifted from Professor Rumlock to Gabriel as the vampire prowled from the training mat he'd been on. Hatred flashed across his face, sharp and raw, a reminder of the bond he'd somehow marked me with that we never spoke of, though neither of us wanted it. My stomach clenched, bile threatening to rise in my throat, and I swallowed hard, forcing it down.

"Move it, Knight." Rumlock barked, pointing toward my usual training mat.

I scrambled forward, my feet hurrying across the grassy pitch. Gabriel was already there, waiting at the edge of the mat like a predator lying in wait, his arms crossed as he glowered at me. Stepping onto the warded square, I let my body sink into the stance we'd been practicing, knees bent, fists up, weight balanced, and watched him warily. The last time we'd trained together, he'd thrown me around like I was nothing. Not even the fire magic I now had at my disposal had been able to help me against his superior strength and speed.

Gabriel smirked, like he remembered every second of it, too. "Try to keep your feet under you this time." His voice was low enough that Rumlock wouldn't catch it, but laced with venom sharp enough to slice.

"Enough posturing," Rumlock snapped from the sidelines. "You're not here to socialize."

Gabriel's smirk widened. His body blurred with speed as he lunged. It didn't matter how ready I thought I was; it could never be enough. His speed made it impossible for me to track his movements. One second, he was on the opposite side of our mat, the next, his fist connected with my stomach. The blow stole my breath and folded me in half. I staggered back, sparks flaring from my fingertips in a wild arc. They fizzled out, as if my stolen breath had yanked the oxygen they needed from them, too, before they could touch him.

"Too slow," he taunted. His grin widened, sharp and merciless as though every failed strike confirmed his belief that I didn't belong at the academy.

I braced myself, eyes roaming his body for any hints that would help me anticipate his next move, but he was a blur of motion. Pain bloomed in my shoulder as he clipped me from behind, spinning me off balance. I caught myself before I hit the ground, a frustrated growl breaking free of my lips. Heaving myself upright, I called forth a ball of flame and desperately launched it in his direction. Gabriel tucked under it, the heat singeing the air above his head as he drove his knee toward my ribs. By some miracle, I twisted at the last second, catching only a glancing blow, but it had been hard enough to leave my side throbbing.

In a blink, my back hit the mat, his weight pinning me down before I could even gasp. My chest heaved, fury and humiliation warring as I tried to buck him off. Gabriel was immovable. His speed had put us in this position, and his strength kept us there. And then he lowered his head. Warm breath brushed my skin a heartbeat before sharp fangs grazed my throat. Just enough pressure to sting, but not enough to break skin. My mind slipped back to the day he'd bitten me, my heart thundering painfully against my ribs. Every instinct screamed at me to shove him off, to burn him, to do something before he followed through on the threat he'd made that day, but I couldn't move.

"Dead." He whispered, the word vibrating against my pulse.

For the barest heartbeat, I wasn't on the training mat. I was back in the haze of those dreams. The ones Gabriel had accused me of using magic to cause, the ones I hated myself for having, where his speed and strength weren't weapons but something else entirely. Where his hands on me, his mouth at my throat, didn't feel like humiliation but heat. My pulse hammered against my throat, right where his fangs grazed, each beat a mix of defiance and something dangerously close to want. I hated him for it. Hated myself more.

And then his body seemed to tense like he felt it too. His chest rose sharper against mine, his fangs dragging that fraction deeper against my skin, not piercing but lingering. His eyes flicked to mine, and for a split second, they burned with something rawer than mockery. The moment shattered as quickly as it came. Gabriel jerked back, lips curling in disgust, eyes narrowing with fury that looked as much inward as outward. He pushed off me like I'd burned him, rising to his feet with unnatural grace.

"Pathetic," he spat, voice sharp enough to cut. "The only thing that saved you is the spell on the pitch that won't allow me to kill you."

The words cracked across me harder than any blow. My throat still tingled where his fangs had grazed, my pulse racing in a sick, traitorous rhythm. Fury surged hot in my chest, clashing with the unwanted heat that coiled low in my belly. I hated him. Hated the way he looked at me like I was less than nothing. But worse—so much worse—was the pull I couldn't explain. The way my body still responded to him, reeling from the ghost of that split second where his mask had slipped. I didn't fear him. I refused to, but I couldn't deny that something in me leaned toward him as if pulled by some tether I neither wanted nor understood. Guilt gripped me in its fist. I *had* a mate, and my body's response to the vampire felt like the ultimate betrayal.

I forced the words out past the tightness in my throat, sharp and steady. "If you're trying to scare me, you'll have to try harder. All you've proven is you know how to pin someone down and gloat. Though, I seem to recall the last time you had your fangs at my throat, I came out on top."

Gabriel's eyes narrowed, his jaw tightening as if he had to grind his fury back before it could crack loose.

Rumlock's growl cut through the air like thunder. "Enough talking. Stance. Now. Use your magic, Knight."

Giving the professor a tight nod, I scrambled to my feet, sinking into the fighting stance once more, calling flames to my hands. The rest of combat class blurred into a grueling rhythm of strikes and failed counters. Gabriel was too fast, and his raw strength outmatched me at every turn. I reverted to dirty tactics I'd used on the streets as a child, combining them with the fire magic that was becoming easier for me to call forth with each attempt. None of it mattered. Every move I made, he slipped past, punishing me with effortless precision.

When Rumlock finally signaled the end of class, Gabriel looked as infuriatingly composed as ever. I refused to give him the satisfaction of so much as a passing glance as I limped off the training pitch to the locker room. I worked quickly to scrub away the sweat and grime that coated my battered body before tugging on clean clothes and making my way across campus to the library.

I spotted Shadrie almost immediately. She sat at a corner table, staring at a stack of books as if they'd offended her. She didn't look up until I dropped my messenger bag next to them and sank into the empty chair across from her.

"What are all these? Where's Miles?" I asked.

"You look rough." She chuckled before jerking a thumb toward the stacks. "He vanished over there just before you showed up. I found him and this stack at the table when I arrived."

As if summoned by her words, Miles strolled out of the stacks, his face scrunched as he skimmed the open book in his hand. A grin suddenly split his face before he looked up and raced over to where we sat.

"I knew it!" He cheered, slamming the open book on the table between us. "Tinu nall, it makes so much sense."

Curiously, I peered at the open book. "Tinu nall?"

"Starcaller." Miles grinned, sliding into an empty seat beside Shadrie. "My coven had a story about the time before the realms were separated. It took some searching," he paused to gesture at the stack of books in front of Shadrie, "but I finally found the same story. Back when elves still ruled the supernatural world and the realms weren't separated by the veil, there was a king who sought to consume everyone's power."

"Wait, elves?" I frowned.

"I think I know some of this story," Shadrie interjected. "They don't teach about elves here because they've been gone from the realm for millennia, but there are stories our parents tell us as kids to scare us into not misbehaving."

"Right, well, my coven tells us this story for a different reason," Miles replied, waving his hand as if to wave her words away. "So, this Elven king, he got power hungry to the point it was hurting all the realms. It wasn't until a Starcaller arose, that he was defeated. The story goes that she was half mage, half elven; the mage half being why my coven tells the story.

Anyway, she was fated to the most naturally powerful males in the realms and somehow was able to use their power as her own. When their power wasn't enough, supernaturals banded together and allowed her to borrow from them as well. She managed to subdue the Elven king and strip him of his stolen abilities, but his queen begged for his life. So, the Starcaller erected the veils that separate the realms and allowed him to keep his life as long as the elves left and never returned to the supernatural or human realms. She became the first non-elven monarch after that."

For a long moment, none of us spoke. The library's silence pressed in close, broken only by the faint scratch of a pen in some far corner. My pulse thundered, hot and unsteady. Starcaller. I didn't know why the word settled into me like it belonged there, heavy and immovable, but it did.

Shadrie leaned back slowly, studying me. "B... you okay?"

I tore my gaze from the open book, but the word clung to me, whispering through my veins like it already knew my name. Starcaller. I shook my head in disbelief.

"I–this... How can we be sure?" I stammered. I wasn't ready to believe this was what Geordie had been pushing for me to discover.

Miles didn't hesitate. He tapped the page with his index finger. "Because what you're experiencing lines up with the story. It can't be coincidence that you've exhibited abilities exclusive to certain supernaturals after coming into contact with them. The real question is, why?"

The room seemed to tilt, the weight of Miles' certainty pressing down on me. Geordie's warnings slipped through my mind, colder, more insistent. My chest tightened, heat prickling across my skin. I didn't want to believe this. I was just a girl from the human realm. I couldn't be some supernatural being of legend. But deep down, I already knew the truth. The name had resonated with some secret part of me. Too right for Miles' theory to be wrong.

CHAPTER THIRTY-ONE

Bechora

The next few weeks slipped by in a haze of denial and longing. Zypher still hadn't returned to campus, and with each passing day, I missed him more. I'd done my best to ignore the discovery of what I was, hoping he'd return with news that Miles had been wrong. Shadrie and Miles tried to coax me into a few experiments that I somehow managed to put off. When they realized I wasn't going to give in, they threw themselves into hunting through the library for more information. That was how I found myself in the living room of my dorm, alone, with my textbooks spread out on the coffee table as I attempted to focus on homework.

A knock on the door came as a welcome interruption from the thoughts that kept overtaking every attempt to focus. Standing from where I'd been hunched over my books, I stretched with a groan and strolled to the door. Zypher stood on the other side when I pulled it open, and I found myself flinging my body at him.

Zypher caught me with a chuckle. "I am pleased to see you as well, Dilectus," he rumbled.

In his absence, my budding acceptance of our bond had blossomed into something more. I almost felt foolish for holding him at arm's length for so long, my protests about not having a choice seeming more like an excuse than anything else.

"I'm glad you're back. Come in," I smiled, pulling free of his hold and allowing him room to step inside.

He smirked, stepping past me and taking in the state of the

coffee table before moving to settle onto the couch where I'd been before he knocked. I moved to join him, letting myself lean against his much larger body.

"I'm sorry I was away for so long," he said, lifting his arm to tuck me further into his side. "My mother wanted to consult with my cousins about your situation. It took a while for them to search through their archives and find the answer."

I sucked in a breath. "Did they find it?" Cautious hope that Miles was wrong bloomed in my chest, only to be wiped away by the furrow of Zypher's brows.

"Yes. Though I fear the answer brings nothing good for us," he murmured before clearing his throat. "They believe you are a tinu nall."

"Shit," I hissed. "I was hoping Miles was wrong about that."

Zypher shot me a curious glance and squeezed me tighter to his side. "The mage is correct. My mother even consulted with the oracles. They confirmed the truth of what you are."

My body stiffened as if waiting for a blow. Zypher's arm shifted so his large hand could rub soothing patterns across my back. "What does that mean for me, though? The story Miles showed me about Starcallers wasn't exactly great."

Zypher's lips pinched into a thin line, and a muscle ticked in his jaw before he relaxed. "I fear that is the case, Dilectus. Tinu nall are said to only rise during times of great need. They're meant to restore balance to the realms."

"But things seem fine here," I protested. "It doesn't make any sense."

"Things have not been right in this realm since the Dreadgrave line betrayed demon kind, Dilectus. Though the situation is much more dire than we believed for you to be a Starcaller." His free hand reached across his lap and took mine, giving it a reassuring squeeze. "We will uncover the truth together. You are not alone in this, Dilectus. You never were."

I let his words settle into my mind, mingling with Geordie's insistence that I claim my "mates." Everything I'd learned about myself since arriving at the academy seemed to point toward having a full Vinculum, as Zypher called it. Except I only knew who two of my mates were—the male beside me offering comfort and support, and the cruel vampire who seemed to derive pleasure from hurting me.

Sensing my overwhelm, Zypher motioned to my textbooks. "How fares our group project in my absence?"

I huffed out a laugh. "Not great. I've been working on research on my own for the most part. The only time Vallynn deigns to speak to me, even about the project, is during class when we're split off into our groups. I'll be glad when we're done, so I don't have to deal with that stuck-up fae."

Amusement twinkled in Zypher's eyes, the corner of his mouth tilting up in a smirk. "Why don't we take a break? I seem to recall I still owe you a date. It is nearing dinner time, and it seems as though you could use a distraction."

Before I could argue, he was tugging me to my feet and leading me out of the dorm. I followed, confused but curious, as he led me toward Daemonium House. He gestured for me to wait once we reached the door to his dorm, slipping inside and returning shortly after with a picnic basket in hand. His free hand slipped into mine, the warmth spreading from my palm to my entire body and led me back out into the fading daylight. We wound our way across campus under the streaks of pink and gold sky until we reached a secluded garden behind one of the ancient stone halls.

Zypher released my hand and pulled a thick blanket from the basket, spreading it across a patch of grass with care. Something like fireflies blinked to life in the growing dusk, adding a faint enchantment to the air as he produced an assortment of food. Soft rolls, sliced fruits—both familiar and unfamiliar to me—and savory meats were placed around the blanket along with a bottle of something that seemed to shimmer like liquid starlight.

"Our date is a picnic?" I asked, a giggle threatening to burst free despite the weight of our earlier conversation.

Zypher's eyes widened. "Is this not a proper courting ritual in the human realm?"

I rushed to where he knelt on the blanket, arranging the dishes, and placed my palms on his cheeks. "No, this is perfect. I was just surprised. Nobody has ever put this much thought into a date with me before... not that I really date much in the human realm or anything. I mean, I'm not inexperienced, I just —"

"You're rambling, Dilectus," he chuckled, shifting one of my hands to place a chaste kiss on my palm.

"Sorry," I grimaced before turning my attention to the picnic. "This is amazing, really."

Zypher pulled my other hand away from his face before tugging me down to sit beside him. "Then I am pleased. Shall we eat?"

I nodded, shifting to get more comfortable while Zypher filled a plate he'd pulled out of the basket with a little of everything. He handed it to me before producing a goblet and pouring a generous amount of liquid. I sniffed it cautiously before taking a small sip. Sweet warmth slid down my throat, leaving a faint tingle on my tongue, almost like it truly was starlight bottled for mortals to taste.

"Careful," Zypher warned, his smirk returning. "That has been known to make humans a little... light-headed."

I threw my head back with a laugh before narrowing my eyes at him playfully. "Are you trying to get me drunk?"

He leaned closer, his gaze dropping to my lips for a brief moment before flicking back up. "I would never need to do such a thing, Dilectus."

Heat crept up my chest and into my face, my stomach somersaulting. He was teasing me, the same way he had that first day when I'd asked about his horns. Only this time, I was certain I wanted him. I wanted the bond between us and everything it meant. Zypher pulled away with a soft chuckle, turning his attention to filling his own plate and goblet.

I ate slowly, savoring both the familiar and unusual flavors, but it wasn't the food that kept stealing my attention. Every time Zypher moved—whether to pour another glass, brush the crumbs from his fingers, or shift closer—the space between us seemed to thrum with life. His presence was overwhelming, not just because of how much larger he was than me, but in the way goosebumps pricked along my skin when he looked at me.

"You've gone quiet, Dilectus," he observed after a stretch of silence, tilting his head in a way that made him look both curious and dangerous. "Are you not enjoying the food?"

"No, I love it," the words came out in a rush, my cheeks flushing pink. "I was just... thinking."

"Of?" he prompted, his voice a low purr as he leaned toward me.

Heat burned my already flushed cheeks, but I forced myself to hold his gaze. My tongue flitted out to wet my lips. "Us, the bond." I forced myself to answer honestly.

The corner of his mouth curved, and he reached out, brushing his knuckles across my jaw. The feather-light touch sent a jolt through me. "Would you care to share those thoughts with me?"

My breath caught, but I nodded. "I was thinking that I want it. The bond. I know I fought against it, but I was wrong. I want this, I want you," the words tumbled out of me, raw and unpolished.

Zypher stilled, his hand lingering against my cheek as his eyes darkened. For a moment, I thought he was going to kiss me. His chest rose and fell sharply, and the conflict radiating from him seemed to saturate the air around us. He'd been so certain from the beginning that his sudden hesitation caused me to pull back.

"Do... do you not want that anymore?" I asked, casting my eyes to the ground and picking at the food on my plate. "I can't say I blame you if what you found out from your family is true. I'm not sure I'd want to tie myself to someone with so many complications either."

He gripped my chin softly, forcing me to face him. "I want our bond more than anything else in all the realms, Dilectus. I hesitate because I am not certain you will still want me once you've seen my demonic form. You need to know fully what I am before you accept our bond; you must know what it is you are choosing. I planned to show you, but I must confess, I am afraid."

My eyes widened with the revelation. Zypher had been a source of quiet confidence the entire time I'd known him. I couldn't imagine the male beside me ever being afraid of anything. "Show me," I whispered.

Worry flitted across his face, but he pulled away, standing to his full height. He looked down at me, sadness clear in his eyes.

"You think I'll be afraid," I said, interpreting the look on his face.

"I know you will not run," he admitted, a humorless smirk tugging at his lips. "You are brave, but you are still human, and humans have been taught to fear my kind's true form."

I rose to my feet and craned my neck to look him in the eyes. "I won't be afraid. Now, show me, Zypher."

His smirk faltered, and I could tell by the press of his lips that he was gritting his teeth. Stepping farther away, he pinned me with his gaze. The air around him seemed to shimmer and wave for just a moment. The hair on my arms stood on end as power permeated the space between us. His unnaturally blue eyes seemed to glow in the twilight, alive with something both primal and eternal.

A sound like a bone-splintering crack and silk ripping all at once rent the air, and his horns lengthened. Smooth, ridged spirals arched back from his temples, dark as polished onyx. They were regal, deadly, and yet somehow fitting, like the crown he was always meant to wear. Broad, leathery wings unfurled from his back, stretching wide enough to block out the dying sunlight. They flexed once, sending a gust of wind across the blanket, before snapping closed and folding tight against his body with surprising grace.

A tail followed, long and sinewy, curling outward with a serpentine flick before wrapping lazily around one of his legs.

But it wasn't just the horns, wings, or tail. It was the sheer presence of him. He seemed larger, his features sharpened. Beautiful, terrifying, and unmistakably otherworldly. Zypher watched me take him in, vulnerable in a way I'd never seen, as if my reaction to this form held the power to undo him.

My body moved on instinct alone, launching toward him. His eyes widened in surprise before he dipped down to catch me. I wrapped my legs around his waist, trusting him to hold my weight, and grasped his face between my hands.

"You're fucking amazing," I breathed, crashing my lips against his.

For a split second, he went still, like I'd managed to shock even him. Then he responded with a hunger that stole my breath. His mouth moved against mine with a raw intensity, his hand sliding into my hair while the other anchored firmly at my waist, pulling me flush against the heat of his body.

The taste of him was fire and starlight, dangerous and intoxicating. His wings arched high behind him, flaring wide before curling in, cocooning us in shadow. The leathery brush of them against the ground made the world shrink until there was only him, only us. I moaned into his mouth, fingers fisting in the front of his shirt as if I could drag him even closer. His lips parted, deepening the kiss, and my pulse roared so loudly I barely registered when his teeth grazed my lower lip. A sting of pain, quick and sharp, followed by the warm slide of his tongue soothing it away.

When he finally pulled back, we were both panting, foreheads pressed together, his eyes burning with something fierce and unyielding. "Careful, Dilectus," he murmured, his voice rough. "You have no idea what you just started."

I smiled, breathless and trembling but certain. "Then don't stop. Bond me, Zypher."

Zypher shot me a devastating smirk and launched us into the air. My stomach dropped as the ground fell away in a blur of stone and grass, the sudden rush of wind stealing the breath from my lungs. I clutched at his shoulders on instinct, burying my face against the solid heat of his chest as his massive wings beat once, twice, propelling us higher.

Cool air tangled my hair, carrying with it the scent of earth and smoke that clung to him. Despite the dizzying height, I felt no fear. His arms cradled me close against his chest, firm and unyielding, his tail curling around my thigh in a possessive brace that made it clear I was not going anywhere unless he allowed it. I dared a glance down and gasped, awe chasing away the last of my nerves. The ancient halls and towers of Blackthorne stretched below like a living map, the stone walls glowing faintly under the enchantments woven into them.

Zypher's wings shifted, angling with effortless precision as he banked toward Daemonium House. My pulse spiked with every tilt and dip, but the thrill of it lit something wild inside me. For the first time, I understood what it meant to be carried not just in his arms, but into his world.

He dipped lower, the shadow of his wings spilling across the upper windows before he landed on the stone balcony outside his dorm with predatory grace. His wings snapped shut behind him, and the moment his boots hit stone, he loosened his hold just enough to let me slide down the front of his body, steadying me with hands that lingered at my waist.

"You didn't want to come in the front door and make sure your roommate wasn't around?" I asked as he opened the balcony doors and motioned for me to step inside. I tried not to gawk as I truly took in the parts of Daemonium House that I could see for the first time.

"I'm a prince, Dilectus. These rooms are mine and mine alone," he replied with a smirk.

"Oh."

It was the only word that had a chance to leave my lips before Zypher bent down and captured them with his own. Our tongues tangled together as his hands dropped to my waist, and he guided me backward into the room. I was so consumed by him that I barely noticed the click of the balcony door shutting behind him.

My thighs bumped into the soft end of a mattress, and Zypher tore his mouth from mine. Straightening to his full height, he stared down at me. His eyes roamed over my body, heat ratcheting higher under his slow perusal.

"Strip and then lie back." The words were a rumbled command that I was eager to obey.

Zypher took a step back to give me space to undress. His eyes never left my body as I tore off my clothes. The reverence in his gaze stole my breath, but the look on his face said he wanted to devour me, causing the space between my thighs to grow slick and achy. The moment my body was bare, I eased myself back onto the mattress, supporting my upper body on my elbows.

"You're a goddess." A growl of approval rumbled from Zypher's chest, and he dropped to his knees. His large hands gripped my knees, wrenching them apart, and he licked his lips. "Use my horns to direct me, Dilectus. Do not be afraid to guide me in how to best worship you," he ordered, his voice rough with need, before he leaned down toward my aching sex.

The first swipe of his tongue along my slit caused my back to arch off the bed. My hands moved to his horns, gripping them to anchor me as he worked me over with his skilled tongue. My fingers tightened around Zypher's horns, their smooth, curved surfaces warm under my palms. His tongue, hot and relentless, traced slow, deliberate circles, teasing every sensitive inch of me. A shudder rippled through my body, my hips bucking instinctively toward his mouth. He growled again, the vibration sending a jolt of pleasure straight to my core.

His dark eyes flicked up to meet mine, glinting with primal satisfaction, as if my desperation was exactly what he craved. His hands slid up my thighs, fingers digging into my skin with just enough pressure to make me feel claimed, grounded, yet utterly at his mercy. Zypher's tongue dipped deeper, exploring with a hunger that made my head spin. He alternated between soft, teasing licks and firm, purposeful strokes, each one unraveling me further. My grip on his horns tightened, guiding him to linger where the heat coiled tightest. He obeyed instantly, his low hum of approval buzzing against me, amplifying every sensation.

"Dilectus," he murmured against my skin, the word dripping with reverence and desire. "You taste like ambrosia." His voice was a rough caress, and before I could respond, he sucked gently, drawing a cry from my lips. My thighs trembled, threatening to close, but his strong hands held them open, his dominance gentle yet unyielding.

The room spun, the world narrowing to the heat of his mouth and the rhythm of my ragged breaths. I tugged harder on his horns, pulling him exactly where I needed him, and he groaned, the sound raw and feral. "More," I pleaded, my voice barely a whisper, lost in the rising tide of pleasure.

Zypher's pace quickened, his tongue working with devastating precision, as if he'd mapped every inch of me and knew exactly how to push me to the edge. My body tensed, teetering on the brink, and with one final, perfect flick, I shattered, a wave of ecstasy crashing through me. My grip on his horns anchored me as I rode out the tremors, his name spilling from my lips in a breathless chant. He didn't stop, not until every aftershock had faded and I was a trembling, sated mess beneath him. Only then did he lift his head, his lips glistening, his eyes burning with a mix of triumph and untamed hunger.

Zypher's eyes gleamed with a wicked promise as he shifted, his large hands sliding under my hips with effortless strength. "Come here, Dilectus," he growled, his voice thick with desire. In one fluid motion, he lifted me, the height difference between us stark as he moved us so that he was lying on his back and my trembling body straddled his thighs. I shifted slightly, feeling the length of him pressing against my soaked entrance. My breath hitched, and his lips curved into a slow, predatory smile.

One of his hands gripped my hip, the other positioned his

cock, before pulling me down. A throaty moan ripped free as he filled me in one brutal motion. The stretch of him was almost too much, and I had to pause to catch my breath.

"So perfect, Dilectus," he murmured, his other hand claiming my other hip. The words dripped with reverence, but the glint in his eyes promised something more primal.

His hips lifted slightly, dragging a gasp from my lips. Emboldened, I rocked against him, setting a rhythm that made his breath catch. His fingers dug into my flesh, hard enough I knew I'd bruise, as he fought to let me keep control. His strength anchored me as my body wound tighter and tighter. Tension built deep in my core, spiraling me higher with every roll of my hips.

My movements became jerky as I neared the edge. Zypher rose from the bed so that we were chest to chest, with me in his lap as I rode him, one large palm slipping to my back and guiding my movements as the other slipped between our bodies. His thumb pressed against my clit at the same moment his teeth pressed against the fleshy junction where my neck and shoulder met. The dual sensations threw me over the precipice. I shattered, crying out his name as waves of pleasure crashed over me, dragging him over the edge with me.

I slumped against his chest, panting as I worked to catch my breath. The bond I'd been so uncertain of in the beginning felt like a living thing between us. It seemed to pulse in time with my heartbeat. A shudder rolled through me as I felt his power fill me, tangling with the fiery magic in my well. The sensation was overwhelming.

Zypher gently pressed a kiss to my head, his arms locking around my waist as if to anchor us to our new reality. Tears pricked my eyes at the absolute certainty that bloomed between us. The bond left no room for questions or doubts. For the first time since I'd arrived at the academy, I didn't feel lost. I was his, and he was mine, and with him, I was home.

CHAPTER THIRTY-TWO

Gabriel

I was sitting at my desk, pen scratching against paper as I tried to outline my portion of the Human Studies project. The words blurred in front of me when a sudden surge of lust ripped through my body with enough force that I nearly toppled from my chair. A strangled groan escaped me before I could stop it, and I doubled over, bracing against the desk. My fingers clawed at the wood as my fangs dropped with a sharp ache. Heat flooded my veins, scorching, insistent, every nerve ending screaming with want. Pressure built inside me with a ferocity I couldn't explain. One moment, I was clawing at my desk, trying to regain my composure. The next, it tore through me.

A violent, shuddering wave of ecstasy crashed down, dragging a guttural sound from my throat. My body convulsed, my back bowing as pleasure ripped me apart from the inside out. My fingers dug deeper in the desk, leaving deep grooves behind, desperate for something to anchor me as the sensations dragged me under.

Pleasure raced through me like a fire, consuming everything in its path. My fangs ached, my skin flushed hot, and I felt as if every nerve ending had been set alight. The intensity left me trembling, panting like a starved beast, as it crashed over me. When it finally released me, I collapsed forward. My chest heaved, and sweat dampened my brow. I stared down at my lap in shock as the evidence of my release soaked through my pants.

"What the fuck," I panted, trying to make sense of what

had just happened. My mind whirred as I tried to determine what sort of magic could cause this—what vile magic could grip me so tightly and make me come in my pants like an inexperienced teenager. "Shit," I hissed, realization slowly dawning.

Shoving away from my desk with enough force to topple my chair, I stood and tore through my room to clean up and change. Anger coiled in my gut, burning away the lingering vestiges of desire as I snarled my disgust at my soiled pants. The feelings that had ripped through me weren't the doing of a spell—no—they belonged to Bechora Knight. The bond had chosen to force them down my throat, to make me feel what she was feeling. The lingering understanding that the bond granted me was enough to know she'd claimed another mate. Jerking my clean pants up, I let them hang, undone, on my waist and stalked to my dresser to retrieve my hidden phone. This bond had to go. I refused to be held captive to the sensations of a woman I loathed.

"Rafe," I hissed the moment my brother answered my call. "Tell me you've found something to help me."

"What happened?"

"Is it not enough to be bonded to someone I don't want?" I snapped.

"You wouldn't have called me if something else hadn't happened," he replied. "You know how risky this is for us both."

I sighed and moved to the wall, leaning my forehead against the cool stone. "She's bonded another. I felt it. As if it weren't enough that the bond drags us together in my dreams, it deemed it necessary that I experience her bonding, too."

"Gabriel," Rafe hesitated. "Are you sure?"

"Of course, I'm sure!" I snapped. "I was given the same education about the bond that you were. This cursed bond I've somehow created with that— that female—will ensure I feel it every time she bonds with another."

"You sound almost jealous, little brother." Rafe chuckled.

"Are you sure your feelings aren't changing about your mate?"

"Absolutely not!" I snarled.

Rafe's laughter softened into something almost sympathetic. "I'm only teasing. You're wound so tight a breeze could snap you in two." He paused, taking an audible breath. "I've found nothing about breaking the bond. What I have found... I'm not sure you want to hear it."

My chest tightened. "There has to be a way. Maybe in whatever it is you're withholding."

"There isn't," he said firmly. "What I've uncovered—"

"Tell me." I insisted. "I need to know."

Rafe exhaled, long and reluctant, before speaking. "All our lives, we were taught that vampire mates are chosen—that a spell must accompany the bite to create our bond, and without it, the bite means nothing. But that's not the whole truth."

My blood ran cold, dread washing over me. "What do you mean?" I demanded.

"If the texts I've uncovered in my search to help you are true, our kind doesn't need spells to bond. Not when it's fated." The words carried a weight that crushed the breath from my chest. Even as my mind railed against them, some part of me knew them to be true. "If she's your fated, the bite alone would have initiated the bond. The bond forms instantly because it's blessed by the gods and ordained by fate herself. You don't choose a fated mate, Gabriel. You find them. Or they find you."

I squeezed my eyes shut, pressing my head harder into the stone as nausea rolled through my stomach. "So, you're saying..."

"This is permanent. The bond will continue to draw you to her until it's completed. There is no breaking it, not that I've found. Every text I've uncovered implies that once a fated bond is initiated, that's it. Deny it all you want, but the pull will get stronger, more insistent, until fully sealed. You bit her, and that was enough. That can only mean she was fated for you from the start."

My hands curled into fists, nails biting into my palms. "No.

No, I refuse to believe that. There has to be a way—you just haven't found it yet."

Even as I spoke, I recalled my interaction with the demon prince. He'd made similar claims—gone so far as to outright state I was bound to Bechora Knight for all eternity—adding weight to my brother's words. The truth settled into my soul like an anchor dragging me to the deepest depths, drowning me in an unwanted bond.

"You can refuse to accept it all you want," Rafe replied, pulling me from my thoughts. "That doesn't make it any less real. Whoever this woman is, she's your fated. You can spend eternity trying to fight it, or you can do as I suggested when you first called me for help. Get to know your mate. I have faith that the fates wouldn't have given you this bond if she weren't worthy."

"I can't accept this," my throat tightened. "Dina needs me. Father—"

"To hell with Father," Rafe snarled, his voice a growl that vibrated down the line. "He's ruled our lives with fear long enough. It's time you stand up to him."

"You don't understand," I spat. "You ran. I'm the only one left to keep her safe. You know as well as I do—one wrong move, one sign of defiance, and he will dangle her safety in front of me like a noose." My throat burned as the words spilled out. "Every step I take, every decision, it's all to keep her safe. If I fail to uphold his expectations, Dina will suffer. You may be able to live with abandoning us to Father's whims, but I can't leave her behind the way you left us."

Silence crackled through the line, heavy and suffocating. For a long moment, all I could hear was Rafe's breathing —measured, forced, like he was holding himself back from unleashing the storm I knew brewed inside him.

"I didn't abandon you," he said at last, his tone low and ragged. "I left because it was the only way to fight back. If I'd stayed, he'd have ground me into his obedient lapdog, the same as he's doing to you. I wouldn't have just had the threat of

Dina's safety hanging around my neck, but yours as well."

My jaw clenched with anger. "Easy for you to say when you're not here. You left and nothing changed, except that I became the one choking on his leash."

"And yet, you're still breathing," Rafe shot back. "You have no idea the weight I carry. The guilt that threatens to drown me because I left you there. I had no choice." His voice cracked before he bit it back, steel sharpening his words. "Don't mistake my absence for apathy, little brother. Everything I've done has been for you and Dina. I needed to leave so I could find a way to end that monster for good. I won't stop looking until I've found what I need to end him. I promise you that."

I pressed my head harder against the stone, forcing back the burn in my eyes—another weakness Father would punish me for. "If he finds out about this bond, if he discovers I've managed to shackle myself to a mate who isn't powerful, he will see me as weak. You know weakness has only one price in his house."

"He doesn't get to decide what's weak," Rafe growled. "He never did. You want to keep Dina safe, stop letting him use her as a cage. She's a child, Gabriel. She should be laughing, playing, dreaming about nonsense, not existing as the blade he holds to your throat. I swear to you, I will find a way to keep her out of his reach, but you have got to stop pretending your bond is the enemy when the real monster is the man who sired us."

"You make it all sound so simple." I huffed.

"It could be," he replied softly. "Do you truly think fate would saddle you with a mate that's a liability and not a source of strength?"

I opened my mouth to snap back, to spit another denial, but the words stuck like ash in my throat. Against my will, an image of Bechora surged to the forefront of my mind—not fragile, not weak, but standing her ground in combat class. I could still see the way she'd been knocked down, dirt smearing her face, only to rise again with that same infuriating fire blazing in her eyes. She had fought back, again and again, long past the point most would have yielded. Stubborn. Reckless. Relentless.

"You don't know her," I forced out, though my voice had lost its sharpness. "She isn't—she can't be—"

Rafe let the silence stretch as if he sensed my denial crumbling to dust. When he spoke, it was clear he'd chosen his words deliberately. "She already is, Gabriel. Otherwise, you wouldn't be fighting so hard to deny it. The fates don't make mistakes, little brother. She may not be what Father would deem worthy, but what is his opinion compared to the gods?"

A shudder ran through me, and for the first time since the call began, rage gave way to something heavier: fear. Fear of my father, fear of the truth, fear of the ways he could use the bond thrumming through my veins like a second heartbeat.

"I can't..." My voice broke, rough and weak. I swallowed hard, hating myself for it.

"You can, Gabriel." My brother's voice was laced with comfort. "Everything I've found in my search to help you tells me so. Fated bonds aren't just a blessing; they're a source of strength—one our kind has seemed to have forgotten. I envy you. What I wouldn't give to be handed such a gift."

I let out a sardonic laugh. "A gift? More like a curse."

I could practically hear Rafe roll his eyes on the other end of the line. "Always so stubborn," he chuckled. "Only you would start to accept the truth and then shove it away in a box."

"I'm not—" I started, my protests cut off by my brother's laughter. "This isn't funny, Rafe."

"Oh, but it is." He breathed, reigning in his laughter. "Let me worry about Father. You stop being a stubborn ass long enough to see what's actually in front of you."

"And what, exactly, is it you suggest I do?" I demanded through clenched teeth. "It's not as if I've been kind to her. Should I show up at her door with gifts like a love-sick puppy and beg her forgiveness?" The thought seemed preposterous.

"Not forgiveness," Rafe countered. "Not right away. If I know you as well as I think, you've made a mess of things, and it will take time to recover from it. Get to know her. Show her the real you—the one you keep hidden away so Father doesn't discover you're not the cold-hearted bastard he demands you be."

I scoffed, but the sound came out hollower than I intended. "Why would she give me the chance to prove I'm anything other than what I've shown her? She's the most infuriatingly stubborn female I've ever encountered."

"Do I hear a hint of admiration in your voice, little brother?" I could hear the smirk in Rafe's voice before he grew serious again. "You won't know until you try. If everything I've learned is anything to go by, the fates don't care how many times you've snarled at her or pushed her away. If she's truly your fated, the bond will find a way—you just have to let it."

I shoved away from the wall, forcing out a bitter breath. "If she spits in my face, I will make it my life's mission to find where you've hidden away and make Father's cruelty look like a pleasant dream."

Rafe chuckled, unshaken by my threat. "Then I'll be waiting. But something tells me it won't come to that."

CHAPTER THIRTY-THREE

Bechora

A sharp rap on the door startled me awake. I jerked upright off Zypher's chest, where I'd been snuggled, and a shield burst free of my chest. Zypher chuckled, one hand soothingly running up my back, dragging his fingers across the barrier with the other.

"I wondered before why it felt so like mine," he whispered. "Now I understand. You're drawing the ability from me."

The magic recoiled at his words, snapping back into me as if it were a rubber band pulled too tight, and I turned my head to frown at him. At some point in the night, my demon had hidden his demonic form and reverted back to his human features. He winked at me before climbing out of the bed and stepping into a pair of pants he grabbed from the floor.

My eyes tracked my newly bonded mate as he stalked to his bedroom door and opened it just a crack. I couldn't make out what he said in his low murmur, but whoever he spoke to on the other side passed an ancient-looking book through the crack before Zypher promptly shut it and moved back to my side.

"This should help us as you learn to control your abilities, Dilectus." He smiled, turning back to where I sat in the bed with the sheets pulled up around my chest. "When I confirmed what you are, my mother asked my cousins to continue searching their archives for anything that could help. Now that our bond is complete, you will be able to use some of my power at will." He tilted his head in my direction slightly. "What you must learn now is how to control not only my magic, but how to control siphoning abilities from others who are not your bonded."

His words were enough to pull me fully from my sleep-induced stupor. "I'm stealing your abilities?"

Zypher's smile turned soft, and he prowled toward me, easing himself up the bed until he settled beside me. Pulling me into his side, he kissed the top of my head and laid the ancient text on his bedside table. "Not quite, Dilectus. I would have felt the absence of my magic if you were taking it from me. What I uncovered before I returned to the academy implied that the Tinu Nall copied the abilities of their mates and even others beyond their mating circle."

My mind flashed back to the one time our Human Studies group had met in Vallynn's dorm. Something powerful and outside of my control had taken over me and three of the males in the room. Only Zypher had been able to withstand the allure I'd somehow conjured. I swallowed hard, forcing my embarrassment at the memory aside.

"How do I control it when I don't even know how I'm doing it?" I asked.

"That I cannot tell you with certainty, Dilectus." His hand stroked up my arm, a motion meant to soothe me. His eyes flicked to the leather-bound tome on his bedside table. "That is an account of the last known Tinu Nall. My family will continue to search for answers while we use the tome to find our own."

"And if we can't?"

Zypher squeezed me gently before easing us back down and positioning my head on his chest. "Whether in the tome or somewhere else, we will find them, Dilectus. For now, let us rest."

The next few weeks flew by in a flurry of classes and studying the book that had been delivered to Zypher in the middle of the night. Professor Thrackborne was still absent from our sessions, and for some reason, that left me feeling rejected. I felt the rejection like a weight pressing on my chest. Worse, it wasn't just the scowling dragon professor that seemed to have my attention. Between the dreams of Gabriel that taunted me nightly and the inexplicable draw to Dante and Vallynn, who both seemed set on pretending I didn't exist, I was stretched taut—pulled in too many directions when I should be firmly focused on my mate and studies.

Though we'd been assigned to work on a project for Human Studies together, Vallynn's summons came as a surprise. After the disaster of our first and only group session, I'd fully expected the fae prince to expect me to carry the full weight of the project.

Magus House was quiet when Zypher and I arrived after dinner, our messenger bags with our notes and books slung over our shoulders, as if smothered by Vallynn's annoyance. We made our way to the top floor of Magus House to the dorm that Dante and Vallynn shared, each step feeling heavier than the last as we drew closer to the males that seemed to call to me unknowingly. Zypher wrapped an arm around my shoulder and pressed me into his side, sensing my nerves. When we arrived, the door was already ajar.

Dante leaned casually against the side of one of the couches in their living area, arms crossed, looking like he owned the place instead of sharing it. His eyes flicked from where Vallynn paced in front of their coffee table to Zypher gently guiding me into the room with a hand at the small of my back. Gabriel was already seated in a recliner, hunched forward with tense shoulders as he scribbled something on the paper in front of him. He didn't bother looking up when we entered, but I didn't miss the way his shoulders grew impossibly more tense.

Vallynn paused his pacing, his head snapping in our direction as his eyes narrowed. "You're late." His posture was straight-backed and commanding as he moved to settle onto the sofa Dante was propped against. "Sit. We need to finalize our project. It's due next week."

Zypher's hand slipped from my back and down my arm, taking my hand in his. He gently tugged me into the room, easing us into the loveseat across from Vallynn before sprawling out with his arm on the back of it behind me. "Careful, Vallynn. It wouldn't do for a crown prince to lose his temper." He smirked at the scowling fae. "A few minutes hardly matter in the end."

Vallynn's lips pressed into a thin line, his jaw ticking as if he were holding back a retort.

"Bechora and I have done more than enough to make up for anyone who's chosen to slack off," Zypher drawled lazily, his eyes sliding to Gabriel.

Gabriel gripped his pen so tightly it snapped, ink leaking out of his closed fist. "I've done my share," he hissed.

Dante chuckled, letting himself flop onto the couch beside Vallynn. "Well, this should be entertaining."

Vallynn's eyes cut to his friend. "Enough. Let's get this done. Our last session was a waste, and we're running out of time if we're going to complete the assignment. I refuse to fail because a worthless mage decided it would be more fun to play with her magic than do the work."

Vallynn's insult burned through me. I had half a mind to tell him I wasn't merely a mage, but I held my tongue. Zypher tensed beside me, leaning forward with a menacing look on his face, poised to retort.

"Careful, Prince," Gabriel drawled before Zypher could speak. "It's unwise to taunt a woman who's proven she can control you with her magic once already. I'd much prefer not being caught in the crossfire if she chooses to do so again."

The air thickened, heavy with Vallynn's restrained fury. The fae prince went rigid at Gabriel's words, his black hair gleaming as shadows pooled in his hands. Dante's chuckle broke the tension, low and amused, while Zypher smirked, settling back against the loveseat like he was preparing to enjoy the show.

I sat frozen, staring at Gabriel. Disbelief gripped me as I studied the vampire. This was the male who never missed an opportunity to tell me how worthless I was, that I didn't belong at the academy. The same male who took some sick sense of pleasure from putting me on my ass every time we were paired together in combat class. His defense of me, while presented as a subtle dig, didn't compute with what I knew of him at all. My mind whirled with possible reasons, wondering if this was some new form of torture he'd devised to screw with me.

"If you don't mind, I have somewhere to be. I'd like to get this done so I can go about my evening," Gabriel spoke, tearing me from my spiraling thoughts.

"As do I," Zypher added, his eyes sliding to me. Shooting me a wink, he shifted his messenger bag to his lap and pulled out a notebook. I moved to do the same.

I flipped through my notebook, nervous energy coiling through me as I tried to ignore the tension in the room. Finding the page of my most recent notes, I tapped a finger under the first line and cleared my throat. "The Greeks used myths to explain what they couldn't understand, right? The same way a lot of modern fairy tales in the human realm are just stories about supernaturals. The gods were just... the first attempt to explain supernaturals in their world."

"Look at that, our charity case finally has something useful to say," Dante smirked.

Zypher growled low in his chest, and I patted his thigh, forcing myself not to rise to the gargoyle's bait. "As I was saying —"

"Not every myth points to a supernatural being," Gabriel interrupted.

Zypher's growl cut off in a snort. "Please, vampire. Half the underworld myths come from your kind; the rest come from mine."

"Enough," Vallynn said sharply. "We're supposed to compare customs, not argue over who inspired them. The Greeks honored their gods through ritual, sacrifice, and ceremony. We can trace some of those to modern day. That's the angle we'll take."

Dante leaned forward, resting his elbows on his thighs as he waggled his brows at me. "Maybe we should reenact some of the rituals. I'd look good in a laurel crown, don't you think, Red?" he smirked.

My face grew hot as I flushed under his gaze, but I pressed my lips together, refusing to respond. Vallynn seemed to tense beside him, and I couldn't help letting my gaze move to his face. The fae kept his mouth firmly shut, his eyes anywhere but on me. Dante laughed, breaking the growing tension, and my eyes slid back to my notes so fast I nearly missed the way Vallynn's eyes flicked to me for the span of a heartbeat before turning away again.

By some miracle, we managed to focus on our assignment after that. Zypher stretched with a lazy grin after marking down a final note in his notebook. "It appears we've managed to be productive for once. Bechora and I will ensure our sections are prepared and sent to you for the final document." He snapped his notebook shut, slinging his bag across his chest before rising from the loveseat. His hand stretched out toward me in offer. "I'll walk you to your room, Dilectus."

Vallynn scoffed. "She's not likely to get lost in the hallway."

Zypher's grin widened as I slid my hand into his and let him help me from the loveseat. "Then you shouldn't have any objections to me escorting her to her room. Unless you believe you deserve the honor." His tone was a clear challenge. Vallynn scowled and pursed his lips, causing Zypher to chuckle. "Come, Dilectus."

I gathered my bag, allowing Zypher to lead me toward the door. Dante's sudden movement in our direction caused us both to freeze just before the threshold. A glint of mischief flashed in his eyes as he stopped beside us. "Why don't you go on ahead, Demon? I need to speak with Red about our astrology assignment. I'll be sure she makes it back to her room." The drawl in his voice was smooth as honey, and I fought the shiver threatening to crawl up my spine.

Zypher's entire frame stiffened as he let his gaze rove

over the gargoyle. His smirk faltered for the briefest second, turning to a pensive frown before he leaned down and whispered in my ear. "I'll wait outside your dorm, Dilectus." His lips brushed my temple, deliberately ignoring the gargoyle's grin, and then he was gone.

The moment he was gone, Dante proffered his elbow, tilting his head to indicate I should take his arm. I shot him a glare and stomped through the door. Somehow, my demon mate had managed to move too fast for me to catch up to him, leaving me to deal with Dante.

"What do you want?" I hissed when the gargoyle caught up to me. "And don't tell me it's about class. I know damned well you don't need my help with an assignment for astrology."

His hand gripped my bicep and pulled me to a stop. Dante glanced toward the closed door of his dorm room before crowding me against the wall. "You're always either running or look like you're about to," he murmured, the corner of his mouth curving up. "I can't help wondering, Red, are you running because you're scared of me"—his head dipped lower, so close his breath ghosted across my lips—"or because you want to know what would happen if you let me catch you?"

My throat went dry. I should have shoved him away and snapped back with something sharp and cutting. Instead, my body betrayed me, swaying slightly in his direction as if pulled toward him by an invisible thread. Heat crept up my chest until it burned my face, my skin likely the same shade as my hair. Dante chuckled, low and rough around the edges, before letting his eyes sweep over me in a way that made me shudder and press my thighs together.

"Selir, you blush so easy." He dragged his thumb across my bottom lip, slow and taunting. "One of these days, Red, I'll see just how far that blush goes." His eyes traced down my body, a heat in them I was afraid to accept.

A door creaked down the hall, and reality came crashing back, bringing a hefty dose of guilt with it. "In your fucking dreams," I hissed, shoving my hands against his chest. Dante didn't budge. It was as if I were pushing against a brick wall rather than the firm contours of his muscles beneath his shirt.

He finally stepped back, flashing me a wolfish grin and tilting his head further down the hall. "Run along now, Red, before your demon prince comes looking for you."

My head jerked back. The sudden change in his demeanor hit me like whiplash. I blinked at him for a second before twisting my lips in an angry scowl. "Fuck you, Dante," I hissed, slamming my shoulder into him as I stepped away from the wall and started toward the stairs at the opposite end of the hallway.

"That's the goal, Red," he called after me with a laugh.

I stomped the rest of the way to my dorm room, muttering to myself about the entitlement of asshole males.

CHAPTER THIRTY-FOUR

Dante

"What was that?" Vallynn demanded as soon as I stepped through the door to our dorm. "Why are you flirting with my mate?"

I forced my expression to remain neutral and shrugged. "It keeps her off kilter. The more I do it, the more she wants to stay as far away from me as she can. Since I'm usually with you, it helps keep your distance."

Vallynn pressed his lips into a thin line and stared at me. For a moment, I thought he was going to call me out on the lie — maybe he'd figured out she was mine too, and I'd been hiding it from him. "Fine," he hissed finally. "The bond is urging me to rip you to pieces, but you're right. She can't know what we are to each other, and if this keeps her in the dark, I'll allow it."

Shadows leaked out from around his feet, lashing up his body as if to illustrate his meaning about the bond. I remained rooted in place, in hopes it would help him keep them under control. It seemed every hard-won ounce of control he had over his ability had been slipping from his grasp since the start of the school year. His fists curled at his sides, trembling slightly as if in response to the direction of my thoughts.

"I'm going to bed. If Daena shows up, you know how to deal with her," he bit out through clenched teeth.

I watched Vallynn turn on his heel and stomp to his bedroom, slamming the door behind him. My breath whooshed out of me, and my shoulders sagged in relief. Part of me wanted to confess that I had my own mate bond to the tiny redhead riding me hard to claim her. The rest knew Vallynn would do the honorable thing if I did and insist I claim her. He wouldn't allow me to wallow in my own unhappiness, even though it would rip him apart trying to fight his own bond with her so close.

The truth lingered on my tongue, bitter and heavy. Mine. She was mine as much as she was his. Lying about it, even to protect him, was slowly shredding me from the inside out. My only reprieve was the stolen moments I tried to tempt her, knowing she would never accept. I could feel Vallynn's power pulsing from behind his bedroom door, and my lips tugged into a humorless smile. "We're both fucked, brother," I muttered to myself as I turned and made my way to my own bedroom.

The next week seemed to drag by. My gargoyle instincts had me tailing Bechora when I wasn't busy working on assignments or coaxing Vallynn into focusing on our mission. She was rarely without Zypher, and the riot of sensations I'd felt the night she'd claimed him as her mate threatened to drag me into that memory each time I saw them together. That only strengthened my resolve to get to the bottom of the King's treachery. If we could uncover his plot, maybe I could tell Vallynn the truth, and we could both claim her as ours.

Probably the most curious thing I'd seen as I stalked her from the shadows was the way Gabriel Dreadgrave seemed to hover just beyond her notice. Rumors had flown around campus the day after he'd bitten her. Daena had even made sure to mention them with her snide, high-pitched trill any time she caught Vallynn's focus on Bechora. It was whispered that he'd made her his thrall in an attempt to put her in her place. Except he'd never made her do his bidding, and the way he'd been hovering lately made absolutely no sense. The entire campus knew he hated her for her lack of power.

Needing to sate my curiosity, I slipped from the rooftop where I'd been perched watching him follow her to the building where our Human Studies class was held and dropped to the ground behind him. Gabriel whirled around to face me with a snarl, poised to attack.

"Careful," I drawled, crossing my arms over my chest and letting my stone form slip away. "You've been trailing little Red like a lovesick puppy for weeks now. Not exactly giving 'fuck her' vibes." I paused to smirk at him. "Well, not the ones you want to be giving anyway. Want to tell me what gives, or should I assume the Dreadgrave heir simply needed remedial stalking practice?"

Gabriel's eyes narrowed into slits. "What I do is none of your business, gargoyle. Shouldn't you be guarding your prince?"

"Prince Vallynn is capable of handling himself," I shot back with a smirk. "Which means I have time to harass whoever I want. And I gotta say, Gabey, you're making it really easy. Strange how you seem to be hovering around her, though. Word around campus is you hate her guts, but here you are shadowing her like some broody bodyguard."

"I said what I do isn't your concern," Gabriel snapped. "That means this isn't your business either."

I whistled low, rocking back on my heels. "Oh, so it's a secret. That just makes it even juicier. Don't worry, I won't let anyone know you're pining away over the little mage. You might want to try smiling once in a while, though. Or blinking. The whole following-her-around-like-an-unblinking-predator thing screams 'serial killer' more than secret admirer."

Gabriel snarled, turning his back on me with deliberate disdain. "You really don't know when to shut up. I suppose it's true what they say about your kind having gravel for brains."

I threw my head back with a laugh and fell into step beside him. "You want to know what I think, Dreadgrave?" I asked, not bothering to wait for a response. "I think you want her. Maybe the story about you cornering her to make her your thrall was rooted in truth, but somehow our little redheaded mage managed to get away from you, and now you're obsessed with her. It would make sense. Don't vampires obsess over things they can't have?"

"You're worse than the damned demon," he snapped.

My eyebrows rose in question. Gabriel was clearly referring to Zypher. It was well known around campus that the demon prince loved to meddle in things that interested him, and sussing out the remaining members of his mated bond group had become a special interest of his since finding Bechora. The vampire didn't seem to realize what he'd given away by mentioning the male.

"I know you'd rather chew glass than admit why you're really following her around. Which means..." I called out, causing Gabriel to look at me as we walked toward class. Something like panic flashed across his expression, there and gone so fast I would have missed it if I hadn't been trying to draw it out of him. "...I'll keep asking until you snap and spill. It's only a matter of time until you find me so frustratingly annoying that you tell me everything."

Gabriel sneered, his tone pure venom. "You'll be waiting until your wings crumble to dust, Vazgurr, since there's nothing to tell."

"Such a drama queen," I chortled, clapping him on the shoulder before he shrugged me off like I'd burned him. "I do have some notes if you wanted that to be more believable, though."

"Fuck off, Dante," Gabriel snapped, putting on a boost of vampiric speed to get away from me.

I followed behind him with a laugh. I nearly laughed again when I made it to Human Studies and spotted the vampire staring angrily at Zypher as the demon played with Bechora's hair. A zip of my own jealousy ripped through me, forcing me to tear my eyes away from them and stalk to my seat. Vallynn was already seated in our usual place, waiting for me.

"Where did you vanish to?" he asked.

"Looking for Thrackborne," the lie rolled off my tongue with the taste of ash, but I wasn't about to tell my oldest friend I'd been following our mate around lately. That would require telling him truths he didn't need to hear.

"And?"

I shrugged. "Not sure where the overgrown lizard has gotten off to." That at least wasn't a lie. Thrackborne had made himself scarce the last month, and I didn't know why. I had a vague memory of him showing up in our dorm the night Bechora enchanted all of us except for Zypher with siren allure, but beyond that, I could only recall my burning need for her.

Professor Kragmane called the class to order. One by one, groups were called up to give their presentations on their assigned region. I found my gaze drifting toward Bechora more often than not, needing to soak in the sight of her. I was working out ways I could get her alone, just so I could have her to myself for a few fleeting moments, when our group was called to the front. Vallynn jabbed me in the side with his elbow, sensing I was distracted, and I jerked my head in his direction. He cleared his throat and gave a pointed look at the front of the room.

I had to force myself to move, but once I was out of my seat, the bond seemed to seize all my common sense. Shouldering my way past Gabriel, I planted myself next to Bechora, my arm brushing her side. She frowned up at me, her lips pursed as if she wanted to make a sassy remark, only to snap her eyes to the front when Kragmane commanded us to proceed with the presentation.

Vallynn stepped forward and started speaking. His words seemed to fade into the background as Bechora became my sole focus. It took every ounce of willpower for me to keep my eyes forward. Her sweet scent taunted me with each movement she made, and I couldn't stop my arm from pressing against hers. I didn't bother moving to the front when my turn to speak came; some miracle allowed me to recite the words I'd memorized for my part. When I finished, Bechora stepped forward for her section, and my hand tried to reach for her. It was only at the last moment that I realized what was happening and forced it up to run through my hair.

I could feel Zypher's eyes boring into the side of my face, but I couldn't take my eyes off my mate, no matter how badly I wanted to see the look on his face to figure out what could be going through the male's head. I nearly sagged in relief when he stepped forward to present the final part of our project, before Kragmane clapped his hands and directed us to return to our seats. My hands lay curled in my lap in tight fists, head bowed for the rest of class as I fought against my impulses to look at Bechora again.

"I'm going to look for Thrackborne again," I said in a rush as soon as Kragmane dismissed us for the day.

Vallynn gave me a tight nod. "Let me know if you find him. I found something in our studies I'd like to discuss."

I nodded back, making my way from the classroom as a wave of guilt threatened to drag me under. Vallynn had taken me seriously when I'd gotten on him for forgetting our mission, and now I was the one letting the bond control me and not doing my duty.

CHAPTER THIRTY-FIVE

Bechora

"What's with him?" I asked, nodding toward Dante, tearing from the classroom like someone lit dragon fire on his ass.

Zypher frowned and shrugged. "I could not say, Dilectus."

I studied my mate for a second, trying to determine if that meant he didn't know or he did and wasn't going to tell me. His expression gave nothing away, and I finally gave up when he started gathering my belongings into my messenger bag.

"I've got this," I insisted.

"It is my pleasure, Dilectus," he replied with a heart-stopping grin. It had every fiber of my being screaming to take him to my room and climb him like a tree. I shook my head to clear away the lust-induced haze just in time for him to put the strap of my bag over my head with a knowing smile.

"I shall walk you to combat class before I return to the library," he said, placing his hand at the small of my back and guiding me toward the door.

We'd spent countless evenings after dinner gathered in the library or one of our dorm rooms with Shadrie and Miles, working through the ancient tome that had been delivered to Zypher. It hadn't been much help in figuring out how to use my Starcaller gifts. Everything written was vague suppositions based on legend and stories passed down from those who'd been alive during the time of the last *Tinu Nall*. Zypher had somehow managed to befriend the academy's librarian, and she had started seeking out books kept in the school's archives on the subject.

Even with her help, the only thing I'd managed to

accomplish was sensing the abilities that already lay in wait deep in my inner well. Since I'd accepted and completed the mate bond with Zypher, I could now feel his shield ability, and if I focused hard enough, I could trace it back to him. Same with the flames I'd been able to summon since I'd received the pendant. The thread of fire magic settled in my well led back to the necklace I wore. If I removed the pendant, the magic didn't last long, leaving only the magic I'd copied from my demon mate at my disposal.

"Do not worry, Dilectus," Zypher spoke in a reassuring tone as we drew near the stadium where combat class was held. "We will find answers, and you will master your abilities."

"I know, big guy," I sighed, patting his chest. "I just wish we had them already."

Zypher smiled at me, dipping down to tuck a strand of hair behind my ear as he placed a gentle kiss on my lips. Lust zinged through me, and I fought the urge to wrap myself around him like a koala, much to his amusement.

"We will see what we find this evening, Dilectus," he promised, pressing his lips to mine again before stepping back.

I watched him turn and walk toward the main quad, half tempted to race after him and take him to the ground. A giggle to my right forced me to tear my attention away from his backside.

"You're a lucky girl, Bechora." Kiri, the lightning mage from my combat class, sighed. "I'd compliment your mate, but I'm not sure being your friend could save me from the level of possessive jealousy I've heard exists over mates."

I laughed, smiling at her. "I haven't quite felt like ripping anyone's hair out over him, but yeah, I don't think I want to test it with someone I like either."

Kiri beamed. "Come on, we should get changed and on the pitch before Rumlock loses his shit."

I followed her into the stadium to the locker rooms to change. Kiri and I hadn't spent time together outside of class —what time we had was limited to the locker room and the occasions we were partnered for sparring—but we'd still managed to become something close to friends. I couldn't help marveling at how quickly I'd adjusted to my new life as I changed into my training leathers and hurried to take my place on the pitch. Professor Rumlock ran us through our warmups, watching us with a stern expression, before ordering us into pairs to spar. Kiri gave me a thumbs up, bouncing on her toes with a grin when we were paired together.

"Yes, girl!" she cheered as we reached our square sparring mat. "Now you can fill me in on alllll the dirty details while we spar. I've been wondering what those demons are like in the sack."

I giggled, opening my mouth to respond as a shadow fell over us. "Move it. She's with me today." Gabriel snarled, stopping just behind Kiri.

To her credit, the lightning mage didn't flinch as she twirled around to scowl at him. "Rumlock paired us together, Dreadgrave. Take it up with him if you have a problem."

Gabriel leaned toward her, flashing his fangs. "Do you see him stepping in now?" he demanded.

Kiri went pale with a nearly audible swallow, but didn't move.

"Leave her alone, Gabriel," I snapped. "She's my partner for today, and that's that. Whatever your malfunction is, it's not my problem."

Gabriel's eyes slid to me before focusing back on my friend. "You will find another partner if you don't want to be made into my thrall, mage," he hissed.

"Hey, asshole," I yelled at him. "I said leave her the fuck alone."

Kiri turned toward me slowly, her hands trembling at her side. "No, it's okay, Bechora. I'll... I'll just swap partners with him."

I turned my head to search for the professor and found him staring at our trio with his arms crossed, watching. "Aren't you going to do something about this?" I demanded.

Rumlock raised a brow and shrugged one shoulder, and I growled to myself. Our professor seemed to think this was a situation for us to sort out on our own.

"Run along, little mage," Gabriel barked.

My attention snapped back to the vampire, and I opened my mouth to speak, but Kiri cut me off. "It's fine, I promise. Just let it go and spar with him."

I pursed my lips and studied her face as I considered what to do. "Fine," I nodded after a beat. "Why don't you join my friends and me for dinner since we aren't going to get to go over all the fun uses for demon anatomy in bed?"

Gabriel stiffened at my words, and I smirked at him. Kiri nodded with a smile before taking off in the direction of the vampire's abandoned sparring partner.

Gabriel stepped into her place on the mat, planting his feet and letting his gaze travel over my body. "It's no wonder you're not improving if you spend your time in class gossiping," he snapped. "A shame really— all that lean muscle and you don't know how to put it to use defending yourself."

I plastered a saccharine smile on my face and waved a hand down the length of my body. "My muscles were used for climbing a pole in a strip club, and let me tell you, they were effective."

Gabriel went still at my words, his face twisting into a snarl as they sank in. An enraged sound left his mouth, and I was on my back beneath him with his fangs at my throat before I could even consider summoning a shield. His snarl vibrated through my throat; his fangs close enough to break skin if I so much as breathed the wrong way. Rage ripped through me, and I slammed both palms against his chest, summoning flames to my hands. Heat flared between us, the desired effect dampened by the magic that kept us from killing each other on the combat pitch. The flames were still hot enough to make him rear back, his lips curling into something between fury and amusement as burnt impressions of my handprints sank into the chest of his training leathers.

"Better," he muttered, on his feet and circling me before I could blink. "At least you're not lying down waiting to die this time."

"Fuck you, Gabriel," I snarled.

"Only in your dreams," he replied with an arrogant smile before winking at me.

My fury sputtered out as I realized he was referencing the dreams that haunted me nightly. The last time the asshole had mentioned them, he'd all but blamed them on me. I couldn't wrap my head around why he was bringing them up again. The answer came nearly as soon as the thought formed. My feet flew out from under me as Gabriel's leg swept them away, and I landed on my back, the air rushing out of me in an oof.

"It's like you want to get hurt," he snapped. "Found your magic and you're still fucking worthless in a fight." My chest still ached from having the wind knocked out of me when Gabriel barked. "Get up. You're embarrassing yourself."

I wheezed out a breath and pushed to my feet, glaring at the arrogant vampire. "I'd say you could be less of a dick about it, but you're... well, you."

Gabriel ignored me, his eyes glinting as he circled, weight balanced perfectly on the balls of his feet. "Square your stance before I drop you again."

My anger flickered back to life, and I forced my body into the fighting stance Professor Rumlock had drilled into us since the start of term. Tracking Gabriel with my eyes, I called flames into one hand and made a come-hither motion at him with the other.

Gabriel tilted his head, a smirk tugging at his lips. "You must enjoy it when I put you on your back." His words dripped with innuendo, and I couldn't help the flare of lust that tingled up my spine.

"Do you ever shut up, or do you just enjoy the sound of your own voice so much that you find it impossible?" I taunted, embarrassment at my reaction coiling in my stomach.

This time, I thought I was ready, tossing the flame in

my hand toward him as I called my shield forward. Gabriel rushed, and though he couldn't reach me through the shield, that didn't stop him from using his momentum to shove me backward, using my own power against me. I went airborne, my heart stuttering as the shield around me snapped back into my body. My arms reached out on instinct to break my fall as the ground rushed up for my face. Something jerked me to a stop at the last second, leaving me a hair's breadth away from hands touching the ground before letting me drop the rest of the way. Looking over my shoulder, I found Gabriel standing over me, another infuriating smirk on his face.

"As entertaining as it would be to see you break your arms, I'm not quite done having fun with you yet."

"Asshole," I bit out, shoving myself off the ground. Stomping back to our training mat, I called fire into my hands and sank back into my stance. "One of these days, Gabriel, I'm going to roast your ass."

His smile was razor sharp as he took his position opposite me. "Good. Then maybe you'll finally be a worthy sparring partner."

Gabriel alternated between tearing me apart with sharp words and throwing me around just hard enough to rattle my bones for the remainder of class. Every time I managed to singe his leathers, he'd find a way to sneer it into nothing. Every time he put me on my back, he made it a point to call out my failure in a tone that left me furious and humiliated. It was only as we returned to our starting stances that he'd hiss out what seemed to be helpful tips, but I couldn't fathom why, aside from using them to keep me off-kilter. By the time Rumlock barked our dismissal, my body ached, and my pride was shredded. I didn't bother sparing the infuriating vampire a second glance as I stormed into the female locker rooms to shower and change.

Gabriel was just leaving the stadium when I emerged. At the sight of him, my anger boiled over, and I couldn't stop myself from chasing after him.

"Gabriel!" my voice cracked across the cobble path like a whip, but he didn't slow. "I know you can hear me, you fucking bastard!"

This time, he slowed to a stop, his shoulders tensing as he turned to face me. His expression was twisted into something dark I couldn't decipher, but I refused to let that stop me from confronting him. It had been his choice to spar with me, all so he could belittle me, and I was done with it.

"You finally decided to chase me," he said, mockery curling through every word as I stomped toward him. "Careful, little mage. I'm not sure you could handle playing that particular game."

I closed the distance between us; my fist balled at my side. "What the fuck is wrong with you?" I demanded, stopping within arm's reach.

Gabriel cocked his head in a predatory tilt. "Wrong with me?"

"Yes, asshole." I seethed, jabbing my finger into his chest. "You're a complete jerk to me one minute, then standing up for me the next to fucking Dante. Not to mention the fucking mating mark you put on my neck that you blamed me for. And the dreams, for fuck's sake, those damned dreams. You know those aren't because of something I did. God, it's like you enjoy flip-flopping how you treat me! I refuse to stand for it. I demand to know what the fuck you're playing at, and I want it to fucking stop!" my voice rising with each word.

Gabriel moved, grabbing my arms and pressing my back against the side of the stadium so fast I didn't have time to react. "What am I playing at?" he growled. "You have no fucking clue, not a one. You have no idea what it means to be chained to me, and yet the fates have made you mine."

"I. Am. Not. Yours." I bit the words out, but even as I spoke them, some part of me knew they were a lie.

Gabriel's eyes narrowed and his nostrils flared. "That mark on your neck wouldn't be there if you weren't. It doesn't matter that I didn't want it, that you're fucking dangerous. If I let myself have this, Selir knows what terrible things will happen, but the gods don't care!"

"What the hell are you even talking about?" I demanded.

"Did you know I have a sister?" Gabriel asked, his voice softening. "My obedience is the only thing that keeps her safe from my father, and yet you've shown up and torn away my common sense. I tried to find a way to undo this, but I can't— it doesn't fucking exist."

My body swayed as my mind worked overtime to make sense of his words. As if pulled by the same force that drew me toward him, Gabriel leaned down, his lips a breath away from my own. Realizing what was happening, he slammed his fist into the stone wall of the stadium with a snarl and jerked away from me, his chest heaving.

"Stay away from me, Bechora. I mean it," he snapped before turning on his heel and speeding away.

My body slumped against the stone, and my hand flew up to press against my racing heart. I stayed like that for several minutes, working to steady myself as my mind spun with everything Gabriel had said. With a final heavy breath, I shoved away from the cold stone and trudged toward the dining hall, still unsure what to make of the exchange between the vampire and me.

CHAPTER THIRTY-SIX

Bechora

After another evening of fruitless searching through the books the librarian had found, I returned to my dorm with Shadrie. Part of me wanted to tell her what happened with Gabriel after combat class, but for some reason, the words wouldn't come. Instead, I said goodnight and made my way to my room.

The days became routine as they slipped into weeks that slipped into months. The pull I felt toward the four males who weren't my mates only seemed to grow stronger and more insistent as time went by. I did my best to ignore it, going through the motions of attending class, completing assignments, dodging the snide remarks of Daena and her crew of mean girls, and working with my friends to find answers about my abilities.

There was something odd in the behavior of those same four males. I'd spotted the scowling dragon professor a few times around campus, but he seemed to avoid me, not even bothering to resume our sessions. For his part, Gabriel had initially left me to my assigned sparring partners before slowly demanding their spot the way he'd done with Kiri. He seemed intent on giving me emotional whiplash with the way he so easily alternated between cruelty and kindness.

Dante continued to ignore me or encourage Daena's taunts, only to corner me in private with innuendo-laced words. Vallynn's behavior was the strangest of them all. He generally seemed content to pretend I didn't exist, but I'd noticed him watching me when he thought I wasn't looking. On more than one occasion, he'd moved toward me, his body taut with intent, only to catch himself before he stalked away. I didn't know what to make of any of their strange behavior, but it soon became clear it hadn't gone unnoticed by the pack of rabid mean girls.

I should have trusted the prickle on the back of my neck when I left the library to head to my next class, but exhaustion had dulled my instincts. I moved onto the empty path between buildings, too focused on making it to class on time to notice the faint shimmer that clung in the air like a spider web.

"Going somewhere, trash?" Daena's syrupy voice cut through the silence.

I froze mid-step. She and her flock of harpies — as Shadrie referred to them — fanned out across the entrance to the walking path. Glancing over my shoulder, I noted the fae females were blocking both ends, effectively cutting off my escape. The smirk curling Daena's lips told me she'd been waiting, silently gathering intel on my routine, all for this moment.

"I'm not in the mood, Daena," I snapped, trying to edge past her most loyal sycophant, Maera.

"Oh?" She smiled, tilting her head slightly. "Things not going well for you with the demon you conned into taking you as a mate? I'd say that's a shame, but we've all seen how you lust after the powerful males in this school — following them around panting and begging for any scrap of their attention."

Daena snapped her fingers, and two females emerged from thin air. I recognized one of them as the succubus I'd collided with on my way to the first group meeting in Vallynn's dorm. Zypher hadn't responded very well to her insinuation that I'd used magic to trick him. She'd seemed contrite in the moment, but the look on her face now was anything but. I was staring into the face of a female out for blood — mine, specifically. The air thrummed with unnatural weight, and I reached for my magic. It skittered away like water off oiled glass, causing panic to claw at my chest.

Daena's smirk widened as if she could taste my fear. "Feel that? I paid quite a bit for this. This little pathway belongs to me now. No one will hear you. No one will save you. And best of all, your pathetic little magic tricks are useless." She snapped her fingers, and the air pulsed with an ominous shimmer.

Cruel laughter ripped through her friends as they moved to circle me. Their eyes shone with anticipation, a frantic sort of energy building around them and threatening to suffocate me as they moved closer. Daena nodded at the demon female I didn't recognize.

"Just the bond with Zypher," Daena instructed. "Leave the thrall bond alone so Gabriel can enjoy her suffering. Who knows, maybe he'll even join us to help put the little bitch in her place."

The female's face split into a vicious grin as she nodded. The air around her seemed to contract, drawing inward around her body as she gave me her complete focus. The demon raised her hand, and heat slammed into my chest like a battering ram. Pain exploded through my ribs, hurling me backward into the shimmering barrier of the spell Daena had cast around the pathway.

My knees buckled as the nearly invisible tether that always hummed in my chest went silent. My breath hitched, a strangled sound scraping out of my throat. It wasn't gone — it was still there, faint and muffled like a candle snuffed beneath glass — but muted. I couldn't feel Zypher, couldn't lean into that thrum of strength, and worse... I knew he couldn't feel me.

"Do you feel it?" Daena crooned, stepping closer, her eyes gleaming with vicious delight. "The demon prince can't feel or sense you anymore. Whatever little spell you cast on him is broken now. Snuffed out just like that." She snapped her fingers to illustrate her meaning. "You're alone, just as you should be."

Their laughter rang out again, sharp and cruel. The muted bond left me hollow, trembling as if they'd torn away everything in my chest and left nothing but fear behind. I tried to call my magic again, desperate to protect myself, but it slipped through my grasp like grains of sand. The magical thrum of the warded path pressed down around me, sealing me off from everything but the females intent on harming me.

"Without a demon prince to hide behind, what are you?" Maera sneered, stepping around Daena and thrusting her palm forward. A searing jolt of heat slammed into my ribs, throwing me face down against the rough cobble.

Another fae flicked her fingers, and a lash of wind snapped around me, jerking me upright as it squeezed my body, crushing the air from my lungs.

"You're nothing," Daena hissed, circling me. "A pathetic little dud, chasing after any male that might spare you a glance. Your little spells to bind them to you have no power here, not anymore. We've made sure of that."

I gritted my teeth, refusing to give her the satisfaction of a response, and the air coiled tighter around my chest.

The succubus stepped forward, her beauty sharpened into something cruel, her eyes glowing faintly as her lips curved in a mocking smile. "Poor little mage," she purred, her voice dripping venom. "Did you really think you could keep him? That a demon prince would ever lower himself to you?"

The other demon moved to her side, flicking her hand out, and a lash of sharp magic cracked across my cheek. I choked on a scream as the sensation of blades slicing my skin tore through me. The succubus tilted her head, studying the damage with a satisfied smirk.

"Zypher belongs among his own kind," she hissed, stepping closer until her perfume and the roiling power of her allure made me want to retch. "Not tangled up with some powerless mage from the human realm. Did you really believe you could steal him? That we'd let someone like you claim our prince without uncovering your twisted little game and making you pay for it?"

She thrust her palm against my chest, a pulse of energy ripping through me, rattling my ribs and wrenching a cry from my throat. My knees would have buckled if it weren't for the air forcing me upright, coiling tightly around my body like a boa constrictor. The succubus smirked as I writhed in agony against her magic.

"Pathetic," she drawled. "So focused on stealing our prince that you didn't bother learning about the rest of our kind. I'm more than happy to educate you." She sent another pulse of energy through me, causing my body to strain against the hold as the sensation of a thousand knives tore through me. "My kind is known for their allure. It's always assumed our allure only incites lust and a desperate sort of need, but there is another side to it — a side meant to inflict the most deliciously wicked sort of pain."

She took a step back, pulling her power with her, and my body slumped, my head falling forward as I panted. My body trembled as I forced my head up to look her in the eyes.

"Fuck. You." I panted, refusing to let my fear get the best of me, no matter how stupid it was to taunt the group surrounding me.

Daena lashed out at my words. Her hand cracked across my cheek, her nails digging into my skin as she clawed my face. The sting burned down my cheek, hot blood dripping along my jaw. She leaned in close, her breath fanning against my skin as she sneered. "You really don't know when to shut that filthy mouth of yours, do you?"

I forced my head to turn and bared my teeth. "At least I'm not panting after a male who so clearly despises me." The taunt left my lips before I could stop it, even as some small part of me screamed to shut up before I got myself killed.

Daena jerked back as if I'd slapped her and narrowed her eyes. She snapped her perfectly manicured fingers, causing her magic to lash out. Cuts littered my body in the wake of her abilities. My skin split open across my arms, shoulders, and thighs — shallow at first, enough to sting and leave thin ribbons of blood trailing down me. I bit the inside of my cheek, hard enough to taste the copper tang of blood, refusing to cry out. Her friends' laughter rang out like a chorus of cackling hyenas.

"You should beg," Daena cooed. "It'll make it sweeter when we tear you apart."

I forced myself to meet her eyes and spat out the blood pooling in my mouth. "I'd rather choke on my tongue," I hissed.

The fae gripping the wind spell that held me tight snarled and twisted her hand. Agony speared through my chest as my lungs compressed violently; I wheezed and buckled against the invisible hold. I slammed to my knees on the hard cobblestone as the magic released me.

Daena crouched in front of me, her fingers reaching out to take my jaw in an iron grip. She tipped her head as she held me in place, studying me like a bug caught in her net. "Let me tell you a secret," she whispered, leaning closer as her grip tightened. "We're going to make sure every one of those males you covet so much sees you broken. When we're finished, you'll be nothing but a pathetic smear they'll turn away from in disgust. It won't matter what spells you cast to try and snare them — they will have seen you for what you truly are: a weak, pathetic little creature. Someone that no male could ever want standing by his side."

She released my chin with a sharp jerk and stood, nodding to her friends. The air whipped around me once more, yanking me to my feet as it squeezed me so tightly my body felt like it was about to pop. My vision grew dim around the edges, hazy as magic lashed at my skin. I lost track of the sensations causing my pain, left with only the knowledge that my body was being battered and broken. It overwhelmed my senses until I sank into a numb place in the recesses of my mind.

A sound like shattering glass rent the air, dragging the world around me back into focus. The barrier's shimmer shifted, pressing outward. All at once, the magic holding me snapped away, and I collapsed onto the cobblestones, gasping raggedly as blood dripped from my body. A low growl rolled through the path, dark and dangerous, raising goosebumps on my arms and forcing me to lift my head. A figure stepped through the shattered barrier, eyes burning with rage.

Gabriel looked like a dark angel of vengeance as he strode toward me. Every cruel taunting word he'd thrown at me seemed forgotten. He didn't look smug, or amused, or conflicted. He looked furious. I trembled under the weight of his glare, but it wasn't aimed at me — it was aimed at them.

"What is the meaning of this?" he hissed, baring his fangs at the females gathered around me.

Daena stepped forward, a placating smile plastered to her face. "We're merely showing the dud her place."

Gabriel moved too fast for my eyes to track. One instant, he was yards away; the next, he was standing in front of me, his hand wrapped tightly around Daena's throat.

"Touch her again, and you'll beg me to end you quickly," he snarled, his voice low, guttural, laced with threat.

"You can't," Maera cried, her voice trembling. "She's Vallynn's betrothed. If any harm comes to Daena—"

Gabriel turned his attention to her, his eyes blazing. "And yet the prince doesn't seem to care much for his betrothed. In fact, I'm almost certain he would thank me for ridding him of any responsibility toward this harpy."

Gabriel squeezed Daena's throat, causing her breath to come out as a wheeze. Her eyes bulged, and I could practically taste the fear rolling off her in waves. I shifted without conscious thought, wanting a better view for the moment he snuffed her out. The movement caused a pained whimper to tear from my lips, and Gabriel's head snapped in my direction. His eyes narrowed as he took me in — bloodied, battered, broken — and then he tossed Daena aside with a carelessness that spoke to his anger.

"Leave," he snarled as he stalked toward me. "All of you before I change my fucking mind."

The females scattered, carrying Daena with them as they raced away. The echo of their hurried footsteps faded, leaving me alone with Gabriel. Fear licked up my spine as I studied him, his body taut with unspent rage. The most primal part of me understood I was in the presence of a predator, and even though I could feel my magic once more, I knew from past encounters that I was outmatched.

"Fuck," Gabriel breathed, squatting to my level. I shrank back on instinct, pressing my lips together to contain the whimper that threatened to escape. His eyes softened, worry creasing his brow. "I'm not going to hurt you."

I flinched as he reached for me. Gabriel went still, horror flashing in his eyes. The sight of his horrified expression caused a twinge in my chest, and my body swayed toward him. My body collapsed under the weight of the movement, but before my face could hit the stones, he'd swept me into his arms. He stood carefully and let his eyes take in my tattered uniform and blood-soaked skin.

"I should have killed them," he muttered, drawing a whimper from my throat. "Fuck, you need a healer, but if I take you to the infirmary, those worthless females will get exactly what they want."

I shifted in his hold, letting out a pained groan. Darkness was encroaching on my vision, and my body ached too badly to care that I was now at the mercy of a male who'd made it his mission to hurt me. I gave in to the strange pull, too tired and injured to fight it, and let my body go lax against him. Gabriel's gaze moved to my face, and I barely made out the determined expression he wore.

"I'm going to fix this, Bechora," he murmured. "As long as you'll let me."

I didn't bother responding. There wasn't anything I could say. As if my silence were all he needed, Gabriel put on a burst of vampiric speed and carried me across campus to Daemonium House. For a moment, I thought he was taking me to Zypher, but then he carried me into a room I wasn't familiar with.

Gabriel's scent filled my nose as I lifted my head and looked around. It became obvious by the disarray that he'd taken me to his room. Unlike the room I shared with Shadrie, his held a lone bed, a desk, and a small living area with a loveseat all in the same space. It was almost like what I'd imagined a human college dorm would look like. Gabriel muttered to himself as he carried me toward his bed and gently placed me on it. I whimpered, not sure if it was from the pain or the sudden absence of his arms.

"You have to take my blood, Bechora," Gabriel said, stepping back from the bed. "It's the only way to heal you without taking you to the infirmary. Selir knows if I take you there, Daena will find a way to get word around the school about what she and her little band of deviants did to you." He paced at the foot of the bed, one hand raking through the curls at the top of his head. "She'll have someone from the infirmary confirm that you were treated, and it will only lend credence to her words. More will try to hurt you if I let that happen. I can't let that happen, do you understand?"

He froze, turning toward me with his face twisted in agony. I could only nod as that strange pull tightened its grip on me.

"This will change everything," he whispered. "I need you to understand that. My... my brother found something that told him as much and he passed the information on to me." My eyes stayed pinned on the vampire as he continued to ramble. "If you take my blood, our bond will be complete. That's what he said. But it's the only option, and Selir, I'm so tired of fighting this. You haunt my every moment, making me ache for you. Every bit of coldness I've thrown at you has only served to rip me apart. I shouldn't want this, shouldn't give in, not when I know what my father will do when he finds out, but Gods! I can't deny you anymore. Not after..."

Something came over me as Gabriel laid himself bare. Maybe it was that strange pull that drew me to him, whether I wanted it or not, maybe it was the desperation in his tone. Or maybe it was sheer insanity. Whatever it was didn't matter as his words struck a chord deep within me. I forced myself upright, my body trembling from the pain as I reached my hands out for the male who'd wasted so much time shifting between hot and cold toward me.

"Heal me, Gabriel." The words were thick with pain as I spoke. "Whatever comes next, we will figure it out. Together."

CHAPTER THIRTY-SEVEN

Bechora

Gabriel went still, his face morphing from disbelief to awe before he moved toward me. There was an air of caution to his movements as he settled onto his bed next to me and brought his wrist to his lips. My eyes never left him as he bit down hard enough to draw blood and offered his arm to me. I expected to feel revulsion at the thought of wrapping my lips around the wound, but instead, a sense of rightness settled deep into place.

My lips brushed his skin, and my tongue darted out, tentative at first before the copper tang of his blood filled my mouth. Heat surged through me, searing and alive, flooding every nerve ending like a lightning strike. Gabriel hissed sharply, but his other hand moved to cradle the back of my head, anchoring me to him. The world narrowed to that single connection. The heat spread outward in a wave and slammed into the invisible tether between us. The pull I'd been fighting for months roared to life, no longer something I could ignore.

With each draw of his blood into my mouth, the pain in my body ebbed. Whatever magic his blood held washed over me in a warm, healing embrace, filling me with renewed strength. I felt it settle deep in my well, nestled next to the power I'd gained from Zypher and the flames that constantly flowed from my pendant. I tore my mouth from his wrist with a gasp as the weight of our new bond settled into my chest. I suddenly understood why I'd never truly been able to refuse the pull toward him, why I unconsciously sought him out even at his cruelest. This male was mine. He'd always been mine.

Gabriel's forehead pressed against mine, his breathing ragged. His lips parted as though words were impossible, pupils blown wide, hunger and reverence warring in his expression. "Mine," he whispered, his voice raw and broken. The word was a vow, binding us together for eternity.

Need pulsed through me, the bond driving me to claim my mate fully. Without thought, my lips crashed against his in a ravenous kiss. Gabriel's lips met mine with equal ferocity, a hungry edge to the kiss that set my entire body on fire. His hands found my waist, pulling me closer until our bodies pressed flush against each other. The heat of him seared through my tattered clothing, causing the bond to thrum happily between us. My fingers tugged at his hair roughly, and he growled against my mouth.

"He broke the kiss only to trail his tongue down my jaw, lapping up the blood left behind from my now-healed injuries. "Bechora," he murmured against my skin. "Gods, why did I deny myself this for so long?"

My hands roamed his chest, trailing down his taut abdomen as he continued to clean the blood from my body with his tongue. Impatience gripped me, and I reached for the hem of his shirt, forcing him back as I ripped it over his head and tossed it away. He mirrored the motion, tearing away the tattered fabric of my ruined uniform shirt and unhooking my bra before tossing it aside. His gaze raked over my bare chest, dark and reverent, as though I were a sacred thing that only he was allowed to worship.

My hands moved to the waistband of his pants, and he captured them, forcing me to be still. "Are you sure?" he asked, his voice rough with the same overwhelming need roaring in my veins.

I leaned forward, pressing a soft kiss against his jaw before pulling back to look him in the eye. "Yes," I whispered. My certainty was absolute, leaving no more room for doubt.

That was all he needed. In seconds, the rest of our clothes were gone, discarded in a frenzy of need. His hands explored every inch of me, worshipping, claiming, as he lay me back against the bed. The sheets were cool against my heated skin, but Gabriel was a furnace above me, his body a perfect weight as he settled between my thighs. His lips found mine again, softer this time, a tender counterpoint to the fire building between us.

When he finally moved, it was slow and deliberate, every motion stoking the inferno inside me. The bond flared brighter, weaving us together until I couldn't tell where I ended and he began. My nails dug into his back, urging him closer, faster, and he obliged, his rhythm building to match the frantic pulse of our connection. Pleasure coiled tight in my core, each thrust pushing me closer to the edge until I shattered, crying out his name as the bond burned white-hot in my chest.

Gabriel followed moments later, his own release a guttural groan against my neck, his arms trembling as he held himself above me. We stayed like that, tangled together as the bond settled into a warm, steady hum. He pressed a soft kiss to my forehead, then my lips, his eyes glowing with a quiet intensity as we worked to catch our breath.

Angry pounding shattered the peaceful aftermath of our completed bond. "Dreadgrave, what have you done to my Dilectus?" Zypher's enraged voice came through the door to Gabriel's dorm.

I realized then that the bond between my demon mate and me was still muted, and guilt coiled heavy in my stomach, threatening to make me sick. Gabriel carefully peeled himself from my body, covering me with his sheet before he pulled on his discarded slacks.

"If you've harmed her, I swear to the gods, I will end you," Zypher bellowed, still pounding on the door.

Gabriel didn't respond as he strode toward the door and yanked it open. Zypher stood on the threshold, his anger making him appear much larger than his 7'1" frame. He narrowed his eyes on my vampire mate and sniffed the air.

Suddenly, his eyes snapped to me over Gabriel's head. He took me in slowly, his tense muscles relaxing as he stepped around Gabriel into the room. Gabriel closed the door behind him and turned to face me, crossing his arms over his chest just as Zypher's anger melted into a pleased smirk.

"It seems you've finally come to your senses, vampire," he chuckled, shooting me a wink. "I'd suggest an orgy to celebrate, but you look thoroughly ravished, Dilectus. You haven't collected enough of your males for one either."

I was hit by a sudden and intense bout of insecurity as Zypher prowled toward me. "You're not mad?" I asked.

Zypher frowned, easing himself onto the edge of the bed. "Why would I be mad, Dilectus? It is your right to choose which mates you claim. Only you can decide who completes our Vinculum." He paused for a moment, taking in the blood that still painted my shoulders and dipped down my exposed chest behind the cover of the sheet I still clutched tightly. "I admit, I was worried when our bond became dull and muted and went in search of you. I scented your blood and followed it here." His gaze slid to Gabriel before returning to me. "I feared your vampire had sought to sever his bond with you through force. I am quite pleased to find I was mistaken."

Gabriel grimaced. "It was Daena and her fucking lackies," he said. "They trapped her in a magical barrier and very likely spelled her so you wouldn't feel what they were doing through your bond. I suppose my behavior led them to believe I would revel in the pain they were causing."

Zypher hummed, his brows dipping down as his expression turned pensive. "I am pleased you saw sense rather than choose to continue denying our Dilectus," he murmured before returning his attention to me. "Let us get you cleaned up and dressed. I cannot undo the spell muting our bond, but I suspect our mage friends may be able to help."

"How do you plan to get her to the communal showers without anyone seeing her?" Gabriel asked, folding his arms across his chest. "I don't have a private bathroom for her to use, and I'm fairly certain that if anyone sees her like this, Daena will find a way to use it to her advantage."

"I'm healed, though; your blood healed me completely," I interjected. "Why does it matter if I'm a little bloody on the way to the showers? It's not like I have wounds for anyone to comment on."

Zypher reached up and tucked a strand of hair behind my ear, gently caressing my cheek before he pulled away. "Gabriel is right, Dilectus. It does not matter that you are not injured. The fae female knows how to twist things to her advantage. But this is Daemonium House, and while the vampires in residence may not bow to me, the demons do. I will ensure they keep the halls clear long enough for Gabriel to escort you to my rooms to bathe and dress." I opened my mouth to protest, but Zypher cut me off, his attention on my vampire mate. "I will send an illusion to let you know when it is clear."

Gabriel gave him a stiff nod, and Zypher rose from where he sat on the edge of the bed, strolling from the room. It didn't take nearly as long as I expected for Zypher's illusion to appear, letting us know the coast was clear. Gabriel bundled me into his arms, the sheet wrapped around me, and sped from his room, not stopping until we arrived in Zypher's bathroom.

"As much as I loathe the idea of you washing my scent off you, I'll leave you to shower in peace," Gabriel said as he set me on my feet. "I need to contact my brother and hopefully find a way to get ahead of any retaliation from my father for claiming you as my mate."

He'd mentioned his brother in his rambling just before we'd completed our bond, but he hadn't really told me anything about him. As much as I wanted to push him to explain, something inside me told me it wasn't the time. That sensation was only confirmed as the blood drying on my skin started to itch as Gabriel leaned into the shower to turn on the water. He kept his hand under the shower spray until he was satisfied with the temperature. Pulling his hand back, he pressed a gentle kiss to my lips and sighed.

"Clean up and let Zypher sort out the spell interfering with your bond. I will find you later, okay?"

"Okay," I whispered with a nod. Gabriel hesitated for just a moment before he turned and left the bathroom. The water falling from the showerhead called to me, and I tore my gaze away from the door he'd left open behind him and climbed into the tub.

By the time I was clean and wrapped in a fluffy black towel, Zypher was waiting for me in the open doorway to the bathroom. His eyes heated as he took me in, but he didn't make a move to act on it. His hand raised in offering, and I noticed the clothing he'd brought for me. I took them with a smile and dressed under his watchful gaze, the muted bond the only thing tempering my desire for my demon. As soon as I was dressed and had shoes on my feet, Zypher pulled me into his arms and strode to the balcony outside his bedroom. His leathery wings burst into existence with a sharp snap, and he launched us into the air.

"Miles is waiting for us in your dorm," he said over the sound of the rushing wind in my ears. "I've already spoken with him about the spell, and he's certain he can undo it."

"Good," I replied, letting relief wash over me as I leaned into Zypher's hold, letting his nearness comfort me.

We arrived at my dorm without incident. Shadrie and Miles were already waiting for us. There was a cauldron sitting in the center of our coffee table, steam rising from inside of it, tinted with an unusual, but not unpleasant spell. Miles was hunched over it, stirring with a wooden spoon. The sight caused a laugh to burst from my lips.

"All you're missing is the beak-nose and warts," I laughed as Zypher gently eased me to my feet.

Miles grinned at me. "Well, humans weren't exactly going to let us look good when they wanted to use us as cautionary tales," he replied, before tilting his head toward the cauldron. "This is almost ready."

I moved toward my friends, eyeing the cauldron with

curiosity. "Why is it bubbling like it's boiling hot without a heat source?" I asked.

Miles shrugged, pushing his glasses up his nose with his free hand. "It's spelled to do so."

"Oh," I replied lamely. "And you're sure whatever it is you've got cooking up in there will undo what that bitch did to my bond with Zypher?"

"Positive," he replied. "There's really only one type of magic that can mute a bond, which means there's only one way to remove it."

"I want names, B," Shadrie hissed, moving to stand beside me. "As soon as Miles is done fixing this, we're going to start plotting to make their lives a living nightmare."

I studied my friend for a second, taking in the barely leashed rage that caused her entire body to vibrate with tension. "It was just Daena and her little band of bitches," I shrugged, hoping to play off what they'd done to me. "They're all miserable enough already; they aren't worth the time it would take to plan our retaliation."

"Fuck that," Shadrie bit out. "Every one of them is going to fucking pay. You don't fuck with mate bonds, B. That's like the one rule that all supernaturals follow. I have half a mind to put aside my distaste for Vallynn and tell him exactly what sort of fae he's betrothed to."

"She's right," Miles added, using the wooden spoon he'd been stirring the mixture with to ladle it into a glass. "Mate bonds are sacred. Most supernaturals wouldn't dare interfere with one, but those who do usually end up being killed for it. Daena would have known the risks of meddling with yours. She'd have to know her days were numbered as soon as Zypher found out it was her."

"That bitch is banking on her status as Vallynn's fiancé keeping her protected," Shadrie hissed. Her jaw snapped shut so hard I could hear her teeth click together. "You know what, fuck it. I'm ratting her ass out. Not even Vallynn would stand for what she did to you."

Shadrie whirled on her heel and stomped toward the exit before I could respond. Miles shoved the glass he'd been filling into my hands at the same time.

"Drink up. It works pretty fast, so you should feel your bond normally within a few seconds of drinking the whole glass."

My nose scrunched at the slime-green liquid inside the cup. It smelled pleasant enough, but it looked like it tasted terrible. Zypher shifted his weight behind me, and I took a deep breath before upending the glass into my mouth. The flavor caused me to nearly drop it, minty and refreshing as it touched my tongue. With each swallow, my bond to Zypher became more vibrant. Just as Miles had said, the bond returned in full force within seconds of me setting the empty glass on the coffee table.

"Thanks," I said, smiling at Miles. "I appreciate you helping me with not just this, but everything. You didn't have to do any of it."

Miles just shook his head. "That's what friends are for, B."

"Speaking of friends, we should probably find Shadrie and stop whatever she's putting into motion. Daena really isn't worth it."

A growl rumbled in Zypher's chest at my side. "On this, Dilectus, I do not agree. The ice mage is right in her actions. Had my concern not been with you and our muted bond in the moment, I would have sought out the fae prince myself. We are owed vengeance, and we shall have it."

CHAPTER THIRTY-EIGHT

Vallynn

I was hunched over the coffee table in my dorm, meticulously decoding the message that arrived from Linoran only an hour before, when Shadrie Nightshade stormed into the room. The door slammed against the wall, bouncing under the force of her rage as the petite ice mage stalked toward me, crystals forming under her feet as all the heat was sucked from the room.

"You," she hissed, a finger jabbed in my direction.

Repositioning myself upright on the couch, I adopted my usual relaxed posture. "Hello, Shadrie. How nice to see you again."

"Oh, fuck all the way off, Vallynn." She snarled. "This isn't a social call."

"What is it then?" I asked, arching a brow at her.

"Your fucking fiancé is meddling with people's mate bonds." Her words were practically a growl as she stood in front of me. Her eyes promised violence, something I'd never seen in the mage in all the years I'd known her.

My lips tilted into a frown. "I find that unlikely," I drawled. "Daena knows the consequences of meddling with mating bonds."

Shadrie slammed her fists against her hips and scowled. "Tell that to Bechora and Zypher."

My breath caught in my throat, and I forced myself to appear unaffected. "Explain," I managed to grit out, waving my hand toward the recliner to indicate she take a seat.

Shadrie didn't budge, staring at me with a glare that

promised my death before she spoke. "Your betrothed," she spat the word like poison. "Cornered Bechora with her gang of harpies, and one of them muted her bond to Zypher so he wouldn't know they were attacking her."

For the briefest flicker, my vision tunneled. The image of my mate cornered, hurt, stripped of the protection her demon mate provided, seared through my chest like a blade. My fists curled tight against my thighs, nails biting into my palms until the sting became sharp enough to anchor me. I wanted to storm across campus, tear Daena and her vapid entourage limb from limb, and remind them why my shadows were to be feared. But I couldn't. Not without revealing what Bechora was to me and painting my father's target firmly on her back.

I forced my lips into the arrogant, lazy smirk I'd perfected in my father's court, the kind that hid everything I was truly feeling. "Muted?" I drawled, as though the thought didn't make my stomach churn. "Sounds like a clever trick. Hardly anything to worry over."

Shadrie's ice magic spread, turning the condensation in the air into sharp crystals of ice. "You know it's more than that, Vallynn. Zypher and Bechora have the right to take their revenge. It's the way of our realm."

I shrugged, deliberately slow, though I could hear the blood rushing in my ears. "It's not that serious. They couldn't actually break a mating bond, and reversing the magic that muted it is simple enough. I'm sure Zypher has already taken care of that."

Her eyes narrowed into icy slits, the pale blue glow of her magic refracting off the walls like daggers. "Not that serious?" Her voice cracked like a whip. "You've changed, Vallynn. The boy I grew up with would never have brushed off something like this. Muting a bond is an egregious slight—it's blood for blood, life for life. You know that."

I leaned back further into the couch, feigning indifference though my heart thundered against my ribs. "You always were so dramatic, Shadrie. Couldn't handle the jokes we played on you as children, so you cried to your uncle and made them out to be worse than they were. If I lost my temper over every slight in this academy, I'd have no energy left for anything else. Daena's little game doesn't matter." I paused, steeling myself for the next words. "Someone had to put the dud in her place— who better than her future queen?"

Shadrie's scowl deepened, and frost cracked across the floor and over my shoes. "So, you're not going to rescind your protection for the bitch, then? I should have known. The second that females started to notice you, you lost any hint of the honorable male you'd been. You're as bad as your father."

The words felt like a strike to the gut, bile threatening to climb up my throat. I swallowed down my instinct to prove Shadrie wrong, keeping my expression carved into my usual mask of bored detachment. "Honor is overrated," I said smoothly. "Strength, however, is worth cultivating. My betrothed is simply doing her duty to the kingdom by culling the weakness here in the academy."

Shadrie clenched her jaw, her teeth grinding until I thought they might crack. The air grew colder until my breath came out in white puffs. "You fucking disgust me," she spat, her own breath fogging between us. "Even when I hated you and Dante for what you did to gain the attention of your fawning females, I thought you'd turn out better than your father. I should have known you'd let him twist you into a reflection of himself."

Shadrie's magic receded in a woosh as she spun on her heel and stormed toward the door. She slammed it behind her, shaking loose shards of ice from the ceiling. They scattered across my half-decoded message. The smirk melted from my face in the silence that followed, and my hands trembled faintly against my thighs. My shadows curled hungrily at my wrists, begging for release from the loose hold of the mental leash I kept them in check with. My eyes flicked to the coded message, a stark reminder of why I had to act against my own desires and play the role my father had cast me in. As much as I hated protecting Daena from the retaliation she deserved, I knew I needed to use her actions to keep myself separate from Bechora. I couldn't give in to the mate bond, not as long as my father sat on the throne. And definitely not before I stopped whatever wicked plot he was playing out against our people.

I drew a slow breath, forcing my shadows away, and lowered myself back into the rhythm of translating the coded message. I'd just finished decoding it when the door creaked open again, quieter this time, followed by the familiar cadence of Dante's footsteps.

"Selir, the temperature in here is like a crypt," he muttered. "What did you do, brood yourself into frostbite?"

"Shadrie paid me a little visit," I replied. "Daena was meddling with Bechora's bond to Zypher, but I decided it was better to use her actions to keep Bechora away from me. As much as I loathe the female, she practically handed me a new tool to keep my mate safe on a silver platter."

Dante arched a brow at me and frowned. "If you say so."

"I do," I drawled, tilting my head toward the decoded message as he plopped into the recliner. "Linoran's message. Coordinates with today's date and a time."

Dante leaned forward and scanned the page. "Some seriously short fucking notice."

"I agree, but we raised my father's suspicions when we helped the sphinx. Linoran likely couldn't get this message to us any sooner."

"Good thing I found the fucking dragon. It would take us hours to get there without him. As it is, I'm already losing out on my beauty rest with the time being after midnight."

"You found Thrackborne?" I asked, turning my gaze toward my friend.

"Yeah, the grumpy lizard was holed up in some secret archive. I had to bribe a few brownies to tell me where he was. No clue what he was doing down there. I didn't even know the place existed."

"Make sure he knows when to meet us. Whatever is going down at this location is important."

It was a quarter to midnight when Dante and I arrived at the clearing in the woods on campus. Caulder was already waiting, his arms crossed over his chest, scowl etched on his face.

"Dante tell you where we're heading?" I asked.

Thrackborne nodded before stepping back and undressing so he could shift into his dragon. Once his shift was complete, I climbed onto his back. Dante shifted into his gargoyle form, his stone wings beating against the night air as he rose to settle behind me. Caulder growled low, a puff of smoke leaving his nostrils as he snapped at Dante.

"Really? You're going to make me fly the whole fucking way?" Dante grumbled. "Aren't professors supposed to care about the well-being of students?"

Caulder blew out another puff of smoke with a grumble. His wings snapped wide, and he launched us into the air. Dante followed, complaining about favoritism and threatening to file a formal complaint with the dean. The dragon ignored him as he angled his wings toward our destination.

Worry coiled in my gut as we flew across the realm. When he angled his body toward the ground and I spotted the nearly empty desert below, I let myself relax a fraction. A small shack stood in stark contrast to the sand stretching beneath us. There wasn't the shimmer of magic to indicate illusion. Another strong sign this wasn't a trap laid by my father. Caulder landed with a thump that made the shack tremble. I eased myself to the ground so he could shift back to his human form. Dante, for all his grumbling, was silent as he stalked forward to meet us, hand outstretched with Thrackborne's clothing.

"I don't sense anything amiss, but be on your guard," I clipped before knocking on the door of the rickety building.

It creaked open to reveal a slim, dark-haired fae male. His irises were shot through with lines of white, the mark of a strong seer. He motioned for us to come inside, shutting the door quickly behind us.

"I'd say it's a pleasure to meet you, but I'm not sure it is." He grinned.

"Who are you?" I demanded.

"Geordalis Caelthir Fenrithiel," he said with a slight bow. "I believe you three are familiar with my half-sister from the academy, and since you are, I shall allow you to call me Geordie, as all my friends do."

"There are no Fenrithiels enrolled at the academy," Thrackborne's gravelly voice rumbled.

The fae smirked and shrugged. "Never said there was."

Dante chuckled, causing Caulder to scowl over his shoulder.

"Why are we here?" I demanded.

"You're here to receive a warning. War is coming, and you will be forced to openly choose a side. I believe your gargoyle friend and dragon companion already received such a warning from the sphinx. And yet none of you are moving as fast as you should."

"Damnable seers, always speaking in riddles," Caulder growled.

The fae, Geordie as he'd asked to be called, simply grinned. "You know if we spoke in direct terms, the future would shift." The smile fell, and he turned to me. "You won't be strong enough on your own, Princeling. Not even with these two. You need to accept this is her fight too. Stop fighting what you know to be true."

My heart plummeted to my stomach. He hadn't needed to say it aloud—his vague references were enough to tell me he was talking about my mating bond. "I can't. You know what will happen if I do." The words left me in a breathless whisper.

Sadness crept across his face, and his shoulders curved inward as if the weight of what he foresaw was too heavy to bear. "Old, forgotten magic is rising. The king gathers his generals in secret, teaching them the whispered spells of the elves. Your future, my prince, is splintered into too many paths and will remain so until you choose for good. There is still time, but it is quickly running out."

"So just tell him the path to take, fucking hell," Dante snapped.

Geordie gave him his full attention. "You play a dangerous game, gargoyle. Your fate is tied to his, yet you keep your secrets. So shall I keep mine."

"Is that all you have for us?" Caulder demanded, smoke pouring from his nose.

"For now." Geordie shrugged.

"Then we don't have any reason to linger," Caulder snapped, storming from the shack.

The fae lifted a hand and waggled his fingers at the dragon's back, tilting his head for us to follow.

"Fucking useless seers," the dragon grumbled as he stripped off his clothes. "Their visions rarely ever matter because they're always meddling, steering things the way they want them to go."

I didn't speak as he shifted into his dragon form and flew us back to the academy. Caulder wasn't wrong. Seers meddled and altered the future in ways even they couldn't foresee. That knowledge didn't stop the dread that started simmering in my gut the moment the seer mentioned my mate.

CHAPTER THIRTY-NINE

Bechora

To my surprise and delight, Gabriel was leaning against the outer wall of Magus House, waiting alongside Zypher the next morning. We hadn't spoken since he'd deposited me in Zypher's bathroom, and I wasn't sure he'd behave any differently than before the bond was completed. Shadrie filled me in on the details about Gabriel's father after she'd finally calmed down from her confrontation with Vallynn. Knowing the sort of cruelty my mate endured at the hands of a man who should have loved and cared for him left me with a deeper understanding of his motivation to push me aside.

Zypher smiled and handed me a cup of coffee in silence while Shadrie hung back, and I continued to stare at Gabriel in disbelief. My vampire mate pushed off the side of the building, his shoulders slumped as he crept toward me. Uncertainty filled his face, mirroring my own.

"I didn't think you'd be here," I said quietly.

Gabriel shrugged. "Where else would I be?"

"I thought you might be somewhere regretting things and planning your next move to push me away if I'm being honest. Shadrie... she told me about your family, what she knew at least. Knowing what I know now, I wouldn't blame you if you went back to pretending our bond doesn't exist."

"No," Gabriel hissed, shaking his head sharply. "I was wrong to ever do that, and I'm going to do everything in my power to make it up to you."

"But your mother—your sister. Won't your father—"

"I spoke with my brother. I don't know what he has

planned, but he assured me he will see to their safety. The only thing left in this world my father can use against me is you, and you're too damned stubborn to let him do that." His lips curled into a smile, and Zypher laughed.

"Well, I guess if B forgives you, I do too," Shadrie piped in. "But just know, Dreadgrave, if you hurt my bestie, I will end you."

"Your friends are vicious, Dilectus. I quite enjoy it," Zypher interjected, causing me and Shadrie to laugh. Gabriel shook his head with a soft smile, and we made our way to the dining hall for breakfast.

The massive space went silent as soon as we stepped through the door. Every head turned to face us, studying me before returning their attention to a table in the center of the room. Daena sat perched there like a queen, her perfectly styled hair spilling over her shoulder as she leaned close to Vallynn. She'd wedged herself at his side, her hand brushing his arm as she laughed at something only she seemed to find amusing. Her merry band of harpies clustered around her, smug expressions fixed as they hung on her every word.

"Poor little Bechora Knight." Her voice lifted above the soft din. "You should have seen her. Absolutely trembling. One teensy bit of magic and she pissed herself, right there in front of everyone."

Shadrie snarled at my side, and I glanced at her. My friend's gaze was pinned to Vallynn as he sat there in brooding silence. Gasps and laughter answered Daena's words, her friends eating them up. I felt Gabriel tense beside me and reached for his hand.

"You really should have seen it. It was just meant to be a fun little test, you see. Something to determine if the pathetic little mage from the human realm was really worthy of the academy without her demon interfering. Poor dear was like a frightened little bunny. If I'd pushed her any harder, I suspect her heart might have given out. Not what I'd call academy material. Not at all." Daena's words marked me as prey among predators, something I knew couldn't be left to stand if I didn't want the entire academy out for me.

"If anyone isn't worthy of being here, it's you, Daena." Shadrie's voice rose above the cruel laughter before I could defend myself, silencing it and dragging everyone's attention back to us. "You interfered with a mating bond."

The words hit the hall like a thunderclap. The scrape of chairs, the sharp intake of breath. Gasps rippled through the crowded space as the weight of the accusation sank in. Dozens of eyes swung toward Vallynn, seeking the reaction of their crown prince, expecting him to condemn Daena. His dark gaze swept across the dining hall, lingering on me with disdain before cutting to Shadrie.

"Daena didn't commit a crime. She did the kingdom a service. My father would have approved of my betrothed's methods of culling the weak; he may still reward her for it. If Ms. Knight truly can't stand on her own without the help of her bond, then she is neither worthy of this academy nor her demon mate."

He spat the word mate like it disgusted him, and I couldn't help my involuntary flinch. My heart seemed to rend in two alongside it. Neither reaction was something I could understand or wanted to dig into. Shadrie took a step toward them, the temperature dropping rapidly as the males at my side snarled. I grabbed her arm and shook my head before deliberately moving my gaze across the dining hall.

"It's funny you call me weak, Daena, but I'm not the one who has to pretend the male at my side enjoys my company. Maybe if you pet his arm a little harder, he'll roll on his back and let you cuddle." I lifted my chin defiantly, my eyes sliding to Vallynn. I could have sworn his lips twitched as if he were fighting a smile before his arrogant mask fell back into place. "And I find it strange how you, *my prince*, talk about culling the weak, while hiding behind a female who needed her friends to help take me on."

Daena's face flushed crimson, her mouth flapping open and shut like a fish as the cruel laughter turned on her. Vallynn held my gaze, his jaw ticking as I stared him down. It felt like an eternity stretched between us, though it was barely seconds, before his chest heaved and he turned his face away.

"Come on, let's find somewhere else to eat this morning. The dining hall reeks of desperation and cowardice," I snapped, turning on my heel and striding through the doors.

"Well done, Dilectus." Zypher grinned as we reemerged outside.

"Sure, if the goal was to have Vallynn coming after you," Gabriel hissed, his words a worried counterpoint to Zypher's praise. "He's the crown prince. You can't just insult him like that and expect to get away with it, Bechora."

"Oh, fuck him!" Shadrie snapped. "It's not like he's going to get his hands dirty, and I can ice any bitch he sends B's way."

I huffed out an annoyed breath. "It's too early to argue about this. I get that what I did probably wasn't the smartest move, but it would have been worse if I'd let the rest of the school think I'm weak prey. I know exactly how the students at this school treat prey."

Gabriel flinched as if I'd struck him. I hadn't meant to hurt him, but neither of us could deny he'd been the one to teach me that lesson.

"Fine," he said after a moment. "But you're shit at fighting —"

"What does that have to do with anything?" I demanded, interrupting him.

"If you'd let me finish. I was saying, you're shit at fighting, but I can help you improve enough to defend yourself. We'll start first thing in the morning and work on it outside of class."

"I can't," I said, biting my bottom lip. My bond with Gabriel was completed, and he seemed all in now, but I wasn't sure I could tell him what I was, and that I spent all my free time in the library or working with Zypher to hone my magic. As my mind worked to decide, Shadrie spoke, taking the decision out of my hands.

"She has to practice her Starcaller shit with Zypher. And we need her help going through the books the librarian finds about her abilities." Shadrie paused, turning to me. "Speaking of, now that you and Fangs, over here, are totes bonded, any new abilities in the well?"

"Her what?" Gabriel asked.

"I'm not sure," I replied at the same time.

Zypher clapped Gabriel on the shoulder and smiled at me. "Allow me to educate my bond brother on what you are, Dilectus. That will allow you and the ice mage to determine what new skills you've gained."

"I knew I liked you, Triple D." Shadrie grinned and winked. "You're officially my favorite out of B's mates."

Zypher let out a full belly laugh while Gabriel stood there looking lost. "Well, I still need to feed her, but I will take your favoritism, ice mage."

Miles came barreling toward us before anyone else could speak. When he reached our group, he pitched forward, placing his hands on his knees. His face was flushed, sweat dotting his brow as his entire body heaved with his effort to breathe. Miles raised a finger—the universal signal to wait—and gulped down another breath before taking a puff from an inhaler.

"Professor Thrackborne," he panted.

My forehead scrunched in confusion. "What about him?"

Miles straightened to his full height as his breathing eased. "I was in the library reading over some loose pages Mrs. Fiodh gave me. They were some sort of journal entry, or something written in a language I didn't recognize, but there was an old translation with them. I barely had a chance to skim the first page when Thrackborne startled me. He was just standing there, glaring at the pages. Demanded to know what I was doing with elven texts and why I was reading about Tinu Nall. I told him it was just academic curiosity, but I don't think he believed me."

"Tinu Nall?" Gabriel asked. I shot a glance at Zypher, catching his eye. My demon mate gave me a knowing nod and murmured an explanation to Gabriel, quietly.

"So, he was mad about it, but that doesn't sound warpath-y to me," Shadrie spoke.

Miles' expression grew serious. "You didn't see his face. Smoke was pouring out of his nose, and I swear I saw scales crawling up his arms. I was sure he was about to dragon out on me, but someone started yelling at the other end of the library. The second his head was turned, I got out, but it's not like we can leave the academy. He's going to catch up with me eventually."

As if to add credence to his words, a loud roar sounded across the cobblestones. Miles' eyes widened in fear, and his breath stuttered.

"That is definitely a pissed off dragon," Gabriel said, causing Miles to blanch.

I swatted Gabriel's chest before turning my attention back to Miles. "We should probably get you somewhere that isn't out in the open."

"Class," Miles offered. "We have spellcasting, and Professor Snowthistle doesn't allow students to be pulled out of her class."

"Okay, that will do for now. We'll figure out what to do once we've gotten you into the classroom." I looked at my mates. "Zypher, Gabriel, can you two try to figure out why Thrackborne is so angry about those papers and see if you can... I don't know, distract him or give him something else to focus on so he forgets about hunting down Miles?"

Zypher smiled, reaching into the messenger bag slung across his shoulder and pulling out a fruit bar. "Of course, Dilectus. Take this as well, since I was not able to feed you this morning."

Gabriel frowned. "You just carry around snacks in your bag?"

"Of course." Zypher smirked as I took the fruit bar from his hand. "You don't?"

"Guys," I interrupted. "We don't have time for this. I'm going to get Miles to class. I'll meet you at lunch to find out if it's safe for Miles to show his face around campus. Zypher, don't forget to get Gabriel up to speed. And the two of you work together to distract the very pissed off dragon."

My mates nodded, their expressions serious. Shadrie stepped forward and gave Miles a hug, murmuring something I couldn't make out. Whatever it was seemed to calm him slightly before we turned and hurried to class.

CHAPTER FORTY

Bechora

By some miracle, we managed to avoid Thrackborne. When lunch rolled around, none of us wanted to risk having Miles out in the open. We grabbed food from the dining hall—or rather, Zypher insisted he and Gabriel grab it and bring it to his dorm in Daemonium House after assuring me it was the safest place on campus to hide from a dragon shifter. While we ate, he and Gabriel told me they'd gone straight to the library when Miles and I headed to class that morning, but the professor and papers Miles mentioned were gone.

We answered Gabriel's lingering questions about my status as a Starcaller—the ones we could. He offered thoughts on connecting with my abilities, walking me through techniques vampires learned as children to test their limits. One exercise required me to push against him with everything I had, pulling magic from my well and guiding it to infuse my muscles. I thought he was playing a trick on me, but my palm shoved him back several feet. His boots skidded across the floor with a startled grunt.

"Fuck, I think you broke one of my ribs," he hissed, an arm wrapping around his side.

"That doesn't make sense. All I did was push you. I didn't even have momentum behind it." I frowned.

"Vampires have enhanced strength," Gabriel grunted, stepping toward me. "We don't need momentum to break bones." He paused, eyes narrowing at nothing. "Fuck, that's it! When I bit you, you threw me into the side of the other building—remember?"

My mind slipped back to the day he'd cornered me between buildings, threatening me before accidentally initiating our mate bond. "Yes," I clipped, not wanting to think about that day.

"It makes so much sense," he continued. "After I bit you, you were suddenly strong enough to fight me off. And then just now..."

"Your strength," Zypher picked up as Gabriel trailed off. "That's the ability she has from your mating."

Miles scribbled notes as Shadrie's gaze flitted between me and my mates with glee.

"Let's go again. We have to test it to be sure. Try to pull more magic into your muscles this time," Gabriel demanded.

"But your rib."

"It will be fine. I'm a vampire; we heal fast." He shrugged.

My eyes sought Zypher, hoping for a way out of potentially harming Gabriel again. Shadrie offered a reprieve instead.

"As excited as I am to see B absolutely kick your ass for being such a dick, she's going to be late for class if she doesn't get moving."

I gave her a grateful look, then followed her gaze to the clock on Zypher's wall. "She's right. We have class, and I don't want to find out how Kragmane deals with tardiness."

"Fine, we'll continue this in combat class later," Gabriel replied.

The three of us hurried across campus to Human Studies. I expected Gabriel to take his usual seat as Zypher, and I claimed ours. Instead, my vampire stalked behind us and snarled at the female at the desk next to mine to move. Hushed whispers rolled through our classmates as he claimed the seat, eyes pinned on the front as if he hadn't done something gossip-worthy. Professor Kragmane cleared his throat, ending the chatter.

"Today's lecture will be the last that isn't focused on the end-of-year trials," he began, eyes scanning the room. "We will be discussing human mating rituals—an area in which, I assure you, I am quite the expert. Some of you will want to pay close attention, as you may find yourselves in the human realm seeking your mate."

The excitement among my classmates was palpable. A male wolf I recognized, thanks to Shadrie, cupped his hands and howled.

"Settle down!" Kragmane snapped, turning to the blackboard and sketching a diagram that looked suspiciously like two potatoes holding hands. "With the exception of our mage brethren, humans do not use mating as a form of pleasure. In fact, the females of the species are naturally opposed to physical intimacy of any kind. Yes, Mr. Welvern," Kragmane paused, calling on the wolf who'd howled.

"My brother just came back from his mate hunt in the human realm over the summer. He said that isn't true and plenty of women in the human realm are employed at strip clubs because they really like getting naked and fucking."

Kragmane arched a brow. "Language, Mr. Welvern!" He waited for the shifter's muttered apology before continuing. "There are outliers in every species, but research tells us the majority of human females in that profession do so because they have been shunned from polite society and are essentially unmateable."

I stiffened, biting the inside of my cheek until I drew blood. Wherever the professor got his information, he was wrong. The wolf hadn't been correct either, but at least he wasn't claiming to be an expert. My gut told me the rest of the lesson would be worse.

"As I was saying," he continued, unaware of the storm brewing within me. "It is well documented. Human females will go to great lengths to avoid consummation, citing mysterious headaches, religious calendars, or fleeing into the night. Entire marriages can pass without a single coupling, as the male resigns himself to a life of frustration."

"You have no idea what you're talking about." The words

were out before I could stop them.

"I assure you, Ms. Knight, I am the foremost expert on this subject. The facts are irrefutable. Why, only last year I observed a pair of humans at a tavern. The male repeatedly offered to 'buy her a drink,' and the female rolled her eyes. This clearly indicates reluctance. The data is flawless."

My palm slapped my desk, the sharp crack echoing through the room. "You're wrong. So wrong it's painful to listen to. I don't know how the academy allows you to teach this bullshit when you clearly don't know what you're talking about."

Kragmane's brows shot up, his chalk hovering midair. "Excuse me?"

"No. You're excused." I leaned forward, every nerve alight with indignation. "Human women are not opposed to sex. We don't go out of our way to avoid it. We don't consider it a terrible burden that we reluctantly allow when a man whines long enough. In fact—" I let my gaze sweep the room as I stood, then back to Kragmane, "—human women enjoy it. We desire it, crave it, and—when it's with someone we actually want—it's one of the most pleasurable experiences we can have. Human women love to fuck."

Zypher let out an amused chuckle, and I felt Gabriel stiffen on my other side.

"I've done decades of research, young lady," Kragmane began, face flushed with anger.

"And I've spent decades living in the human realm as a human," I cut him off. "Plenty of those years were spent enjoying a man in my bed." My feet carried me to the front until I was bent, face-to-face, with the ignorant dwarf. "If he was good enough, we wouldn't even make it to the bed. Sometimes a man can make a human woman so desperate to fuck that she has him bend her over and take her right there. Contrary to the bullshit you're teaching, if our partner is worth a damn, human women fuck. And, speaking from personal experience, we fuck a lot."

Kragmane's mouth worked like a fish on land. "This is...

this is utterly disgraceful behavior!"

"Disgraceful?" I barked a laugh. "What's disgraceful is that you're up here teaching nonsense about a subject you clearly know nothing about. And do you want to know why you think women hate sex, Professor?" I leaned closer, my voice dropping into a sharp whisper that carried to the back row. "Because no woman alive would climb into bed with you."

The class broke into chaos—howls of laughter, shocked squeals, someone pounding a desk in glee. I turned back to my classmates. I spotted Zypher first, leaning back, the picture of casual elegance, an amused smirk on his face. Gabriel, on the other hand, glanced around the room as if looking for someone to murder. That strange, unwanted pull forced my eyes to Dante and Vallynn next. Both males looked as murderous as my vampire mate.

Kragmane was nearly the color of boiled beets when my attention returned to him. "I'll have you disciplined for this disruption, Ms. Knight! You cannot speak to me in such a manner!"

"Oh, but I can," I cut in, straightening and stepping back, arms crossed. "While you're scribbling potatoes on the board and pretending to understand human intimacy, I've actually lived it. From where I'm standing, your decades of research don't amount to a damn thing if they're filtered through your failure to attract a woman."

The laughter grew louder, rolling like thunder through the lecture hall. A wolf shifter at the back fell out of his chair, howling with delight. I barely noticed Zypher and Gabriel moving from their seats toward me.

"You're not an expert on mating, Professor Kragmane," I added coolly, voice sharp enough to cut glass. "You're just bitter no one's ever wanted to mate with you."

Kragmane's sputtering fury was drowned out by the uproar. His stubby fingers clutched his lecture notes as if they could shield him from the reality crashing down; the room wasn't laughing with him anymore. It was laughing at him.

"Time to go, Dilectus," Zypher purred in my ear as he gently took my elbow and guided me toward the door. Gabriel flanked my other side like a wall of simmering violence, his fangs flashing when anyone so much as snickered in my direction.

"That was reckless," Gabriel muttered, lips turned down in a scowl.

"Reckless?" I shot back. "That man was spreading straight-up lies. Lies that get women in the human realm hurt by human men. Not to mention the damage from him teaching it to supernaturals who visit the human realm."

"I believe you set the record straight, Dilectus. Word will spread through the academy after your... memorable delivery." Zypher grinned, eyes twinkling with mischief.

Before I could decide whether to be concerned about how my actions might be twisted as word spread, a deep voice cut through the corridor.

"What are the three of you doing?" Caulder demanded as he moved toward us.

My heart squeezed at the sight of him, and my body threatened to sway forward. I gritted my teeth and focused on the open book in his hands to keep from lunging at him. Whatever draw he held wasn't something I wanted to explore. It only left me feeling guilty and unworthy of the two males at my side.

Zypher shrugged, grin widening. "Ah. Professor Thrackborne, Bechora has just finished giving an impassioned speech on the sexual desires of the human female."

Thrackborne's brows dipped as Zypher's words sank in. A puff of smoke blew from his nose on a heavy exhale. "What exactly have you done, Ms. Knight?" he grated between clenched teeth.

"Someone had to put that stupid dwarf in his place," I snapped, the flames of my anger stoking anew. "He seems convinced human women don't enjoy sex at all, but he's so fucking wrong."

"What my Dilectus is neglecting to say is that she made it

quite clear she thoroughly enjoys fucking," Zypher said, humor lacing his words.

Thrackborne's grip on the book tightened as more smoke poured from his nostrils. Before any of us could comment, he tore the book clean in two. That seemed to amuse even Gabriel, who chuckled alongside my demon mate at the sight of the two halves hanging from the dragon's hands.

"Detention. All three of you," Thrackborne snapped. "Report to my office at dusk."

I stared at his back as he stomped away, not sure what to make of his strange behavior.

"Well, it seems we have successfully distracted him from Miles," Gabriel said.

Pressing my lips together, I turned to Zypher. He seemed pleased with Professor Thrackborne's reaction, though I wasn't sure why. Noticing my attention, he smiled and slipped a hand into mine.

"We should return to my dorm and tell Miles the good news," he said, tugging me along behind him.

CHAPTER FORTY-ONE

Bechora

Word of my outburst in Human Studies spread across campus like wildfire. Daena's little group used it to spread nasty rumors. I did my best to ignore them, but the males propositioning me in increasingly bold ways whenever I was alone made it difficult. By the time the first snow blanketed the grounds of Blackthorne, the rumors that persisted had dulled into background noise. For the most part, students had shifted their focus to the end-of-year trials.

The end-of-year trials weren't just a test of knowledge or skill. With each class that passed, our professors drilled into us that they were a way of weeding out the weak. Only those of us who could endure the pressure, competition, and danger of each trial would move forward. Whispers in the Magus House common room spoke of elaborate challenges—mental, physical, magical—that pushed even the most gifted students to their breaking point. Everyone seemed to know someone who knew someone who'd failed and lost their life in the previous years' trials.

Zypher and Gabriel insisted on working with me to master my new abilities, both barely concealing their worry about my chances. We hadn't found anything useful in the tomes the librarian found about Starcallers, so research turned into action. Most nights and early mornings found me shivering in a clearing in the woods. My mates took turns sparring with me and forcing me to call forth my magic until my bones ached and I longed for sleep.

"Again, Dilectus," Zypher said, rolling his shoulders like he was preparing for battle. "As much as I enjoy having you in my arms, try not to look as though you're about to fall over this time."

I scowled at him, causing his smirk to grow. Summoning the strength I'd copied from Gabriel when we completed our mate bond, I infused it into my muscles until my body vibrated with power. When I lunged, Zypher let me push him back a few steps before anchoring himself like stone. He chuckled, low and warm, as I stumbled from the recoil. My feet tangled, and I barely regained my balance in time to avoid landing on my backside.

"Better," he praised, steadying me with a gentle hand on my arm. "But you must learn to fight through the exhaustion, Dilectus. There are all manner of beasts used in the trials, and they do not care whether you are tired."

"I'm trying," I gritted out between clenched teeth. "Doesn't mean I'm not wondering why I put up with the two of you, though."

"I cannot speak for the vampire, Dilectus, but I believe you put up with me because of my dashing good looks," he replied without missing a beat, flashing me a grin that warmed me from the tips of my toes to the top of my head. "And because I only push you because I believe you are capable of this."

Gabriel's voice drifted from the shadows at the edge of the clearing, clipped as ever. "Less flirting, more focus." I turned my head in his direction and snapped my teeth in the air.

Zypher laughed at my antics, winking before stepping back into position, utterly unbothered. "Ignore him. He's brooding because he has no sense of humor."

Despite the ache in my arms and the frost numbing my fingers, I found myself smiling. Zypher's relentless optimism and playful jabs wrapped around me like a shield, taking the sting out of the dread that clung to every whisper of the trials. Where Gabriel's sharp criticism pushed me to sharpen my edge, Zypher's warmth reminded me I wasn't alone. I expected my vampire mate to stay in the shadows, content to throw out clipped remarks, but instead, he stepped forward. His expression was unreadable as he crossed the clearing.

"You're pushing too much strength into your arms, and not enough into your legs," he said softly. "It's making you unstable when you attack."

Even though it had been months since we'd sealed our bond and his behavior toward me was kind, I couldn't help bracing for the sneer. Gabriel noticed the slight flinch and sadness leaked into his expression. He slowed until he stood a breath away, and his hand rose with a hesitance that made my chest tighten. He gently brushed his fingers down my forearm before sliding his hand into mine.

"I wish I could take back everything I did to you, Bechora," he whispered, low enough that only I would hear. "It shreds me into pieces seeing you so unsure of me even after all this time, but I know I only have myself to blame."

"I know," I whispered back.

My mind slipped across the last few months, pulling forth all the ways the male before me had changed. Beyond the way he took my ability to survive the trials to heart, he'd stood up for me. Once, in the dining hall, Daena attempted one of her thinly veiled insults—something that would have been a whisper and a ripple last month. Gabriel didn't let it slide. He rose as if the comment had branded him and answered not with fury but with a quiet, irrefutable statement of fact that made the table's chatter fall into embarrassed silence. He didn't humiliate her; he made it clear he wouldn't permit her to carve me into a punchline.

He spoke to me differently, too. Where his words had once been careful and measured, they were now patient and plain. He listened to my complaints about aching muscles, the overload of classwork, and my frustration over not having the information I needed about my abilities. He'd spent countless nights in my dorm, working out the kinks in my shoulders, arms, and legs as I completed assignments. Even Shadrie had stopped treating him like an outsider, accepting him into our little group as if he'd always been there.

"Trust takes time, Bechora," Gabriel said, pulling me from my thoughts. "And I know I have to make up for all the cruel things I've done to you. I will prove myself to you, whatever it takes. Ensuring you survive these trials is only the start."

I let myself believe him, a little. Not because the past was erased, but because he kept showing me, in a hundred small ways, that the man beside me had been changed by what we were to each other. The trials could take many things from us —but if Gabriel was truly all in, then perhaps I might step into the storm with something other than fear.

Once my mates were satisfied I'd trained enough for the morning, we made our way back to our separate dorms to shower and dress for classes. When I strolled into Intro to Supernaturals, I was met with an unfamiliar sight. I blinked at the front of the class, surprised. Professor Sabelus generally didn't rise from his desk, simply rattling off the day's assignment before lying his head down and drifting off to sleep. But today he was awake, standing behind the lectern with his sleeves rolled up and eyes gleaming black as polished obsidian.

Murmurs ran through the room as everyone settled into their seats, rustling the papers laid out waiting for us. The heading across the top read: Bestiary of Trial Subjects: Observed Patterns and Weaknesses. My stomach sank as I read the bold print; in all the whispered rumors about the trials, not once had beasts been mentioned.

Sabelus rapped a knuckle against the desk, and the noise cut the whispers short. "The trials," he began, voice clipped and resonant, "do not care about your pride or your pedigree. They care about your blood. They care about your resolve. And they will use beasts to measure both."

He began to pace, pausing to gesture at the illustrations on the printed pages. Each monstrous animal was more terrifying than the last, and I was beginning to wonder if the purpose of the trials wasn't simply to kill us all off. For a moment, I missed

Professor Thrackborne. The dragon's steady, albeit grumpy, presence at the beginning of term had somehow turned into a comfort I longed for. My brow furrowed in irritation at the thought. Thrackborne ended our sessions abruptly and without warning. The strange draw I felt toward him made no sense. It only served to deepen the guilt that seemed to be my constant since mating Zypher and Gabriel.

"Shadow maws," Sabelus continued, pulling my attention back to him. "They will show you things you fear. Hallucinations, manipulations of light and shadow. If you allow panic to dictate your response, you will not last. Anchor yourself. Breathe. Trust your allies."

The professor pointed at a student behind me.

"So, we can work with allies in the trials?" a female I only knew from class asked.

"In some cases, yes," Sabelus replied. "The nature of the trials is not revealed until the trial arrives. However, in past years, they have tested students both on their own and as a team. It is unlikely you will face all three alone."

"Are we allowed to work with people outside our Year?" a male asked.

"First Years are limited to their own Year. It's a tradition that dates back to when the academy was a war college, and the first year was meant to test whether you belonged at the academy or not. While we no longer prepare our students for war, we have kept the tradition of the trials. Should you pass all three and advance to Second Year, you will be able to form teams with students from Third and Fourth Year. It's encouraged that Fourth Year students build teams they prepare for and lead through the trials."

The room went still, a hush settling over the rows of desks as the weight of his words sank in. Encouraged to form teams. Led into the jaws of death by older students who'd already proved themselves. My stomach twisted. It wasn't just about strength, knowledge, or even surviving one terrifying night —it was about belonging to something larger, proving you weren't just an individual who stumbled into Blackthorne by mistake.

Sabelus's gaze drifted across the room, sharp as a blade, before landing on the packet in his hands. "Each of you will study these creatures—their habits, weaknesses, and strengths. Some of you will overestimate your ability to outwit them. Some of you will underestimate their cunning. Both mistakes will cost lives."

"Professor," the male from before called out. "Surely if we're expected to fight beasts, the academy will provide us with appropriate weapons. It would be rather... unfair to pit us against things designed to slaughter without offering proper defenses."

"Fair? This is not a game of fairness, Mr. Ashbourne. This is the trials. You will live or die by your skill and wit. Beyond that, you are expected to rely on your training and education. Those of you who have relied on anything other than yourself to survive will fail." A ripple of unease spread through the room, but Sabelus continued as if he hadn't just ripped away any hope of a safety net. "The trials are meant to test your ability to survive Blackthorne itself. The academy was built to forge the strong and break the weak. It is up to you to prove you are the former."

I forced myself to steady my breathing, unsure when it had grown ragged and uneven. I still didn't understand why the academy upheld such a barbaric tradition, but I refused to be one of the names whispered in the common room next term. One way or another, I was going to survive the trials.

Sabelus snapped the packet closed and looked out over us one final time. "Dismissed. Take the rest of the week to familiarize yourselves with these creatures. We begin practical demonstrations when we reconvene next week. And pray that you are not the first to bleed."

Chairs scraped against the stone floor, the room buzzing with nervous energy as students gathered their papers and hurried out. I tucked mine under my arm, the words Observed

Patterns and Weaknesses staring back at me like a threat. As I stepped into the corridor, a chill ran through me. The trials were no longer some future possibility—they were a rapidly approaching reality that could very likely mean my death.

CHAPTER FORTY-TWO

Bechora

It seemed like I blinked, and the trials were upon us. Shadrie, Miles, Zypher, Gabriel, and I were gathered in the living room of my dorm, spending the evening together before the first trial the next morning. Part of me wanted to grab them all and run to the human realm, even though I knew it wasn't possible.

"So, what do you think the first trial will be like?" Miles asked, snagging a Twizzler from the package in Shadrie's hands. Shadrie scowled and swatted his hand.

"My First Year trials were difficult," Zypher said. "The Labyrinth of Lies was probably the worst of them, though I doubt that will be something you face this year."

"The Labyrinth of Lies?" Shadrie asked.

Zypher inclined his head, his expression as grave as I'd ever seen it. "A maze woven with illusions so real you could not tell what was truth and what was fabrication. Every wrong turn showed you a vision crafted to break your will. Some students never made it back out."

I shivered and pressed myself deeper into Gabriel's side. "But we won't have to go through that one, right? All of my professors said the trials are different every year."

"Correct," Gabriel answered. "They don't want us able to prepare. I've heard rumors the academy itself creates the trials, so students are faced with their deepest fears and greatest weaknesses."

"My coven spoke of the sentient nature of the academy before I was accepted," Miles said, pushing his glasses up his nose. "But it can't create all three trials if we're meant to work as a team through some of them."

"Not every student faces the same three trials," Zypher said, wrapping an arm around my shoulder. "My first trial, I was alone with only my shielding and illusion abilities to aid me. My access to my inherent demon magic was cut off. I couldn't summon hellfire or shift into my demon form."

"They can cut off your magic?" I gasped.

Zypher's arm tightened around me. "Yes, and they did. Though it was only demon students who experienced such a trial."

"That's not right," Shadrie hissed. "They shouldn't be allowed to treat demon students like that."

Zypher shrugged, the motion almost careless, though I could feel the tension in the arm still looped around my shoulder. "Fairness is not part of the academy's design. It never has been. The trials are meant to expose weaknesses, and for demons, that weakness is overreliance on the abilities we hone from birth."

"That's still barbaric," Shadrie scowled.

Gabriel gave a humorless laugh. "That is precisely the point. For all my father's faults, he drilled that into my head before sending me to the academy. As much as the professors harp on using our abilities to pass them, it's usually cunning and preparation that mean survival."

"We won't know what our first trial is until tomorrow. How are we supposed to prepare for that?" I asked, a weight settling in the pit of my stomach.

"You can't, Dilectus," Zypher said simply. "Not in the way you want. The academy is designed to strip us bare, break us down, and build us into something stronger."

"Well, that's depressing," Shadrie scoffed. "I say we forget about our impending doom and enjoy our evening before we work ourselves up and are too nervous to stand a chance tomorrow."

We did just as Shadrie suggested. The evening drifted

by in a haze of laughter, teasing, and the kind of easy companionship that made the looming trials fade to the edges of my mind. We played a few silly games with the leftover candy, Miles and Shadrie bickering in the background, while Zypher and Gabriel occasionally traded sharp remarks that almost—almost—sounded like humor.

Eventually, the room fell into the quiet that only came with exhaustion. Miles and Shadrie said their goodnights, but I was reluctant to move from where I was sandwiched between my mates. The idea of walking into whatever trial I'd face tomorrow without them made my chest ache.

"You should get some rest," Gabriel murmured against my ear. "We all should."

I tilted my head to look at him, then at Zypher on my other side. The thought of being alone in my bed with nothing but my thoughts for company made my throat tighten.

"Stay with me." The words slipped out before I could second-guess them. My voice was softer than I meant, almost pleading. "Both of you. Just… don't leave me alone tonight."

Zypher's blue eyes softened instantly, and he reached up, brushing a knuckle gently along my jaw. "If that is your wish, Dilectus, then nothing in this realm can keep me away."

Gabriel hesitated, his uncertainty about his place written plainly on his face. I stared at him, my eyes pleading with him to see the sincerity of my request. Finally, he gave a short nod. "If that's what you want." His tone was quieter than I'd ever heard it, stripped down to raw longing.

I threaded my fingers through his and squeezed. "I do."

We stood and walked the short distance to my room in a small, clumsy procession. Gabriel lingered at the door as if unsure whether to cross the threshold, while Zypher moved with quiet certainty to my bed. The lamp in my room threw a warm pool of light across my comforter, leaving the rest of the space in shadows. For a moment, the world felt unbearably fragile and ridiculously ordinary all at once.

I climbed into my bed, folding back the comforter and

motioning for my mates to join me. Zypher shed his T-shirt, leaving him in a pair of black sweatpants as he slid in on one side. A satisfied sigh escaped me as he wrapped an arm around me, tucking me into his side. Gabriel hesitated at the other edge, clicked off the lamp, and then eased himself down with a soft curse. He moved as if he were negotiating with himself —half refusal to cross my boundaries, half wracked with his own need to be near me. His entire body went stiff as he settled under the blanket, and I moved from Zypher's side to lay my head on my vampire's chest. My hand found his in the dark, and I curled my fingers tightly around his. His chest was solid beneath my cheek, but his body stayed stiff, as if he didn't believe he had the right to be here.

"Gabriel," I whispered into the dark. "I want you here. Not because I'm scared. Not because I need protection. Because I want you."

His breath hitched. For a long moment, he didn't answer, his hand twitching beneath mine like he wasn't sure if he should hold on or let go. "Selir, I want this more than my next breath, but you shouldn't want me here," he said finally, voice rough. "Not after everything I did to you. There hasn't been enough time to prove to you that I've truly changed. I haven't done enough to earn a place in your bed."

I lifted my head to look at him; even in the darkness, I could make out the raw uncertainty in his eyes. His jaw was tight, as if he were bracing for me to agree with him. My heart clenched at the thought, having forgiven him before my mind had caught up.

"You were cruel," I admitted softly. "You pushed me away when I didn't understand why. And yes, it hurt." His eyes flinched at the word. I reached up, cupping his cheek, forcing him to see me. "But you're here now. You've been at my side when you didn't have to be. And I don't care about what you think you deserve, I care about what I choose. And I choose you."

Something in him cracked then, a tremor running through

his body as though my words had landed in a place he hadn't dared open. His hand squeezed mine back, tentative at first, then firmer, almost desperate. "Gods, I don't deserve you, but I will spend the rest of my existence trying to."

For a heartbeat, silence stretched between us, thick, vulnerable, honest. Then Zypher spoke. "Our Dilectus has chosen well, bond brother." His voice was low and teasing, but threaded with something warmer than mockery.

Gabriel grunted something that might have been a retort, but it had lost its edge. His fingers tightened around mine, then relaxed, as if he were finally allowing himself the small, treacherous luxury of trust. Zypher shifted, pulling me a little closer so my back was flush against his chest without forcing me to leave my position sprawled across my vampire. Gabriel's other hand came to rest over ours, an awkward, polite claim that somehow made the three of us fit together like pieces that had been waiting to be snapped into place. Sleep pulled me under in soft, warm waves of security where I lay wrapped in the arms of my mates.

Morning came too soon, and I had to fight the urge to stay tucked beneath the blankets with Zypher and Gabriel. It was only their insistence that they needed to return to their rooms and prepare for the first trial that allowed me to let them go and prepare myself. We met for a light breakfast in the dining hall before Zypher split off to join the Third Years, leaving Shadrie, Miles, Gabriel, and me to merge with the crowd of First Years making their way to the cathedral where we'd had our magic unveiled the first day of term. The building seemed to exude an ominous air as we made our way inside to take a seat.

"Greetings, First Years," a woman I didn't recognize spoke from the front of the room, her voice magically carrying throughout the building. "For those of you who haven't met me, I am Dean Femirea. For the last few centuries, I have had the pleasure of overseeing this academy and watching generation after generation rise—or fall—within these walls. Today, you will face your first true test at this academy."

She paused, letting her words settle as hushed whispers rolled through the space. "Today, you will face the Labyrinth of Shadows. This is not a trial you can survive with brute strength; you must rely on your wit and will." A portal shimmered into existence behind her. "Once you step through this portal, you will be faced with a maze of mirrors and illusions, where only the academy knows what you will be shown. Some of you may see truths you wish to remain hidden; some of you may be confronted with your deepest fears. If you manage to overcome whatever it is you see, you will emerge stronger. Those of you who do not," her lips curved, though there was nothing kind in their shape, "will find your minds broken beyond repair."

A ripple of unease passed through the gathered students. My pulse pounded in my ears, but I kept my chin held high.

"When your name is called, you will enter alone. There is no aid, no escape but forward. Remember: fear can rule you, or you can rule it. The choice, as always, is yours," Femirea said with one last glance across the crowd before stepping back for a professor to take her place.

One by one, students were called, swallowed by the portal. Some returned mere moments later, ashen and shrinking, but alive. I could only guess what the ones who didn't were experiencing, though the trial sounded similar to the one Zypher told us he'd been through. My stomach coiled tighter with each name called until mine finally rang out across the dwindling crowd.

"Bechora Knight."

I forced myself onto unsteady feet, sparing a final look at my friends. Gabriel's gaze burned into me as I moved forward, the echo of Femirea's warning chilling me more than the portal itself. I hesitated at the edge, forcing a shaky breath into my lungs before stepping through. The air shifted immediately, cool and damp, carrying a metallic tang that set my teeth on edge. Before me stretched a chamber lined with mirrors, endless corridors branching into reflections of reflections. My own face multiplied into dozens, each set of eyes sharp, accusing.

"Bechora Knightvale," a cacophony of voices hissed in unison. The name rattled through the space like a curse as a crown of black iron materialized atop my head in the reflections. "Heir to the stolen throne. Born to rule. Born to right the realm. Too weak to take it."

I shook my head. "That is not my name," I snapped, taking a step forward.

"Weak." The voices hissed in defiance as the mirrors rippled.

In their depths, a new scene replaced my reflection. I recognized myself as a toddler, cradled in the arms of a human woman who held a striking resemblance to me. Beside her stood a fae male, his emerald-green eyes the same color as mine. I knew with every fiber of my being that these were my parents. Geordie moved toward them; his usually cheerful face twisted in agony.

"This is the only way," he said. "She has to survive." He turned to the male, his eyes pleading. "I promise, father, I will keep her safe."

Tears slid down the woman's face as she reached an arm out to embrace Geordie. "You are not of my blood, Geordalis, but you are the son of my heart. You will keep your half-sister safe until it is time for her to return to this realm and set things right."

Geordie's jaw clenched as he sagged into her hold for a moment before he pulled back with a tight nod. The woman pressed a kiss to my hair, releasing Geordie as the male I recognized as my father tore open a portal. Her shoulders shook with grief as she stepped forward. "This is the only way," she sobbed. "Selir willing, I will see you again, my little star."

I watched as she released my small body through the portal. Geordie stepped forward to follow and stopped abruptly, his eyes going completely white.

"No," he bellowed as the sound of a door being battered down rang out.

The scene shifted almost too quickly for my eyes to follow —shadows wrapping around my parents as they bade Geordie to run. A blade flashed, blood splattering across my parents' clothing as screams ripped through the glass before the vision cut away.

"No," I cried out, begging my feet to move. "This can't be real!"

"Descendant of the last Starcaller Queen," the voices droned. "Blood of the throne. Child of a slaughtered line. You are the heir. The realm bends to you. War follows you. These are the truths we whisper."

The images came faster now—armies clashing under banners of flame, the Fae King laughing over a mountain of corpses. Zypher's body, crumbling to ash. Gabriel's head lolling in death. Shadrie, torn apart. Miles' lifeless eyes staring up at me. I screamed, pressing my palms to my ears and slamming my eyes shut as I forced my feet to carry me forward. I stumbled until I slammed into the hard, cool surface of another mirror and was forced to open my eyes.

I saw them then—the three males who weren't mine, but I felt drawn toward anyway. Vallynn, Dante, and Caulder, dragged in chains, their expressions carved from fury and betrayal. The executioner's axe fell once, twice, three times. Their heads rolled across the mirrored floor. Finally, it was me, kneeling at the block. My own execution reflected endlessly in the glass until I couldn't breathe.

I could feel the weight of the crown in my reflection pressing heavier and heavier on my skull. Every whisper drove the blade deeper into my chest. "Too weak. Too small. Too afraid."

For one terrible moment, I believed it all, sinking to my knees as despair tore at me. The voices taunted me with the destruction I would bring, the endless death. But then

I remembered Zypher's arms around me, Gabriel's reluctant hand in mine, Shadrie's inappropriate jokes, the studious way Miles attacked every problem. They had all believed in me even when I didn't believe in myself.

The labyrinth wanted me to believe in a future where I let my own fear consume me. One where I refused the truth it spoke and led my friends and mates to their bloody deaths. I forced myself upright, every part of me trembling. "I will not accept this," I whispered—then louder, stronger.

The mirrors rippled, cycling through vision after vision. I forced myself to look closer; some of it was true. The woman sobbing had been my mother. I'd dreamed of her voice more nights than I cared to recall. The fae male with emerald eyes—my father—his face setting off a twinge of undeniable familiarity. That I was the Starcaller was another undeniable truth. A deep, knowing acceptance settled into me as I considered the possibility that the throne belonged to my family—that I was the rightful ruler of this realm. But the rest —the crown crushing me, the endless corpses, the betrayal in the eyes of those I cared for—those were possibilities, shadows twisted into inevitability by fear.

"I see it now," I whispered, pressing my palm against the cold glass. "You show me what was and what could be, but I'm the only one who can decide what will be." The crown in my reflection flared, heavy and gleaming, but I refused to bow beneath it. My voice grew stronger, steadier. "I am Bechora Knightvale. I am the Starcaller Queen. That much is truth," The images of war and ruin screamed louder, trying to drown me out. Their weight caused me to stumble, but I refused to give in, my feet carrying me forward one step at a time. "I am not too weak. I am not too small. And I am not afraid." The last word tore from my lips in a roar.

The mirrors around me shattered, shrieking as shards of glass exploded through the air. My arms flew up to protect my face, and the sensation of being jerked forward shot through me. The illusions' screams were ripped away, and quiet chatter reached my ears, causing me to peek through my arms. I was back in the cathedral—whole and unharmed.

CHAPTER FORTY-THREE

Bechora

We gathered in mine and Shadrie's dorm room again that evening. We'd all survived, but the mood was more somber than the evening before. Even Zypher lacked his usual cheer after whatever he'd faced in the upper-classmen's trial. None of us could bear to share what we'd experienced, each of us too lost in the haunting memories of what we'd survived. Zypher and Gabriel joined me in my bed again that night. We clung to each other as if we could survive the next two days by force of will alone.

"A package came for you," Shadrie mumbled when we finally stumbled out of my room the next morning.

Zephyr and Gabriel followed close behind as I moved to the counter where she'd left the package. It was wrapped the same as every other gift I'd received throughout the term, but my demon mate's presence was enough to tell me it hadn't been sent by him. My hands trembled as I opened the small box, realization washing through me that if he hadn't sent this one, he hadn't sent any of the others either. Inside sat several small vials of liquid, but there wasn't a note to tell me who my secret benefactor was.

"Someone is helping you, Dilectus," Zypher said softly.

My brows dipped as I frowned. "What do you mean?"

Gabriel gently nudged me aside and peered into the box. "He's right. These each have a specific purpose." He lifted a vial of deep green liquid from the box. "This is meant to mimic earth magic in people who don't have access to it. Based on the coloring, it's quite strong, too. If you use this, you should be able to control earth magic for hours and with the strength of a natural wielder." He gently set the vial aside and pulled another one free. This one was a milky white substance with a slight shimmer. "This is called Obscuration powder."

"But it's a liquid," I interjected.

"Only until it's exposed to the air," Zypher offered in explanation. "The moment you uncork that vial, it becomes a powder that will temporarily hide you from sight."

Gabriel nodded as he continued to remove vials from the box. "Ice magic, storm magic, speed. Someone has provided you with tools to give you a leg up in today's trial."

"We don't even know what it is; how could someone possibly know what I'd need to help me?"

Gabriel shrugged, and Zypher shook his head. Shadrie cleared her throat and pushed my mates out of the way to study the vials lined up on our counter. "It has to be someone on staff," she said. "That's the only way they'd know how to help in advance." I looked at her in disbelief, opening my mouth to argue, but she held up a hand, silencing me. "I know it doesn't make sense, B, but you should still stick these in your pockets just in case."

The look on her face didn't leave room for argument, and I grabbed the vials, putting them in the pockets of the sweats I'd put on before leaving my bedroom. I'd decided the moment I opened my eyes that if I were going to die today, I was going to go out comfortable.

Nobody said another word as we left our dorm in a slow, fragile procession and headed to the dining hall. The tables were packed tighter than usual. Everywhere I looked, students sat in clusters, some with a dazed, empty expression on their faces, others crying softly. Zypher led us to our normal table before he and Gabriel headed for the buffet line to gather our meal.

They'd barely returned, setting the plates in front of us as Professor Snowthistle flitted into the hall. Her face was drawn as she made her way to the front of the space. She didn't have to call for quiet. Everyone's attention had gone to her the second she arrived, only the occasional sob or sniffle breaking the heavy silence. With a sad look, she cleared her throat and began calling off the names of the students who hadn't survived the first trial. My stomach lurched, my food turning to ash on my tongue. I tried to force another bite down, and it threatened to come back up, so I pushed my plate away. Shadrie's hand gripped my arm, her nails digging deeper into my skin with each name called. I counted them all, seventy-three students lost by the time the last name was called.

When we were dismissed, the movement toward our assigned meeting points for Trial Two felt like a march. No one laughed, no one joked. Zypher wrapped his arms around me before he had to split off toward the Third Year meeting point. I had the overwhelming urge to cling to him, as if keeping him here a moment longer could keep him from whatever he would face in his own trial. The thought of losing him had silent tears spilling over my lashes.

"Do not fear for me, Dilectus," he murmured, pulling back and swiping tears from my cheeks with his thumbs. "We will endure."

He looked over my head at Gabriel before stepping back. My vampire mate took Zypher's place as the demon turned and strode away. Gabriel's hand slipped into mine with a reassuring squeeze, and he led me in the direction of the cathedral.

The space was eerily silent for the number of students sitting in the pews. The heavy oak doors boomed shut behind us, and the air inside the cathedral tasted of ozone and smoke, as though it already carried a warning. Dean Femirea stood on the dais once more; her hands folded loosely in front of her as her eyes scanned over us. When she spoke, her voice filled every corner of the room.

"First Years," she began, her emerald eyes sweeping over us. "You have survived the Labyrinth of Shadows. Now you will face the second trial: the Elemental Trial. You will be cast into a pocket realm of shifting terrains and volatile magic. For one hour, you will endure. Survive the threats the elements place in your path, and you will be permitted to return. Fail, and you will not." Her lips curved faintly, though the expression didn't reach her eyes. "It will be up to each of you whether you aid one another or not."

A ripple of unease passed through the pews. Someone whimpered; another muttered a hurried prayer. Gabriel's hand was steady in mine, though I felt the faint tremor beneath his skin. Shadrie and I shared a glance before turning our attention to Miles. Words weren't needed to know that whatever waited for us in the pocket realm, we'd face it together.

Femirea raised her hand, and the dais split open to reveal another portal. "Step forward when your name is called. The trial awaits."

Names began to echo through the cathedral, each student stepping forward and dropping into the portal swirling in the raised floor. Some strode forward with their head held high, confidence radiating off them. Others dragged their feet as if the few seconds of delay could save them from their fate. None refused, the portal swallowing them whole. When my name rang out, Gabriel released my hand reluctantly, his gaze burning into me.

"Stay alive long enough for me to find you," he murmured. I nodded, steeling my spine before marching forward and dropping into the waiting portal.

The world slammed into me with a force that knocked my breath from my lungs. I staggered onto rough stone, jagged cliffs rising all around me. The air was thin, sharp, and laced with the scent of lightning. From somewhere far below me, the sounds of waves crashing against the unseen shore pounded out with a fury that echoed like war drums. I barely had time to find my footing before the wind howled, whipping hard enough to nearly hurl me over the edge. My hair ripped across my face, stinging my eyes. A sharp crack split the air as lightning cleaved the ground a few feet away, shattering rock and sending sparks skittering like living fire. Heart hammering, I stumbled back. My hand brushed the vials hidden in my pocket. Someone prepared me for this.

I forced myself to remain steady and scanned the horizon. The realm around me seemed endless, with different terrain just barely visible in the distance. There weren't any sounds of life, and it only took me a moment to realize that wherever I had landed, I was completely alone. The air crackled again, my hair raising on end as the scent of ozone thickened around me. I needed to find shelter, somewhere to hide from the violent elements.

I reached for my well of power and grabbed the strength I'd copied from Gabriel, coaxing it into my limbs as my eyes searched for a way down from the cliff I'd landed on. Hidden among the shrubbery to my left, a dirt path beckoned me forward. It took all my focus to hold the magical strength in my limbs as I picked my way down the rocky cliffside. Rocks skittered off the sharp face of it under my feet as I moved. I was nearly halfway down, sweat dripping down my back and between my breasts, when the temperature suddenly shifted.

Snow slammed into me, biting cold searing across my skin. My legs stiffened, every muscle fighting to keep moving. From somewhere up ahead, a student screamed. The sound was pained and terrified; a warning that whatever they'd encountered was not something I wanted to face. It was the first sign of life around me, and it sent a shiver of fear up my spine. My numb fingers fumbled around in my pocket as I tried to grasp the Obscurement powder. By some miracle, I pulled it from my pocket. My teeth chattered against the bitter cold as I yanked the cork free. The liquid burst into a shimmering powder, cloaking me in a veil that bent the air around me. The storm continued to howl, driving ice shards sharp enough to flay skin, but at least I was hidden from whatever had caused that scream.

Clenching my jaw, I forced my feet to keep moving. The

cliffside path gave way to blackened stone. Heat slammed into me as the storm died, and the air grew heavy with sulfur. Lava surged between jagged cracks, lighting the terrain in an angry glow. My sweat slowly washed away the powder, keeping me invisible as I trudged along. A lone figure moved carefully across the terrain, hair matted, clothes singed.

"Miles!" I shouted, my voice raw.

His head whipped toward me, wide-eyed. Relief broke across his soot-streaked face. "Bechora!" He staggered toward me, stumbling over the unstable ground.

We barely had time to embrace before the lava shifted. A beast rose from the fissure itself—molten rock pulling into the shape of a wolf with burning eyes. It lunged, spewing fire across the stone.

"Down!" I shoved Miles aside, pulling the green vial from my pocket. The earth's strength surged through me the moment I uncorked it. I slammed my palms into the ground, jagged walls of stone rising to block the searing spray.

Miles recovered, his magic flaring. Blue electricity licked across his arms before arcing out, striking the molten wolf in the chest, stunning it. I willed the earth to rise and harden around the creature, praying to whatever god was listening that it would be enough. Inch by inch, the flaming beast sank back into the ground until it was swallowed whole. We didn't celebrate. We kept moving.

"I don't think time works here like it should," Miles noted as we trudged forward.

"What do you mean? The Dean said the trial lasts an hour; why wouldn't time be the same?"

He held his arm out toward me, tapping the watch strapped to his wrist. "According to this, only a handful of seconds have passed. You were through the portal at least three minutes before my name was called."

"Shit," I hissed.

"Shit indeed."

We fell into a companionable silence as we pressed forward.

Our eyes were constantly scanning for threats, ears echoing with the distant screams of our classmates. Eventually, the lava plains bled into a swamp. Thick mud clung to our shoes, threatening to pull us down with every step. Mist coiled over the still water, and serpentine heads darted up, striking at anything that moved.

"Fuck you, you fucking thing!" a sharp voice rang out from the fog.

Shadrie emerged, ice magic swirling at her fingertips. Frost spread across the water, locking the serpent creatures into place. She shattered them with a vicious snap of her wrist before turning to face us.

"Selir, I thought I was never going to find you," she breathed, rushing to hug us both. "This place is... It's something."

"Have you seen Gabriel?" I asked, my vampire mate the only one still missing.

Shadrie shook her head solemnly, and Miles grabbed my hand, giving it a gentle squeeze.

"He's a vampire. He'll be alright," Miles murmured. "But we won't if we don't find somewhere safe to hole up."

I swallowed and forced myself to nod. I couldn't let my fear get the better of me, not here. Together, the three of us pressed on once more until the swamp gave way to desert. Heat beat down, the horizon bending with mirages as thirst clawed at my throat. A sandstorm whipped up so fast it nearly blinded me. Through the grit and wind, I caught a flash of movement. My heart surged into my throat as I realized Gabriel was fighting against two towering beasts made of sand and wind. His hands clawed them apart, but they reformed as quickly as he struck.

"Gabriel," I screamed, surging forward as fear for my mate ripped through me.

He turned, eyes burning at the sight of me. The momentary lapse cost him. One beast swung its arm, a pillar of wind knocking him to the ground. I froze, unable to do anything as my heart stuttered to a stop. Shadrie and Miles dove forward, Miles' voice ringing out over the raging wind.

"I'll hit the sand beast with my electricity, and if I'm right, it should turn it to glass. You try to freeze the air beast."

"How am I supposed to freeze air?" Shadrie called back as she stalked forward.

"Pray that the beast has water droplets within it like normal air!" Miles yelled back as his electricity arced from his hands toward the sand creature.

Seeing my friends act broke me from my panic. My fingers dipped into my pocket, and I pulled out the remaining vials, hunting for the fire magic potion. I let out a silent cheer as I found it, stuffing the others back in my sweats before uncorking it and swallowing it down. I felt the potion hit my well of power, mingling with the fire magic that lingered there from the pendant I wore. It twisted and twined together into something nearly uncontrollable, bubbling up until it burst out of me in a line of deep blue flames. It trailed across the sand, leaving glass in its wake until it wrapped around the sand beast, crystallizing it as it let out a final hissing shriek. Gabriel shoved off the ground and sprinted forward, slamming his fist into the creature, causing it to shatter.

"Uh, guys! This thing isn't freezing!" Shadrie yelled. "What do we do?"

"Run!" Gabriel called back.

We didn't hesitate, sprinting back toward the swamp lands the three of us had just left. Somehow, we managed to reach the muddy terrain, and the air beast turned back into the desert rather than follow us. Miles bent forward, hands braced on his thighs as he sucked down air.

"We need shelter," I said, fighting the urge to launch myself at my mate.

Gabriel frowned, his eyes raking over me as if he were fighting the same urges I was. "The three of you stay here. Bechora, start a fire. I'll find something we can use to build a structure for cover."

"Be careful... please," I replied, as I took in the firm set of his jaw that told me he was going whether I wanted him to or not.

Just as I thought he was going to turn away, he strode toward me and grabbed my shoulders. Pulling me against his body, he pressed his lips to mine, and I felt myself melt into him. "Don't fucking die, Bechora," he demanded when he pulled away.

I watched him disappear into the swamp before turning to find my friends smirking at me. Shadrie had the audacity to laugh before she pointed at the small pile of sticks she'd managed to gather. Shaking my head at her, I called my fire magic forth, more controlled now, and lit the fire. The fire snapped and popped, spitting sparks into the misty air as the three of us huddled close. I couldn't say how long we waited there, each of us on edge, waiting for the next threat to emerge, before branches cracked in the distance. All three of us summoned our magic, ready to defend against the next elemental beast. A shadow emerged from the mist, striding purposefully toward us, and relief surged through me so violently my knees nearly buckled.

"Gabriel." My voice broke on his name.

He carried an armful of scavenged branches and broad fronds, his shirt torn, black smears across his jaw. His gaze found mine instantly, relief flashing across his sharp features before his usual control snapped back into place. "Good. You built the fire." His voice was low, gruff. But the way his eyes softened when they raked over me told a different story.

I couldn't stop the laugh of disbelief that broke free. "I built a fire. That's the first thing you say after going scavenging through this place?"

He shrugged, a smirk tugging at the corner of his mouth. Dropping the pile of supplies he found, his eyes scanned the landscape behind us. "There's a rise just there," he nodded behind where I stood. "We'll use this stuff to build a lean-to. Shadrie, you'll use your ice magic to reinforce it. We'll have to leave the fire, but Bechora is skilled enough with her flames that it shouldn't be an issue."

I couldn't help the warm pride that swelled in my chest at his words before he ushered us into motion. We made the short trek in the direction he'd indicated, Gabriel carrying the fronds and twigs. As soon as we reached the rise, we set to work, quickly crafting the lean-to under my vampire mate's guidance. Shadrie sealed it over with her ice magic, and we crowded inside. For a fleeting moment, it felt like safety. Then the screams started.

They weren't close, not at first. Distant cries carried across the warped landscape—sharp bursts of terror that cut off too quickly. A shiver slid down my spine, every instinct urging me to cover my ears. One scream rose higher than the rest, echoing inhumanly before it was silenced with a wet, final sound.

Miles squeezed his eyes shut, whispering a curse. Shadrie buried her face against her knees, her icy bravado cracked. Gabriel stayed utterly still, jaw clenched, gaze fixed outward as if he could hold back the horrors beyond with sheer will. I pressed my hand into his, lacing our fingers together. His knuckles were white, but his grip loosened just enough to return the pressure.

And then, as suddenly as it had begun, it ended. A deep hum thrummed through the ground, rattling the lean-to and breaking Shadrie's ice away in sheets. The mist outside shimmered, pulling like a tide. My stomach lurched as invisible hands hooked into my chest, yanking me forward. I yelped as the world seemed to tear apart. The swamp, the storm, even the air itself collapsed in on itself in a swirl of light. My body stretched and folded in ways it shouldn't before I slammed back onto solid stone. We were back in the cathedral.

Gasps and groans filled the cavernous space as students reappeared one by one, some limping, some bloodied, too many not returning at all. I lay sprawled on the cold floor, chest heaving, the screams from the trial still ringing in my ears. A hand cupped the back of my neck, strong and grounding. Gabriel's face swam into view above me, pale and fierce, his relief so raw it nearly undid me.

"We survived," he breathed, pressing his forehead against mine.

Miles and Shadrie pressed close, the four of us standing in an awkward semblance of a group hug. Around us, other students gathered in trembling clusters. The Dean's voice echoed over the cavernous space, calm and detached as if we hadn't just been fighting for our lives.

"Congratulations, students. The second trial is complete."

CHAPTER FORTY-FOUR

Bechora

When I returned to my dorm room, another package was waiting. This time, it held five of the restoration potions I'd been receiving nearly daily. The meaning was clear—one for each of us, except Zypher hadn't arrived yet. Smothering my worry, I handed a potion to Miles, Shadrie, and Gabriel. The four of us downed them quickly before Miles muttered something about needing to shower and wanting to sleep for a century.

"You should get cleaned up too," Gabriel said as Shadrie slipped into her bedroom to gather clean clothes and her shower caddy.

"I–" The words caught in my throat, but something in my expression must have told him the thoughts swirling in my head. After what we'd just been through, I couldn't bring myself to be away from him.

"We'll go together. Zypher will probably be here by the time we get back."

The tension in my shoulders relaxed a fraction, and I nodded. Gabriel didn't wait for me to move, using his vampiric speed to gather clean pajamas, a towel, and my shower caddy before stopping in front of me to grab my hand. We made our way to the communal showers in silence that dragged on as Gabriel situated my things and turned on the water in a stall. Wordlessly, he led me inside and stripped both our clothes away before washing the grime from my body. There was nothing sexual in the way his hands moved over my skin, only the quiet comfort of being cared for. My entire body felt lax and heavy with fatigue by the time he started on my hair.

"Let me," I insisted, as he raised the soapy cloth to his chest after rinsing the conditioner from my hair.

My hand curled around his wrist, and after a heartbeat, Gabriel relinquished it. I moved the cloth slowly across the planes of his chest and shoulders, my touch careful, reverent almost. He didn't flinch, only watched me with those fathomless eyes, the tension in him leashed but ever present. The silence between us wasn't heavy this time, though—it was grounding. By the time we stepped out, steam curling in the air, I was warm to the bone and impossibly drowsy. Gabriel wrapped me in my towel before securing his own around his waist, then dried me off as though I might shatter if left unattended. I didn't protest—the exhaustion in my muscles wouldn't have let me if I tried.

He dressed me with the same care before tugging on the sweats he'd slept in the night before, then led me down the dimly lit hall toward my dorm. Masculine snores carried faintly from Shadrie's room, and I moved to peek inside. She and Miles were curled up on her bed, both fast asleep. My heart twinged at the sight of my friends as I stepped back and quietly shut her door. When I turned, the sole remaining potion vial on the counter seemed to stare at me like a silent reminder. Zypher still hadn't shown up after the trials, and I had no way of knowing if he'd survived whatever it was the other Years had faced today.

"He'll come," Gabriel murmured softly, as he guided me toward the couch. I sank into the cushions with a sigh, my head lolling against the back. "I don't think there's anything in this life or the next that could keep that demon from returning to you," he continued as he settled beside me.

Minutes stretched into hours, and still no Zypher. My eyelids grew heavier with each blink, the pull of sleep nearly irresistible as I fought to wait for my missing mate.

"Bechora," Gabriel said softly, crouching before me. I blinked, trying to remember when he'd moved. "Don't fight sleep, you need to rest."

I tried to shake my head, but it barely moved. "Not until..."

"Shh." He scooped me up as though I weighed nothing, my limbs too sluggish to protest. My head slumped against his chest, the steady thud of his heartbeat urging me closer to sleep. My eyes fell closed, and when they opened again, Gabriel was easing me onto the mattress with care. "Rest. I promise, Zypher will come."

I sank into the soft bed, letting my eyes close again as I felt him climb in beside me. The bed dipped under his weight before his arms wrapped around me, pulling me closer. My head instinctively found a place on his chest, my hand settling on his abdomen. It was almost perfect, but my demon was missing. Tears welled behind my eyelids at the thought.

"I'm scared," my voice cracked. "What if he didn't make it out of his trial?"

"He's still alive. You'd feel it if he wasn't," Gabriel spoke, conviction laced through his words.

"How do you know?"

Gabriel tightened his arms around me and blew out a shaky breath. "The first trial." He paused, but his tone told me not to press. To let him gather himself and continue on his own terms. After what felt like an eternity, his voice broke the silence again. "At first, it showed me my mother and sister. Their fate at the hands of my father, because I accepted our bond instead of rejecting you for someone outwardly more powerful. It felt like I lived every second of their torture and death as those fucking mirrors played them out in great detail."

My breath hitched at the pain in his voice. "Gabriel–"

"That wasn't the worst of it." His grip on me tightened as if he feared I'd vanish. "The mirrors showed me a future where I hadn't come to my senses and accepted our bond. You died, beheaded by the fae king for reasons I can't even begin to fathom." I stilled at his words, the vision so eerily similar to what the mirrors had shown me. "I felt the moment of your death. Our bond wasn't complete in those visions, but I'd still initiated it with my bite, and when it snapped, it shredded through me. It was torment, and for a brief moment, I considered ending myself to make the pain stop. If our real bond hadn't flared inside me when it did, that trial might have claimed my life."

Hot tears slid down my cheeks, and I lifted my head enough to see his face. "None of that was real," I whispered fiercely.

Gabriel eased my head back down to his chest and stroked his hand over my hair. "No, it wasn't. But I knew—I know—the pain that threatened to tear me apart when the bond broke is only a fraction of what I'll feel if something happens to you. That's one truth I can't escape, and it's why I know you would have felt it if something happened to Zypher." His words hit me square in the chest. He kissed my temple, gentle as a benediction. "Sleep," he said. "Let your body fix what your head can't right now. Zypher will come, and I'd prefer not to fight with him about letting you wait up when he does."

I curled tighter against him, letting out a soft snort, exhaustion finally overtaking my resistance. Gabriel's fingers threaded through my hair, and he hummed under his breath. My body went completely lax, my eyes falling shut as sleep pulled me under.

Morning came too soon, but I allowed myself a moment of thanks as I recognized Zypher's body curled around mine. Carefully rolling to face him, I noted the way worry lines cut across his brow even in sleep. Whatever he'd faced the day before still weighed on him. My fingers inched up, and I gently smoothed them over the lines. Zypher's eyes blinked open, and he smiled.

"Good morning, Dilectus." He grinned, his arms pulling me closer, causing Gabriel to grumble in his sleep behind me. "I must say, I've quite enjoyed waking in your bed these last few days. I'm not certain I can go back to waking alone after these trials are done."

I pulled back just enough to playfully swat his chest as someone pounded on my bedroom door. Gabriel bolted upright with a snarl, and Zypher let out a booming laugh.

"Get up!" Shadrie called through the door. "You've got another package from your secret admirer, and we're going to be late!"

Gabriel huffed, practically throwing himself out of the bed as I shoved Zypher into motion. I moved to my closet to quickly grab a fresh t-shirt and another pair of sweats, noticing the neatly folded clothes sitting on my desk. Zypher moved to the stack, grabbing his own from the top before handing what was left to Gabriel.

"I thought we both could use something to wear today without having to leave our mate's side until absolutely necessary," Zypher said to my vampire.

I smiled to myself as Gabriel grunted out a thanks. We lapsed into silence as we quickly dressed and made our way into the living area of my dorm. Shadrie and Miles were both dressed and waiting. Miles wore a pained expression, his eyes flitting to the watch on his wrist every few seconds.

"Open your package and let's get moving before you cause Miles to stroke out," Shadrie called, causing the mage in question to shoot me a sheepish smile and shrug his shoulders.

I waved my hand at Shadrie and moved to pick up the plain package from the counter. Like all the others, it only had my name, nothing else. Ripping it open, I tipped it toward the counter, and a bracelet of sapphire blue gems, glowing slightly with magic, clattered onto the countertop.

"Odd," I murmured, picking it up to study it.

"Another trinket from your mystery benefactor?" Zypher asked, leaning over my shoulder to examine it. "A powerful one at that. The gems will enhance your shields."

"But aren't they already basically impenetrable?" I asked, frowning at the bracelet. "I copied them from you, and yours are."

"Yes, but someone thinks yours need assistance. Given

their last gifts helped you through yesterday's trial, I'd be hesitant to question it, Dilectus."

"Just wear the damned thing, you lucky bitch," Shadrie snapped playfully. "We need to get moving. You three already missed breakfast and the death toll, and I don't want to find out if we end up on tomorrow's for being late to our last trial."

We hurried across campus, Zypher not leaving my side until we arrived at the cathedral. He kissed me softly, wishing me luck before vanishing in the throngs of students back the way we'd come. I let the crowd move me forward, one hand clutching Gabriel's as the other reached for Shadrie. The closer we got to the threshold, the more my gut screamed that something wasn't right. I tried to convince myself it was just my nerves, but the moment we finally stepped inside, the floor beneath us gave way. My hands were ripped from Gabriel and Shadrie's as the world spun out around me. I landed with a thud on my backside, towering walls rising up on either side.

I pushed myself back to my feet and moved to study my surroundings. Grass covered the ground beneath me, the strange walls spanning every direction, the sharp corners in places signaling turns. I was still trying to sort out where I was when Dean Femirea's voice boomed out.

"Welcome, First Years. Today marks the third and final trial —the Maze of Allegiance." It sounded like she was standing right next to me, but she was nowhere to be seen. "Inside these walls, you will be tested not only on your skill and endurance, but on your choices. Loyalty and survival rarely walk hand in hand. Today, you must decide what matters most. Those of you who survive the maze and reach its center will advance to Second Year."

"Fuck," I hissed to myself.

The air felt charged, pulsing faintly with magic, and the silence pressed in thick enough to smother a scream. I knew I had to move if I wanted to make it out of the maze, and I forced myself to cautiously start walking forward. My hand trailed along the cool stone wall, and I'd nearly reached the first turn when a growl cut through the stillness. My heart lurched. From the shadows, a beast I recognized from the packet Professor Sabelus had given us slithered toward me. My mind raced as I tried to remember the weaknesses of the basilisk.

It hissed, the sound scraping down my spine like nails on stone, before lunging. I flung my shield up, sapphire light sparking into existence around me. The serpent slammed into it, scales screeching across the barrier. The impact rattled my bones, but the bracelet I wore pulsed, feeding strength into the shield, thickening it.

"Fuck this," I panted, sprinting around the writhing mass.

My feet thudded against the soft ground as I ran, taking corner after corner in my blind attempt to flee the monster. Around the time the hissing sound stopped, I realized I was as good as lost. Tilting my head back, I looked to the sky as if it could tell me where to go.

"Maybe I should have gone with Geordie to those classes when he got weirdly into navigating without a compass," I muttered to myself.

"Bechora?" A familiar female voice called out. "Thank Selir, it is you." Shadrie raced toward me from an opening in the maze to my left.

Relief flooded my system, causing me to sway on my feet. "Shadrie!"

She skidded to a halt in front of me, her hair askew, frost clinging to her sleeves where she'd clearly thrown up walls of ice to slow something down. Her chest heaved as she bent forward, catching her breath.

"I'm so fucking glad I found you. This maze is nuts. I ran into two different minotaurs and barely made it out alive," she panted.

Before I could respond, a distant scream echoed through the maze, chilling the air between us. It was abruptly cut off, leaving only silence. Shadrie and I exchanged a look, both of our bodies tensing.

"Let's not stick around to find out what did that," I said,

urging her forward.

We moved quickly but cautiously, taking turns that felt more like guesswork than strategy. Once, a deep snarl rattled the walls just a few feet away, shadows shifting as some enormous beast prowled the other side. Shadrie grabbed my wrist, tugging me faster. We didn't stop running until the sound faded. The sun dipped below the towering walls as we wandered, trying to find our way to the center. I was starting to think this trial would be the end of us when, finally, we stumbled into a clearing. At its center rose a black stone altar, its surface pulsing with power. Dean Femirea's voice boomed above us, and a transparent copy of her materialized beside the stone.

"Illusion," Shadrie muttered.

"Congratulations, First Years. You have reached the center of the maze. There is one final task before you can be transported to safety. You must choose—loyalty or survival."

The stone hummed louder, the air pulsing around it. I could practically taste the threat building in it.

"They can't be serious." Shadrie's voice hitched.

My stomach turned as the hum built further, raising the hairs on my arms. "They are."

Shadrie's fingers brushed mine. Her jaw was tight, but her eyes—bright with fear and resolve—locked on me. "Leave me, B. You have to. Everything we've found about what you are tells me you have to survive this, or we're all screwed anyway. It has to be you."

"Don't you fucking dare," I snapped, tears burning in my eyes. "No way in hell I'm sacrificing you."

"I don't want to die, B," she shot back. "But this test was pretty damned clear that it's you or me." Shadrie paused, swallowing thickly. "The first trial... Those mirrors showed me things, B. I'm pretty sure it was what happens if you don't make it out of this trial. If I'm right, I'm dead anyway. At least this way I won't have to suffer."

Power pulsed from the stone altar, the ground trembling

beneath our feet.

"I can't!" My shield flared instinctively as another wave of power crashed over us. "Neither one of us is dying here. You fucking hear me?"

Shadrie gave me a pleading look and took a step back. I channeled strength to my legs and raced toward her, grabbing her shoulder before she could sacrifice herself. The bracelet on my wrist heated against my skin, shooting searing pain through my arm. My shield stretched in response until Shadrie was safely inside it with me. The ground quaked, a violent rush of power exploding from the stone altar and blinding me with white light. My legs buckled as it battered my shield. As quickly as it happened, the light faded, taking the walls of the maze with it. Shadrie pulled me to my feet and wrapped her arms around me as we took in the familiar sight of the cathedral.

"You stupid, stubborn bitch," she whispered hoarsely, her voice breaking.

"You're welcome," I rasped back as I squeezed her tightly.

A throat clearing pulled our attention to the Dean standing on the dais with a soft smile. "You ladies have learned the most valuable lesson," she spoke. "The options you're presented aren't always the only choices at hand."

I blinked at her dumbly, fairly certain she'd just complimented us on not sacrificing the other and finding a way out for both of us. I bit my tongue to keep from losing my temper and telling her exactly what I thought of the barbaric trial we'd just endured. Dean Femirea waved her hand toward the pews, and I almost thought better of keeping my thoughts to myself.

"If you don't mind taking a seat while we wait for the trial to come to an end."

"Come on, B," Shadrie said, tugging me off the dais.

My eyes stayed pinned to the dean, glaring daggers at her smiling face as Shadrie led me to an empty pew. We took our seats, my anger at the dean steadily rising. Students began to emerge from nothing at her side, some in worse shape than others.

With each new student that appeared, my rage twisted into worry for Gabriel and Miles. The cathedral pews were half-filled when Miles finally appeared. He was spattered in blood, his face ashen, and his hands trembling as he clutched his glasses between his fingers. Shadrie slipped from her seat and grabbed his arm, gently leading him to sit with us.

Dread slowly spread through my body, causing my limbs to grow heavy with each new student that appeared. Time seemed to tick by slowly as I waited for Gabriel to appear. A gasp of relief ripped free when he popped into existence beside the dean. His eyes blazed with murderous rage as they scanned the space. Dean Femirea leaned to say something to him, but he stomped away before she could, his eyes finding me. Tension melted from his entire body with each step toward me until he collapsed in the empty seat next to me. His hand reached out and took mine as if to reassure himself I wasn't a hallucination.

My entire focus moved to where our hands clasped together. The low murmur of the Dean's voice as more students emerged from the final trial faded into the background. The only thought I could hold onto was that we'd survived. My friends and my mate made it through the last trial. I only needed to know Zypher made it through whatever trial he'd faced, and then I could breathe.

"Congratulations," Dean Femirea's voice rang out. "You have all survived the trials. When you step outside the cathedral, you will find your family waiting to greet you. Celebrate with them. Enjoy your victory. Each of you has proven you have what it takes to advance to Second Year at the academy."

She shot us a final smile before sweeping forward from the dais and floating from the cathedral.

CHAPTER FORTY-FIVE

Bechora

"That bitch is mental," I muttered, nodding in the direction the Dean had gone as Gabriel stood and helped me to my feet. "You'd think we all just passed a multiple-choice exam the way she acted."

"It's the way things are here," Miles said softly from behind me.

I looked at him over my shoulder, taking in his appearance once more. "Are you okay?" I asked as we merged into the crush of students making their way to the exit.

"I'm alive." He shrugged, slipping his grime-covered glasses back onto his face.

"Thank Selir for that!" Shadrie replied.

I shook my head, not sure I could say anything to ease the trauma we'd endured over the last three days. Gabriel tugged me forward with the crowd, and my free hand shot behind me to grab Shadrie's. I barely heard her say something to Miles over the growing sound of chatter, but a quick glance told me she'd taken his hand in hers. We held tightly to one another as we weaved through the throng of students, and I couldn't help searching over their heads for Zypher.

The blinding light of midday caused me to blink furiously the moment we stepped outside. Time had moved differently in the third trial, like it had in the second. Students fanned out, moving toward their families as my vision adjusted.

"There's Zypher," Gabriel said, pointing through an opening in the crowd toward the far side of the quad.

I sucked down a breath of relief as I took in my other mate.

He stood next to a male who bore a striking resemblance to him. Zypher wore an exasperated expression as he gestured wildly at the man's clothing. I let myself take in the new male and almost laughed as I noted his khaki cargo shorts, the striped polo tucked into them, and the white sneakers on his feet. He was the epitome of the suburban dad stereotype.

"This is not what I meant by casual, Father!" I heard Zypher hiss as we drew near.

The male simply rolled his eyes. "Fine," he sighed, waving his hand in front of his body. His clothing changed in an instant, leaving him standing in a sleek black suit.

"Thank you," Zypher drawled just before he turned and spotted me. A smile split his face, and I tore my hands free from Gabriel and Shadrie's hold. I ran the remaining distance between us and launched myself at my demon, my arms and legs wrapping around him as he caught me.

"You're alive," I sobbed, burying my face in his neck.

"Of course, Dilectus. I told you I would return to you," Zypher replied, one hand supporting my weight as the other rubbed soothingly across my back.

"Ah, this is the female who has deemed my son worthy of her *Vinculum*." The male beside him spoke, causing me to stiffen.

I slowly peeled myself off Zypher, embarrassment causing my skin to flush red as he allowed me to slide down his body to my feet. Tucking me against his side, Zypher turned us to face the male.

"Dilectus, allow me to introduce you to my father, Lucifer Morningstar."

"The pleasure is mine, I assure you." Lucifer smiled before his eyes flicked to the others. "Am I correct to assume this is the rest of your *Vinculum*?"

Shadrie cackled, and I noticed Miles' face turning red. Gabriel moved to stand at my other side, his arms crossed over his chest.

"Can you imagine us with B and these two?" Shadrie

laughed, elbowing Miles as she pointed at Zypher and Gabriel.

"Shadrie, Miles, this is my father," Zypher interjected, motioning between my friends. "Father, these are our friends." Zypher gestured toward Gabriel as Lucifer nodded at them. "This is Gabriel Dreadgrave, my bond brother."

"It is a pleasure to meet you all," Lucifer replied before addressing Zypher. "I will leave you to comfort your Dilectus with your bond brother. As I recall, the trials are rather traumatizing. When you're ready, I will be speaking with the Dean."

We watched the crowd part as Lucifer strolled toward the administration building. Zypher and Gabriel both pressed closer to my sides as the male vanished from sight.

"I apologize for him," Zypher spoke, finally. "My father can be a bit much."

"It's fine," I assured him. "I honestly thought he was kind of sweet." Gabriel scoffed but didn't say a word. I leaned forward, peering around Zypher to find Shadrie.

"Should we find your parents now?"

"We can try, but it's probably better if we stay put and let them find us." She shrugged.

I was about to ask Miles the same question when I spotted a familiar face moving through the crowd toward me. His hair was a vibrant blue, and his clothing was in an unfamiliar style, but there was no denying the shape of his hazel eyes or the silly grin plastered on his face.

"Geordie?" I croaked.

"Hello, Bechora," he said, drawing to a stop in front of me.

"What the fuck, asshole?" I snapped, punching him in the chest. "Six fucking years and you never told me a damned thing. You were my best friend, and you were lying to me the entire time!"

His lips twisted into a frown. "I had to. It was the only way to ensure you ended up here when you needed to," he replied.

"Did you know the whole time? That I am... what I am?" I demanded.

"I've known since before you were born, Bechora. Before your mother fell pregnant with you, I foresaw what you would be. I tried to warn our father, but my meddling kept changing the future. I didn't realize how badly I'd fucked things up until the day you were sent through the portal. I was supposed to follow right behind you. You were never supposed to be alone in the human realm."

The words tumbled out of him, the weight of the truth breaking through the dam that had kept them back for the last six years. "I barely made it out of our home that night. Your mother and our father... they died buying time for me to escape. It took me years to find another way to the human realm without being detected."

"So, it's true then. The things I saw in the first trial."

"Some of it, yes."

"The part about you being my half-brother?" I asked, arching a brow.

"That is true," he replied. "I was seventeen when you were born. We share a father, though my mother died in her birthing bed and your mother was the only one I ever knew."

"What else are you keeping from me? How are you even here? I thought you couldn't come to the academy!" The words came out in a rush of demanding questions.

"I won't be able to stay here, Bechora. I'm only here now because I have to warn you. And because I needed to speak with you." His eyes moved to Zypher, who stiffened at my side. "Tell your father to use *Aegis Maleficarum*. You will know when he needs to use it."

"The law that claims mated females as a familial ward?" Zypher frowned, and I glanced between him and Geordie in confusion.

"Yes. That is the one," Geordie replied, his head turning toward Miles and Shadrie. I opened my mouth to question him, but he held up a finger to silence me and moved toward my friends. "Hello, mate," he purred, taking Miles' hand in his and pressing it to his lips. Miles flushed, his mouth opening in stunned silence.

"Oh, you lucky asshole," Shadrie laughed, slapping Miles on the back.

Geordie turned to her, and she narrowed her eyes at him. "You have done well protecting and helping my sister, ice mage. Before you give me your brilliant speech about being good to Miles, I have one more request. I must ask that you look after my heart now, too. I won't be able to do it myself for some time, and I trust that you can keep him safe. You must pretend he is yours. Promise me, mage."

"Well, damn. I guess I don't need to give the speech now." Shadrie gaped. "I promise. Miles can be my fake mate as long as you need him to be."

"Excuse me!" I snapped. "I'm not done getting answers from you, Geordie. You owe me explanations."

Geordie moved to stand in front of me again and let out a heavy sigh. "I can't give you the answers you want. Not yet, at least. The only thing I can tell you now is that you're still moving too slow. You should have claimed your third mate by now."

My eyebrows shot to my hairline. "Excuse me? My what?"

Geordie ignored my outburst, tapping one finger on his chin. "Hmm, I don't think that one is quite ready. Perhaps it's for the best you claim your dragon next."

"My... my dragon!" I shrieked.

"Yes, the professor. Very broody that one, but he's been sending you all those little gifts all year. It won't take much to sway him into giving up his fight against the bond."

Clarity crashed over me. The strange pull I felt toward Thrackborne, the way his behavior toward me seemed to run hot and cold, his sudden disappearance and cessation of our tutoring sessions after the incident with the succubus allure. "That bastard," I hissed.

"Indeed," Geordie chuckled. "I must be going now, but you should go ahead and tell the dragon exactly what you think about him hiding from your bond."

I snarled at Geordie, causing him to laugh before he turned on his heel and vanished into the crowd. My feet moved of their own accord, and before I knew what I was doing, I was stomping toward Thrackborne's office, friends and mates following in my wake. I didn't bother knocking when I reached it. The heavy oak door slammed against the stone wall as I shoved it open. Thrackborne straightened where he sat behind his desk and shot me an unamused look.

"Ms. Knight," he drawled, his voice deceptively calm. "To what do I owe this—"

I stomped to the opposite side of his desk, the others filing in the room behind me. "Don't you dare," I snapped, cutting him off. "You've been lying to me this whole time! Mates. We're mates and you thought you could hide that from me?"

Zypher chuckled, the sound filled with mischief. Thrackborne's composure cracked for the first time since I'd met him in the parking lot of Sinful Seduction. Scales rippled along his exposed forearms, and I felt Gabriel tense beside me as Zypher laughed harder.

"Everything I have done has been to protect you," Thrackborne snapped, surging to his feet. "If I had acknowledged our bond, one of us would have been forced from the academy! Neither of those things is an option, not when there are forces at play you can't comprehend. Dangers that will rip you to shreds!"

"Fuck you," I gritted out. "You're what, thirty-something, and rather than tell me that like a fucking adult, you chose to hide what you are to me? How fucking childish!"

"Two-hundred-thirty-five, actually," he replied, the calm in his voice betrayed by the smoke curling from his nostrils.

"What?" I demanded.

"I'm not thirty. I am two-hundred-thirty-five, though the lifespan of my kind would put that on par with a human in their thirties."

"Jesus Christ! I thought Shadrie was joking when she said you were two-hundred-something." I snapped, throwing my hands in the air and whirling on the others. "Anyone else want to drop an age bomb on me, now's the time."

"I'm only twenty-two," Gabriel shrugged.

"I told you my age when we met," Shadrie added.

"I'm nineteen," Miles said meekly.

"I am twenty-four, Dilectus," Zypher said before grinning at the professor. "I knew you were a bond brother."

"Are you serious right now?" I demanded, causing Zypher's smile to drop. "You knew and you didn't tell me either?"

"After what my mother experienced with Adam, I refused to risk putting you through that, Dilectus." Zypher's tone was soft enough to temper my anger.

My shoulders slumped forward as I turned to face the dragon again. I leaned forward, my hands curling into fists on the edge of his desk.

"You could have told me," I said, quieter in the wake of Zypher's admission. "You could have trusted me enough to tell me the truth. Instead, you sent me gifts in secret and lied to me. This whole time, I've been drawn to you, thinking something must be very wrong with me to be attracted to another male when I already have two mates. It was all I could do to keep the guilt from consuming my thoughts." My voice cracked. "You could have told me the truth at any time, and I wouldn't have had to spend all this time thinking I was a horrible mate to them."

"You think I wanted to hide the truth from you?" he asked, pinning me with his amber eyes. "I have waited for you for centuries. I searched the human realm for you and came up empty. It wasn't until I caught your scent in that parking lot that I finally found you. It nearly destroyed me to realize I couldn't claim you without risking your life."

"You stole the choice from me, Thrackborne," I snapped.

"Caulder," he murmured. "If you're going to address me as anything now that you know the truth, it will be my first name."

"Fine," I spat. "Caulder. I know the truth now, so you have

to decide. You either want this bond, or you don't." I held my hand up, silencing him before he could speak. "I'm not saying I forgive you, but no more hiding from it. No more lying to me about it. We get to know each other. You prove you're worthy of being mine, and then I'll decide if I'll accept you and the bond." I could practically feel Zypher's pride in me rolling off him from where he stood behind me.

Caulder's jaw clenched, and he nodded in understanding. "Then, come what may, I am yours."

The sound of a siren tore through the room, causing me to jump.

"What is that?" Shadrie yelled to be heard over the sound.

"Something is wrong," Caulder called back, moving to stand between me and the door to his office. "We need to get to the quad now."

"Isn't it safer in here?" I yelled, my hands pressed to my ears in an attempt to drown out the noise.

"No, the quad is the only place all the students can be gathered and informed of the reason for the alarm," Caulder answered before pinning his gaze on my mates and jabbing his fingers in their direction. "Keep her safe. The Dean's shield should hold, but we don't know what we're about to walk into."

Without another word, he stormed into the hallway, leaving us to chase after him. Zypher and Gabriel flanked me as we raced behind the dragon toward the quad. We arrived to find it full of students and their families. I caught sight of Lucifer over the crowd and motioned toward him. Zypher nodded in my peripheral and waved a hand above the mass of people surrounding us. Lucifer seemed to sag with relief as he pushed his way through until he reached us.

"Do you know what's going on?" I asked, my words echoing over the crowd as the sirens cut off abruptly.

Lucifer shook his head, just as a screen shimmered into existence above us. Dean Femirea's voice rang out, quieting the worried whispers, as a scene began to play out over the projected illusion.

"Attention students and staff of Blackthorne Academy. Effective immediately, students are prohibited from leaving campus."

My eyes focused on the illusion as a shimmering wall came into focus. As it panned out, thousands of humans appeared, military tanks and planes peppered throughout their growing numbers.

"The supernatural realm is under attack. In order to assure the safety of all Blackthorne Academy students, the King has ordered us into lockdown. Parents will be permitted to return to their homes and are expected to shelter there," Femirea's voice continued.

"Something's not right," I muttered, reaching around Gabriel to tug on Miles' shirt sleeve. "Do you see it? Those people, they don't... they don't look right."
Miles frowned and squinted at the screen.

"Father, you must invoke *Aegis Maleficarum.* You must invoke it now," Zypher hissed.

I didn't bother sparing the exchange any attention. I was too focused on the strange shimmer that seemed to wrap around the humans on the summoned screen. "Please tell me you see that, Miles."

"I see it," Miles said finally. "I don't think those are real humans."

"Then what are they?" Gabriel asked, having overheard us.

Miles squinted harder. "They... they look like illusions, but I don't understand why nobody else seems to notice they're not right."

Caulder growled low in his throat, a thick puff of smoke blowing from his nose. "The King," he snarled. "This is his doing."

"Why would—" Shadrie started.

Caulder shook his head. "I can't explain that here." He turned to face me, his hands reaching out as if he meant to grab me before he caught himself. "You must go with Lucifer now, Bechora. Only demon law can get you off academy grounds now, and if the things I uncovered while looking into your magic are true, you need to access their archives before you return."

"I can't leave. What about everyone else?" I demanded.

"I will keep your friends safe. Your... mates will be able to leave with you. As long as Lucifer invokes *Aegis Maleficarum*, you and your claimed mates will become his wards. You will fall under his rule. The demons were smart in their negotiations with the academy. None of their kind are subject to the Fae King's orders on these grounds."

Caulder nodded toward Zypher. My demon mate pulled me into his side and turned to his father. "Do it. Do it now."

I opened my mouth to speak. To argue for another way. I couldn't just leave Shadrie and Miles behind, not after everything we'd endured in the trials. I lurched forward, reaching out for Caulder, my soul screaming that I couldn't leave him behind either. Not when I'd only discovered he was mine. Not when I knew something was seriously wrong outside the academy's wards. I barely heard Lucifer's voice, clipping out a melodic cadence as Zypher and Gabriel pulled me back.

A sob tore from my throat as I struggled against their hold. Caulder watched me with sad eyes as the pitch of Lucifer's voice rose, his words whipping into a frenzy. I heard the ground crack open before I felt it, the stone warping beneath my feet, before I fell. I screamed, my hands lashing out to grab anything I could find. The darkness swallowed me whole, air whipping past me for what seemed like hours, and then it just... stopped. My mouth snapped shut, my throat raw from screaming, as I took in my new surroundings.

"Welcome to my home, Dilectus," Zypher spoke from beside me. My lower lip trembled, and tears threatened to spill over my lashes at the realization that I was no longer at the academy, my friends and dragon mate left behind. "I promise we will find the answers you need and get you back to them."

BONUS CHAPTER

Detention: Bechora

I stood outside Professor Thrackborne's office just after dusk, Zypher and Gabriel flanking me. The lights threw long shadows across the stone hall, and I couldn't keep myself from sneaking glances at the vampire by my side. Gabriel hadn't complained once about being given detention in the wake of my outburst in Human Studies. I'd braced for sarcasm, for sharp remarks meant to belittle me—just like he'd done so many times before—but instead there was silence. Controlled, brooding silence that pressed heavier against me than any insult ever had. His eyes, when they caught mine, no longer held the venom I remembered. Was it resignation? A truce? Or had something shifted in him as much as it had in me? I wasn't certain I was ready to press for answers.

Zypher reached up and knocked on Thrackborne's door, the sound echoing through the heavy silence. I could hear the grumpy professor moving around on the other side just before the door swung open. Professor Thrackborne stood in the doorway, a leather satchel dangling from his fingers, as he stared at us. My body threatened to sway toward him, that irritating pull to the dragon shifter coming to life.

"Follow me," he clipped, stepping around us into the hallway. His boots struck the stone floor with sharp finality, each step daring us to keep up.

I exchanged a glance with Zypher, then fell in line between him and Gabriel as Thrackborne led us across the quad. The night air was cool, carrying the faint scent of damp grass and the lingering ink-and-paper tang of classrooms shuttered for the evening. For a moment, I thought we were being dragged to the library, but Thrackborne veered sharply toward one of the lesser-used academic wings.

The building loomed ahead, its windows blackened and cracked open just enough to let an eerie sound filter through —a faint, incessant chit-chit-chit that prickled along my skin like crawling ants. Thrackborne stopped at the doors, swung the satchel off his shoulder, rummaged inside, and pulled free three pale nets, their strands shimmering faintly with script I didn't recognize. He shoved one at each of us before speaking.

"Chitterfae infestation," he grumbled, as if it were the most ordinary thing in the world. "They've claimed this building. You'll clear them out."

"Chitterfae?" I echoed, turning the net over in my hands.

"The nets are spelled," Thrackborne continued, ignoring me. "They'll daze the creatures long enough for you to toss them into the cages. You'll find those in the first empty classroom. Don't damage the building, and don't come back until it's done." He shoved the satchel at Gabriel, who caught it with effortless precision, then gave us one last scowl before striding away as if this entire mess was no longer his problem.

I opened my mouth, then shut it when Zypher leaned close, his tone patient as he explained, "Chitterfae are small— smaller than your hand. They have wings, sharp teeth, and a temperament fouler than a demon with a toothache."

"They're relentless," Gabriel added, voice low. "Always in swarms. Their chittering never stops, and their bites are venomous. Not deadly," he amended at my raised brows, "but enough to leave welts that take weeks to heal."

"Magical cream is usually required," Zypher said with a grimace. "And even then, the sting lingers."

I glanced at the darkened windows of the building, the sound of that incessant chittering crawling into my ears and under my skin. Tiny, vicious, winged beasts. Of course, Thrackborne thought tossing us into a nest of them was an appropriate punishment.

Gabriel pushed the doors open first, the hinges groaning in protest as the stale air inside hit us like a wave. The smell of dust and mildew was sharp enough to sting my nose, but it was quickly drowned out by the shrill chorus of chit-chit-chit erupting from the shadows. The moment we stepped into the hall, movement exploded above us. Tiny shapes darted across the ceiling, their wings beating so fast they blurred. The swarms' glittering eyes caught in the light as Gabriel put on a burst of speed to flip on the light switches. Something smacked against the side of my head, a crumpled notebook tumbling to the floor at my feet.

"They throw things?" I yelped, ducking as another one lobbed an empty glass bottle that shattered against the wall beside me.

"They throw anything they can get their claws on, Dilectus," Zypher said grimly, raising his net. "Be prepared."

Before I could respond, pain lanced across my scalp. "Ow!" I yanked downward only to find a Chitterfae tangled in my hair, its sharp teeth nipping gleefully at my ear.

I swung wildly, but the creature screeched and tugged harder, pulling my hair until my eyes watered. Gabriel's hand shot out, tossing his net with practiced ease. He whipped it through the air, the glowing strands flaring as they tangled around the Chitterfae in my hair. The little beast shrieked once before going limp, dazed by the spell. He yanked it free and tossed it toward the open door of a cage Zypher had retrieved while I'd been dealing with the creature in my hair.

"One," Gabriel said simply, as though keeping score.

Another swarm dove from the rafters, pelting us with erasers, broken chalk, even a cracked desk leg one had managed to haul into the air. I ducked again, swinging my net clumsily and nearly snagging nothing but air. But one of the creatures veered too close, and the shimmering strands wrapped around its wings. It tumbled to the ground with a hiss, stunned, and I scrambled to shove it into the cage before it regained its senses.

The chittering rose to a fever pitch. They were everywhere —clawing at Zypher's shoulders, buzzing in Gabriel's hair, snapping their needle-sharp teeth as they dive-bombed us from the ceiling beams. My arms already stung from shallow bites, each welt burning as if set aflame.

"Keep them distracted!" Gabriel barked.

"Distracted? They're already throwing a classroom at us!" I shouted, flinching as a Chitterfae hurled a chair that splintered against the wall inches from his head.

The vampire didn't flinch. He snared three at once with a single sweep of his net, expression cool despite the blood beading at his temple where one had clawed him. He shoved them into the cage with efficient precision, his voice calm as he said, "You're terrible with the net, and your shouting is only exciting them. Just keep them busy and let me and Zypher catch them."

"Oh, excuse me for not being composed while bugs try to scalp me!" I snapped, swiping another off my arm. Both of my mates smirked at me before returning their full attention to the task at hand.

The hours bled together in a haze of wings, claws, and stinging bites. Every time I thought the swarm might finally be thinning, another wave spilled out of the classrooms and stairwells, their shrill chittering echoing so loudly I thought it might never leave my ears. My arms and shoulders burned with welts, my hair tangled where claws had ripped through it, and my net was frayed at the edges from how many times I'd swung it. By the time the first blush of predawn light seeped through the dusty windows, the building had gone quiet. The last of the Chitterfae lay dazed in the cage at Gabriel's feet, the once-writhing mass of furious wings reduced to an exhausted, angry heap.

I sagged against the nearest wall, dragging in deep breaths as sweat clung to my neck. My arms throbbed. My scalp ached. My voice was hoarse from swearing at the little monsters. "If this is what detention looks like," I croaked, "I'd almost rather be expelled."

ABOUT THE AUTHOR

Zoe Dunn is an American romance author with a lifelong love for stories that dance between shadows and light. Growing up devouring horror, she discovered how much a good twist can change everything—and she's been weaving that sense of suspense and surprise into her books ever since.

Zoe writes across a variety of romance subgenres, from paranormal to small-town and beyond, creating stories where passion, resilience, and unforgettable characters shine.

When she's not plotting her next twist or bringing new couples to life, Zoe can be found wrangling her kids, doting on her dogs, and laughing with her husband—the kind of love story that inspires every happily-ever-after she writes Stay Connected

Stay Connected

Newsletter:

Get exclusive updates, early cover reveals, sneak peeks, and bonus scenes.

Sign up here.

Website:

For book lists, reading order, FAQs, news, and upcoming releases, visit

www.zoedunnauthor.com

Facebook Reader Group:

Join Zoe's community of readers for behind-the-scenes content, teasers, discussions, and more.

Join here.

BOOKS IN THIS SERIES

Blackthorne Academy

Blackthorne Academy: Year One

Bechora has always lived life on the edge, surviving day by day as a twenty-three-year-old stripper, with no memories of her past before the foster homes she was placed in at age two. Her world is one of poverty and struggle, until a mysterious night changes everything. Taken from the club's parking lot, Bechora finds herself thrust into the enigmatic Blackthorne Academy, a school for the supernatural.

At Blackthorne, Bechora is initially classified as a fire mage, but it doesn't take long for her to realize her powers are unlike anything the academy has ever seen. As she navigates the perils and wonders of her new life, she forms deep, unexplainable connections with several intriguing individuals who seem to hold the keys to her destiny.

In a world where ancient powers are awakening, and dangerous secrets lie in wait, Bechora must uncover the truth about her origins and embrace a power that hasn't been seen in millennia. With her heart and the fate of the supernatural world hanging in the balance, Bechora's journey is just beginning.

Blackthorne Academy: Year Two

Bechora Knight survived her first year at Blackthorne, but the academy she's returning to is unrecognizable. The gates are locked. The King's soldiers patrol the grounds. Curfews silence the courtyards that once thrummed with magic and laughter. Combat drills and tactical lessons are taught alongside spellcraft, and every student is being prepared for a war no one understands.

Bechora isn't the same girl who first walked these halls. Her Starcaller power has awakened, steady and growing stronger with every connection she makes. Two bonds claimed. A third revealed. And when a wolf arrives at Blackthorne, his first words to her are a declaration of fate—another thread in the tapestry pulling her toward something greater than destiny itself.

But beneath the academy's silence, prophecy is stirring, and Bechora stands at the center of it all. If she can't find her mates and master her ability, she might burn down Blackthorne long before the war ever reaches its gates.

BOOKS BY THIS AUTHOR

Meddliing Memaws

A voicemail from her grandmother's best friend has Harley suspicious. The woman's grandson, and Harley's childhood sweetheart, is in town, and she has been specially invited to a party he will be attending. Harley knows this scheme. It's one their grandmothers cooked up when they were kids. Get Harley and Jackson together. Amused that they think they can play her so easily, Harley agrees to attend the party. She is her grandmother's ride after all. What she doesn't expect is the sparks that fly when she sees Jackson again for the first time in fifteen years. Or how damaged the last few years have left him since the death of his wife. After learning about everything Jackson has been through, Harley is set on being just friends. The grandmas have other plans though, they see the connection Harley and Jackson share, and intend to see it through. Will Harley stay true to her decision, or will the meddling memaws prevail?

The Wolf's Bite

Samantha has been on the run for ten years, ever since the night her father tried to sell her to a mob boss's son to settle his debt. Drifting town to town under an assumed surname, she thinks she might just outrun them. That is until one fateful night when she's attacked by a wild animal when taking out the trash for the diner she's been working at. Samantha finds herself in the clutches of reclusive billionaire, Aiden Black, and he's convinced she's being turned into a werewolf. He claims he and his people are werewolves themselves, but Samantha knows they only exist in movies. Or that's what she thought, before another voice began speaking to her from inside her mind. The voice claims to be her budding wolf, claims that everything Aiden has told her is true, it also claims she's his mate - whatever that is. Samantha is sure she's going crazy. That Aiden Black and his weird wolf cult have done something to her to drive her insane before they hand her over to the mob. But the voice in her head keeps getting stronger, and she's not sure what the truth is anymore. All she knows is this whole nightmare started with the wolf's bite.

The Rebound Rule

Emmerson McAllister wasn't looking for a second chance. She was just desperate for an escape.

Fleeing an abusive ex-fiancé—former minor league hockey star Maverick Thorne—Emmerson runs to the only place she feels safe: her twin brother Lincoln's home, clear across the country. Lincoln's not just her brother, though—he's a powerhouse in the NHL. And his roommate? Ryan Reeves. The league's most notorious playboy. Inked, cocky, and way too charming for his own good.

He's also the one guy she's supposed to stay away from.

But rules have never been Ryan's thing.

As Emmerson finds her footing again, Ryan becomes the one person who makes her feel strong. Wanted. Safe. Except Maverick isn't done with her yet. And he'll do anything to drag her back—whether she wants to go or not.

Now Emmerson has to decide if she's ready to fight for herself... and if she can trust Ryan with her heart before her past destroys her future.

www.ingramcontent.com/pod-product-compliance
Lightning Source LLC
Chambersburg PA
CBHW061514020726
47502CB00006B/2061